(continued on next page . . .)

JACK, KNAVE
AND FOOL

Bruce Alexander

BERKLEY PRIME CRIME, NEW YORK

JACK, KNAVE AND FOOL

A Berkley Prime Crime Book / published by arrangement with the author

PRINTING HISTORY
G. P. Putnam's Sons hardcover edition / 1998
Berkley Prime Crime mass-market edition / October 1999

The Penguin Putnam Inc. World Wide Web site address is
http://www.penguinputnam.com

ISBN: 0-425-17120-5

Berkley Prime Crime Books are published
by The Berkley Publishing Group,
a division of Penguin Putnam Inc.,
375 Hudson Street, New York, New York 10014.
The name BERKLEY PRIME CRIME and the BERKLEY PRIME CRIME
design are trademarks belonging to Penguin Putnam Inc.

PRINTED IN THE UNITED STATES OF AMERICA

10 9 8 7 6 5 4 3 2 1

For the Kesslers, Jascha and Julia

JACK, KNAVE
AND FOOL

ONE

*In Which We Visit
the Crown and Anchor
and a Lord Falls Dead*

Because I have taken it upon myself to write of Sir
John Fielding's feats of detection and of the most
notorious matters which came before him as Magistrate of
the Bow Street Court, I fear that the picture I have presented of him and his little household is somewhat unbal-
anced at best and most crudely distorted at worst. Each time
I have taken up my pen, I have drawn a portrait of the man
in crisis, so to speak, obsessed as he could indeed become
with the solving of some puzzle and the apprehension of
some malefactor. It was not always so. Indeed, through the
years that I spent in the warmth of his association, Sir John
was quite generally of an even and pleasant temper, a just
and gentle ruler of his household.

Of the time I write, early in the year 1771, that household
did consist of four: he, the master; his mistress, Lady Fielding; the widow Katherine Durham, whom he had taken as
his second wife; Annie Oakum, our most capable cook,
who had then just turned sixteen years of age; and I, Jeremy
Proctor, a few months younger, Sir John's "man Friday,"
or so he called me, a fellow of all work—porter and house

cleaner for Lady Fielding, and for Sir John scribe, reader, runner of every sort of errand, and whenever needed, a ready pair of eyes. (It must be remembered, reader, that all of his remarkable accomplishments were made more remarkable still by the fact that he was blind.) We two younger members of the household were treated as near like the children of Sir John and Lady Fielding as ever any could be. True, we had our duties, but so also do the children of any proper family. Yet we sat at table with the elders not only in our quotidian routine, in the kitchen, but also when guests did attend in our modest dining room. On such grander occasions we were permitted to join in table talk, respectfully, as children should, when we were addressed directly. There were never two who counted themselves to be as lucky as Annie and me.

We went oft to the theater, all in a great party of four, and always to the Drury Lane, where David Garrick did hold forth. He and Sir John were well acquainted and greeted each other as friends. Yet it was not merely Mr. Garrick's generosity with tickets that took us so frequently to his performances. No, more, it was that he brought Shakespeare so often to the boards. None excelled him in his love for the Great Bard—save perhaps for Sir John Fielding. It was to Mr. Garrick's productions of Shakespeare that Sir John would take us, and to none other. No matter what hints Annie would drop in his path, he could not be moved to test what he called "the new plays." And when Lady Fielding rather pointedly read an enthusiastic notice given the Drury Lane's production of Vanbrugh's *The Provok'd Wife* (not, certainly, a "new play," but rather revived after a space of some fifty years), she found that it availed her nothing. Sir John refused to take the bait.

"Ah, Kate," he had replied to her, "it may be a very good play indeed, but surely not of the *best* quality. Why not wait a bit for the best?" Then, after a moment, as if the thought had just struck him, said he: "You know, Kate,

I do believe that David is doing *Hamlet* again next week. Now, how would that suit you, eh?''

So it was that we had the best—or nothing at all. And we were, to my mind, all the richer for it. I do well recall Annie Oakum's introduction to the theater. It came not long after she had entered Sir John's employ and shortly after the departure of Tom Durham, Lady Fielding's son, on his first voyage as midshipman. Annie was so plainly heart-broken at Tom's farewell that Sir John thought to cheer her—indeed, to raise all our spirits—with a dose of Shakespeare, the best medicine he knew for spiritual elevation.

Not *Hamlet* but *Othello* was the fare on the Drury Lane's menu that night. Mr. Garrick's preference for the tragedies over the comedies was well known, or at least widely sus-pected. It came naturally to him, I believe, for he was a man of serious mien; there was nothing about him of the fool. Yet there can be no doubt that the best roles in Shake-speare are to be found in the tragedies, and as manager of the company, he did not hesitate to choose those plays for presentation which showed him off as actor to the best ad-vantage. He was certainly in grand form as the Moor for Annie's introduction to the theater. As any who saw him will admit, he was not so much a great physical actor. Which is to say, he did not leap around the stage and throw his arms about as he spoke those great lines; such behavior, he would no doubt have said, befitted the dignity of neither the character nor the playwright. But never was there one who, with a matchless voice, could find such music in the words of Shakespeare. It was that quality which so pleased Sir John. And it was that quality, too, which on the night in question struck dear Annie utterly dumb.

In his generosity, and because it was a slow night at the end of the run, Mr. Garrick provided us with a box quite near the stage. It seemed indeed as if we were upon it, and the actors played their parts left and right around us. I was next to Annie, and we two sat in front, hanging over the rail a bit, with Sir John and Lady Fielding behind us. Therefore was I able to observe closely the effect of this new experience upon her who had become like a sister to me. It was indeed quite remarkable. At first I thought that it was the physical beauty of the scene revealed to us when the curtains parted which so impressed her—the richly painted flats, the costumes of the actors. But no, it was more. A bit later, after a few glances her way, I noted that she was silently mouthing phrases and shorter lines spoken by the actors; not *with* them, of course, for she heard them for the first time, but just after, testing them upon her own lips. She paid no heed to me, and during breaks between the acts when I sought to engage her in conversation regarding the play and the performances of the actors, I found her quite unable to speak, so rapt was she in all that she had seen and heard. Lady Fielding, who had also been watching Annie closely, caught my eye and, smiling, shook her head; then did she whisper quietly in Sir John's ear.

Though I would not have thought it possible, Annie became even more deeply absorbed as the play progressed. At certain points her mouth gaped at Iago's evil lies. And when, believing him, Mr. Garrick, in the blackface guise of Othello, rumbled forth that awful malediction, "Damn her, lewd minx! O, damn her!" she caught her breath in horror. At the murder of Desdemona she cupped hand to mouth and let out a little shriek; but such was the power of David Garrick's performance that hers was not the only voice raised in shock. With the final curtain, our brave spectator showed herself completely overcome; tears streamed down her cheeks and flowed so freely from her eyes that she was near blinded by them; she failed to see the handkerchief offered her by Lady Fielding until it was pressed into her hand.

Though I myself was uncertain of what would be the result, Sir John insisted on taking us all backstage that we might congratulate Mr. Garrick on the production and his performance and thank him for his generosity in providing us a box to ourselves. I led our party down into the bowels of the great building, knowing the way well from previous visits. Sir John kept his hand firmly on my shoulder as we descended the stairs, and the women trailed after, Annie seeming somewhat reluctant, perhaps wishing not to end the state of rapture in which she had dwelt these last hours.

As we approached his dressing room, a couple emerged, man and woman, dressed quite grandly and speaking together in a tongue I took to be Dutch or German. The gentleman and I exchanged bows, his lady smiled, and the two moved rather swiftly past us.

When we appeared at his open door, Mr. Garrick leapt from the chair on which he sat at his dressing table. As he greeted us, he made a rather strange appearance, for on one side of his face—the left side, as I recall—he wore still his dark stage makeup, and on the other, which had been wiped clean, his natural ruddy complexion shone forth. He looked half a Moor and half an Englishman. I happened to glimpse Annie's face as she beheld him; she seemed quite shocked. Had she supposed the man onstage truly to have been a Moor?

Sir John inquired after the couple who had preceded us. "German, were they?" he asked. "I'd known you had a following in France. Has your great reputation traveled even farther?"

Mr. Garrick smiled modestly and bowed his head a bit. "I know naught of France," said he. "And in general, I would say that when I am introduced on the Continent, I may as well be a greengrocer for all they have heard of me. No, Sir John, the two, man and wife, are Austrian, distant cousins of my wife. But as you say, they are Germans more or less, and as such are greatly gifted at finding fault. They offered a number of suggestions as to how my performance might be improved, even offered a bit of advice to the playwright."

"To Shakespeare?" Sir John gave a short, scoffing laugh at the notion. "Well, I daresay they must be taught respect.

One wonders how much they truly understood.''

"Indeed, but their objection was more fundamental. They thought it all wrong that this tragic hero should be African.''

"Ah, how little they know of the world—or of human nature. But David, dear fellow, I know I speak for all of us when I say that your performance could not have been bettered.''

We joined in general agreement to that. And again, Mr. Garrick blessed us with a smile, perhaps a little less modest this time, yet the bow he offered was truly a bow; his hands were clasped before him in a gesture of earnestness.

"You're too kind, all of you. In truth, I am no judge of my own performances, for once I am up there on the stage I become quite transported in the beauty of the great poet's language. I do feel, though, that I played well enough, considering I did the whole of it on a gouty foot.''

(I had, by the bye, noted that standing before us he seemed to favor one leg over the other, supporting himself on the left side by keeping a firm grasp on the back of the chair from which he had risen.)

"We'd no idea!'' said Sir John. "Do sit down, please.''

"Yes, I fear I must take next month off and give it a rest.''

In the moment it took him to resume his seat upon the chair, Lady Fielding ventured to say, "Mr. Garrick, there is one of our number who exceeded us all in her appreciation of the play and the player. I have never seen such copious tears.''

"All shed in good cause, Lady Fielding,'' said he, "for it is indeed a beautiful and terrible tragedy. But who is this person you speak of?''

So saying, he fixed his eyes upon Annie, who seemed to shrink back almost in terror at being presented to so grand a personage. Nevertheless, Lady Fielding put her hand firmly on the girl's elbow and brought her forward.

"She is our cook, Annie Oakum, and very capable she

is, notwithstanding her young years. This night was her first experience of the theater.''

Annie stumbled slightly as she bobbed down in a curtsy. For a long moment she was quite tongue-tied, but then at last: "Pleased I am to meet'cha, sir.''

"Ah, a good cook are you, Mistress Annie?'' said Mr. Garrick, smiling indulgently. "Then you shall have no trouble making a good marriage, rest assured.''

"I . . .'' Annie began, stopped, then blurted out: "That is not my intention, sir.''

"Not marry? What a shame, a pretty girl like you.''

"Perhaps someday, sir, but I have an ambition.''

"And what is that?''

"To be an actress on the stage. One day I shall be Desdemona.''

At that we all laughed—and I with the rest. It was not meant cruelly, of that I am certain. We did but laugh in surprise.

Always considerate, Lady Fielding hastened to make things right. "Do forgive us, dear Annie, but we had heard naught of this before.''

Annie turned to her with a great blush reddening her cheeks. "You could not've, mum, for I've decided just tonight.''

Then did Mr. Garrick fix her with a most sober look. "I must say, my dear girl, that half the young ladies who visit me after a performance make declarations such as the one you have just made. I tell them, as I tell you now, that to be on the stage is not near so grand a lark as it looks to be. To be an actor or an actress requires more than a wish. You must needs have talent. You must be willing to work hard. And you must learn to take disappointment. It is a harder life than ever you'd guess.''

Annie returned to him a look ever as grave as he had given her. "I thank you for your caution, sir,'' said she to him, "but I shall be chosen.''

Of all of us assembled there, I believe it was I who took her words most in earnest.

Next day she would have me read *Othello* to her. That took hours snatched from our tasks parceled out over a few days. Then would she hear *Romeo and Juliet,* which she adored. And so on, through most, if not all of them. I did not begrudge her time spent thus. I quite enjoyed reading the plays aloud, for Shakespeare's words are, after all, meant to be spoken. I had performed the same service for Sir John. I had read to him *A Midsummer Night's Dream* and had begun his brother's romance *Tom Jones,* though we had not got beyond the first volume of that long book when his marriage to Katherine Durham intervened—and there we had left it, though I pressed on alone and finished it.

But as the year 1770 drew to a close and I continued with Annie our journey through the works of the Great Poet, she got it in her head one day to dispense with my services. Here is how she put it to me:

"Jeremy," said she, "if I'm to be an actress, it will not be enough to know the plays from having heard them read, now will it?"

"I suppose not."

"I must know how to read them myself." Then did she give me a hard look. "I want you to teach me how to read."

Thinking upon that, I had not the slightest notion of how to go about it. I myself had no memory of how I had come by that knowledge; it seemed to me that I had simply begun to read—and at quite an early age. I could recall going to my mother or my father and asking what this word meant, or that, but as to when or how any sort of fundamental instruction had taken place, that was simply lost to me. All this I explained to her, yet she was not to be so easily denied.

"An idea has come to me," said she. "Here we sit face-to-face at the kitchen table. You read, and I listen. What if

I sat next you, and you were to point to the words as you read them? Then I would remember them and soon be able to read them myself. How does that strike you?''

Absent any better method, I thought hers worth a try. And so we rearranged ourselves at the table and began. With what play we made the experiment I cannot recall. Yet I do well remember the tediousness of working through it line by line and word by word. She would often stop me and demand to know why a word—oh, such as ''bear'' or ''will''—would mean something in one place and something quite different in another, or ''the'' was written thus most of the time, but sometimes expressed simply as ''th'.'' Because she had a quick mind and a good memory, she interrupted constantly and quite drove me to distraction. She asked questions that I couldn't properly answer, and that made her distrust my abilities as a teacher; I distrusted them myself. Gone was the considerable pleasure I had derived from reading the plays aloud. Each day with her became a struggle and a torment. We were often cross with each other.

Finally, Christmas put an end to it. I received a gift from Sir John and Lady Fielding of the four volumes of Sir Edward Coke's *Institutes of the Law of England*. This was to be the beginning of my education in the law. I started at once to read through it, using those hours which I had previously devoted to Annie's lessons. When she protested, I reminded her rather priggishly that I, too, had an ambition, and that mine was as dear to me as hers to her. We argued. She sulked. She attempted to push forward on her own, but would come often to me to ascertain pronunciation or meaning. I would then often become short with her, and again she would sulk and sometimes we would quarrel. So is it often with brother and sister in proper families. So was it early in the year 1771 with our own.

Sir John and Lady Fielding could not but notice that some ill feeling had arisen between Annie and me. He, being the just and gentle ruler I have named him, thought to cheer us and bring peace between us by offering a treat. As it happened, Shakespeare was unavailable (and since he was indirectly the cause of our falling-out, might only have complicated the matter between us), and so Sir John looked elsewhere for our diversion. He turned his attention to the Crown and Anchor. It was then, as it is now, a tavern of great dimension in the Strand; in those days it was the site of the Sunday concerts sponsored by the Academy of Ancient Music under the direct patronage of Lord Laningham. If Shakespeare would not do for us, surely a dose of Handel would serve as well. Annie, who had lately turned snappish and glum, would surely be cheered by the mighty choral strains of that late, great master. We knew her, after all, to be the best musician of us all; as a singer of ballads and old songs learned in Covent Garden she knew no peer.

And so it was set: we would be off to the Crown and Anchor for an early dinner with Mr. Donnelly and Mr. Goldsmith, to be followed by a musical entertainment the equal of any in London. It would be an evening to remember, Sir John assured us. And so it was, reader, though not for reasons that any one of us could have foreseen.

Because of the limited capacity of the Bow Street Court's strong room, it was necessary for Sir John, as magistrate, to hold a short session on Sunday. Saturday night brought him always a rich harvest of drunks. He dealt with them swiftly so that he and Mr. Marsden, his court clerk, might be on their way to enjoy the rest of the day. This usually meant that he dealt with them leniently. There were sometimes complications, of course. And as I remember, one such arose whilst I sat taking my ease on one of the back benches of the Bow Street Court, listening as the magistrate heard one case after another of public drunkenness. Having had part of the night and all the morning to return to themselves, they were now sober and repentant, though they appeared much the worse for their experience. The last of them, tall and thin and dressed in brown linsey-woolsey—

but with a plaid waistcoat in the Scottish style—could not pay the fine of ten shillings which Sir John imposed, for as he explained, he'd "drunk up" all he had in his pocket. His name he gave as Thomas Roundtree, and he claimed to be gainfully employed as a journeyman carpenter, one of a gang working on improvements to one of the great houses on Bloomsbury Square.

"Which great house is that?" asked Sir John.

"It's that of the Lord Chief Justice," said Mr. Roundtree.

"And what sort of improvements are you making?"

"We're puttin' in a new water closet, sir, makin' it nice for the ladies of the house, we are. I'm a good worker, sir, I am truly."

"Ah, well, I suppose in that case you would prefer not to spend thirty days in the Fleet Prison in lieu of fine. That is customary in this court."

"No sir, indeed I would not, for I am a workingman and would have no job of work when I came out."

"You put that quite reasonably, Mr. Roundtree. What, then, do you suggest?"

"Ah, well, I could pay it to you bit by bit, p'rhaps."

"I have a better idea. Why not remain as our guest here at Bow Street for one more night? Then in the morning you may go to your place of work in the company of one of our constables and ask the master carpenter for whom you work for the loan of the ten shillings. If you are as good a worker as you say, then he should not hesitate to advance it to you. Him you can pay back bit by bit, as you proposed to do with me."

Thomas Roundtree stood, hesitant, rubbing his chin. "Well, sir . . ."

"Have you family?" asked Sir John.

"Nooo," said he, though he hesitated a bit.

"Then you've no one to remark your absence one more night." Sir John at last became impatient: "Come now, sir, it's either that or the Fleet Prison."

"Well, when you puts it so, I accept your invitation. I

do hope for a better dinner than I got a breakfast, howso-
ever.''

"We'll feed you. That is our obligation." Sir John
slammed down his gavel upon the table. "Mr. Fuller, conduct the prisoner back to the strong room. And Mr. Marsden, are there more?''

"None, sir," said the clerk of the Bow Street Court.

"Then this Sunday session is done." He beat down his
gavel once more, stood, and stretched. "I'm for a nap before dinner," he declared. "It will be a long evening ahead,
and I wish to be fit for it."

Fit for it we were and dressed for the occasion as we set
off by foot for the Crown and Anchor a little before five.
It being January, the day was all but gone; sunset had gone
to twilight and twilight to dusk. But the lamplighter had
been out upon his rounds, and our way—Russell Street to
Drury Lane, Drury Lane to the Strand—was well lit and
filled with London folk enjoying the last of their day of
rest. Sir John, well refreshed by his afternoon nap, led the
way with Lady Fielding upon his arm. As long as he was
here in the Covent Garden district that he knew so well,
there was little chance that he would make a misstep, but
should he perchance do so, his good wife was there to put
him back on course. Annie and I followed at a near distance.

"What of this Handel music we go now to hear, Jeremy?
What do you think of it?" Annie asked her questions as
we marched along Russell Street.

"Well," said I, "from what I've heard, I think it quite
fine. Gives you a sense of the grandness of nature, it does.
Raises your spirits."

"All that? To me it just seems terrible loud. I can't make
out the words."

"Sir John certainly loves his Handel," I said, making a
mild reproof of a neutral comment.

"Oh, indeed he does. Me, I like a good ballad, a street song."

"You know them all."

"I know many," she agreed. Then, with a sigh: "Still, be it good or foul, I look forward to eating any meal cooked by another. Sir John and the good lady wish us to be well entertained this evening, and I, for one, am determined to be so."

So saying, she lapsed into a silence which lasted until the hanging sign of the Crown and Anchor was in sight. There was, in any case, no mistaking our destination. Closed carriages, coaches, and hackneys crowded the entrance of the place, discharging their passengers, ladies and gentlemen, onto the walkway. There was a bustle of excitement to the scene before us which seemed to bespeak our entrance into the great life of our great city.

"Oh, Jeremy," said Annie beside me, "this is indeed exciting. Just look at them all, how fine they are dressed! How they seem to glide, like they was walking on air, you might say. Damn me, but I must work on my walk if I'm to look the part of a lady."

"On your speech, as well," said I. "Ladies don't say 'damn.' "

She stopped and turned upon me, looking as if she was about to give me a sharp retort. But then she softened and said most seriously: "Right you are to correct me. I know I speak like a slut more often than not. I must learn better. I *will* learn better."

Having halted even so briefly, we had fallen somewhat behind Sir John and Lady Fielding. They now stood at the entrance to the tavern. They waited, I supposed on us, yet our lady seemed to be staring ever so intently at a coach which four matched horses had just drawn up to the walk.

It was indeed a remarkable coach. It rode upon carved, gilt wheels, and as we drew nigh I saw that it had upon its door panels scenes of the countryside in winter and spring most beautifully painted, clearly the work of an artist of great skill. Somehow, without running round to make sure of it, I knew that the two panels on the far side of the coach would display similar scenes depicting summer and autumn. When the footman jumped down to open the coach door and assist the occupants to the walk, I saw that he (as well as the driver) was dressed in a remarkable silver livery which glittered and shone even in the dim light of the streetlamp.

Lady Fielding was whispering a description of this garish vehicle to Sir John as Annie and I came up to them. I could tell from the amused expression upon his face that he recognized it from the likeness she sketched with her words.

"That coach," said he, full-voiced, "can only belong to one man. Let us linger here a moment and greet him."

I should not have been surprised had the Prince of Wales himself emerged from the coach with a party of his royal siblings. Yet one man only descended from the interior of the coach; and though richly dressed, he did not appear to me a prince—though perhaps a duke. Nevertheless, he was well acquainted with the Magistrate of the Bow Street Court.

"Sir John!" cried he. "You're looking well, I must say."

"Though I can't, alas, say the same to you due to this fault of my eyes, I will say your voice, Sir Joshua, has never sounded heartier."

"Well said, well said, and you may take that as an outward sign of my inward health."

The two shook hands warmly, and Sir John presented us to Sir Joshua Reynolds, the great painter of portraits. Annie and me he introduced as "members of his household." A few pleasantries passed between them as we moved toward the door of the Crown and Anchor. Once inside, we proceeded at a good pace, yet Lady Fielding kept a good, tight hold on her husband's arm, guiding him gently through the uneven row of empty tables toward the inner doorway which led to the site of the evening's festivities. Annie and

I kept very close so as not to miss any titbit of interest that might pass between them. We were not left unrewarded.

"When, pray tell," asked Sir Joshua Reynolds, "will you allow me to paint your portrait, Sir John?"

At that Sir John let forth a booming laugh. "Never, I fear. The modest budget I am given by the Lord Mayor's office includes no allowance for personal vanity."

"Nothing of the kind, sir. Vanity's got little to do with it. A good likeness is a gift to posterity."

"He's right, Jack," put in Lady Fielding.

"I doubt posterity will have reason to remember me," said Sir John.

"Not so, sir. And putting all that aside, you've a face whose strength I should like to capture. It appeals to me as an artist."

"Be willing to put aside your fee, would you?" Sir John said it in a teasing manner.

"*Jack!*" scolded his lady.

"Ah, now there you have me. I am an artist, true, but I am also a man of business. Yet an adjustment of some sort would not be out of the question."

The three stood at the entrance to the ballroom. Before them was a great multitude seated at tables and milling about.

"Ah, but here we are," said Sir Joshua. "My table is at the far side with some of my colleagues of the Royal Academy, and so I shall leave you here. Delighted to meet you, Lady Fielding, and you two young people, as well. Always a pleasure to see you, Sir John."

He danced down the three stairs leading into the ballroom, and at the last he turned. "Do give some thought to what I suggested," he called back.

"Oh, we shall, sir," Lady Fielding replied. "Indeed we shall."

Then with a wave, he was away, weaving through the crowd.

"Kate, please," grumbled Sir John. "Don't encourage

the fellow. Have you any idea what he would ask? A hundred and fifty guineas, or so I have heard.''

"Oh dear," said she. "Well, we may speak of it later."

"But not a word of it at table."

"Agreed."

The Crown and Anchor is like unto many a tavern and inn in London, though more respectable than most. What sets it apart from all, however, is the great ballroom at its rear. At the head of it there is a stage, where at that moment, music stands and chairs were being assembled for the evening's entertainment. The floor of the ballroom (on which there would be no dancing that night) was crammed with tables set so tight there was barely room enough for servers to pass between. Yet pass they did, for dinner had begun at many of the tables, and at the rest wine flowed freely. Arranged so, as many as four hundred could be seated in the grand ballroom, and it appeared that near that number were already present.

Annie and I stepped forward, for our eyes were keener than Lady Fielding's, who was a bit shortsighted. We swept the assembly back and forth until at last my gaze fell upon a familiar figure, standing and waving to us from a near-empty table quite near the stage. It was unmistakably that of Mr. Gabriel Donnelly, formerly ship's surgeon, now recently appointed (through Sir John's intercession) as medical advisor to the coroner of the City of Westminster. I waved back and bade all follow me.

Wending our way through a narrow, devious path, squeezing past servers and many engaged in idle conversation, we came at last to the table where Mr. Donnelly and Mr. Oliver Goldsmith, the noted author, awaited us. Both were standing, smiling, greeting us in the most welcoming manner. How good it is to be among friends on such occasions. We seated ourselves, and at once the talk did bubble up as from a fountain.

Mr. Goldsmith jested about Mr. Donnelly's sudden rise

in society: "So many invitations has he now that he has quite forgot the taste of his own cooking."

"What was ill to the taste is well forgotten," said the surgeon. "In all truth, dear friends, you should know that Noll here—that is, Mr. Goldsmith—has connived most of these invitations for me, certainly those to the grandest houses."

"But do tell, Mr. Donnelly," inquired Lady Fielding, "are you now well set in your new surgery?"

(At year's beginning, Gabriel Donnelly had moved from his small place located in a walk-up in Tavistock Street to more spacious and altogether grander quarters in Drury Lane, formerly the surgery of the late Dr. Amos Carr.)

"Ah, very well indeed," said he. "There is a waiting room of larger size for my patients—and the living quarters are separate and quite commodious. It is indeed a proper surgery for a better clientele."

"And has such begun to appear?" asked Sir John.

"Oh, certainly, yes. I seem instantly to have inherited all the late Dr. Carr's patients."

"And shocked they must have been at his—" Sir John searched a moment for the proper word. "At his sudden passing."

"Ah yes, each must discuss it with me."

"And has his ghost come to visit?"

"Not a bit of it. I've erased all trace of him—with alcohol and strong soap."

"But," said Mr. Goldsmith, "he is far too modest. Already his ascent into polite society has brought him patients of the gentler sort."

And though his eyes twinkled at having spoken thus, his meaning eluded me, and perhaps it was so with the rest in our party, as well.

Perceiving this, Mr. Goldsmith leaned across the table and said in a stage whisper loud enough to be heard over the din of the crowd, "The . . . ladies, friends, the ladies. They seem to flock to him with all manner of ailments—a positive epidemic of female troubles of every sort seems to have hit the best houses in London. He brings it with him wherever he goes.''

A distinct blush did then appear upon the cheeks of Mr. Donnelly. We all laughed wickedly at his discomfiture. Thus was he forced to confirm Mr. Goldsmith's tale-tattling. "There is some truth to it," he admitted. "I've had a dozen new patients this past week. All but two of them are women. It's taken some effort and no little study to keep up with their complaints. After all, I began my career in medicine as a ship's surgeon, and there was precious little call for such knowledge aboard a man-of-war. Apart from birthing a few babies in Lancashire I'd not had much experience.''

"There was my dear wife Kitty," put in Sir John. "You alone diagnosed the truth as to her situation.''

"And, as I have heard often from Jack," said Lady Fielding, "you greatly eased her passing, may God rest her soul." There were solemn grunts and pious nods around the table until she resumed on a note no less serious but not so somber: "Indeed, I believe Mr. Donnelly should do well as a doctor to women. I observed him during his visit to the Magdalene Home just before Christmas. He has a sympathetic manner with his patients, but above all, he listens. What women want most is to be taken seriously.''

"Hear! Hear!" came the impetuous cry from her who was seated next to me.

"Thank you, Annie," said Lady Fielding with a gracious nod.

Then from behind, a new voice: "Jack, dear fellow, is it you?''

Yet Sir John recognized the voice before I could turn and identify the face. He was up on his feet, thrusting out his hand toward the speaker. "Alfred Humber! How good to meet you—and where better to find you than here at the Crown and Anchor.''

"We were regular Sunday attendants for a while.''

"And then I found my Kate. You met her at our wedding reception."

"Of course, of course," said Mr. Humber.

He bowed as low as his considerable girth permitted and bestowed a kiss upon her hand. And then did Sir John introduce him around the table and invite him to take a place with us. As it happened, he chose to sit next to Mr. Goldsmith just as two servers came our way and, without a word, slammed down our dinners before us; they left as they had come, at a run. It all happened so swiftly and with so little ceremony that we could not but laugh.

"Well, Mr. Humber," said Mr. Goldsmith, "we seem to have exhausted a bottle of wine already. Will you open another?"

"I should be happy to do so, sir."

As Mr. Humber busied himself with cork and corkscrew, Mr. Goldsmith asked him if he was in trade.

"In a manner of speaking, yes I am, sir. You might say that I am in the money trade. I am a broker at Lloyd's Coffee House."

"Money, is it? Now, that is a topic which interests me greatly. I sometimes have sums to invest. How might I put them best to work?"

Thus did Messrs. Humber and Goldsmith begin a conversation which lasted through dinner. The unfortunate Goldsmith, who died deep in debt but a few years later, ever had dreams of making a great fortune. The investments he spoke of were mere fantasies, I fear. But poor man, he did wish to be well informed when and if the opportunity to invest should ever come his way.

The meal put before us was something better than I had expected. In order to serve so many, plain fare must be offered, and plain fare was what we got. It was not such as we were used to at home from Annie, whose ordinary stews were spiced to a delicious piquancy. Yet our plates were well heaped with good English beef, and beside was a good chunk of pudding and atop all a sauce of beef drippings; there was bread on the table for sopping. And so, while what we were offered may have been no feast, we were given plenty, and what we ate was good.

As we dined we watched preparations proceed upon the stage for the concert. The musicians began to file out from a door in back to take their places. At last the clatter of hundreds of knives and forks upon plates began to subside, and a round and red-faced man came forward whom I presumed to be the master of the ceremonies. He held up his hands, asking for silence, and waited until the deep hum of conversation had subsided somewhat. We sat so near the stage that I was able to make out the veins that showed upon his swollen nose.

"Ladies and gentlemen," he shouted out to the audience, "and especially ladies, as you no doubt know, the *Ode for St. Cecilia's Day,* by George Frederick Handel is on our program for this evening. But due to the inclement weather we have had lately this winter season, the soprano section of our choir has been some little depleted. In short, I appeal to you, the ladies of our audience, for volunteers to augment our soprano section. The choirmaster informs me that even if you have not previously participated in the singing of this great work, music will be supplied, and you will be drilled in your part before the performance. So . . . please? Are there some of you out there? Volunteers who wish to take part in this great occasion?"

At first there seemed to be none. But then a woman, no longer young, rose from a table at the far side and marched resolutely up the stairs her side of the stage.

Then did Lady Fielding lean forward and say most earnestly: "Oh, Annie dear, you go. You have such a lovely voice. Yours would help them immeasurably."

"Oh, ma'am, I can't! I couldn't!"

Then, from the stage: "Are there no more? I'm told we need at least two more, and five in all would be best."

Another came forward from the rear of the ballroom.

"Please, Annie, do it for us," said Lady Fielding. And

Mr. Donnelly and Mr. Goldsmith, who to my knowledge had never heard Annie sing, joined the importuning chorus.

"But I don't read music," wailed Annie quite miserably. "I've never even heard the piece."

"We have one here!" called out Lady Fielding loudly. *"We have a volunteer!"*

And so, with the reluctance of one condemned, Annie was forced to rise. Saying nothing more, she left our table and climbed the stairs our side of the stage as one might to the scaffold. In spite of repeated invitations, no further recruits could be pulled from the great crowd, so at last the three were trundled off through the door at which the musicians had entered.

Then did the master of the ceremonies look about him, and making certain that the members of the orchestra were all in their places, he took a step forward and then he bellowed forth even louder than before: "To those of you who come regularly to these Sunday concerts, the man I am about to introduce needs no introduction. He is a great patron of the arts in general, to the art of music in particular, and to these concerts in specific. For two years now he has inspired and guided us with his interest and, not least, has supported us generously from his pocket whenever attendance flagged and it became necessary. We at the Crown and Anchor Tavern, and you who are supporters of the Academy of Ancient Music, owe him a great debt. Let us all give witness to that with a great sound of applause for our patron, Christopher Paltrow, Earl of Laningham. Ladies and gentlemen, I give you Lord Laningham."

The applause that followed this fulsome introduction seemed somewhat meager and merely polite. Nevertheless, the man for whom it was intended took no offense at that. He bounded up from his table at the far side of the stage and, bearing a ceremonial staff of some sort, hopped up the stairs with surprising agility. He was a man who had, I judged, entered his eighth decade, or so the deep lines in his face did suggest. His movements, while not those of a

young man, were somewhat forced, as if he were one who
wished to appear young and vigorous still.

"I must apologize for him," said Mr. Humber to the
table, in a voice perhaps too loud. "He does make an awful
fool of himself."

Lord Laningham would then speak his piece before the
music could begin. Yet it was brief. "Dear friends of ancient music, we have a fine program for you this evening,
we do, and all of it by our favorite, Mr. Handel, may the
good Lord keep his soul. Well, there's the *Ode for St. Cecilia's Day,* of course, but that's a bit later." He stopped a
moment, hemmed and hawed, then turned and sought the
aid of the musicians. "Ah yes, we begin with two of Mr.
Handel's grand concertos, the first two, I'm told, of . . .
what is it now?" Again he turned to the orchestra. Then:
"Of Opus three, I'm told. Mr. Concertmaster?"

With that, Lord Laningham withdrew to a chair of honor
placed before the orchestra and facing out toward the audience. He seated himself but kept in hand that staff with
which he had ascended to the stage; it was gilt-painted and
had at its upper end a round bulb of good size, such as
would fill a man's hand.

The concertmaster, which is to say the violin player nearest us, stood, taking the attention of the musicians, and
began them on the first piece of the program. Remarkable
it was how all managed to start together under his direction;
once they were playing, however, he seated himself and
played as one of the many. Indeed there were many—
thirty-three, as I counted them—divided between strings
and horns of every sort, with stringed instruments somewhat in the majority. Remembering Annie's objection to
the loudness of the music, I admitted that while that was
true, there was a certain grandeur in that greatness of sound.
I liked the way it changed from loud to soft and back to
loud again; thus also with the pace of the music, going for
a stretch at a dignified, funereal gait, then unexpectedly

breaking into the swift movement of some dance, a jig or
an allemande.

Lord Laningham himself had a great preference for these
sprightly parts. When they came, he was moved to jump
from his chair and begin beating his staff upon the stage
floor in time to the music—though not, alas, in strict time.
I noted that often the musicians would look up at him in
annoyance as he banged and capered about. Yet he, it
seemed, was having a grand time of it; so completely did
he give himself to his performance before the orchestra that
in the space of two concerti grossi (which may have taken
half an hour to perform) he had quite exhausted himself.
Beckoning a server to him, he gave quite detailed instructions to the fellow and then pointed back to the table
whence he, Lord Laningham, had come. In a moment the
server had returned with a newly opened bottle of wine and
a glass. The lord did wave away the glass but took firm
hold of the bottle and took a deep swig from it. With his
thirst temporarily slaked, he sat and rested as the choir began to file in.

There was a space of ten minutes, perhaps as many as
fifteen, between the first and second parts of the program.
(I later learned that there was a third part planned, selec-
tions from the *Water Music,* always a great favorite with
attendants of the concerts.) During this time musicians left
their chairs and milled about. A few left the stage altogether, perhaps answering calls of nature. The choirmaster
conferred with members of the choir who had grouped
around him. Annie, a bit shorter than most, was near invisible in the crowd. Through it all, Lord Laningham sat,
fortifying himself from time to time with a swig from the
bottle.

As we waited, Mr. Alfred Humber regaled us with tales
of the patron's past foolishness: how he did, on one occasion, become so carried away with the pomp of the *Royal
Fireworks Music* that he descended the stairs from the stage
and led a parade through the audience; and on another,

wishing to show his appreciation to the orchestra for what he judged a superlative performance of something or other (and lacking a hat), he doffed his wig to them, revealing a head quite bald except for a bit of fuzz at the ears.

"He is such an embarrassment," said Mr. Humber. "Some come just to laugh at him. I don't know why the Academy puts up with the old fellow—though I suppose they must. It's all that wine he drinks, I suppose."

All the members of the orchestra had reassembled and were back in their chairs. The choir had taken its place on a platform to the left of the musicians, with the sopranos, Annie among them, at the far end.

I half expected Lord Laningham to make some sort of announcement—but no, he remained seated. He seemed subdued somewhat, yet bothered, shifting frequently and, it seemed, somewhat uncomfortably in his chair of honor.

Perhaps he was merely bestirring his old bones, limbering them up to perform, for sure enough, once choir and orchestra had begun he was up on his feet, no doubt inspired by the booming sound of the great kettledrums. Yet this time he did no more than beat his staff upon the floor. He wandered about a bit uncertainly; then he found his way over to the choir, where he did ogle the sopranos—pretty Annie, it seemed, in particular. The choirmaster was openly annoyed by this.

I cannot, by the bye, say that I actually heard our Annie singing on that occasion. Certainly I heard the choir, and she was one of them. Her lips moved, and her mouth opened. I watched her closely until Lord Laningham drew near to her, at which time she put her music up before her and hid behind it.

Still he wandered, yet with faltering step. The ceremonial staff he simply dragged after him, bringing it down only now and then upon the floor. He had paled. Sweat stood upon his face. A murmur of comment at his condition went through the crowd as he found his way back to his chair and collapsed into it. He dropped his staff, and it rolled a few feet from him across the stage. Then did he lean forward as if to retrieve it. Having so leaned, he could somehow not stop himself, and quite out of control, he toppled lengthwise upon the floor. His lower body quivered and jerked, knocking down the chair from which he had fallen and sending the half-consumed bottle of wine spinning across the floor, spilling its contents. Then, in what may have been his last willed act, he raised his head—but only to vomit. Beef, bits of pudding, and a good deal of nasty red liquid, which I took to be wine, spewed forth from his gaping mouth. It was a most unpleasant sight to behold.

For a moment there was silence. The orchestra had halted, and so, too, the choir. Those in the audience were too stunned to do more than gawk. Yet only for a single eye-blink of a moment did that silence last, for in the next instant all onstage seemed to be converging upon the fallen figure. There were shouts and screams from them, as from the great crowd in the ballroom. Of a sudden all was chaos.

"What a disgrace!" shouted Mr. Humber. "He's fallen drunk and vomited out his guts before us. This certainly exceeds the limit."

There were others all around who joined him in similar cries of disgust.

Mr. Donnelly, however, already on his feet, put a different interpretation upon those actions all had witnessed. "Dear God," said he, "the man is ill. I must do what I can to help him." And so saying, he left us at the table and ran to the steps nearby leading up to the stage. I saw him pressing through the crowd that suddenly surrounded Lord Laningham.

There was shouting:

"Give him room!"

"Do not push so! You'll crush my violin."

Then just as Mr. Donnelly reached the figure on the floor of the stage and knelt down to him, I felt a tug at my sleeve. It was Sir John, who had come round the table to seek me out special.

"Jeremy," said he to me in a hoarse whisper, "you've a good pair of eyes and mind enough to note peculiarities. Tell me quickly, boy, exactly what you saw from the time Lord Laningham appeared on the stage."

That I did in no more than a minute's time. Sir John listened, concentrating carefully on what I had to say. He nodded when I finished.

"And the last you saw of that bottle of wine, it was rolling around on the floor up there?"

"That's true, sir," said I, "spilling its contents all round."

"Then take me up to the stage, for we must restore order somehow, clear the area, and find that bottle."

"Yes, Sir John. Grab hold my shoulder."

The crowd up on the stage seemed to have increased threefold by the time Sir John and I arrived. He tried shouting them down. Yet his considerable voice was lost in the tumult. Then had I an idea of what might be done. We stood in the midst of the orchestra, or where the orchestra had been minutes before. If I might but . . .

"Here, Sir John," said I, "let me help you up on a chair. If I can reduce them to something like silence, you may deliver one of your magnificent threats."

"Well and good," said he. "Do what you can."

Taking my hand, he made it up to the seat of the chair. I then helped point him in the right direction and urged him not to move, lest he fall. Then did I go right swift to the orchestra's loudest instrument, which stood untended.

I picked up the mallets—covered in sheepskin they were—and I began beating upon the kettledrums as Tom O'Bedlam might, making them boom forth like cannon, then rolling them out long and loud like thunder, then booming and banging again and again.

When I looked up and saw all turned toward me, open-mouthed in surprise, I knew that I must stop. Reluctantly, I did so. Then rang forth the stentorian voice of the great man himself.

"I am Sir John Fielding, Magistrate of the Bow Street Court. I order you all to clear the stage at once. With the exception of Lord Laningham, members of his immediate family, and Gabriel Donnelly, the doctor in attendance, all must leave immediately. The Bow Street Runners have been sent for to enforce this order. All who remain in defiance of it may expect to spend the next month in Newgate Gaol."

What a rush there was! Musicians and chorus fled out the door at the rear of the stage. Those of the audience who had come up out of curiosity or concern left, as they had come, by the steps at either side. In less than three minutes, only Lord Laningham, Mr. Donnelly, and a grandly dressed woman whom I took to be Lady Laningham, remained there with us.

But look as I might—and I spent the next ten minutes poking in every corner—no bottle of any sort was there to be found.

TWO

*In Which I Play
the Constable
and Am Embarrassed*

The men of our table at the Crown and Anchor assembled once again in Sir John's chambers back of the courtroom at Number 4 Bow Street. It had been over an hour since Lord Laningham had fallen so sudden ill upon the stage and died so ingloriously before hundreds of witnesses. While some had filed out immediately, aware that the musical entertainment was not likely to resume, which of course it did not, most remained, some no doubt out of concern for the aged noble, but the greater number simply to gawk at a man in the throes of death. At last death had come and taken him. Lady Laningham, who had knelt beside him through all, then gave the word and two servers of the Crown and Anchor hauled off the body between them to an embalmer nearby on Fleet Street.

That done, Sir John had allowed back the musicians and members of the chorus to retrieve their instruments and music from the stage; then did he send me off to find the innkeeper and bring him hither. It did not surprise me that he who had acted as the master of the ceremonies proved to be the one I sought. He went most willingly to Sir John;

I merely trailed after. Yet I was then sent off to find Annie and bring her to the table, so that I heard nothing of the question and answer that passed between them. Instead I found her with the choirmaster, he giving her a stern talking-to, one complete with finger shaking and frown. Whatever she had done seemed to have displeased him greatly. Nevertheless I heard no details, for as I approached close enough to listen there was, of a sudden, nothing to be heard. He turned from her and stalked off, perhaps in search of some other poor soprano he might abuse. All this took place in the space behind the stage reached through that door through which both orchestra and choir had passed. Asking simply if we were ready now to return to Bow Street, Annie came along, music in hand, accepting my response that it would be soon.

And so it was. Sir John was at the table with the rest—his interview with the innkeeper could not have lasted long—and we all set off together, among the last to leave the scene of that unhappy event. He declined to discuss it, saying that he wished to give it some thought as we made our way home. "If, however," he had said on the walkway before the Crown and Anchor, "you gentlemen wish to accompany us, I would be curious to hear your comments and observations on the matter. Perhaps we might do that at Number Four."

They had indeed wished to come along, and though they could not wait to talk of the death amongst themselves, Messrs. Donnelly, Goldsmith, and Humber trailed our party at such a distance that they could not have greatly disturbed Sir John. Upon our arrival at Bow Street, Lady Fielding and Annie had mounted the stairs to our quarters, and I, on Sir John's orders, had gone ahead to light candles in his chambers and otherwise prepare it for his guests.

Thus, when they entered, the place was well lit, and upon Sir John's desk stood a bottle of good brandy (fetched from the bottom drawer of his desk) and four glasses, wiped clean and ready.

"Ho!" crowed Mr. Goldsmith in celebration. "What have we there? Is it the Spanish fundador or the French cognac?"

"I know not its country of origin," said Sir John, "only that it has a pleasant taste and warms the stomach well."

"Well and good," spoke Mr. Humber.

I filled glasses for all but myself and handed them out. They took chairs scattered about the room and pulled them close. I, not being asked to leave, found one for myself, as well.

"Sir John?"

"Yes, Mr. Goldsmith?"

"Your interest in this matter seems to indicate a suspicion that Lord Laningham did not die of natural causes."

"Oh . . . not necessarily. As described by Jeremy, the scene upon the stage following Laningham's collapse was one of great disorder. At the very least, I thought it wise to clear the stage that Mr. Donnelly might minister to the poor man. That, following Jeremy's solo on the bass drum, I was able to do."

"And grateful I am to you both," said Mr. Donnelly.

"On the other hand," said Sir John, "the order of events prior to his collapse, again described to me by Jeremy, were such that the possibility of an unnatural death cannot be dismissed."

"But why?" said Mr. Goldsmith, ever the doubter.

"Yes, why?" echoed Mr. Humber. "Lord Laningham was most certainly of an age for dying—seventy-five years, as I understand. He'd a bad heart and one attack of apoplexy known to me."

"You seem to know a good deal about his former state of health," said Sir John.

"That, Jack," said Mr. Humber, "is because I had been critical a year past of Laningham's behavior at the concerts, and I was told all this by a medico who happened to be at my table. It was his opinion that Lord Laningham was attempting with all his foolish jumping about to prove himself fit and hale in spite of his years.''

"There, you see, sir?'' said Mr. Goldsmith. "That seems well vouched for. In light of all that, how is it you still harbor a suspicion—be it even a mild one?''

"Well, first of all, Mr. Goldsmith—and you also, Alfred—because I am a magistrate, it is my place and my duty to harbor suspicions of all sorts. It is true that I often put a dark interpretation upon a set of facts—yet also true that as often as not such a view is proven justified. When in the back of my mind I have some doubt—not a thought but a feeling—there is usually good reason for it. I have come to trust my doubts.''

"But at this point,'' said Mr. Goldsmith, "you have merely feelings . . . doubts? Not yet a good reason for such?''

"Well, let us consider the sequence of events, shall we? As I understand them, Lord Laningham quite hopped up to the stage when introduced by the innkeeper. He frisked about the stage for a good half of an hour until there came a break, at which time the choir came upon stage for the singing of the Saint Cecilia ode. As this transpired, he sat himself upon a chair to rest, and having developed a thirst, hailed a server and sent him off to fetch a bottle of wine. Now, where that bottle came from we cannot at this point be absolutely certain, for I have not yet had the opportunity to speak with the server. The innkeeper, however, volunteered to me that he was near certain it would have come from Lord Laningham's own table, for it was Laningham's habit to bring wines from his private stock to the Crown and Anchor on concert Sundays. The innkeeper has promised to ask among the servers until he has found the one who brought the wine and then to send him to us. Why should this be of such importance? Because Lord Laningham drank greedily of that bottle of wine, and it was only after he did so that he began to show signs of distress.''

"But," objected Mr. Goldsmith, "those signs were by no means immediate. The better part of an hour passed before the spectacle of his collapse upon the stage."

"Oh? Truly? I had judged it to be not near so long as that, myself," said Sir John. "How long would you estimate the time that elapsed between the lord's first taste of the wine and the moment he fell to the floor and vomited, Alfred?"

Mr. Humber considered. "Closer to half an hour, I should say, perhaps less." Then, giving the matter a moment's further thought, he added: "We could find out from the choirmaster or the concertmaster just how far along they were in the piece. That might help in making a more accurate estimate."

"Indeed it might," said Sir John. "If it becomes a point of prime importance, we might consult with them. But leave it that it was only after he had drunk of the wine that he began to act, according to Jeremy's description, 'queer'—to wit, that he wandered a bit aimlessly, let drag his staff, and staggered about before returning to his chair and suffering that final episode which we have chosen to call his 'collapse.' "

"Yes, I seem to recall those earlier signs that all was not right with him," said Mr. Humber. "You're saying, Jack, that he was at least affected not long after drinking from that bottle? Well, it was indeed plain that he was less lively after the wine than before."

It seemed that Mr. Humber, who had begun in doubt, was coming round to Sir John's way of thinking on this matter. Mr. Goldsmith, however, remained firmly in opposition.

"The wine! the wine!" he blustered. "If you will forgive me, Sir John—and I mean no disrespect—but your argument is not reasonable. It is based upon a logical fallacy—" And here did Mr. Goldsmith raise a finger and point above him as he quoted: *"Post hoc, ergo propter hoc."*

"I have little Latin," said Sir John, "but enough, I think,

to English that. Roughly, what you have said means, 'after which, therefore because of which.' Am I correct?''

"Indeed. You seem to feel—''

"Oh, I understand right enough,'' said Sir John, cutting him off sharply. "You suggest I argue that the bottle of wine from which he drank accounts for his death. Nothing of the kind! I offer no argument, neither fallacious nor logical. I merely seek to account for my doubts. Yet I do concede, Mr. Goldsmith, that if the appearance of that bottle of wine were all I had to support my doubts, then it would certainly not be enough.''

Thinking he had won a point, Mr. Goldsmith puffed up a bit and smiled a smile that could only be termed self-satisfied. "Good of you to say so, Sir John,'' said he.

"Nevertheless,'' continued the magistrate, "when we consider the appearance of that bottle of wine along with its sudden and complete *dis*appearance during that space of time when Lord Laningham was stricken and all did crowd around him, then—*then,* I say, there is quite sufficient support for doubt.''

"Come now, Jack,'' said Mr. Humber. "A 'disappearance,' you say? Is that not too strong, too dramatic a word? Say, rather, that it was not afterward to be seen.''

"Yet it was searched for. Jeremy—I take it that you are still here—did you not search?''

"I did indeed, sir,'' said I, "for ten minutes' time and over every foot of the stage.''

"But good God,'' said Goldsmith in evident exasperation, "there must have been near a hundred people up there—musicians, singers, Lord Laningham's family, some of the Crown and Anchor staff, and the . . . the merely curious—all of them crowding in. I daresay a server may have picked up the bottle which we saw rolling around on the floor and spilling its contents, picked it up and simply disposed of it. That would be the most logical explanation for what you call its disappearance.''

Sir John then let forth a sigh, a rather melancholy sound

in that room lit by only three candles. The depth and force of it extinguished the one on his desk and made the number two. Silence for a moment; then said he: "I shall, however, hold to my doubts. But Mr. Donnelly?"

"Yes, Sir John?" The surgeon spoke up almost reluctantly. He sat somewhat apart from the rest and had listened to the debate abstractedly, as if his mind were elsewhere.

"We have not heard from you. I had hoped you could enlighten us a bit on the nature of Lord Laningham's death, a few facts perhaps. For instance, if you will indulge this maggot that nags at my brain, how long after he drank of that bottle of wine did he die?"

"About an hour, I should say."

"Would you describe the nature of his death—his symptoms, so to speak?"

"Well, you noted the vomiting, of course."

"Aye!" crowed Mr. Humber. "Like it or not, we all saw *that!*"

"Alfred, please, let Mr. Donnelly continue."

And continue he did: "Like Jeremy, I'd noticed earlier signs—apparent dizziness and discomfort—but I counted them to his drunken state. Following his collapse and vomiting— By the bye, it was a true collapse, for he seemed to have little control over himself afterward, and it seemed there was nothing I could do for him. But after the collapse, I turned him over and loosened his collar to aid his breathing, which gave him obvious difficulty. There he lay, conscious but quite overcome, for a good many minutes. His wife arrived and tried to communicate with him, but he was unable to answer. Whether or not he grasped what she said to him—messages of endearment and encouragement they were—I really have no idea. He went into convulsions and then a state of coma, from which he could not be roused. I should say that last stage was of a duration of near ten minutes. His pulse grew weaker, and finally his heart stopped altogether."

"Thank you, Mr. Donnelly," said Sir John. "I should

call that grim description up to your usual high standard—precise, graphic, and dispassionate. Now, again, simply to indulge me in this matter, do you know of any poison—to utter the word at last—which could cause a death such as the one you described?"

"No, Sir John, I do not."

"There! You see?" hooted Mr. Goldsmith. "He knows of *none!*"

"*But*," said Mr. Donnelly, raising his voice, overriding him somewhat, "I must make it clear that I know next to naught of poisons. They did not figure in my career with the Navy as a ship's surgeon. As for my abortive practice in Lancashire, who knows? Perhaps some of those deaths I deemed natural may have been hurried on by henbane or foxglove. I had no reason to suspect, in any case."

"I quite understand," said Sir John. "But you have at your disposal books such as might give some light on the matter?"

"I do, yes, and I mean to study them tonight in order to explore this possibility, this 'doubt' of yours. In all truth, I was quite dissatisfied with the opinion I gave to Lady Laningham as to the cause of her husband's death. I told her that her husband had died of circulatory failure. This is very like saying that he died because his heart stopped beating. That, of course, is the ultimate cause of all death."

"Would you hazard a guess as to the penultimate?"

"I should be reluctant to do so. It seemed to be a gastric disturbance of some terrible proportion. What might cause such has me quite baffled. Barring further study of the kind I mentioned, and barring an autopsy of Lord Laningham's corpus, there would seem to be no way . . ." Mr. Donnelly paused, a frown upon his face, a look of frustration.

"What is it, sir? Something has occurred to you."

"Indeed something did occur—though now quite useless to us. It came to me that had we saved that which Lord Laningham vomited from his stomach and brought it to a competent chemist for analysis, he might have told us if there was some foreign element in it which could have caused such a violent reaction. But you, Sir John, gave permission to the innkeeper to clean up the stage after the body had been removed.''

''Ah, so I did. It seemed only proper.''

''As we left, I happened to notice one of his servers with mop and pail making rid of the mess.''

''Well, perhaps another time—though indeed I hope there be no other time.''

Through this conversation which took place between Sir John Fielding and Mr. Gabriel Donnelly, the two other gentlemen had remained silent—yet their attitudes differed greatly. For his part, Mr. Humber was clearly fascinated by all that passed between them. Mr. Goldsmith, on the other hand, seemed merely tolerant, bound by his affection for his friend Mr. Donnelly and his respect for Sir John to let them have their say. When a brief silence ensued upon their conclusion, I was in no wise surprised when it was Mr. Goldsmith who broke it.

''I have but one more objection to make, if I may.''

''Make it then, by all means,'' said Sir John, flapping a hand indifferently in the air.

''It is this, a simple appeal to good sense: If one were to wish to poison another, one would *not* choose a setting as public as these Sunday concerts. After all, up there on the stage? With hundreds looking on? It makes no sense, sir.''

''Yes, yes,'' said Mr. Humber, swayed once again in the other direction, ''Mr. Goldsmith brought that up on our walk from the Crown and Anchor. It does seem a good point, Jack.''

''Ah, but is it?'' questioned Sir John. ''What was it that those hundreds saw? An old man of seventy-five who had probably eaten too much and certainly drunk too much, up there before them, prancing about as one his age should not have done, playing the fool as he had often done in the past, overexerting himself. Many there knew he was not a well man. There could have been little surprise at his collapse. Some indeed may have made such dire predictions, attending simply in the expectation that it would one day happen just as it did and they might be there to see.'' He shook his great head and quaffed the last of his brandy. ''No, I reject Mr. Goldsmith's final point more emphatically than his others. I believe contrariwise, that if one were to wish to poison another—that other being Lord Laningham—he would choose just such a time and place as the Crown and Anchor stage within the process of a Sunday concert.''

As we climbed the back stairs to the kitchen, I heard the voices of Annie and Lady Fielding raised in such a way that it seemed they were quarreling. While that proved not quite to be so, they were certainly in disagreement.

''But Annie, you must!'' Lady Fielding's voice rang insistently as we reached the top of the stairs. ''It is a great honor to be chosen.''

Then, as I opened the door and Sir John followed, Annie, her back to us, responded vehemently, ''M'lady, that is just what I was told by Mr. Wills, the choirmaster. But how can it be an honor when it will only lead to my shame?''

We two walked into the kitchen, and the two females fell silent for a moment—but only for a moment, for both turned to us, each to argue her case. Sir John stood in bafflement, preparing himself for the assault.

''Jack,'' said Lady Fielding, ''you must talk a bit of sense to this girl.''

''Sense, is it? It seems just now to have come in high fashion. Forgive me that remark, Kate. I have just now left a discussion in which many appeals were made to good sense. My adversary seemed to think I lacked all trace of it. But let that pass. What is the trouble?''

''Annie here was invited to join the Handel Choir specially by the choirmaster. The other two volunteers were dismissed with thanks after the sadly aborted performance.

But our girl Annie was asked to become a permanent member of the choir. He was most flattering about her voice—she admits that—told her it was quite outstanding. And do you know how she replied? She told him that she was employed as our cook and had no time for such things.''

''Well . . . does she? That is to say, we do depend upon her for our meals, do we not?''

''Of course we do. But it seems that she told him in such a way as to offend him—I hope not overmuch—as if to say that music was of little importance when put against her daily duties.''

''Why, I think that quite admirable. Bravo, Annie, good, loyal girl!''

''Jack, no! She has a talent. It has been recognized. She should be given the opportunity to cultivate it. I have put myself forward to fill in for her here in the kitchen on those Sundays on which concerts are to be given. There are rehearsals, but they take place during the day.''

''Well, yes, I see what you mean, Kate. Only on Sundays, eh?''

''And not *every* Sunday—only on concert Sundays in the season. In fact, we have taken advantage of her willing nature since she has been with us. In many households, cook is given Sunday—or allowed to prepare an early meal so she may have the rest of the day to herself.''

''Ah, yes, hmmm, I see.'' Sir John rubbed his chin in thought, nodded in much the same way as he might when weighing testimony in his courtroom. ''This must, however, be Annie's matter to decide. We cannot force her to go off Sundays and sing Handel merely because we think she should. Perhaps it was not because she wished to serve us better that she gave this as her reason to the choirmaster. Perhaps that was merely an excuse to cover another, more personal.'' Then did he turn in her direction. ''Annie, tell me, as I entered just now, did I not hear you mention 'shame'? I believe you asked, 'How can this be an honor

when it will only bring me shame?''—or words to that effect. You did say that?''

"I did. Yes, Sir John.''

"What did you mean? How would it bring you shame?''

"She cannot read music,'' put in Lady Fielding.

"No, it's true I can't. When they handed me the music
sheets, all the notes was like so many flyspecks upon the
page. One of the ladies sang me my part, and I got it right
enough as far as she was able to take me—I've a good ear
for a tune—yet we had soon to go on the stage, and she
could only take me so far. No farther could I go. Mr. Wills,
he said he knew right when I quit, for the life went right
out of the sopranos. Which was meant as flattery, but indeed it made me feel ashamed that I could only open and
close my mouth and pretend to be singing with the rest.''

"I see. Well, perhaps at a proper rehearsal you could be
taught the rest and sing it entire.''

"P'rhaps,'' said she, "but it is long and has many tunes
in it. But then, there's this other thing that shames me even
more.''

"And what is that?''

Her lower lip trembled, she sniffled a bit, yet she plunged
on: "Even when I was singing I could only go ah-ah-ah,
for I could not even read the words upon the page. Some
of them I made out, for Jeremy has worked with me a bit,
but I fear I'm not a good scholar.''

"She is a good scholar,'' said I, seized by guilt and blurt-
ing it out. "It is I who am not a good teacher. I lack patience.''

"I often do myself,'' said Sir John. Then did he return
to rubbing his chin as he considered the matter. "You wish
to learn reading, do you?''

"More than anything, sir. I feel such a dunce in this
house having no letters.''

Then did a thought strike me, one that should have come
months before. "Sir John,'' said I, "there is a Mr. Burnham
who has worked a wonder in tutoring Jimmie Bunkins.

With no more than a few months' instruction, he has Bunkins reading from the *Public Advertiser* and has just put
him to work on *Robinson Crusoe*. No teacher before him
could bring Bunkins even to the beginnings of literacy.''

"Is it so?" said he. "Then perhaps you might make an
inquiry of this Mr. Burnham. If he were willing to take on
another scholar, I would be willing to pay for her tuition—
within reason, of course.''

"Oh, Sir John," said Annie, "I should be the happiest
cook in all London.''

"And would you then accept the invitation to join the
Handel Choir?" asked Lady Fielding, pressing her sudden
advantage.

"Oh, I would, I would. If I could but read the words, I
would gladly sing the song.''

"Fair enough, then. Jeremy," said Sir John. "Visit Mr.
Bilbo's domicile tomorrow and make inquiries of this fellow Burnham.''

The next day began as many another. Waking about six, or
a little before, I dressed hurriedly to warm myself against
the damp winter cold; then did I descend to light the kitchen
fire, as was my morning duty. Annie appeared, rubbing her
arms and doing a dance upon the kitchen floor to set the
blood a-flowing, and then did she set to work. Whilst she
put the water on and made tea and hauled down the flitch
of bacon to cut from it the rashers for breakfast, she did
gush her excitement at the prospect of learning letters from
a proper teacher.

"Not that I don't appreciate what you did for me, pointing at the words and saying them, as you did, Jeremy old
friend.''

"Yet I cut you off when the *Institutes of the Law* came
to me. I had only time for what *I* wished to do.''

"You'd a right. Each has his own purposes. Besides, I
was then forever after you for this word or that. I know I
was a bother.''

"And I was often ill-tempered when you came to me. It was good of you not to mention that to Sir John."

"What would have come of it? Anyways, 'twas you thought of Mr. Burnham." She hesitated then and gave me a most inquiring look. "Oh, Jeremy, do you think he'll take me?"

"Well, I hope so." Then, thinking upon it more, I said, "Yes. Yes, I think he will."

It was about that time that Lady Fielding came down the stairs, dressed as was her usual at breakfast, in slippers, nightgown, and a warm wrapper. She sat down upon a chair and huddled close to the fire, warming her hands. She was early. Sir John usually preceded her, dressed for the day. I wondered at his absence. She accepted a cup of strong tea from Annie with thanks and explained that he had been called downstairs by Constable Benjamin Bailey to attend to some matter but had promised to return for breakfast.

"It was not so long ago," said she. "I heard you, Jeremy, on the stairs shortly after. I've been in that half-waking state since then, unable quite to rouse myself, unable quite to return to sleep."

"Did he go out?" I asked. I was nearly always called to assist him on such expeditions.

"I think not," said she. "He did not return for his cloak, and he would indeed need it on such a morning as this."

And so, cutting off a great chunk of bread and topping it with butter, I took it with me for fear I might have no more for breakfast. I said I would summon him to breakfast and discover the nature of the matter. If there was to be action that morning, I wished to be in the very thick of it.

All was hubbub as I descended the stairs. It seemed, looking about below, that near half the force of red-waistcoated Bow Street Runners were milling about. They had organized themselves in pairs, each armed with pistols and cutlass, and were receiving instructions from Constable Bailey, their field commander. Each pair, having got their assignment, would then strike out for the street. Close to

Mr. Bailey, but a step or two behind, was Sir John, Magistrate of the Bow Street Court and general to the Runners. He would, from time to time, put in a few words of encouragement to his departing soldiers. I stood somewhat at a distance, chewing on my chunk of bread, as this business was negotiated. I had no wish to interrupt during what I clearly, and rightly, judged to be an emergency. When the last two had gone forth, I came forward. Mr. Bailey, I perceived, was also about to depart.

"We'll have covered all the likely places one such as this Slade might go on the sneak," said he to Sir John. "He'll be in the strong room in an hour, or I miss my guess."

"I dearly hope so," said the magistrate. "We cannot allow an attack upon a man of the law to go unpunished. Tell the men tonight how grateful I am to them for extending their time to make this search."

"Not a bit, sir. Cowley may not be the best of us, yet he is one of us." Looking about him then as if taking stock of the situation for a final farewell, Mr. Bailey spied me nearby and gave a sober nod. "Hullo, Jeremy," said he. "What news do you bring?"

"News of breakfast," said I, perhaps a bit too facetiously. "I am sent to bid Sir John to come and eat, if he's a mind to."

"Well and good then," said Mr. Bailey, turning to leave. "I'll be on my way."

"Good luck to you, sir," Sir John said. Then to me: "Eat, is it? Well, I suppose I must, for there is little more I can do here."

"What is it has happened?" I asked.

He sighed. "Late, quite late, last night, Constable Cowley came upon a robbery, as one might say, in the very act. He subdued the robber right enough with his club and took from him the knife with which he'd threatened the victim. Yet as Cowley bent to frisk him, the fellow drew a dagger from his sleeve and stabbed poor Cowley in the thigh—the meaty part. It did not do terrible damage nor make the blood to spurt, but it was enough to make pursuit impossible, for the villain took to his heels the moment he had stabbed the constable. The robbery victim remained and assisted Cowley to Mr. Donnelly's surgery, which, thank God, was not far off. He's well enough and resting there now.''

''But the identity of him who did the stabbing is known, I take it?''

''Yes, known to Cowley, for he had arrested him twice before on charges of drunkenness and robbery. Jonah Slade is the name of our villain. I also know him, for he came before me on both charges. He could not be bound over for robbery, for his supposed victims refused to testify against him—threatened, I should suppose. Many of the Runners know him from some encounter. Mr. Bailey is right. He should not be hard to find.''

''Could I help in the search?'' I asked.

''I doubt you could do much, since you know him not by sight, nor have you snitches to whisper in your ear where he's gone to.''

''I suppose you're right, Sir John.''

''There is, however, one service you might perform for me—not beyond your capabilities, I'm sure. Were you yesterday in my courtroom?''

''I was, sir, yes.''

''Then you may recall a fellow named Thomas Roundtree, whom I allowed to remain in our charge a second night that he might borrow the amount of his fine rather than pass a month in the Fleet Prison.''

''Indeed I do recall him—tall and thin, unshaven and seedy.''

''Well, there you have the advantage of me, but I'm sure you've described him accurately. In any case, it was my intention to ask Mr. Perkins to convey him to the residence of the Lord Chief Justice, where he is doing carpentry work. Mr. Perkins, as you well know, lives nearby. However, he's off on the hunt, as are all the constables save Mr. Fuller, who must tend the prisoners.''

"You wish me to accompany him?"

"Yes, if you would not mind accepting the responsibil- ity. You would be unofficially a constable *pro tempore*. We shall deck you out in a brace of pistols, though I think we may dispense with hand irons for the fellow. He seems docile enough. So, are you up to such a task?"

"Indeed I am," said I, "and proud to be asked."

Thomas Roundtree did certainly seem to be a docile fellow once away from Number 4 Bow Street, even quite likable. No more than a few steps onto the street, and he moved me to laughter by stopping suddenly to scratch himself on every part. Morning pedestrians passed him by, giving wide space, thinking him quite daft—or worse, possessed of some awful itching ailment. Yet he cared little, pulling faces as he rubbed and scraped away beneath that plaid waistcoat he wore.

"You've quite a flea farm there in your strong room," said he. "I believe I'm leaving with a hundred of your herd." He scratched again. "Ah! Make that a hundred and one."

I could but laugh at the fellow. He was a rustic clown. He could be one from Nick Bottom's troupe of players.

"I'll not be prosecuted for flea theft, nor even blamed, for as you can see, young sir, they've come with me quite willing." He left off his earnest activity at last, then wig- gled his narrow shoulders as if in great satisfaction. "Aahh!" said he.

Taking him by the elbow, I urged him forward. "Come along," said I. "We must be on our way."

"Yes, I s'pose, but caution, young sir. Get too close, and you may find them pasturing on you."

I dropped my arm from his and found myself rubbing uneasily at my wrist as we set off together. We had gone but a few steps when he turned to me and said, "I have a question for you."

"And what is that?"

"Where are we headed?"

"Why, to Bloomsbury Square," said I, "and the house of the Lord Chief Justice. That is where you have your employ, is it not? Where you must borrow ten shillings from the chief carpenter?"

"True enough," said he, "but I go there to start my day of work and not merely to borrow. And to do that, I must have my tools. You've yours, right enough—a club for breaking nappers, pistols to shoot me should I try to throttle you, which God's honor I never would do. I also needs the tools of my trade—hammer, saw, axe, awl, and such—for without them I cannot work."

He had succeeded in halting me, which was his intention. I gave a great sigh of annoyance. "And where are these tools of yours?" I asked.

"In the room where I dorse. I would not go walking about with them, lest some scamp rob me of them, and with them take away my livelihood. Ah no, I may be new to London, but thus much I have learned of life on your streets."

"And where is this room of yours?"

"In Half-Moon Passage—off in t'other direction."

"All right," said I, turning about where I stood, "let us go there quick as we can so I may be done with it. You may not credit this, but I have matters to attend to other than your own."

We started off again toward Half-Moon Passage. In this direction there seemed a greater swarm of pedestrians moving in one direction and the other. Roundtree managed well enough, moving swiftly along on his long legs, yet I was forced to hop to keep up. I had to keep close to him, fleas be damned, else I was not his guard but rather his attendant. I thought we might manage better by cutting through Covent Garden, and so when we came to Russell Street, I gave him a proper nudge and a nod, and up we went, immediately leaving that teeming mass of men and women behind.

"Aye now, that's far better, ain't it?" said he. "I had to stretch my legs just to keep up with the crowd."

"And I to run just to keep up with you."

"Did you so? Sorry, chum, didn't notice."

He slowed to an amble, and it was not long till we were in Covent Garden. In another hour or two it would be packed with buyers. There were only a few about then, however, those who had come early in the expectation of finding fresh greens just in from the farms; yet what they were more likely to get was that which was left over from the day before. What was fresh was saved for the later throng. I had not lived hard by the Garden near three years without learning the ways of its sellers.

We passed close by a bake stall, one with a working baker who was just then pulling loaves and buns from the depths of the oven. The smell of the fresh-baked bread wafted to us and stopped Thomas Roundtree as sure and swift as if he'd bumped up against a wall.

"What say, young sir?" said he, clasping his hands before him in a gesture of supplication. "I've had naught to eat this morning. You would not send a man to work on an empty belly, would you now?"

It was just possible that indeed he had not eaten. Things had been turned topsy-turvy by the sudden search for Jonah Slade. I might be tempted to have a bun for myself if I could get one fresh from the oven. And so I haggled with the woman who hawked the goods—not on the price but on the particular buns I would buy. She would have none of that; she alone would choose what she sold.

"If that be so," said I, "then I will have only one bun, and that for him"—pointing at Roundtree—"even though it be cold and most likely a day old. If you wish to sell two, then they must be from that batch just pulled from the oven."

"Well, you'll have none, you rude boy. Out of my sight with you."

She would have continued and no doubt called down a curse upon me, but then did the baker himself shout her down: "Maggie, give him what he wishes. Can't you see the lad is from Bow Street?"

And so we got our ha'penny buns, and she her penny, though taking it in bad temper. They were warm to the touch and steamed in the cold air. We retired to a place just beyond the bake stall to eat them, and it was true I never tasted better than on that morning.

"You're a rum joe for a hornie," said Roundtree, chewing contentedly.

I did not know quite how I might take that. True, he meant it as flattery of a proper sort and no doubt sincere, yet behind it was evident a certain dislike, perhaps even hostility toward constables—"hornies," "Beak Runners." Well, why not, after all? He'd been arrested but two nights before by one of them—I had no idea which—for public drunkenness. He could not but mark that a sad event.

Even so, in responding to his remark, I put all that aside and said, "For one who says he is new to London, you've already managed to learn a bit of flash cant."

"It's them I work with," said he. "They're a rowdy lot, and not near the sort you'd expect to find working in the home of the Lord Chief Justice. I have indeed picked up some of their talk."

"Where are you from?" I asked.

"From Lichfield," he said, as quick as ever you please.

"So was I once," said I.

"God's truth? Now, ain't that a marvel! In what part of the town did you live?"

"I've no exact idea. I was too young to know my way around the place very well. I do recall, though, that there was a very large church nearby."

"That fixes it a bit," said he. "I think I knows what part. So you come to London then, did you?"

"No, not immediate. My mother and younger brother died there in the typhus of 1765."

"Oh, I remembers it—terrible it was, killed many," he interjected.

"My father and I moved to a smaller town"—I would not deign to mention the name of it—"and there he, too, died"—nor would I describe the brutal circumstances of his death—"and I was left an orphan. Only then did I come to London, alone, at the age of thirteen."

"Why, ain't that a sad tale! Yet you made your way in London and stayed on the right side of the law."

"I cannot claim credit for that," said I. "To one man alone I am beholden for my salvation. You have met him. Let me tell you what he did for me."

Whereupon I told Roundtree the longer tale of my first day in London: of how I was gulled by an "independent thief-taker," so called, and his confederate, and brought to the Bow Street Court falsely accused of theft; of how Sir John Fielding penetrated their deception and sent one off with a warning and the other to Newgate; and of how Sir John made me a ward of the court and finally one of his household.

By the time I had done, Roundtree's mouth was quite open in awe. Never had I had a better listener to my story—and I had told it often—than this rough carpenter from Lichfield. He seemed quite moved by it.

"And that be the very same one made it possible for me to borrow my fine 'stead of going off to jail."

"The very same one—Sir John Fielding."

"Oh, I heard of him. He's the one they call the Blind Beak of Bow Street, ain't he?"

"He is."

"Right fair and just."

"He is indeed." I popped the last of my bun into my mouth; his had disappeared some time before. "But now," I said to him, "we must be off to pick up your tools and deliver you with them to the house of the Lord Chief Justice.''

"I s'pose we must. But you tell a good story, chum. God's truth, I could listen to you the whole day long.''

For one of fifteen years to hear that from a man twice his age was heady stuff indeed. I walked along at a steadier pace, buoyed somehow by confidence, a sudden feeling of manliness. We talked—oh, I have no true idea what it was we talked of on our way to Half-Moon Passage. I seem to recall he asked my advice on what new place he might move to, Covent Garden offering too many temptations and bad companions for a simple fellow, such as he was, fresh come from Lichfield. He asked if Southwark would do, and I told him of its bad repute—"no better than Covent Garden, and in some places worse." I recommended Clerkenwell, "out from the city, with much new building—houses and such." He thanked me greatly and said he would go out there for a look.

There were other matters—comments upon places and people we passed; women, especially, seemed to interest him. One exchange, however, I do recall for its later pertinence.

Quite without relevance to anything under earlier discussion, he turned to me and asked, "How comes it you don't wear no red waistcoat like the rest of the constables?''

"That is because I am a constable"—what was Sir John's phrase?—"*pro tempore*.''

"Is that like something special?''

"Noo," said I, searching for some easy way to define my status yet still retain some dignity, "it puts me more in the way of an apprentice constable.''

"Ah," he said, "well I knows 'prenticeship. I was a 'prentice carpenter for six years.''

"As long as that?''

"I had a hard master. Yours, though, ain't near so hard, nor would he want you to be. Why, I'll wager those barking irons you got on ain't even loaded.''

"Oh, but they are. Mr. Baker, our armorer, says there's nothing so foolish as carrying about an unloaded gun."

"But you ain't never kilt nobody, have you?"

"No, nor would I want to." Then, after thinking about that and in the interest of truth telling, I did add: "I once shot and wounded one, however."

"Truly so? A young fella like you?"

"Yes, truly. He died, though not of the wound."

With that he fell silent for a long spell. Still, as we turned down Half-Moon Passage from Bedford, he roused himself and played the rustic clown once again.

"This house wherein I dwells, it was built as an inn a hundred years ago or more, perhaps a thousand from the way it's decayed and ramshackled, like. I don't wonder a good wind will blow it down someday soon. Well, I did not live there long till I began to notice strange comings and goings and hear shouts and ugly laughing at night when a workingman such as myself needs to get his sleep. Well, I keep my ears open and my eyes open, and I asks around a bit, and I come to find this place I'm livin' in is known as a great house for whores. Come summer, I'd go home at night, havin' had my bub and grub, and I'd go down the hall, and here's my women neighbors standin' about in their doorways in their shifts and their altogethers, some of them, bubs hangin' out, just advertisin' what they got to sell. Oh, I tell you it was a sight. And even now, in the winter, I catches sight of them in the hall, visitin' back and forth just so, without a care."

And then did he raise his arms and strut on the street in a female manner and say in mimicking falsetto: "Oh, Moll, may I wear your brown frock? My blue one got all muddy, and I ain't had time to wash it."

I laughed quite in spite of myself, yet hung back, embarrassed, as he attracted gawking attention from the passersby with his foolish parade. Yet he returned to walk beside me. There could be no doubt that he was my companion.

"I have seen them so, nekkid in the hall, or next thing to it. Ain't that enough to give a man care? You can see why I must move to Southwark—or where was that other place?"

"Clerkenwell," said I.

"Ah, so it was—Clerkenwell. Must remember that," said he solemnly. Then did he brighten: "But here we are. It won't take but a minute for me to get my tools. Then we'll be off to Bloomsbury."

The place was as he had described it, certainly no better. I had passed it many times before but had thought it in no wise remarkable. There was a modest entrance, such as might once have accommodated horses and coach. It led into an interior court, whereon all manner of refuse and rubbish had been tossed. From it came an evil stench. Around the courtyard on three sides were two tiers of rooms, top and bottom. It was quite like the court in which poor old Moll Caulfield had lived that later blew down. And it seemed nearer two hundred years old than a hundred. In only one significant way did this court building differ from that one and most others: the surrounding tiers were walled over, so that the hall that Roundtree had described was interior and dark with only a small window to cut the gloom every twenty feet, or approximately so.

We climbed a short flight of stairs to the level of the first tier, and he led the way down the hall.

"Watch out now one of those nekkid women don't reach out and pull you into her room. They can be mightily insistent." He laughed a silly, cackling laugh at that. "'Twouldn't do for a young fellow like you to get caught like that."

More laughter until at last we came to a door about half-way down the hall, and he reached down deep into his coat pocket and pulled out a key. He held it up to me as if it were a sort of talisman or some popish holy relic.

"I keeps the door always locked. Whores is notorious

thieves, and my tools and other b'longings are worth something.''

In the dim light I could tell the key, though large, was old and rusty. If the lock to which it fitted was as old, his tools were not near as safe as he seemed to think them.

He bent to insert the key and turned it in the lock. I must have been bending over him somewhat myself, for when of a sudden he looked sharp to the left, his head was quite near mine.

''There's one of them now,'' he whispered urgently, ''one of them nekkid women!''

To my discredit, I turned to look. That was my great mistake. For with my attention uselessly averted (there was nothing to be seen), he uncoiled his lean body against me with surprising force and sent me sprawling in a heap against the far wall of the hall. Before I could regain my feet, the door was open, he was inside, and the door was shut again. By the time I righted myself and stumbled over to it, I had heard the key turn in the lock.

I beat bootlessly upon the door with my fist. ''Open up!'' I shouted. ''I'm to keep you in sight at all times!''

Laughter was his response. ''I'll be out directly,'' he called.

Through the door I heard steps, movement, a great flurry of activity. It occurred to me that if I could hear through it so plain, the door must not be so very thick. Perhaps I could batter it down. And so, backing off to the far wall, I took two running steps and hurled myself against it, shoulder first.

I felt it give somewhat, but I also felt a stab of pain pass through my shoulder. I might indeed be able to knock open the door, but I should likely cripple myself before I was done. There must be some better, faster method, I thought, then remembered what Constable Perkins had taught me not so long ago: that it was possible to destroy a lock with a shot from a gun. The trick, he said, was in the placement of the ball—not direct into the lock, but between the door and the doorframe, where the bolt of the lock fits into the hasp.

I drew out a pistol from its holster and found the place I thought likeliest. Then, hauling back the hammer, I held the pistol close and pulled the trigger. It was a good-sized pistol which fired a good-sized ball. It jumped in my hand as the shot exploded loudly from it, so that I feared it may have hit above the mark. But no—as the smoke from the gunpowder cleared, I saw the ball was well placed. It had blown a hole of frightening dimension in the wood at just the spot at which I had aimed.

I holstered the pistol, pulled out the club I had been given by Mr. Fuller, the gaoler, and gave a great kick to the door—and then another. Then did the door fly open, scattering bits of lock and ball over the floor of the room beyond.

I leapt inside and looked about. I saw nothing of Roundtree—only a window with both panels opened wide. I ran to it and looked down. Indeed there he was, not more than ten feet below but hurrying without a look back down a narrow dirt passage to the street, toolbox and a few other belongings in hand.

Pulling out my second pistol, I thought I might still get in a wounding shot, if indeed I did not kill him, but . . . Yes, "but" indeed. Was ten shillings worth wounding a man, possibly killing him? Angry as I was at him, furious as I was at myself, I could only answer that in the negative. I eased back the hammer of the pistol and tucked the weapon away.

Though I had no expectation, nor even hope, of finding Thomas Roundtree there, I went direct to the residence of the Lord Chief Justice in Bloomsbury Square.

Having hastened a fair distance in a high state of emotion, I was in a proper sweat by the time I took hold the great knocker and rapped loudly upon the door. As expected, the butler appeared. I resolved I would stand for none of the usual nonsense from him that morning.

"Ah," said he, "it is the boy from Bow Street. If you wish to see the Lord Chief Justice, I am afraid that is impossible dressed as you are. Goodness! You're even wearing pistols—certainly not with pistols! You'd best give me the letter, and trust me to—"

"*No*, I do *not* wish to see the Lord Chief Justice," I shouted at him. "And I have *no letter* to *deliver!*"

In response he stood and blinked three times. At last he spoke, apparently unperturbed: "What is it, then, that you wish?"

"I believe you have a crew of carpenters working in the house installing a water closet."

"That is correct."

"Bring me their chief. I wish to speak with him."

A direct order. Reader, how good that felt!

"Uh . . . well . . . yes, I shall. Would . . . would you care to wait in the vestibule? It's rather chilly this morning."

That surprised me so that I very nearly failed to thank him. But thank him I did and stepped inside, taking a place beside the bench whereon I had waited on those occasions when the butler had deemed me properly dressed to enter the residence of the Lord Chief Justice.

"You may seat yourself, if you like."

"No, I prefer to stand."

"As you wish," said he, backing away. "Uh . . . tell me, is this about the vase?"

"I know nothing of a vase. The chief carpenter, if you please."

He nodded, turned, and hurried off. It could not have been more than three minutes that elapsed before he returned with a short, wiry little man in tow. The chief carpenter was dressed roughly for work; I noted bits of sawdust on his breeches. He looked around him curiously as he approached, and it occurred to me likely that this was his first visit to this part of the house. At a certain point the butler hung back, though well within eavesdropping distance, and allowed the man to proceed to me.

"What can I do for yez?" the fellow asked. He seemed to be Irish. So many in the building trades were.

"First, let me ask you," said I, "what is your name, sir?"

"Dismas Cullen and proud of it. Now you must tell me the what of this matter."

"Gladly," said I to him. "I am from the Bow Street Court. A man held prisoner on a minor matter of public drunkenness has escaped my custody. He said he was in your employ, and was on his way to borrow from you the ten shillings' fine that would keep him out of gaol. I am sure he has not come here, for he well knows this is the first place I would look for him. But I have come to you first, to ask you to hold him for us if he does show his face. And secondly, to ask you for information you may have that will aid us in finding him."

"It's Thomas Roundtree you're speaking of, now ain't it?"

"Did I not say so? Forgive me. Yes, it is."

"Well, let me set you straight. He ain't in my employ no more. Friday night after we left work here, they found a vase of some value, Chinese it was, had gone missing, and they let us know on Saturday morning that we was suspect. Now, I was damn certain I didn't take it. And I was sure about three of the crew because they are my son, my brother, and my brother-in-law. I could vouch for all but Roundtree. So we marched him back to his room in Half-Moon Passage and looked the place through, but no such thing was to be found there. This I reported to the Lord Chief Justice hisself, and he said there was no certain evidence against the fellow, but he wanted him here no longer. Nor did I. So I pays him off, I did, and sends him on his way, all the time him telling us how innocent he is. We four family have worked in many homes of the gentry and the nobility and never had no trouble like this before."

"So you would not have loaned him the ten shillings in any case?"

"Hah! No chance of it. The way the Lord Chief Justice handled the matter, he subtracts the worth of the vase from what he pays me when this job is done—five guineas, if you please! We'll make precious little profit on this water closet. He said it was my fault for hiring him. And you look at it his way, and he's right. Loan Roundtree ten shillings indeed! That'll be a cold day in hell!"

"Well," I asked, "why did you hire him? What did you know of him?"

"Not enough. My youngest brother went back to County Wexford to visit our mother, who's terrible ill and old. He went for the rest of us. But that left us shorthanded for this job, so I posted a notice and several answered. Roundtree looked the best of the bunch, and he'd had journeyman's papers for twelve years, so I hired him. In truth, he wasn't a bad worker. But I rue the day I set eyes upon him."

"But nothing about him that would help me find him?"

"Well, he lives in a terrible place in Half-Moon Passage, a den of thieves and whores."

"I know the place. I've been there."

"And—oh, let me think a bit—he's from Lichfield. That's where his journeyman papers was from."

"I knew that, too."

"Beyond that I cannot help you." He shrugged. "Sorry, young fella, it seems we was both his victims."

As I thanked Mr. Cullen, the butler appeared suddenly at my elbow—materialized, rather, in a somewhat ghostly manner. He opened the door, making it plain that my time had run out. Having no alternative, I accepted that and had no retort to the whispered envoi with which he sent me out into the cold.

"Losing a prisoner," said he, then made a series of sucking pops with his tongue which I shall hereby render, *"tsk, tsk, tsk, tsk."*

THREE

*In Which I View
an Unholy Sight
in a Churchyard*

There was naught to do but return to Bow Street and inform Sir John of my failure. That I did, seated before him in his chambers, shoulders drooping and all apologetic. I told not all in detail, leaving out the device by which he distracted my attention as too shameful to admit, and said merely that Thomas Roundtree had cozened me and won my confidence until he knocked me down, fled inside the room, and locked me out. Then, describing how I had forced my entry, I told how I had raced to the open window and caught my last glimpse of him, running down the foot passage for the street. Yet more to tell, I gave an account of my visit to the residence of the Lord Chief Justice and all that I had learned there.

Sir John listened silently through all, his face so impassive that I was unable to draw any hint from it of his response to this matter which embarrassed me so sorely. At last when I had done, he spoke. "I would not blame myself overmuch in this if I were you, Jeremy," said he. "I no less than you misjudged the fellow. Did I not say that he seemed 'docile'?"

"Well, yes, but . . ."

"These things happen from time to time. In this instance
he will have been the cause of his own misfortune. He will
wish many times over that he had served that month in the
Fleet Prison, for when he is caught, he will be dealt with
far more severely. Yet I daresay his intention in returning
to his place in Half-Moon Passage was to recover that vase
along with his tools."

"You see it so? Mr. Cullen, the chief carpenter, said they
had searched the room thorough."

"Perhaps Mr. Roundtree is cleverer at hiding than Cullen
and his family are at searching. A floorboard perhaps? I
recall you found quite a treasure beneath the floor in one
house in Half-Moon Passage. Was it, by any chance, the
same one?"

"No, Polly Tarkin's was two houses closer to the Strand.
This one was in even worse repair."

"You don't say so," he mused. "Sometime another
great fire or wind may come and take all such ancient and
decrepit buildings. London may indeed be the better for it."
He paused. "You might go back for another look about his
place. There might be there some hint of where he might
have gone."

"Back to Lichfield perhaps," I suggested.

"Possibly—though I doubt it. There was Lichfield in his
voice, though a strong layer of London atop it. I would
venture that he has been here years, rather than months. In
any case, I shall write the Magistrate of Lichfield, whoever
he be, and ask that Roundtree be held for us, should he
make an appearance there. We shall see. There are more
urgent matters before us."

"And what are they, sir?"

"I should like to indite a letter to our new coroner, Mr.
Thomas Trezavant. Perhaps you, Jeremy, would take it
down for me."

Responding that I should be happy to do so, I shifted my
chair closer to his desk and took from him the paper and

quill which he produced from his drawer; the inkwell stood, as it always did, at my side of the desk, at a safe remove from the sweeping gestures he sometimes made. I dipped the quill and told him I was ready.

Yet he did not make an immediate start as was his usual. He sat a long moment, his chin raised, apparently deep in thought. I considered it likely that in this instance he had given no prior attention to the exact wording of the letter and was composing it in his mind ere he gave it forth. But no, I was wrong.

"That fellow Roundtree," said he, "I must say he does intrigue me."

"Oh? How is that?"

"Well, he is actor enough to have deceived us both as to his true nature. I make no boast to say that I am not easily deceived. And bold! Good God, one would indeed have to be bold to steal a vase from the home of the Lord Chief Justice. He has a reputation for severity that must surely have reached Roundtree."

"Yet even he admitted there was no direct evidence against him. Perhaps one of the house staff took the vase, knowing that with carpenters in the house blame would naturally fall upon them."

"That would certainly seem a possibility," said Sir John, "but much less likely considering Roundtree's escape from you. Interesting that the Lord Chief Justice settled simply for the value of the vase." Then, with a shrug, he ended his musing with an "Ah, well," then launched into the letter: "To Mr. Thomas Trezavant, Coroner, City of Westminster. Dear Mr. Trezavant . . ."

Having thus begun, he recapitulated the doubts regarding Lord Laningham's death he had stated the evening before to Messrs. Donnelly, Goldsmith, and Humber, and briefly supported them as he had with questions and an argument or two. Sir John spoke in an easy cadence of phrases which made it easy for me, as his amanuensis, to follow close behind his dictation. His powers of summary were such that when he concluded, asking if an inquest might not be in order and arguing for an autopsy, I had near half the sheet of foolscap left unwritten upon.

"Do you wish to add anything?" I asked.

"Has something been left out?"

"Nooo, but there is much space left."

"Then I shall fill it with my signature."

And he very nearly did. I put the quill in his hand, placed it upon the paper, and he did the rest, even adding a rare flourish beneath.

"How is that?" he asked. "Something better than my usual scrawl?"

"If scrawl it be, then it is a most impressive scrawl."

"Well and good. Signatures are not meant to be read, but rather to be respected."

Then did I fold the letter, seal it with wax, and stamp it with his seal of office.

"You will deliver that, of course," said he, "and ask for a written reply. Since this will be your first visit to the residence of Mr. Trezavant you must get address and directions from Mr. Marsden. He has a record of all such details. I know not what we should do without him."

I hesitated at the door, remembering a matter of some importance. "Sir John," said I, "forgive me. I was so taken up with my own matters that I failed to ask about the search for Jonah Slade. Did it succeed? Has he been caught?"

"Alas, no, but we shall continue to look. We cannot allow an attack upon a constable to go unpunished."

"And Mr. Cowley?"

"He does well." Then did I turn to go, only to be hailed back by Sir John. "Jeremy," said he, "if on your return you pass near St. James Street, you might stop at the home of Mr. Bilbo and inquire of that matter with his Mr. Burnham and our Annie."

"I shall, Sir John."

"Though it be only proper to inquire first of Mr. Bilbo,

since he is the master of the house. Remember that, please.''

Mr. Trezavant's butler greeted me respectfully at the door, made no objection to my attire (I had, of course, left the brace of pistols at Bow Street), and when told I bore a letter to his master from Sir John Fielding, bade me enter. He left me in the vestibule at the door to announce my coming to Mr. Trezavant. I could not but remark the difference in the reception I was given here when compared to that which I had received earlier in Bloomsbury Square.

It was a large house, larger than any I had been in, save that of the Lord Chief Justice. From where I stood, the vestibule opened into a large reception area, one side of which was taken up by a staircase which wound to the two levels above; the other led into a long, dark hall down which the butler had disappeared. Two doors opened right and left from the reception area, and upon its walls pictures were hung. The absence of family portraits suggested to me that Mr. Trezavant was in trade. The fact that such pictures as there were presented harbor scenes and seascapes with distant sails a-billowing made it seem likely that he was in the shipping trade.

It was a very quiet house. For minutes the only sounds I heard within entered through the door from the street. Then at last came the steady, unhurried tread of the butler as he made his way back to me up the long hall. I heard him some time before I saw him. He took a stance in the center of the reception area.

''Mr. Trezavant will see you now, young man,'' said he. ''If you will but follow me?''

I did so, seeking to match him stride for stride. Our footsteps chimed together on the slick, waxed floor. He stopped at the last door on the left and rapped soundly upon it. A call to enter came from inside. The butler opened the door and announced me simply as ''a young man from the Bow Street Court.'' Then he did leave us, closing the door behind him. They certainly observed formalities in this house.

I understood why that should be as I took the opportunity to observe Mr. Thomas Trezavant for the first time. He was not so much a man given to formalities as he was a huge bundle of formalities given the shape of a man. "Huge" in the sense that he himself was hugely fat, overflowing the chair in which he nested in every direction, so that he gave the illusion of being invisibly suspended behind his considerable desk, rather than simply seated.

Yet then he revealed the chair by struggling out of it. He reached toward me across the desk—surely not to shake the hand of one so young whose name had not been given him; that would be exceeding the mark!—to facilitate an exchange.

"I believe," said he, "that you have a letter for me."

"I do, sir," said I, producing it from my pocket, "from Sir John Fielding, Magistrate of the Bow Street Court. He has asked for a reply in writing, if it please you." I handed it over to him.

"Do sit down," said he, gesturing to a chair. "Would you care for some refreshment—coffee, perhaps?"

I had already noted the silver coffee service on a table nearby. "Why, yes sir, I believe I would."

He called in the butler and pointed to the coffee. "Please serve our guest, Arthur."

Nor even then did he seat himself, nor cast his eyes down at the letter. He waited patiently whilst Arthur poured and served the coffee. Only when cup and saucer were in my hands did Mr. Trezavant return his considerable weight to the chair, thus making it invisible once again. He made space for the letter upon his desk, which was piled high with ledgers and account books. Then, after adjusting his spectacles, he gave the letter his full attention.

By the time he had done with it, he wore a frown. Yet as he removed his spectacles, he forced a smile.

"I have had the pleasure of meeting Sir John but once," said he to me, "yet I recollect that he is blind."

"That is true, sir."

Then did he say something most peculiar: "Do tell him for me that he writes a very good hand for one so afflicted."

I happened just then to be sipping the lukewarm coffee I had been served. And upon hearing what he said, I came very near to spewing the contents of my mouth across the room. Luckily, I managed merely to deposit the coffee back into the cup.

"Are you all right?" He seemed genuinely concerned.

"Yes," I said, croaking a bit, clearing my throat, "yes, do pardon me, sir."

"Certainly."

"But I should tell you that it was I who took the letter in dictation from Sir John. The hand is mind. The signature, however, is his own."

"Ah, yes, the signature—very strong. Do pass that on from me, will you?" He smiled again, this time somewhat more tentatively. "But since you took the letter in dictation, you know its contents, of course."

"Of course, sir."

"Then allow me to discuss its contents, well, as one might in conversation, and you may pass on to Sir John my thoughts on the matter at hand."

Should I remind him that Sir John was especially desirous of a written reply? This did not seem quite the moment. He seemed so eager simply to talk about it. "Well," said I, reluctantly, "all right."

He leaned toward me and again smiled quite ingratiatingly. "Really," he said, "this will never do."

"Sir?" I fear that the surprise I felt was all too apparent in my response.

"Indeed, no," said he quite firmly. "I see no need for an inquest. I concede that Sir John raises some interesting questions. I concede also that I was not present at the event in question. Nevertheless I see no point in it unless an autopsy be performed, and an autopsy would certainly be out of the question.''

''But why?''

''Well, if I understand these matters aright, an autopsy consists of cutting open the body and examining the organs, that sort of thing, am I right?''

''Yes sir. Mr. Donnelly is quite expert at such procedures.''

''But they are so messy, so *unseemly*. Such exercises may prove useful upon the ordinary victims of crime, but upon members of the nobility they do not seem suitable— no, not at all. Why, if there were an autopsy, much more an inquest, people would think that there was something questionable about his death. We cannot have that, now can we? Think of the effect it would have upon his poor widow! No, with all due respect to Sir John and his doubts, I see no point to it. After all, Lord Laningham was near fourscore years. High time he died, if you ask me!''

Thomas Trezavant, the recently appointed coroner of the City of Westminster, had indeed spoken; it seemed to me that he had been excessively emphatic regarding the choice he had made, which was, after all, to do nothing. No doubt he was less sure of himself than he wished to appear—or so I see it today, as I write this nearly thirty years after the event. Perhaps he was trying to convince himself.

''Now,'' he resumed, ''any lad who writes as good and clear a hand as you have written here must be very bright, certainly bright enough to convey my arguments against to Sir John. I shall trust you to do so.'' This was said with the most dazzling of winning smiles.

I was flattered, though not deterred. ''But sir,'' said I, ''Sir John did specifically direct me to request from you a written reply.''

His smile faded. It was clear that he would rather not.

''Really,'' I added, ''it is just a formality. And it would be a great help to me in doing justice to what you have said if you were to put down a few words that I might take as notes from which to make plain your position. You might jot them down at the bottom of the letter. The Lord Chief Justice frequently does that."

"Oh?" He considered my suggestion. "Lord Chief Justice, you say?"

"Indeed, sir."

"Just a few words?"

"Just a few."

"Well, I suppose I might do that."

And so saying, he picked up the quill pen with which he had been working, dipped it, and very quickly jotted a few words beneath Sir John's florid signature. A very few. Then did he fold the letter, not bothering to seal it, and called out for the butler. With the same great effort as before, he pushed himself up from the chair. And as I gulped down the remainder of the coffee in my cup and put it aside, I, too, stood and made ready to accept the letter—though not first, it seemed, without a final bit of ceremony.

"May I ask your name, young man?"

"It is Jeremy Proctor, sir."

"Let me assure you, young Mr. Proctor, that I judge my time with you well spent. I look forward to other meetings and to a long and happy relationship with Sir John Fielding. Convey that to him, please do."

With that, he offered his right hand; I shook it and took the letter from his left.

"Thank you, sir. It has been a pleasure."

"Arthur, show Jeremy Proctor to the door and send him on his way with our good wishes."

Arthur bowed his acceptance of the task. I bowed my goodbye to Mr. Trezavant. And Mr. Trezavant bowed his dismissal to me. Such an abundance of bowing!

I returned down the long, dark hall, following the butler as before, and noted that as he opened the door to allow me into the street, he followed his charge exactly.

"Good wishes to you, young sir," said he.

"And to you also," said I, with a wave.

I heard the door close after me and walked on to the next street. And as I walked, I reflected that in an odd way it had indeed been a pleasure. What Mr. Trezavant seemed to lack in plain sense, he made up for in politesse. He was of a type I knew nothing about at that time in my life and do now know only a little better: a born courtier; the sort who, with good manners alone, hopes to overcome all resistance, who with smiles and compliments and a sure sense of where power might lie in any given situation would find his way to the side of power while giving no offense to the rest. The man was no fool. That much was evident. Only great success as a merchant could have provided him with such a grand house. Yet his intelligence was of the sort most comfortable with numbers, debits and credits. For the rest, he stood firmly upon ceremony.

I would not pretend, reader, that all of this had occurred to me during my walk to the corner. It is equally the product of later experiences and observations Mr.—later to become Sir—Thomas Trezavant, who eventually died as Lord Barnwell, Earl of Calder. All I can honestly say is that when I had gone that distance from his house, I thought it safe to open the letter and see what he had written upon it. I give it to you now in all its cryptic brevity:

"See no need. Unseemly. No point.—T."

All that I truly thought then and there was that the man was a perfect ass.

The house I had visited was in Little Jermyn Street. I had reached it walking down Piccadilly. To my surprise, I found that the corner at which I had chosen to read the message appended upon Sir John's letter put me on St. James Street. I knew I was close to the Bilbo residence, yet I'd no idea I was quite so close, for in the past I had always approached it down Pall Mall, paying little attention to what lay in the surroundings. So then did I turn on St. James and make my way to that house which I knew so well.

Jack Bilbo was proprietor of London's largest gaming

establishment. He was a man with a past. There were dark rumors of how he had come by the fortune he had spent in outfitting and opening his now thriving enterprise. Some said he'd got his money smuggling during the French War; others that he'd captained a privateer in the Caribbean and preyed upon all shipping that passed his way but for British; most, however, dismissed such accounts as mere milk-soppery and declared with great certainty (though always behind his back) that Black Jack Bilbo had been nothing more or less than a pirate.

He looked the part. Bald but for a few stray hairs, he refused to wear a wig and wore a great bush of a black beard which covered the lower part of his face completely. Though not of great stature, he carried a substantial weight of muscle and sinew on his powerful body. He would often go through the streets of London, on foot and unarmed, carrying considerable sums of money; never was it known, however, that he was accosted by robbers: his fierce appearance and even more fearsome reputation protected him against all.

Nevertheless, Sir John called him friend. Jack Bilbo had been guest in our home on more than one occasion. He was forthright and honest, and he was generous enough to have taken my friend Jimmie Bunkins off the street and made him his ward. He took him from his life of thievery and taught him honesty, loyalty, and obedience. In only one particular had Bunkins failed to learn, and that was in the matter of letters—failed, that is, until Mr. Robert Burnham came as tutor a few months before the time of which I write. Young Mr. Burnham, with his kind and persuasive manner, his experience in teaching, and his simple and direct method, had achieved immediate results. As I had told Sir John, Bunkins already read from the newspaper and was now taking on more challenging matter—books. It was to Mr. Burnham's tuition that I hoped to entrust our Annie.

So came I to the house in St. James Street which had once belonged to the unfortunate Lord Goodhope. How it came into the hands of Black Jack Bilbo is a tale already told; I shall not further impede this narrative by repeating it. Suffice it to say that under Mr. Bilbo's rule the household was run in a manner more democratic than before. He kept no large house staff of retainers—footmen, maids, servers, and the like—only a cook and a kitchen slavey or two, and a couple of what he termed "house cleaners." Those who lived in the house, most of them on the staff of his gaming establishment, were given the responsibility of maintaining the house and serving themselves insofar as they were able. Since there was no butler, all inside lived by Mr. Bilbo's injunction that he who heard a knock upon the door must needs answer it. For the most part this system, if it be called such, worked well enough. There were often, however, long waits upon the doorstep as one waited to catch the ear of one of the residents. Nor was there any certainty just who might at last appear at the door.

On this occasion I was pleased to find an old acquaintance there to greet me. It was the familiar face of Nancy Plummer that I found a-smiling out at me. Her I had first met near three years before on the occasion of my first (and near only) visit to Black Jack Bilbo's gaming establishment. She worked there as a greeter and hostess. Yet she lived under her master's protection in this house that had once been the dwelling of an earl, and here I had seen her often.

"Jeremy," said she, throwing open the door, "come in, though I must tell you that Jimmie B. is at his morning lessons."

"Well and good," said I, entering, "for I must first talk with the cove of the ken."

"Oh, he's about, ain' he?" Shutting the door. "Though I'll not take you where he is. I would not dare to go for a handful of neds." She said it with a proper shiver of horror.

What was this mystery? I was about to ask when she told all:

"Mr. Bilbo's down belowstairs. The house is bein' ratted. The men is all down there, looking on, hooting and yelling and cheering the ratcatcher on. Cook and I and the other ladies of the house took shelter above just to be away from them terrible creatures. I come down for a deck of cards, else I would not have heard your knock.'' She held the deck up to me as if to prove her claim.

"Then go, Nancy," said I. "I'll find my way to him."

"That's a good lad," she said. "Just down the hall—"

"To the last door on the right and down the stairs," I said.

"You know the way for fair. I'll leave it to you, then." She pranced away toward the staircase. "Oh, sweet Jesus, I do hate them things," she wailed as she took to the stairs.

Indeed I did know the way. I had learned it during my early visits to this house when it was still the Goodhope residence. It seemed to me that it was a very long time ago, though I knew it was not. So much had happened since then, however, that my life seemed utterly changed. I hardly knew that boy who had made his way, alone, to London.

Before I had reached the end of the hall, I heard the rowdy sounds from below. As I threw open the door, there came laughter, shouts and yells, and more laughter, all the deep sounds of male hilarity. I was careful to close the door after myself, for it would not do to allow one of those despised little beasts an exit into the main floors of the house. I followed the stairs as they wound down and round and came out a few steps above the kitchen. A large, though ordinarily fairly dark room, it was as well lit as could be, with candelabra, single candles, even an oil lamp, placed on every flat space of more than a few square inches in size. Still, there were a few dark corners around the place, and it was in those, evidently, that the rats had their holes. A few score lay dead or dying upon the floor, but a good many teemed and squirmed within a good-sized cage over which the ratcatcher himself presided. His terriers jumped about him, eager with excitement.

I was so fascinated by my first glimpse of the scene that

I very nearly fell over a large figure seated upon one of the lower stairs. It was Mr. Bilbo himself. He turned, recognized me, and slapped the empty space beside him on the stair.

"Sit down, lad. Have a look at this," said he to me. "There's a science to it, and a bit of art, as well."

I accepted his invitation and dropped down next to him. From where I now sat a gang of residents and house staff, all male, ranged against the far wall. It was their loud voices I had heard but a moment before. All now had fallen silent.

"He's cleaned out two holes already," said Mr. Bilbo, "and he's preparin' now to go after that one right there." He pointed to a spot just ahead of us, a gap between floor and wall that had been widened to a place of about three inches round, perhaps less.

It was certain that the ratcatcher enjoyed the attention of his audience. He went about his preparations like some performer at a fair, throwing little glances and smiles at the fellows off to the left and dropping a bow now and then to Mr. Bilbo, as master of the house. He delved deep into the pocket of his coat, and from it pulled a small furry animal which I at first took to be a rat. But no, its coat was a lighter, shinier brown, and its fur covered the length of its shorter tail. He held it out, cupped in his two hands, for all to see.

"What is that?" I asked Mr. Bilbo.

"A ferret," said he. "This is where the science does pertain, for the ferret is enemy by nature to the rat. He may be small, but he is vicious, and the rats do fear him, for he kills them well—but not this one."

"Oh? Why not?"

"Look sharp, Jeremy, and you will see his jaws is tied tight together with a bit of strong string. Though he be hungry, he cannot kill, and he cannot eat. Now, just see what he does with this little fellow."

I leaned forward to watch. An expectant hush now—not

even a whisper. The only sound came from the dogs, three of them, whining in agitation, rocking back and forth, dancing hind legs to front. Their master knelt down and released the ferret into the rathole. The animal squeezed through the small opening with no difficulty and quite disappeared.

"But," said I to Mr. Bilbo, "if the ferret cannot kill the rats, why put him down the rathole?"

"To bolt them—but a moment, and you'll see."

It was but a moment, nor more than two or three, until I saw the result: the rats came pouring out—I would not have supposed there could have been so many down that little hole. As soon as one had squirmed through, another was out behind him. Once in the open, they did scatter, rushing off in every direction. Yet there was no hope of escaping the terriers, who went wild as they leapt upon them, one after the other—a paw on his head, a paw on his tail, then the sharp, swift bite to break the back of the little beast, or a brisk shake of the head to break his neck—then on to the next and the next.

Again the kitchen was alive with shouts and roaring laughter. The men who watched the slaughter seemed near as excited by it as the dogs that did the killing. And I admit, reader, that I, too, was stirred by this display of brute nature at work. What a sight it was!

Mr. Bilbo leaned close and said loud so that he might be heard over the noise in the room: "Y'see, lad, the ferret goes down the hole, and he cannot bite and cannot kill. But the rats do not know this, and they fears him so that it throws them into a great panic to escape. Which they do— but only to be set upon by the terriers."

Still they came, and still the killing continued. Then did I notice one of the dogs did not kill as the other two did. The little brown and white spotted fellow was as quick and strong as his mates. Yet once he had a rat in his jaws he held it just tight enough so that escape was impossible; he then ran with it to his master, who took the offering by the tail and dropped it in the cage with the rest. Then back he would go and pounce upon another, which again he would deliver to the ratcatcher.

I pointed at the brown and white dog, engaged as he was, and looked inquiringly at Mr. Bilbo.

"Now that's the art of it," said he, once again in a shout. "That dog is trained by his master not to kill but to deliver them live to him that he might keep them. That took a deal of doing, I'm sure, for it is surely the nature of terriers to kill rats."

"But why?" I asked. "Why does the ratcatcher want them live?"

"Oh, they've their uses. He asked me if he could take some along so he might contribute to the supply for the rat match in the cellar of the King and Castle. You've not heard of that?"

"No, what is it goes on there?"

"There're matches between terriers as to which can kill the most rats in a short amount of time. Taverns and inns all over London have like diversions, cockfights and such, so cods may wager their bobsticks and lose 'em, naturally." He gave me a wise wink. "Ah well," said he, " 'tis no worse than me milking neds and quids from the gentry— and I'm the first to admit it."

Of a sudden he stood up, and pointed down at the floor. I saw that it was no rat but the ferret that was making his exit through the hole dug out between wood and plaster. The ratcatcher scooped up the little beast and dropped him back into his pocket. Things had quieted down once again. The scurrying of the rats had ceased. The dogs had stopped pouncing and growling. The watchers no longer shouted encouragement as they had but a moment before. It would seem that the entertainment had ended.

"Hi, yer lordship!" shouted the ratcatcher. "I mun clean up here, plug the holes and sech. Then we be paid, my boys and me?"

"Then you be paid," said Mr. Bilbo.

We left, he leading up the dark stairs. With his broad

back to me, he continued to talk, his words booming a bit within the narrow space: "Some said we'd do better to use poison on them. But to spread poison about in the kitchen seemed a bad idea to me. Besides, they crawl off to the rathole to die, and you've got a terrible stink through the place."

Emerging into the main hall, I put a question to him that had that moment occurred to me. "What sort of poison do they use to murder rats?"

He thought a moment. "Why, I ain't sure," said he, "but I believe I have heard it is arsenic is most often used."

"And it would kill a person?"

"Oh, it would, right enough. A pinch of it in the stew, and we'd be sick—a goodly bit might kill us all. Dangerous stuff it is." He regarded me curiously for a moment, then let the question go unasked. "I would suppose you're here for our young Master Bunkins. You'll have to wait a short bit till his morning lessons is done. Oh, he did protest at not bein' allowed to watch the rattin' of the belowstairs. But Mr. Burnham was firm. 'Nothing must interrupt the schedule of instruction,' said he, and I stood behind him. A good lesson for the boy, I say."

"Well . . . yes, but there is another matter. Sir John said I should discuss it with you first."

"A discussion, is it? Well, I hold all them in the captain's cabin. Come along, and we'll have this out."

He led the way up the hall to the room that had once been Lord Goodhope's library. Mr. Bilbo had made it his own. Though there were books about, this was plainly the place of a man who had spent a good deal of his life on shipboard. Nautical prints, ship paintings, and seascapes covered the walls. Behind his great desk and above on the wall hung crossed cutlasses—a new touch—and thus he seemed ever ready to do battle.

He caught me looking at them, somewhat in awe.

"They're mine right enough," said he. "I had no need to go out and buy a pair for decoration, so to speak. They ain't for decoration, purely. But pull up a chair, Jeremy. Tell me what's upon your mind.''

I did as he said and summarized quickly the purpose of my errand, making it clear that asking Mr. Burnham to take on a second scholar had been my idea and not Sir John's. For his part, Black Jack listened carefully, stroking his dark beard, leaning back in his chair and nodding like some wise Solomon. When I had done, I asked in particular if he had any objection to my putting the matter to Mr. Burnham.

''No,'' said he, ''I have none, but mine is not the only vote that matters.''

''Of course,'' said I, ''there is Mr. Burnham—''

''And Bunkins, too,'' he reminded me. ''He should have some say in this. He's tight with him, yet in a proper way of scholar and teacher. He may not like sharing his spot.''

I thought about that then—for the first time. ''I shall talk to him alone and let him decide for himself.''

''The only way to do it. And as for Mr. Burnham, he may not want her, neither. With two scholars instead of one, he'll be workin' twice as hard, it seems to me. He may want extra pay if he takes her on.''

''Sir John thought that, as well.''

''I believe you should make the offer without namin' a figure.''

''I will, sir.''

Still he sat, rubbing his beard, considering the matter. ''This would be Annie, your cook, would it not?''

''Yes sir, it would.''

''Her who was at the table when me and Jimmie B. come by for Christmas dinner?''

''Yes sir.''

''I knew her before when she worked in this house for Lord Goodhope.''

''I remember that, sir—or I had guessed it.''

''Well, it may work out, or it may not. Anyways, I have naught against it. You may put it to Mr. Burnham and Bunkins. The matter is settled insofar as it concerns me.''

I stood and thanked him, offering my hand. "The matter is done with you, sir?"

He leaned forward, took my hand, and shook it. "Done and done," said he.

I turned about and headed for the door.

"Hi, Jeremy," he cried after me, "what think you, lad? Would a ned be too much for the ratcatcher?"

"I know nothing of such matters, Mr. Bilbo."

"Well, he did a good job and put on a good show—why not?"

"As you say, sir, as you say."

With a wave, I left the room and wandered up the hall to the front of the house. It was there in the room which had been Lady Goodhope's "sewing room," so called (though I am sure she sewed ne'er a stitch in it), that Mr. Burnham held his school. In its present state I knew it to be a rather bare room with little more in it than a large slate board, a good-sized map of the world, as was known to be the latest, a table and a chair for Bunkins, and a sturdy case well filled with books.

Reaching the closed door of the room, I listened at it and heard Bunkins reading—haltingly, yet reading nevertheless—from the first volume of *Robinson Crusoe,* with which I had gifted him at Christmas. I was most favorably impressed.

I retired to a place nearby, though to the far side of the hall; it would not do to be found with my ear to the door. There I considered what Black Jack Bilbo had said to me about the matter at hand. Indeed, Bunkins must have a say as to Annie's joining the class. He had a great fondness for Mr. Burnham. He might well hesitate; or, giving his assent, later find he wished he had not. Ah, it was a touchy business! Perhaps if I were to remind him that I had gladly shared with him Mr. Perkins's tutelage in self-defense, he would acknowledge that the comparison was a just one and decide accordingly. Perhaps—

But the handle to the schoolroom door had turned. The

door swung open, and out came Bunkins with Mr. Burnham close behind. Both were smiling; it was thus evident Bunkins had recovered from his pique at having lost out on the rat-catching demonstration. So it was, yet hoping some bit of it might remain to be seen, he was sore disappointed to learn from me that it was done but for the cleaning up. Yet he took it in a manner most stoical—in fact, with a shrug.

"Ah well," said he, "I've seen such before. And anytime I want to I can drop in at the King and Castle for a rum session of rat-crapping. If you've a mind, I'll take you along one night."

"Could be, Jimmie B.," said I agreeably. "But I came by thinking you might be for a ramble this fine day."

"That hits me right rum, but I must first ask the cove and grab my toggy and my calp."

Then said Mr. Burnham, who had been witness to our exchange: "And you must be back in good time for your afternoon lessons." Spoke with a smile it was, and not with a frown.

"Oh, I will right certain, sir. Never doubt me."

"Well said," laughed his tutor. "I've had no reason to doubt thus far."

Then with a nod Bunkins left us and hurried down the hall to search for Mr. Bilbo. I looked then to Mr. Burnham, cream-coffee-colored, a true mulatto Jamaica-born, half English and half African; and of a sudden I realized I'd said nothing to anyone at Number 4 Bow Street of that, nor of his history—not to Annie, nor to Sir John, nor to Lady Fielding. Would it matter to any of them? Should I wait and make all this clear at home before bringing up the topic for which I'd come? Then did I decide firmly that it wouldn't concern them, because it shouldn't.

"Mr. Burnham, I have a question to put before you," said I.

"And what might that be?"

Again I summarized the matter; this time, however, I told him more of Annie, mentioning that she was bright, eager beyond telling to learn, and already quite capable in her own regard as the cook for our little household.

"The cook is she?"

"Yes sir."

"My mother is a cook. I believe that of all my accomplishments, that which mattered to her most was my ability to read. From it, she said, came all else. And she was right, of course." It was only then that he turned his eyes to me. "It would be very difficult for me to turn down a cook who wished to learn letters."

"Then you will take Annie?" said I, all excited.

"Then I would *try* her," said he. "I've no doubt she is as bright and eager to achieve as you say, but there is the question of how she will fit with Master Bunkins. I must also ask permission from Mr. Bilbo."

"I've already sought that from him," said I. "He gave it, but said only that he had no objection. He said the real decision must come from you and Bunkins. I mean to talk to Jimmie B. on our ramble."

"Do that," said he. "Let his be the deciding vote."

"There is the matter of money," I said. "Both Sir John and Mr. Bilbo felt that with an additional scholar . . ."

"We'll speak of that later, shall we?"

Bunkins had an especial destination in mind for our stroll that morning. When I heard what it was and what awaited us there, I was reluctant to accompany him. It seemed, as he told it, that a sewer man had made a gruesome discovery in the Fleet up near the Holbourn Bridge. He had taken it direct to Mr. Saunders Welch, High Constable and Magistrate of Holbourn, rather than to Sir John at Bow Street. It was found in such a place as might have been thought to be Westminster, yet he went to Saunders Welch in hope of some reward, for just as Mr. Welch was free with his fines, he was known to bestow rewards for items brought to him which were of criminal interest. The sewer man—Bunkins did not know his name, nor was it of importance—

received a bounty of ten shillings. And now that object had been placed upon exhibit in St. Andrew's Churchyard.

I listened—patiently, I believe—as we trudged upon our way. Yet at last, in exasperation, I demanded to know the nature of this grim object whose worth had been placed at ten shillings.

"What is it?" said I. "What are you taking us to see?"

"Some poor cod's napper. Not the rest of him, just his napper!"

Had I understood Bunkins aright? I thought myself fluent in his flash cant, yet here was a bit of intelligence so startling that I thought it best to ask for confirmation in plain speech. "You mean a head?" I questioned. "A human head?"

"Ain't that what I'm tellin' you? They got it there stuck up on a pole for all to see. Welch is ready to put out another ten shillings to him who can say sure and certain who it is. I hear there's a lot of lookin' goin' on."

"Curiosity seekers attracted by a disgusting spectacle," said I primly.

"Naw, not a bit of it," said he. "They're reward seekers, is what they are."

"Well, I for one will have none of it. I'll go with you to the churchyard, but I shall wait for you without the gates."

"Do it your way. I'll not nap the bib 'cause of it."

I was cross with him, silent, sulking—and he with me—as sometimes happens between chums. Why must he so often descend to the level of the mob? I asked myself. Of course he had not the advantages of family I had had—never knowing his father, barely remembering his mother, out on the street to shift for himself since he was s child. Still, he had advantages aplenty these past two years, now nearly three. He lived in fair luxury there on St. James Street and wanted for nothing—certainly not the ten shillings he might gain by identifying the poor man whose head was spiked upon a pole in St. Andrew's Churchyard. He went merely for the oddity of it.

I was reminded of the time when first I had walked with him from the Strand into Fleet Street. Having passed that way a number of times before and noticing nothing unusual, I was quite unprepared when he stopped me there at the Temple Bar gate and called my attention to the two skulls hung high above on pegs, rattling in the wind. He laughed at my disgust and told me that there had once been meat upon them, but the birds had long ago picked them clean. These were, I later learned from Sir John, all that was left of the heads taken from the traitors of 1745. Originally there had been four up there—or was it five? Sir John was unsure. In any case, all but two of the skulls had blown down or perhaps simply crumbled and crashed to the cobblestones. "I know not," Sir John had said, "if such a display discourages traitorous acts. I am certain, however, that it comes near to justifying them." I myself have ever after had a particular loathing of decapitation as a means of execution. At least when a man is hanged, his body is buried whole.

Yet it would not do to sulk too long, nor to play high and mighty with Bunkins, for I came to him that day as a petitioner. Therefore I broke the silence between us.

"Tell me, Jimmie B., how go the lessons with thee?"

"Right as rain," said he, as we hiked along together. "We're readin' through the *Crusoe* book you gave to me at Christmas. We're up to the part about the cannibals." He paused just long enough to offer me an impudent grin. "Jeremy, old chum, you don't s'pose, do you, that the head's all that's left of that cod in the churchyard? You think he got ate?"

While he made little effort to contain himself, doubling up in laughter so that he could but stagger along as he barked forth a series of great guffaws, I exercised a great deal of restraint, reminding myself that I owed it to Annie to endure any number of his witticisms in bad taste.

(Was I then truly such a prig? At times, reader, I fear I was. It seemed to come upon me in fits and starts.)

Waiting until at last he had calmed himself, I offered Bunkins what I meant to be a rather noble smile; then said I with all good cheer: "No, I think it more likely the rest of him has found a home of some sort in the ground, or perhaps been floated out the river to the sea. But they may now have all of him they will ever find."

"Then admit it, chum. He could've been ate."

"In London all things are possible."

Was this the moment to put to him the question I had come to ask? Though not quite certain of it, I had decided to do so and was searching for the words to make my proposition seem desirable, when Bunkins pointed out the tower of St. Andrew's Church ahead, lying just off Holbourn. My opportunity had passed.

As we reached the open gate of the churchyard, I saw that a great crowd had gathered there. Had admission been charged, I believe there would have been just as many, so eager were Londoners then (as now) to view sights bizarre and ghastly. They were, as I had expected, rowdy and joking in their demeanor, in no wise offering the sort of dignity the dead deserve. To my surprise, however, there were a few women among them, drabs and whores most of them no doubt, their laughter pealing higher and shriller than the rest.

Bunkins came to a halt at the gate. He faced me, hands on hips, a frown upon his face. "Jeremy," said he, "you truly mean to wait here whilst I takes a look?"

"Well . . . why not?"

"You seen worse, told me so yourself, how you looked upon them whores, all cut up so horrible with their innards all hangin' out."

"But that was different. That was . . . that was a criminal investigation."

"Ain't that what this is? They got to put a name on this poor cod before they can find out who killed him, don't they? If this was Sir John asked you to take a look at what's left of him and say if you knew who it was, why you'd do it surer'n anything. Now, ain't that so?''

I glowered at him. ''What if it is?''

''Well, maybe you do know him in the churchyard. Ever think of that?''

In truth, I had not, and so my only answer was silence.

''Look in there,'' he persisted. ''They is women in there, and they ain't afraid to take a look. They're hopin' for their ten shillings like the rest.''

''I'm not afraid.''

''Then, what's holdin' you back, chum? Yer pal Annie, she'd not drag her feet. She'd be up to the head of the line, lookin' and sayin', 'Oh, that's Mr. Whomsoever. I bought greens from him three days past in the Garden.' ''

Annie? did he say Annie? This was my chance!

''Oh, by the bye,'' I blustered in, ''that brings to mind something I wished to ask, Jimmie B.'' Would that do for preamble? ''Annie wants to learn reading. How would it be if she sat in class with you and Mr. Burnham?''

''Ask him, not me,'' said he, put off a bit by my interruption.

''I did. He told me to ask you.''

''Well, course it's good with me. Annie's a rum little moll.''

''Tell Mr. Burnham that, would you?''

''Awright. But now, let's get back to the subjec' at hand, as Mr. Burnham might say.''

''Oh, never you mind,'' said I. ''You've convinced me. This is, as you say, a criminal investigation, and were it Sir John's I would willingly take part.''

''Well . . . well . . .'' Bunkins seemed confused by my sudden concession. ''Then come on. Let's have a look.''

He beckoned me through the gate, and together we marched into the churchyard. On the one hand, I was so relieved at having achieved my purpose that I hadn't it in me to offer further resistance. But in all justice, I had to admit that Jimmie Bunkins had argued well. There might be much of the street boy in him still, and he might be only just past the threshold of literacy, but he was right firm in debate—and that was the sign of a good mind.

We joined a line that had formed. Though there were many ahead of us, they moved along swiftly enough so that I had no need to fear that we should be there overlong. Because of the number blocking our view, there was no chance to glimpse at a distance the object we were to study up close. That suited me well. Even if I had given in to Bunkins, I felt a bit queasy about what lay ahead.

Those in front of us—and now those behind—in the waiting line were, as I had stated, quite boisterous and some to the point of rowdiness. There were jokes—''Anyone yet thought of askin' this joe on the pole his name? Now that'd be a right queer shock if he should answer—ain't it so?'' (This was shouted out by one of the women.) There was jolly talk about what would be done with the ten shillings once it was earned; most such plans included strong drink and loose women. There was braggadocio and swagger of every sort. But off to the left, there was a lesser group—or a few groups, really—of those who had already been through the viewing line. They were altogether quieter, muttering and whispering among themselves; from them I heard no laughter.

For our part, Bunkins and I talked little. He surprised me at one point by speculating that he was sure that he might himself be able to help Annie along, for Mr. Burnham had said he had learned from his own earlier teaching experience that it was the duty of scholars to help one another along. A nice thought, of course, but perhaps Bunkins underestimated Annie Oakum and her great desire to learn. I said nothing of that, however—merely told a little of my own unsuccessful efforts to teach her letters, of my lack of patience and lack of system. Then did Bunkins comment quite confidently: ''We'll teach her, Mr. Burnham and me.''

Throughout all this, I had kept my back turned and face averted from the head upon the pole. Whenever Bunkins stepped forward, I moved with him. As we came nearer it, his eyes seemed to rove back and forth uneasily, and his face took on a more serious mien.

At last he nodded and pointed behind me.

"Our turn, Jeremy."

There it was, the awful thing. In a way, it was not quite so bad as I had feared. The face and hair had been washed, so that none of the filth of the sewer was upon it. Even so, it seemed doubtful somehow that it had ever held a place atop a proper human form. The skin had discolored to a sort of gray-brown cast. The sewer waters had somehow loosened and distorted the features in such a way that the face bore a slack and doleful expression—the sadness of death. The mouth was open, as were the eyes—expressionless, the pupils faded to some pale color, less than a proper blue.

That it was indeed a head separated from a body was evident from the bits of dark gristle hanging down from a spot below the vocal cords where the head had been severed. Yet it was a clean cut. Could a headsman's axe have done so well? Below the chin was the mortal wound—not a gash but a slit which ran from just below one ear, across the throat, to the other.

I shivered. I looked away. There was naught for me to see that I had not seen. Yet Bunkins stayed on, staring in deep concentration until reluctantly he, too, turned away. We walked from the thing together, saying nothing until we reached the churchyard gate. Only then did he stop and take me by my arm as one might in making a declaration of the most solemn sort.

"You know, chum," said he, his voice hardly more than a whisper, "I think I know that poor cod from somewheres, but I just can't think where or how it was."

FOUR

*In Which Sir John
Confers with a
Widow Without Result*

Next morning I saw Annie off for her first day of school. At our parting, I rather presumptuously began to give her instructions as to what route she might best take to reach Mr. Bilbo's house in St. James Street. She looked at me rather queerly and interrupted me with a just reminder.

"You forget, Jeremy, that I worked in that house for over a year," said she, "and most days I tracked back and forth to Covent Garden to do the buying for cook. I ain't daft. I know the way still."

In truth, I had for the moment forgotten. "Of course," said I in chagrin. "It's me must be daft. Yet I believe you'll find the house much changed inside."

"All changed for the better, I'm sure." And with that she gave me a wave and departed.

Off I went then to do our buying for that day from the greengrocers in the Garden. Annie had dictated the list to me, and it had been agreed with us in the household that such responsibilities which usually fell to her would now always be mine. She would attend the morning session only. That one was given over solely to reading. It was Mr. Burnham's custom to devote the afternoon to geography and numbers. Annie declared that her knowledge of London was complete, and she had no need to know more of the world. And as for numbers, she knew enough to count her change, which she always did quite carefully, and that, she was sure, would suffice. So it was determined she would be a morning scholar. The afternoon she would have clear to devote to baking, to special dinners for guests which required more in the way of preparation, and to incidental duties as devised by Lady Fielding. Thus were all satisfied.

Upon returning from Covent Garden, I went at Sir John's request to his chambers, where he did dictate a letter to a Squire Bladgett, Magistrate of Lichfield. The name had been searched out from a list provided by Mr. Marsden, the clerk of the Bow Street Court, that Sir John might communicate with the law in distant parts of Britain in matters such as that of Thomas Roundtree. It was not a very grand letter. It simply stated that while in our custody on a minor charge, the fellow had escaped and as a fugitive was now in much greater trouble than before. Seeing that he claimed to be from Lichfield, he might possibly return there; if he should do so, he was to be held until a constable could be sent to bring him back to London. After signing the letter, Sir John indited a postscriptum, to wit: "Would also appreciate any information you might supply on said Roundtree which might aid us in our search for him here."

I read back the letter to him in full. He listened attentively, rubbing his chin, until I had finished. "That should do it, don't you think?" said he.

"Oh, I do indeed. Nothing more needed."

Still he sat, musing. "This fellow continues to plague me. He could not have made his escape simply to avoid a month in the Fleet. I daresay he wished to make himself scarce so as to avoid discovery in some greater crime. The theft of the vase? Perhaps, but as you pointed out, Jeremy, he had already managed to get himself off the hook on that count. No, there must be something more, something greater. Yet I, for one, do not know what it might be.''

''Nor do I, sir,'' said I. ''It might be helpful if I went to that room of his in Half-Moon Passage and had a look about it. Something might turn up.''

He chuckled a bit at that. ''Something might, though I doubt it. With the damage you did the lock, the place was left open to whoever might wish to enter. I would wager that his room is by now rather bare.''

''So did it seem upon my first visit—yet I took no time to inspect the premises. Still . . .''

''Still it may prove worth the effort. No stone unturned, et cetera. Why not? After you have posted the letter at the coach house, proceed to Half-Moon Passage to continue your investigation.''

''Yes, Sir John, and then I should like to stop in at Mr. Bilbo's house in St. James Street. Since Mr. Burnham declared he was taking Annie only on trial, I would like to see if, perhaps, she has met his expectations.''

''And inquire as to how much it will cost me,'' said he.

''As you say, sir.''

''Again, why not? You've a busy morning ahead of you, lad. Best get on with it.''

The old building in Half-Moon Passage was as I remembered it from the day before. What had been the coach entrance, once cobbled but now broken and covered over with refuse, seemed quite like those country roads of dirt that I had known earlier in my boyhood. The littered courtyard smelled still as foul as before. I found my way up the short stairway, then down the long hall along which I had followed that sly fellow Roundtree.

Oh, how he had gulled me! My cheeks burned with shame at the thought of it. All of it—his foolish clowning in the street, his pretended awe at my storytelling, and especially, oh most especially, his lurid tales of women naked in the hallway—was meant to prepare me for that moment when he knocked me off my feet and against the wall, slipped into his room, and locked the door against me. He had duped me proper. Sir John was right: the fellow had true talent as an actor. Even as I, in my embarrassment, recalled his performance in Bow Street, scratching and jumping about as he remarked upon the ''flea farm'' we kept in our strong room, I could not but smile. Feigned or true, there was indeed something likable about Thomas Roundtree.

I had no difficulty finding the room that had been his. It was, of course, the one with the destroyed lock upon the door. I had half expected to find it standing open, for thus I had left it in my bootless rush to get out to Half-Moon Passage that I might give him chase. He was, of course, nowhere to be seen. Even had he been nearby, he would have been quite invisible, for the crowd in the narrow street—hardly wide enough for a wagon to pass through— was such that none but a giant would have stood out from the mass. Though tall, he was no giant. He had most likely dodged into another court, perhaps sought shelter from a friend, or ducked into one of the many dives and taverns up in Bedford Street. I had seen it was hopeless, and so I had gone on to Bloomsbury Square to seek out his putative employer.

Thus I came to his door and gave it a push with my hand, expecting it to open. It did not. I gave it another, stronger push, felt it give a bit—yet only so far, perhaps half an inch, perhaps less. Had I the right door? Yes, certainly, for there was the hole made by the ball I had discharged into the door. Had the lock been repaired, the room perhaps already rented? That seemed doubtful.

Then did I hear movement inside—light footsteps, like those of a child or a small woman. I pounded loudly upon the door with my fist.

''Hi in there!'' I shouted. ''Open up! I am come from the Bow Street Court with orders to search this room.''

For a moment there was no response. Then: ''Go away.''

It was the voice of a woman or a girl, of that I was near certain.

"Stand aside," said I, "for I am coming through."

I reasoned she must have some piece of furniture pushed up against the door, perhaps a chest. Was there a wardrobe in the room? I had not yet gone against the door with my full strength. I would do that now. Planting my shoulder against the door, I leaned hard against it, dug in my feet, and pushed with my whole body. It began to swing slowly forward. There was resistance from the other side; whoever was beyond the door had not only barricaded herself but was also pushing back as I pushed forward. There was naught I could do but push harder, and that I did—harder and harder—until at last whatever piece of furniture blocked the door was pushed aside with a bang and my adversary was sent sprawling.

I was inside. The piece that had blocked my way was a large chest of drawers now flat on the floor; and indeed, the occupant of the room was flat on her backside, looking up at me angrily as my eyes scanned the room.

"Got no respect for privacy?" she asked.

"Who're you?"

"I asked first."

"I have no respect for them who don't belong—and you have no right to be here."

"Oh yes I have. I'm his daughter."

I was confused. "Whose daughter? What do you mean?"

"Him who made a fool of you." Then, most impudently, did she stick out her tongue.

She was of an age for such brazen foolishness—eleven perhaps, not more than twelve. I saw, when she scrambled to her feet, that she was tall for that age, slender and wiry, yet quite undeveloped in the womanly way. She must recently have taken a spurt of growth, for her frock reached down to a point well above her ankles and its waist rode up above her own.

"What is your name?" I asked in a manner most stern, as befitted my errand.

"Clarissa Roundtree," said she, giving emphasis to her surname, "daughter of Thomas and proud of it."

"You should not be, for he is a fugitive from the law."

"If the law is you, then the law is a ninny. Ain't you ashamed of yourself? Lookin' about for nekkid women? Oh, I heard. I know the whole sorry tale of it."

She stood, arms at her sides, her hands made into fists. The look she gave to me was both belligerent and contemptuous. I should not have been surprised if she had shaken a finger at me like some old shrew.

"Well," said I, cool to her taunts and refusing to blush as she would have me do, "if you know the whole sorry tale, then you have heard it from your father. Has he been back here?"

"I'll not tell."

"Where is he now?"

"My lips are sealed."

"You must tell, for this is a court matter."

"Oh . . . pooh. A court matter, is it? Well, you may torture me if you like, but I'll not betray my father."

At that I burst out laughing. She did not like that at all. Retreating a few steps, she glowered at me most murderously.

"And why should that be funny?" she demanded to know.

"You have got that from some romance or other. We do not torture."

"No?" She seemed truly dubious.

"No. All we need do is put you before Sir John Fielding, who is the magistrate at Bow Street, and you will begin to quake in your boots quite immediate."

"Is he so terrible?"

"No, but he inspires awe in everyone."

"Pooh!"

"Very well, Miss Pooh," said I. "My purpose was to

search this room, and search it I shall. You may sit down in that chair while I do''—I pointed to the only chair in the room—''or you may continue to stand where you are. But do not try to prevent me.''

''Is that a threat?''

''A caution.''

I must have managed to intimidate her at least a little, for she said nothing as I set about my task. She remained standing. Out of the corner of my eye I kept check upon her, lest she make some sudden dash for the door. In truth, there was not much there to search. I looked beneath the bed, first of all, and found naught but a trundle bed—for Miss Pooh, as I perceived, though no doubt a good fit for her in her present proportions. The wardrobe had little but Roundtree's greatcoat, which he had foolishly left behind, the pockets empty, and a suit of clothes for a boy of about the age of Miss Roundtree—and a second frock, which it seemed would fit her as ill as the one she wore. The curtained closet contained no more than a nightgown, a shift, and a smelly chamber pot.

''This pot could use an emptying,'' said I to her.

''You go too far!'' said she.

And probably she was right.

I went to the chest of drawers which I had knocked over in the course of my entrance into the room, righted it, and pulled out the topmost of the two drawers. Then did she fly at me.

''You've no right to look in there. That is *my* drawer.''

I grabbed at her shoulder and held her at arm's length.

''All the more reason to look,'' said I. ''If Thomas Roundtree wished to sequester something, he might indeed mix it with things of your own.''

''What is it you're looking for?''

''Something that will tell me where he is hid—since you will tell me nothing.''

She shrugged loose from my grip and stalked away. ''Go ahead, then. Look, if you must. I've nothing to hide.''

And so I turned my attention to the drawer. Beneath mended hose and undergarments there were trinkets inside, though no more than any girl of her age might keep. I found an odd-shaped stone which glittered of crystal where it was broke and a feather from a falcon's wing. There was a chain and locket; I opened the locket and found the delicate cameo of a woman, perhaps her mother. A doll with a broken china head was there, too. And I found three romances of precisely the kind I had suspected she read. No doubt she was better educated than her father; he, I supposed, was illiterate. I closed the drawer, feeling a bit guilty that I had pried into her collection of treasures.

"My father made that chest," said she. "He is a great craftsman and can build near anything."

"So he says."

"In a while he will furnish a house for us in grand style."

"In a while he will be in gaol."

"Don't say that!" she shouted at me.

"Well . . ." That was rather rude of me, I decided, quite uncalled for. "Then perhaps not. He has not yet pled his case before Sir John."

I knelt and opened the bottom drawer. It was all a jumble of worn hose, dirty linen, a neckcloth stiff with dried sweat, a few wipes, and a lally. It was the more filled of the two drawers, but beneath all there was little to be found but a knife with a broken blade and a collection of paper slips tied together with a bit of twine. I slipped one out for closer examination. There was a number writ upon it, a sum in shillings, and a signature scrawled upon it, no more than initials—an "M" and something else, quite indecipherable.

"You leave those alone," said Clarissa Roundtree. She made to sound bold, even threatening.

"What are they?"

"Never you mind. Just put them back," she ordered.

"You must tell me what they are, or I shall take them with me and show them about until I learn what they are."

There was silence from her as she considered my threat. Then at last did she speak up: "They're pawning tickets is what they are. He's had to pawn a few things for ready money. We'll have them all back soon, though."

"Oh? You're sure of that?"

"Sure as I can be." She said it with certainty to match her claim. "We shall be coming into money before long."

"I daresay one of these is for the vase stolen from the residence of the Lord Chief Justice."

"I know naught of any vase," said she, then pursed her lips in a manner somewhat exaggerated as if to demonstrate her silence.

"Do you know the location of the pawnshop?"

"No."

"Never been there with him, have you?"

"No."

Perhaps she was lying, and perhaps she was not. But if she was lying, I knew of no way to force the truth out of her. And with that came the realization that to question her further would be only a waste of my time. I had come here to search the place, and I had done that. Now I had best be on my way to Mr. Bilbo's. But then, as I was about to take my leave, something occurred to me: it was a matter of what I had *not* found in the course of my search.

"You've neither food nor money here," said I to her.

"That is a matter that doesn't concern you," said she. "This room is paid up to the end of the month, so I have every right to be here. As for how and what I eat, well . . ." She hesitated. "My father provided for me in the past. He'll do it in the future."

"Your father is a fugitive. He ran from me because he had not ten shillings to pay his fine. He had no money at all. I know he has been back here at least once, yet he left you nothing. When last did you eat?"

"That is a matter that doesn't concern you, either."

"Well and good," said I, dipping into my pocket and pulling out a few shillings from my store. I counted out three and laid them atop the chest. "If you are as destitute as you seem and as hungry as you look, then you may take this and feed yourself and perhaps buy a little coal to warm this place a bit."

I smiled at her, expecting thanks. I received none. There was naught to do but leave, and so that was what I did, moving briskly through the door and pulling it shut behind me, tight as it would go. I lingered there for a moment and, as I expected, heard the chest slide across the floor until it bumped up against the door.

Turning up St. James Street, I had the feeling that I would be arriving at my destination a bit later than I had intended. It was, of course, due to wasting time in Half-Moon Passage, asking useless questions. I had learned nothing—or so it then seemed to me. That silly girl who would be tortured rather than betray her shiftless father (tortured! what a notion!) had not even the grace to thank me for providing the means to sustain her wretched life a little longer. (Like so many others, reader, at that time in my life I performed good deeds in large part to receive the gratitude of others; if it was not forthcoming, I felt no little cheated.)

Thus I arrived at Black Jack Bilbo's domicile in a somewhat sullen state, unsure that I should find Annie there still, uncertain that Mr. Burnham would be available for a consultation, for as Bunkins had told me, he often took a midday walk when morning lessons were done. I rapped hard upon the door with the great brass knocker, and very shortly afterward Jimmie Bunkins threw open the door.

"Hello, chum," said he. "You look right done in. What's got you down?" He beckoned me inside.

"Oh," said I, "naught that I wish to discuss at the moment. It'd take long to explain and embarrass me in the telling."

That seemed to satisfy him. As I stepped inside, I heard the sound of music in a room not far off. It was Annie singing one of those ballads she knew so well, this the very

ancient one known to me by the name of "Greensleeves."
Yet in this instance I heard her accompanied upon a harpsichord—no more than chords struck and improvised bits
beneath the sung melody. Whether it be the accompaniment
or no, it cheered me to hear her sing so, for in truth, she
never sounded better.

"Right you are," said Bunkins with a wink. "It's your
Annie. She's a proper chirrupin' moll, ain't she? I'd no idea
of it. That's Mr. Burnham playing alongside. He's right
taken with her, he is, says she got a talent for it."

How this had come about, I later learned, was that Annie
had brought with her the music and text of the *Ode for St.
Cecilia's Day* and asked if Mr. Burnham might teach her
Dryden's words that she might commit them to memory
rather than go la-la-la-ing through the text as she had done
before. He allowed this might be possible, depending upon
her rote powers, but that he would first like to test her voice.
And so, the morning lessons completed, he had taken her
into the drawing room, seated himself at the harpsichord,
and asked her to sing what she knew best; he followed
rather than led her. Bunkins came along and provided them
with an audience of one. Mr. Burnham was well satisfied
by what he heard.

The two had moved on to another as Bunkins led me
into the drawing room. We proceeded upon tiptoes and
caused no disturbance as we settled ourselves on soft chairs
at the far end of the room. Annie, with her back to us, gave
no notice at all to our arrival. Mr. Burnham offered nothing
more than a discreet nod. Her song was now one of Scotch
origin, "Barbara Allan." How she came to learn it I've no
idea, for I'd not heard her sing it before. She had so many
songs and ballads in her head that it seemed her supply was
quite inexhaustible.

It went on a bit, as Scotch ballads will do, yet when they
came together at last to the end, Mr. Burnham struck a final
chord, then rose from his seat at the harpsichord.

"That will do very well, Miss Oakum," said he, smiling

generously. "I should like you to leave your copy of the score with me. I shall need it to learn the piece after a fashion, for as I said to you, to learn the text without the music is both foolish and dangerous."

"Oh, Mr. Burnham, I do thank you so," said she.

"And now your friend Jeremy is here to accompany you home, I believe."

At that she turned round in surprise and found me there with Bunkins. "Jeremy, how long have you been there? Just as quiet as a mouse, I swear!"

"Not long," said I, "though long enough to hear you sing one I'd never heard before."

"I know them all," said she, laughing quite heartily. "Shall I get my cape?"

"Please do."

As she made her way quickly out of the drawing room, I went direct to Mr. Burnham and without preamble asked if he had come to a decision on Annie. "Will you take her on as a scholar, sir?"

"That will be my great pleasure," said he. "She has a quick mind and is hungry to learn. And like so many who have good minds but are ignorant of letters, she has a remarkable memory. I do believe I can teach her the *St. Cecilia's* text before she can properly read it."

"She's learned a good bit of Shakespeare in just that way, sir."

"And I understand you taught her. She said you began her instruction in reading."

"Oh, I was nothing as a teacher. I haven't the patience for what you do so well."

"Perhaps you taught her better than you think. You gave her a good start. It should not be long until she has caught Master Bunkins up."

"And what about you, Jimmie B.?" I asked, turning to him. "Will she do for you, too?"

"No question," said he. "She's a rum one. Make me

work harder, but there's still a thing or two I can teach her.''

"And as you know, of course," said Mr. Burnham to me, "she has quite a talent for singing—though I understand that her heart is set upon the stage."

"Oh, she's told you that already, has she?"

"Oh yes."

So it was decided—but for one matter: "Sir John said that he would be willing to pay for her tuition, within reason, of course."

"Ah yes, well, Mr. Bilbo has been so generous, providing me with salary, room, and board, so that I have both my needs and wants taken care of. You have heard Master Bunkins say that her presence will make him work harder. That should be payment enough for me. You may tell Sir John Fielding that I shall require nothing from him for the present, though in the future there will be charges for books and such like."

I was quite struck by his generosity. "Oh, I will, sir. I shall tell him that. And may I take this opportunity to thank you for him. He . . ." I hesitated. "He is not a rich man."

"No, but I have heard he is a just one."

There was little I could say to that, and as it turned out, nothing was needed, for at that moment Annie's voice rang forth from the rear of the room.

"Ready to go, Jeremy."

She stood in the drawing room doorway, caped, a great smile upon her face.

"And I am, as well," said I.

Then, thanking Mr. Burnham once more and grabbing up my scarf from the chair where I had left it, I made my way out. Bunkins accompanied us to the great door to the street. As he hauled it open, he detained me for a moment.

"Just one thing, chum," said he. "You remembers that thing we looked at in St. Andrew's Churchyard? It's been took down. They said it was going rotten. It's now with that surgeon fella you know—the Irishman."

"Mr. Donnelly?"

"That's him. He's got it in gin, which is said to keep it longer. I'd like to take another look at that mug, for I'm still sure I know that cod from somewheres. Would you take me there to have another look? Tell him I'm not some queer joe looking for a shiver?"

"Right you are, Jimmie B. Let me know when."

"In a day or two. I'll send word by Annie."

"Fair enough."

With that and a goodbye, I left him at the door. Annie waited upon the walkway, still beaming a smile broad as her face. We fell into step together, marching down St. James Street toward Pall Mall.

"I have good news for you," said I.

"Oh? And what is that?"

"Mr. Burnham has agreed to take you on as a scholar."

"Oh ... well ... I knew he would do that." That she said in a most airy and dismissive manner, as if it could not have been otherwise.

"Oh, you did, did you? And what made you so sure?"

"We hit it off remarkable well, I would say, right from the start." She seemed most pleased with herself. "Best of all," she added, "he has offered to teach me the *St. Cecilia's* text."

"So I heard."

"He said I have talent as a singer."

"So did Lady Fielding. So did the choirmaster."

"Oh, I know, but ..."

"But what?"

"Nothing."

What ailed Annie that she had suddenly begun acting and talking so queer? For near two years past, once that matter of Tom Durham was behind her, she had proved to be the very paragon of good sense. Now she was acting both smug and mysterious. What had got into the girl?

"Jeremy?"

"Yes? What is it?" I sounded a bit snappish, even to myself.

"You did not tell me that Mr. Burnham was African."

"I didn't tell you because I didn't think it should matter. Does it? Do you mind?"

"I? Mind? Why, Jeremy, you're bein' quite ridiculous!"

She was becoming more exasperating with each pronouncement. What might I say to her? Perhaps this: "Besides, Annie, he's only half African, the other half being Shropshire English."

"Well, he *looks* African."

"And speaks as a proper English gentleman."

"Yes," said she with a sigh, "isn't it remarkable? He does remind me so of Othello."

My report to Sir John upon my visit to the room of Thomas Roundtree was not delivered until well into the afternoon. His court session intervened, and following that he was cloistered in his chambers with his clerk, Mr. Marsden, for an examination of the court accounts. A financial report on the year past was due by the end of the month at the office of the Lord Chief Justice. I waited patiently, seated upon the bench outside Sir John's door, until at last they were done. When Mr. Marsden emerged, he offered me a nod, and I jumped at my opportunity and rapped at the door left open.

"Who is there?"

"It is I, Jeremy. I've something odd to relate."

"Then come, by all means. I've had quite enough of pounds, shillings, and pence for one day. Tell me a story, and be it rum or queer, you shall have me till it be done."

And so tell him I did, leaving out little or nothing. I described my surprise at finding the door to Roundtree's room barricaded, and my greater surprise at discovering his daughter within. Clarissa Roundtree I described to the life and gave what was virtually a verbatim report upon our conversation, such as it was. Nor did I fail to mention the three shillings I had left for her upon the chest.

"You will be recompensed for that," said he to me when I had done. "It is in our interest to keep her alive, healthy, and in that room. You have only to ask Mr. Marsden for your three shillings."

"Thank you, Sir John. Perhaps more should be given her."

"Oh, I think not. Three shillings should keep her tidy enough for a week or more."

"I was thinking, sir," said I, "that if I were to wait within sight of that court building in Half-Moon Passage, this fellow Roundtree would eventually appear on a visit to his daughter."

"Yes, but he might take days in coming. And suppose he did appear—unless you wore pistols you would have no way to enforce your order to proceed quietly to Bow Street. If you were to wear them—and in this instance I should forbid it, but only suppose you had them by your side— then if he chose to disobey, you would be faced again with the choice of shooting him or allowing him to run. I would not want you to have that choice again, for you might this time choose to shoot."

"I might indeed be able to subdue him with a club."

"You might, then again you might not. This time he may be armed, for all you know. Besides, you lack the authority to arrest, and I refuse to give it you, even on a temporary basis."

"Perhaps I could wait with a constable, and when I iden-tified Roundtree, then he could be properly detained."

"Jeremy, I have better things to do with my constables than send them out on night-long waits with you in hope of capturing a fellow gone fugitive from a public drunk-enness conviction. I would remind you that Jonah Slade has so far eluded us. *He* assaulted Constable Cowley with a deadly weapon, and such an attack is one against us all— a much more serious matter."

I felt properly abashed. "I . . . I'm sorry, Sir John. In fact, I had forgotten."

"Oh, I know, Thomas Roundtree caused you embarrassment by slipping away from you as he did. You feel that it's only by bringing him back that you may be exonerated. Well, there is no need for you to feel so. In truth, I would as leave let the fellow go as not." He paused, gave his chin a stroke, then added: "The girl does give me reason for concern, however."

"I can see that, yes," said I. "What should be done about her?"

"For the present, nothing at all. She was quite right when she said that she had every right to be there so long as the rent was paid up—with or without a lock upon the door." Again he went silent for a moment, and of a sudden brightened a bit as he said, "But at least we now know why he went fugitive rather than serve thirty days in the Fleet— the girl, of course, his daughter. He knew she could not survive with him away so long. He's not an entirely bad sort, you see. Few are."

"Probably not. But . . . but why did he deny having family dependent upon him? I recall that you asked him specifically if he was married—if there was any at home who might miss him if he spent another night in the strong room."

"Yes, that is puzzling, is it not? Had he told me of his daughter, I might indeed have allowed him to pay his fine piecemeal, as he suggested. Yet rather than reveal her to me, he chose to absent himself for an additional night. That gives us cause for wonder, does it not?"

"Perhaps it was not an unusual occurrence for him to be away one night or two," I suggested.

"Perhaps not—public drunkenness was the charge, after all. Uh . . . Jeremy, I know not quite how to put this, but you searched the place—would you say that there were signs that father and daughter shared the same bed? Were there, in fact, two beds?"

That was indeed a detail I had omitted. "There was a sort of trundle bed beneath the greater one. It was bigger than most such. Perhaps he had built it for her special."

"A carpenter, after all. And how old did you say she was?"

"I should estimate that she was about eleven, no more than twelve."

"But near full-grown, you said."

"In height only."

"Well," he sighed, "be that as it may, I must discuss her situation with Kate. She may have something to suggest, may even wish to visit the girl."

As it turned out, Lady Fielding did indeed wish to visit Clarissa Roundtree. That evening, following dinner, she questioned me at length regarding her state. I offered her the same report I had given Sir John, and she asked me a number of the same questions he had put to me. She, however, was particularly interested in the girl's physical well-being.

"There was a fireplace, but no fire? No coal nor wood?"

None, I told her.

"You searched the closet. Was there a cape or greatcoat that might have fitted her?"

"No, I found only a second frock, and uh, a boy's coat, too."

"How odd. Did she seem fearful of the future?"

"Indeed not. She boasted that her father had provided for her in the past and would continue to do so."

And so on. Having interrogated me thusly, Lady Fielding concluded that Miss Roundtree was, in her situation, a child neglected, and that she must herself interview her to determine what might be done to help. That interview would take place next morning, as she informed me, and I would be needed to guide her there and help her gain admittance.

So it was that we set off together the following day shortly after Annie had departed for her lessons. There were no hackney coaches in sight, and in any case, Lady Fielding determined that Half-Moon Passage was only a short distance, one that could easily be reached by foot. She had not reckoned with the morning crowd in the streets, however. Her traveling to and from the Magdalene Home for Penitent Prostitutes, which she oversaw, was usually undertaken later in the day and always by hackney, as its distance from Bow Street demanded.

We set off together, I attempting to keep by her side. Yet, as earlier with Roundtree, that soon became impractical, and so I forged ahead, clearing a path for her through the buffeting mass of pedestrians. This required such effort that I suggested we cut through Covent Garden, again following the route taken with the prisoner whom I had lost along the way. Though we soon returned again to the teeming streets and were forced to dodge drunks along Bedford, we reached the dilapidated court in Half-Moon Passage without serious incident. Lady Fielding's nose twitched at the foul smell of the place, yet she pressed on without comment, following me up the short staircase which led to the enclosed first tier of rooms.

It was on the way to the one occupied by Clarissa Roundtree that a most unfortunate event occurred. I was walking next to Lady Fielding, as the width of the long hall permitted, when a door opened most suddenly and an unkempt wreck of a fellow came stumbling out and collided with m'lady; his hat he wore back to front, in one hand was his coat, and the other held up his breeches. Reaching out, I saved Lady Fielding from being knocked to the floor most unceremoniously. Then, glancing up whence he had come, I caught a brief glimpse of one of Roundtree's notorious "nekkid ladies" before the door slammed shut.

"Ye'll be sorry for that, y'will," he shouted at the closed door. And to Lady Fielding: "Beg yer pardon, mum, but 'twasn't my fault. I was pushed."

With no more than that, he set off down the hall toward

the stairs, waddling ungainly in an effort to keep his breeches up somewhere near his waist.

Lady Fielding was quite livid with anger. "Imagine," said she, "a young girl in such a place as this!"

(I had the day past imagined it and thought that Clarissa must be having quite an interesting time of it. But then, at that point I was not overly sympathetic to her plight.)

Thus we did come to her door. I knocked upon it stoutly and after some delay received a response from not too far within the room, a strong and challenging "Who is there?" I could imagine her at that moment taking her place behind the chest, ready to exert all her childish strength against mine. Let her, thought I. I had won the contest once before, had I not?

Nevertheless I answered in a mild and sympathetic tone: "It is I, your visitor from the day before. I have brought with me one who wishes to inquire into your state."

Then, from her, quite anticipated: "Go away!"

I leaned against the door, not attacking but testing it. It gave very slightly, but then held firm. Giving more pressure to it, then still more, I found I could not budge the door farther. Could she somehow have pushed the bed against the door? Not even the wardrobe would have held the door so well.

I felt a tap upon my shoulder. Lady Fielding indicated silently that I should step aside.

"Clarissa," said she, her voice raised in a distinct, commanding fashion, "this is Katherine Fielding. I wish to meet and talk with you. It is in your interest to do so—and even more in your father's. I have considerable influence with my husband, Sir John Fielding, who is Magistrate of the Bow Street Court. When your father is captured, as indeed he will be, only clemency from Sir John will save him from severe punishment. If you wish me to plead for clemency, then you must open this door immediately. I have an offer to make."

Rather than the scrape and bump of furniture moved

across the floor, I heard a click and a metallic slap, and then did the door swing open. Clarissa Roundtree was revealed, stepping back to make room for our entrance. Lady Fielding preceded me through the door. I entered, shut the door behind me, and examined the device that had blocked me so effectively. It was a simple hasp and staple lock, old and a bit rusty, yet still strong. It was evident that Thomas Roundtree had paid his daughter another visit.

I looked round the room for further evidence of him. There was naught to see but the fire that burned wood and coal together in the fireplace. I doubted that the girl possessed the skill to set it well; he must have started it not so very long before, for it was now a proper blaze. My eyes drifted to the curtained closet. It was only there he could hide himself. I vowed I would throw back that curtain and have a look ere we left the room.

Clarissa stood erect, tense as a string to be plucked, dressed in the same green frock she had worn the day before. She held a book in her hand, one of her romances. The single chair in the room had been pulled over by the fireplace.

"You were reading," said Lady Fielding.

"Yes, mum, I was." Quite in contrast to her way with me, she was courteous, restrained, perhaps intimidated by her female visitor.

"Let us go over to the fire. It's a chill morning. You may sit, if you like."

She edged nearer to the fireplace as Lady Fielding took a place near to her.

"I prefer to stand, mum."

"Jeremy says there was no fire when he visited you yesterday, that it was quite cold in the room here."

"He left me some shillings. I used some of the money to buy wood and some coal."

"And some food, I hope."

"Yes, mum, two loaves and some butter. They'll last me awhile."

"Did you thank Jeremy for his gift?" asked Lady Fielding. She knew the girl had not; I had told tattle on her.

"No, mum," said she. Then with a bit of the old defiance: "I resented his visit."

"You should not resent those who try to help you."

"I resent those who come to make my father prisoner,
who say he doesn't take proper care of me. My father is a
good man, and he takes care of me as best he can."

"And he drinks much of the money he makes, is that
not so?"

Clarissa Roundtree's eyes did truly flash fire in response,
yet she held back what was in her mind to say. After a long
moment's silence, during which she breathed deep once or
twice, she said at last: "He has that habit, yes, but none of
us is perfect, and he does as well as he can. He's a skilled
carpenter, he is."

"I'm sure he is," said Lady Fielding. "When did you
last see him?"

"I'm not sure I should tell you that," said she.

"It could not have been long ago, m'lady," said I, interrupting their dialogue. "He has put a lock upon the door
since yesterday, and it must have been him built this fire."

Lady Fielding then passed me a look which said quite
plain that I was to leave the talking to her. Chastened, I
nodded my compliance.

"What he says is true," said Clarissa. "He was here
early and left just before you came. He left me a few shillings, as well."

"Since he does come to visit and makes an effort to look
after you, I would like you to deliver a message to him
when next you see him."

"And what is that, mum?"

In answer, Lady Fielding raised her voice considerably
and half turned in the direction of the curtained closet, as
if she, too, suspected that the elder Roundtree might be
hiding there. "You may tell him," said she, "that if he
returns to Bow Street and surrenders himself, Sir John will

overlook his escape and his days as a fugitive. Some arrangement will be made on the payment of his fine so that he will not have to spend time away from you in gaol.'' She turned and faced the daughter direct. ''Is that understood?''

''Yes, mum.''

''But now, about you, my dear. How old are you?''

''Oh, sixteen, near seventeen now.''

(A lie! Surely a lie! And it was all I could do to keep myself from telling her so. Only the quizzical smile that appeared on Lady Fielding's face registering her own disbelief prevented me from saying so.)

''And how long have you been here in London?''

''Oh, ever so long—a year, no, two years, perhaps longer.''

(Another lie, of course.)

''And you came here from Lichfield? That, I believe, is where your father said he was from.''

''Uh, no, mum. For a time I lived with an aunt and uncle in . . . Bristol. My mother, you see, died when I was but a child of ten.''

(That last, at least, was no doubt true.)

''And how long were you with them?''

She had been made quite uncomfortable by the questions, worried that her improvised responses might not quite match, one with the previous. She delayed as long as was seemly. Then: ''A few years. Five, I think. Yes, five more or less.''

''Which is it? More? Or less?''

''Then more—yes, a little more than five.''

''With your aunt and uncle in Bristol?''

''*Yes!* Yes, mum.''

Lady Fielding had managed to fluster her, and in so doing had made it plain to her that she knew the girl was lying. Much better that way than simply to accuse her of telling untruths. Had she taken instruction in interrogation from Sir John? If so, she had learned well; if not, she had a great natural talent for it. She began again in a manner at once milder and more sympathetic.

"Tell me, Clarissa, do you have a trade or a craft? Any sort of special skill?"

She considered that a moment, and not wishing to seem utterly incapable, she said, "Well, I can read."

"Many girls of your age cannot," said Lady Fielding.

"And I can write a good hand, as well. My mother taught me."

"Very good. She must have been herself a woman of some skill and learning. But can you cook? Can you sew? Can you weave?"

"No, mum, but . . . well . . . I have an ambition to be an author—a poet, a writer of romances."

"That would be an unusual occupation for a woman," said Lady Fielding, though not unsympathetically.

"But a possible one!"

"Oh yes, my dear. More is possible for women of intelligence and ambition than the world allows. I would be the last to gainsay the possibility."

Clarissa Roundtree considered the statement a moment and seemed to look at the woman who had made it in a new light. She smiled shyly. "I'm pleased to hear you say that."

The smile was returned. "My husband tells me that so long as your rent is paid up here, you have the right to remain, but you must think of the future."

"My father and I are making plans for the future."

Lady Fielding waited, but nothing more was said of them. "I see," said she. "Yet there is also the present. It is winter, and it is cold. Jeremy told me that in his search of the premises yesterday he found no cape or coat of a sort that might be yours. Did he overlook it? Do you have one?"

"Oh, I did, but . . . but I foolishly left it behind in an eating place. We have not yet found one that is suitable."

"Well, until you do, I shall find one for you. You see, I

oversee the running of a charitable house for young women. We receive frequent donations of clothing, and''—looking her up and down—''I believe I may have just the thing for you. Until you find something better, of course.''

''That will be welcome, thank you.''

''My hope is that by then your father will have surrendered himself to Sir John.'' Again she raised her voice: ''He will not be sorry if he does. My husband is a just man.

''Jeremy will bring the cape tomorrow. I shall look in on you later as matters develop. Until then, goodbye and God keep you, Clarissa.''

Then, in turning, as if she had perceived my desire to look behind the curtain and into the closet, Lady Fielding grabbed me firmly by the arm and marched me to the door.

The girl trailed us. I saw, when I turned round in the hall, that she had a stout peg in hand that she might slip it into the lock and make it secure. Catching Lady Fielding's eye, she said goodbye and added, ''You're a kind woman.'' Then swiftly she made the door shut and we our way down the hall.

Nothing at all was said between us until we had left the court and were walking together down Half-Moon Passage. I ventured a look, then gave it as my suspicion that Thomas Roundtree might well have been in the closet, listening behind the curtain to all that was said.

''Of course he was,'' said Lady Fielding. ''That was why I shouted so loud my bid for his surrender. I daresay that trollop two doors down heard me plain and clear.''

''I had not known that Sir John had made that offer to bring Roundtree in,'' said I.

''Neither yet does he,'' said she with a sigh. ''But Jack will honor it, I know he will. Something must be done for that girl.''

''You were far better with her than I. She was saucy and rude with me, and I repaid her with rudeness.''

''She's a plucky girl, Jeremy—and, oh dear me, she does so love her father!''

Of a sudden did Lady Fielding stop and face me. It was only then that I noticed the tears upon her cheeks. "Jeremy," she said, "I've a terrible need for a blow and a wipe, and we left in such a rush that I've nothing with me."

Digging into my pocket, I supplied her need. It was a fair clean piece of linen, too; it had been used by me but once.

It was left to me to make a report to Sir John regarding our visit to Half-Moon Passage. Lady Fielding waved down a free hackney at the corner of Chandos Street and Bedford and departed for her daily visit to the Magdalene Home for Penitent Prostitutes. She waved from the coach door and called to me that she would have that cape for Clarissa upon her return. The matter did seem that important to her, just so. I returned her wave and set off along the way we had come.

Though as I approached Number 4 Bow Street, I confess, I did not look forward with pleasure to telling Sir John of the generous offer of clemency that had been made in his name, in the event I found his response very mild indeed. In fact, when he heard of it, laughter was his response.

"She said that, did she?"

"Uh, yes sir."

"What was the offer again? That if he were to surrender himself, then I would forgive him his little adventure as a truant and work out some means of paying his fine for the original charge—that was it, essentially?"

"That was it, yes sir. She felt sure that you would honor the offer."

"Oh, I will, indeed I will. A man should not willingly make a liar of his wife." Again he laughed; it seemed positively a giggle. He was much amused. "And you suspected, Jeremy, that he was present throughout the interview, hiding in the closet behind the curtain?"

"That is correct, sir. Left to myself, I would have thrown back the curtain and confronted the fellow."

"Well, then it is just as well you were not left to yourself, for all the good reasons I explained to you yesterday. No, I think you did well to hasten back, rather, and explain the matter to me. Otherwise, our friend Roundtree might have preceded you here."

"You believe, then, that he will surrender himself?"

"Oh, I do. Were I in his position, that is what I would do. It is, after all, a most generous offer. And I also admit, a practical way to handle a matter gone quite out of hand. I should have thought of it myself. Perhaps I ought to consult with Kate more often on court matters."

Then did he grow of a sudden more serious. He leaned forward, folding his hands before him, his jaw set and his lips pursed. Then did he speak: "Now, about the girl—Clarissa? is that her name?—that is quite another matter. I shall talk about her to—"

A rather intrusive and noisy commotion commenced at that moment not far beyond the open door to Sir John's chambers. The voice of a woman: "I will *not* be impeded, young man!" The voice of Mr. Marsden: "But it is only proper that you be announced." "I need no announcement. I am who I am!"—and that said with great authority.

"Jeremy," said Sir John, raising his voice above theirs, "go and see what all that is about, will you?"

I rose and went to the door, and there was I near bowled over by a figure in black, hatted and veiled, all in widow's weeds. She bumped past me as she propelled herself forward with all the force of a cannonball and into the room. Stopping only when she had reached his desk, she took an aggressive stance, leaning over so that no more than two or three feet separated their faces.

"Sir John Fielding!" said she with some urgency—and no more.

"That is my name. And who, pray tell, are you, madam?"

"Lady Laningham, widow of the late lord."

Then did Sir John rise as the occasion demanded. He

bowed *pro forma* and murmured that it was ill to meet under such sad circumstances, and I went quietly to a chair near the door and seated myself, not wishing to miss a moment of an interview that had begun so spectacularly. Sir John invited her to sit down, and she dropped heavily into the chair I had vacated.

"In a sense," she said, "we have already met—up there on the stage of the Crown and Anchor. I was most grateful to you for clearing that mob. All those people milling about and poor Chrissie in such terrible distress. I thought I would quite go mad until you sent them away."

"Yet," said Sir John, resuming his seat behind the desk, "you did not come here to thank me—or I am mistaken."

"No, I did not." She took a deep breath. "I have heard something about you that is quite distressing."

"Oh? And what is that?"

She threw the veil up from her face and again leaned forward in a confrontational manner. "I have heard that you have been putting it about that my husband was poisoned."

"Putting it about, you say? Who told you such a thing?"

"Mr. Oliver Goldsmith visited to pay his respects and offer words of consolation. Yet far from consoling me, his words quite inflamed me. I have come to you direct to demand from you some explanation for this . . . this opinion of yours."

"First of all, Lady Laningham," said he, "let me declare that I have in no wise been 'putting it about,' as you said. I have discussed the matter only once, and that was on the evening of your husband's death with Mr. Gabriel Donnelly, the doctor who attended your husband, Mr. Alfred Humber, and Mr. Goldsmith. That conversation took place in this very room. Now, did Mr. Goldsmith actually say that I had been 'putting it about'?"

At that she paused for thought. "No, in truth, he did not. What were his exact words? As near as I can remember, what he said was that you had questioned that Lord Laningham's death came by natural causes, that you thought there were reasons to consider the possibility of poison.''

''Now, that is quite another matter, would you not say so? To question is one thing, and to spread it about to others is quite another. I had hoped my conversation with those gentlemen would be kept private.''

''But *why* do you question?'' she asked most earnestly. ''What are your reasons for considering the possibility of poison?''

Then, offering first a deep sigh, he did launch into a summary of those matters that had disquieted him so on the evening of that Sunday past. He laid them before her in most orderly fashion, as if summarizing a case of law, which in a sense was what he was doing. She, an educated and intelligent woman, listened carefully, nodding her understanding as he talked on for a period of no more than a few minutes. When he had concluded with his summary, he put to her a question: ''Tell me, Lady Laningham, had your husband ever before experienced extreme digestive distress—anything, that is, that might have begun to approach the severity of his attack that night?''

''No . . . no, certainly not. Chrissie had the digestion of a bear. He could eat or drink anything at all, it seemed, without misfortune. I used to tease him about it.''

''Well,'' said Sir John, ''there you have another reason to question death by natural causes. There was no forewarning, no earlier hint of any such difficulty.''

''But for the most part,'' said she, ''it is this matter of the wine, as I understand you.''

''That is correct. He showed no signs of illness, even of discomfort, until he drank from the bottle brought to him there on the stage, and it was not long after he drank from it that he collapsed. Add to that the fact that the said bottle was nowhere to be found once the crowd had been cleared from the stage, and, as I said, we have further reason to question. But now do I have another question for you. And it is this: Whence came the bottle of wine in question? The innkeeper of the Crown and Anchor gave it as his opinion that it had been brought up from your table, though he could not be certain, since he had not located the server who brought it. Do you recall that detail? Did the wine come from Lord Laningham's private stock, as the innkeeper believed?''

''Let me think,'' said she, and think she did, taking near a minute to respond to Sir John's interrogative. ''Yes, I recall it perfectly. Lord Laningham has always kept a good cellar and always made it a point to bring with him bottles of his private stock to these affairs at the Crown and Anchor. The server came to our table, a young man, as most of them there are, and said that Chrissie had requested a bottle, and it was sent up with him.''

''Jeremy Proctor, my young assistant, who I believe is sitting behind you now near the door''—how could he have been so exact?—''saw the bottle brought to Lord Laningham and noted that it was uncorked, but he thought it to have been full. Was it so?''

Before answering, she turned about in her chair and regarded me briefly with a frown. Was it disapproval, or merely a shortsighted squint? The latter, I hoped. She was rather a formidable woman.

Yet in a moment her attention had returned to Sir John. ''As I recall,'' she said, ''it was nearly so.''

''*Nearly* so? Would you explain, please?''

''Gladly. It was the last unopened bottle on the table. I signaled to the server that he was to open it, and he did so. Yet then, just as he was about to leave with the bottle and Lord Laningham's glass, he was stopped by Mr. Paltrow, who asked for a bit more before the bottle left. The server looked at me, and I nodded my assent. He took no more than half a glass, but I remember the incident well, for I thought it most presumptuous and unmannerly of him, and in that way quite characteristic.''

''I see,'' said Sir John. ''And who, may I ask, is Mr. Paltrow? A relative of your late husband, I take it.''

"What? Oh yes. Arthur Paltrow was the late lord's nephew and heir. As you may or may not know, Chrissie and I had no children, to our great sorrow—mine, I believe, most of all. He was near twenty years my senior, and I believed that marrying a younger woman would provide him with a considerable family of children. Yet that I could not give him."

"And so Arthur Paltrow was a guest at your table on that fateful evening?"

"Yes, he, his wife, and their two adolescent daughters."

"He was on a visit to London with his family?"

"No, they moved here some months ago. Until then they had dwelt upon his late father's small estate near Laningham."

"I take it from your earlier remark," said Sir John, "that you are not overly fond of Mr. Paltrow."

"No, I am not. I said that he lacked courtesy. I should say rather that he lacks ordinary human consideration. I give you an example. Mr. Paltrow is the Laningham heir. There is no question of that. Yet he has put me on notice that I am to move out of our town residence in St. James Square at my earliest opportunity after the reading of the will. It's true, I have been well provided for, and the house does go to Mr. Paltrow as part of the estate. But to force me out to look for suitable quarters so soon after all this has happened—that I call damned inconsiderate."

"Oh, quite. I'm in accord with you on that. I, uh, take it that the reading of the will which names him as heir makes him officially Lord Laningham. You must forgive me, I know nothing of such matters."

"And I next to nothing. There is, I believe, a further matter, an invitation of some sort from the House of Lords—an 'investiture,' or some such thing."

"Ah, so." He remained silent for a long moment, rubbing his chin, deep in thought. "I have a question or two for you, Lady Laningham, if you would not mind."

"Ask what you will."

"First of all, did you see Mr. Paltrow drink that half glass of wine he begged? That is to say, did he finish it? Did he gulp it down?"

"No, certainly he did not gulp it, nor do I know that he finished it. I did, however, see him sip it once or twice. I remember he made some fatuous remark about its great quality. In truth, it was not all that grand. We saved our best for our dinner parties."

"So we leave it that he sipped it. Now, tell me if you will, did Mr. Paltrow go with you to the stage of the Crown and Anchor at the time of your husband's collapse?"

"Why yes, yes he did. It was the one bit of kindness that he showed me that evening. The crowd formed about Chrissie most immediately—the chorus and orchestra gathered round and others preceded us to the stage. Mr. Paltrow pushed his way through them and made a path for me. I doubt I could have made it to Chrissie on my own."

What followed was a long—oh, an interminably long—silence from Sir John. Lady Laningham was made uneasy by it. She shifted in her chair, then turned to look at me questioningly. There was naught I could do but nod reassuringly. At last Sir John spoke.

"Lady Laningham," said he, "what you have told me still leaves doubts in my mind. I believe poison cannot be ruled out as a possibility."

"Do you mean Mr. Paltrow could somehow have . . ."

"I point a finger at no one direct. There is another possibility. The server himself might have slipped a potion in the bottle as he brought it to the stage. There are any number of possibilities, yet we cannot consider them until we know if Lord Laningham was poisoned, and there is only one way to be certain of that."

"And what might that be?"

"By autopsy."

"Do you mean cutting him open and examining his inwards?"

"That is just what I mean. A trained medical man like

Donnelly would know from the condition of the organs
how your husband died—that is, if his death did or did not
come by natural means.''

''Oh dear,'' said she.

''If you, as his widow, gave permission, the entire exercise could be handled overnight. It would not even be
necessary to delay the funeral. When is it, by the bye?''

''Saturday,'' said she, and then nothing more until: ''I'm
afraid I should have to give some consideration to this—
cutting poor Chrissie open. It seems such an insult to the
body, so . . .'' She hesitated, looking for the right word.
''Well, *unseemly* is what it seems to me.''

''Unseemly? Well, it could all be handled confidentially,
in a single night, as I said.''

''No,'' she said, rising slowly, as if beneath a great burden, ''I'm afraid I shall have to give a great deal of thought
to this—of the private sort, that is. Thank you for your
directness, Sir John. I must go now and think. Goodbye.''

And with that, she made her way past me and out the
door, perplexed, a bit overwhelmed. Her exit was in great
contrast to her entrance.

FIVE

In Which Shocking
News Is Brought from
the Laningham Residence

The delivery of the cape brought by Lady Fielding
from the Magdalene Home took place next morning.
It was a good warm piece of clothing, one which she was
proud to donate to Clarissa Roundtree, in whom she had
taken a keen interest. I carried it over my arm as I marched
the distance to Half-Moon Passage. Once arrived, I trod the
long hall a bit more carefully than on earlier visits, that I
might not be bowled over by some whoremonger come
flying out a door at me. None did. The knock I gave upon
her door was also a bit less peremptory than before.

"Who is there?" came the voice from beyond the door.

"It is I, Jeremy Proctor from Bow Street."

"What do you want?" That, at least, was an improvement upon her previous invitations to leave.

"I have with me the cape which Lady Fielding promised
you."

She made no verbal response to that, but answered by
pulling the peg from the staple and throwing back the hasp.
All this I heard as I waited impatiently in the hall. The door
came open, though it was not thrown wide to admit me;

rather it was opened a distance of about two feet, which space she herself filled. She reached out an open hand.

"Give it me then," said she.

Yet I held back the cape, fearful that she would slam the door soon as she had it.

"Your father has not yet surrendered himself," said I.

"Oh? Well, I suppose he hasn't."

"Have you seen him? Have you passed on to him the offer made by Lady Fielding?"

"I . . . well . . ." She was flustered, having evidently prepared no reply to a question she should have known I would ask. Would she lie? Tell the truth? And how would I know one from the other? But she managed to regain herself: "No, I have not yet passed it on."

What she said rang as an untruth, but then I saw through her device: she had used the truth to tell a lie.

"I strongly suspect," said I, "that you have not told him because there was no need to. I strongly suspect that he was present during our visit, hidden away in the closet behind the curtain. Now tell me, am I not right? Did he not hear all?"

"Oh, pooh!" said she. "If you suspected so much, why did you not capture him?"

It would have taken too much to give a proper explanation, and at that moment I felt she deserved none. "Let us say, Miss Pooh, that Sir John prefers that he surrender himself."

She peered at me in a sullen manner. "Are you going to give me the cape, or are you not?"

I had nearly forgotten it in my fit of ill temper. "Yes, of course I am. Here." I shoved it at her through the narrow opening she had provided me. "Lady Fielding wishes you well and prays that you will wear it in good health." That was what I had been told to say, and I had said it.

She took it from me and, forcing a smile, said, "You may thank her for me. Tell her I thank her kindly. She's a good woman, is she not?"

"She is, right enough," said I; then, as Clarissa Round-tree began to ease shut the door, I remembered something more. "But a moment. *I* have also brought something for you."

"*You* have brought something? And what might that be?"

"A book." I delved into the pocket of my coat and brought it forth. "It should provide a change from those romances you read—a history and geography of the American colonies with many true tales and anecdotes of adventure." I recited from memory. It was a book I treasured.

Then did she truly smile. She took the book from me most eagerly.

"It is from my personal library," said I. "It is a gift to you and not a loan."

"You have so many?"

"I have a few." Puffing a bit.

"How could you know that we—" She halted abruptly, checking herself.

"That you . . . ?"

"Oh . . . nothing. It was but a childish fancy. My mother and I did oft read such books together. But I thank you, Jeremy Proctor. The gift of a book will ever be the best gift for me."

"Then I am satisfied," said I. "Goodbye to you."

With a wave, I turned and started back up the hall. She called her goodbye to me. I looked back and saw her leaning out the door, still smiling, waving the book. All the way back to Bow Street, I turned in my mind what she had said—or no, it was rather what she had not said. Was it merely, as she had claimed, that she and her mother had read together such books as the one I had given her? Or was America the refuge chosen by her father in some grand plan of escape he had formed? The phrase she had blurted forth, "How could you know," seemed somehow to suggest the latter possibility. But escape from what? Surely not a public drunkenness conviction. The means to settle that had been given him. What more could there be? That question would plague me for some days to come.

Some time after I had returned, whilst I was yet engaged in the onerous task of cleaning out the kitchen fireplace, Annie came back from her morning lessons with Jimmie Bunkins in tow. He had come, he said, in hopes that we might together visit Mr. Donnelly's surgery. Only then did I recall his news that the human head we had viewed in St. Andrew's Churchyard had been taken down and handed over to the medico that it might be preserved against further decomposition.

"I'm right willing to take you there, Jimmie B.," said I, "but I must first finish my charwoman duties."

"I can help," said he.

"It'll go faster if you do."

And so together we finished the task, and together we hauled down two great buckets of ash and burnt coals, which we dumped in a deep hole dug in a corner of the yard for that purpose. After dusting off a bit, we were off to make our visit to Mr. Donnelly.

I had not been to see him since his move to Drury Lane. Yet I knew the location well from earlier trips to fetch his predecessor, Dr. Amos Carr, at that location. It was not far to go. And once arrived, I noted that the new surgery had the undeniable advantage of placement in the ground floor; the windows of Mr. Donnelly's waiting room looked out upon the street; a plaque upon the wall next the door announced his residence in the building.

Within the waiting room three prospective patients sat—two women of middle age and an older man. There was naught that Bunkins and I could do but take our place among them. We had not long until Mr. Donnelly made his appearance. He came escorting a patient from his consulting room, a young woman of quality dressed for the street. Once he had sent her on her way with murmured words of encouragement, he turned to me with a questioning look and beckoned me to him.

"Jeremy," said he in a whisper, "what is the matter? Has Sir John sent you?"

"No, he has not," said I. Then I quickly explained the purpose of our visit in a tone of voice equally quiet. Bunkins, for his part, had risen from his seat upon a chair, yet hung back, hat in hand, waiting hopefully.

"He is your friend?" asked Mr. Donnelly, having heard me out. "You vouch for his serious intent?"

"Oh, I do. When first he looked upon the hideous thing, he told me that he believed he once had known him to whom it belonged, yet could not call him up exact from his memory."

"So many have come in off the street demanding to look upon it that I have begun turning away all but those whom I judge to be here for the true purpose of identification. The rest seem to wish some perverse thrill. But so long as you vouch for him . . ."

Then did he wave Bunkins forward. "This will not take long," he announced to those in the waiting room. "It is a court matter."

He led us through the door into the consulting room, which seemed to me to be grandly equipped with all manner of medical paraphernalia, then took us beyond into his private quarters, consisting of two good-sized rooms and a small kitchen. Into the kitchen we went. Mr. Donnelly produced a key, and with it he unlocked a cabinet. Reaching in with both hands, he pulled out a large and heavy glass jar and placed it carefully upon the counter below. He stepped back to reveal that which Bunkins had come to view.

"There you are, young Mr. . . . . Bunkins, is it?"

"Yes sir."

"Have your look then. It is naught but how all would appear, were their heads separated from the rest of them."

"Yes sir," repeated Bunkins, and he settled himself upon

the counter to stare face-to-face, as it were, at the head which floated in the jar.

I myself took not much more than a glance at it. More I would not have wished. The thing looked to me much as it had looked before, except that in the clear solution the hair attached to the scalp fanned out and floated free around the head in a kind of unholy halo.

Mr. Donnelly seemed impressed by the intense concentration with which Bunkins studied the face in the jar. He saw no trace of a smirk upon his features, heard no sly remark or chuckle from him. This was to Jimmie B. a matter of the utmost seriousness. The surgeon was moved to be helpful.

"You should think of the living face as narrower than what appears before you now," said he. "The time spent in the sewer water, the process of decomposition, and the solution in which it is now suspended would all tend to loosen and thicken the features of the face."

"Is that gin it's in now?" asked Bunkins.

"No, a solution of pure alcohol. The nose, especially, would have been broadened, the cheeks loosened. The face you see now is distorted from the original."

Then did Bunkins shut his eyes and thus concentrate with the same intensity. And opening them, he stood and said with some degree of certainty, "Bradbury."

"You believe you know him? I should be very happy to bury this with the rest of his parts if they can be found. Oh, I would indeed."

"Well, I ain't absolutely sure," Bunkins replied. "But what you said about the face puffin' up, like, gave me the clue. The top of his napper and around the eyes is like him I knew when I was out on the scamp."

"Pardon?" queried Mr. Donnelly with a blink of his eyes. "Scamp? I don't quite understand."

"Thievin'," said Bunkins, "which was my trade in my younger days. I was a proper village hustler. When you said I should think of the cod as thinner, I thought of him

so, and out come Bradbury. He had a pawnshop on Bedford, and he would take naught but ticks and rings and such.
Very particular he was."

"Stolen goods?"

"Oh, he weren't particular about *that*. He was a proper
fence. Every scamp and dip in London knew him."

"You're sure about this, then? This is a positive identification?"

"Well, now, I don't know about that. Positive means
sure certain, don't it, Jeremy?"

"Sure beyond a doubt," said I.

"Well, maybe I ain't that sure. The thing is, I seen him
on the street not so long ago. He was healthy enough then."

"How long ago, Jimmie B.?" I asked a bit breathlessly.

"I'm tryin' to think—a month, maybe more. How long's
he been like this, Mr. Donnelly, sir?"

"It's difficult to be exact, but judging from the degree
of decomposition, probably about a week."

"There, see? Maybe I'm wrong."

"Well," said the surgeon, lifting the heavy jar and re-
placing it in the cabinet, "let us place it, then, at a strong
suspicion as to the identity of this poor fellow. That, I
should think, would be sufficient to report to Sir John,
wouldn't you say so, Jeremy?"

"I would indeed," said I.

He locked the cabinet, pocketed the key, and said, "Now
I must attend to my patients. It would not do to keep them
waiting long."

With that, he led us back the way we had come. Yet in
the waiting room as Bunkins stepped out into the hall, Mr.
Donnelly held me back long enough to say, "I'm much
intrigued by your friend. You must tell me about him when
next we meet."

Bunkins said nothing until we reached the street. Then
did he turn to me and mutter, "I don't think we should go
to your cove just yet, chum."

"You don't? But why not?"

"Well, I'd feel right foolish if the cod was still alive, walkin' the street and tendin' his shop."

"I see what you mean. Well, what do you propose?"

"Simple enough. We go to his shop, and if he comes out, we'll know it ain't him floatin' in that jar. I tell him I was just passin' by and thought I'd inquire how he was gettin' on. I gives him a shake and a wink, and we shove our trunk right on out of there."

"And if he isn't about?"

"Then . . ." He paused. "Then we'll see."

"That sounds like a reasonable course of action," said I, "and it shouldn't take long. I'm for it."

So off we went to Bedford Street—down Long Acre and James Street, cutting the corner of Covent Garden; it was not a long walk, and Bunkins did amuse me as we went by telling tales of his thieving days and particularly of his dealings with Mr. Bradbury. It seemed he only went to him when he was eager to rid himself quickly of stolen goods— "when the hornies was hot after me," he explained. "Reason was ol' Bradbury was a skinflint. He would rather lose a finger than pay an honest thief a fair price."

"In the end he may have lost his head for it."

"Now that's a possibility, ain't it? There's highway scamps wouldn't stop at such if they thought they'd been cheated. But there's so many dips and hustlers workin' in Covent Garden they'd keep him well supplied, most of them too lazy to take a tramp to Field Lane, where there's so many pawnshops which are, truth to tell, just fences."

"And they paid better?"

"Oh," said Bunkins, playing the expert in such matters, "ever so much better. See, each one on that street is playin' against the rest. If you don't like the price you're offered, you go on to the next and get a better one. I been out of the game quite some time, but I'm sure it's the same now there up on Field Lane."

"Do they never get caught?"

"Some do, but not often do they get crapped for it.

Judges seem to look kinder on commerce than out-and-out thievin'. And the fence can always say, 'I never had no idea these goods was stolen. The fellow brought them in said they were his own. I wrote them out a pawn ticket and all.' He can say that, see, and there's none who can prove different.''

With that, my mind did go to that wad of pawn tickets I had found among the belongings of Thomas Roundtree.

Bunkins continued: ''I remember ol' Bradbury never let me leave without a pawn ticket. Once I ran all the way to that shop of his on Bedford with a proper gold tick I'd lifted. I thought him I'd taken it from was right behind me. Bradbury gave me no more than a shilling for it, but he grabbed hold of me and wouldn't let go till he'd writ out the ticket. He slapped it in my hand and made me take it. See, if you get caught, such is evidence against you.''

''What did you do?''

''What did I do? I ate the ticket.''

I laughed in surprise at his ready answer. Yet I wanted confirmed what I hoped and suspected. ''So no true thief would hold on to pawn tickets for stolen goods. They would be, as you say, incriminating.''

''Oh no, you wouldn't keep 'em. No point to it unless you mean to buy the goods back.''

At that I felt relief. I had, because of his daughter and their hapless situation, come round to some degree of sympathy for Roundtree; I no longer wished to think the worst of him.

Thus came we, Bunkins and I, to Bedford Street and to a dingy, dusty little shop which I had passed many times before without notice. Its windows were so dirty that one could bare see inside; but putting my face up close, I made out an assortment of musical instruments hanging from a rack, as well as a clock or two propped upon a shelf, and in the center of the display a delicate china figurine of a shepherdess which appeared to be of some worth. There were more goods within the shop proper, yet I saw no human form or movement in the dark interior.

I turned to Bunkins, who stood beside me at the shop-window. "It seems to be closed," said I. "It's dark inside, and I see no one about."

"It ain't closed," said he. "They live up above the shop, as all shopkeepers do. Ol' Bradbury keeps the place dark because he's such a skinflint, won't keep a lamp or even a candle burnin' unless there's a need. We go inside, somebody'll be out before you know it. Mark me on that."

"All right then, let's go inside."

"Awright, but just you let me do the talkin', clear? If I want to hear from you, then you back me up in what I say. You got that?"

I gave him an emphatic nod, more than willing to leave such discussion to him.

"And one more thing," said Bunkins. "Try to look like a thief."

"How do I do that?"

"Well, your clothes is awright—right dusty after cleaning that fireplace. But look kind of skulky, if you get my meaning. Don't hold your head so high. Don't look nobody straight in the eye."

I hunched my shoulders, lowered my head, and thrust my hands in my pockets. "Will this pass?"

He took a moment to give me an inspection. "It'll do. Come on, then. Let's inside."

And into the pawnshop we went. He led; I followed. A bell jingled above us as we entered. And responding to that signal, a heavy curtain was thrown back, and a woman entered the shop proper from its rear. She carried a single lit candle in a silver candleholder that must once have cost some lord or knight a pretty penny. She was young, in her twenties, and attractive in a lithesome sort of way. Richly dressed was she; what she wore was less a frock than a gown, yet it seemed to hang loose upon her in a number of places. Her face was fixed in a rather haughty smile, the sort that must indeed have been practiced before a looking glass. In her own way, she was playing the grand lady. But then did she open her mouth and greet us, and in a trice the ladylike illusion had vanished.

"Wot kin I do fer you two young gents?" Her voice was like a crow's, at once squawking and shrill. The only human voice I had ever heard make such a sound was that of our departed cook, Mrs. Grudge.

"We come to see the cove of the ken," said Bunkins in a most authoritative manner.

"He ain't available to you, so you must talk to me."

"And who might you be?"

"Who might *I* be?" I am his lawful wife is who—Missus Bradbury, and I'll thank you to address me as such, I will."

She was all ruffled and indignant, as if some great insult had been done to her. As she pouted for a moment in the gloomy room, I glanced round me at its crowded contents. There were a great many clocks about, large and small, tucked into corners and up on shelves. I saw a rack of grand dresses and gowns, some of them quite old-fashioned, an open clothing box from which one might grab what was needed, pieces of furniture of all quality and description—and so on. Upon the counter was a showcase, no doubt locked, containing a great many watches, rings, and odd bits of jewelry. The jumble and amount of goods was such that there seemed little room for the three of us in the place.

"Awright, then, Mrs. Bradbury," said Bunkins, in no wise more respectful than before, "at one time we done quite a lot of business with your husband of a particular kind, if you get my meaning. But we been out of the game for a couple of years now, and I come back to find that George Bradbury got himself married. Well, you can suppose our shock. Ain't that so, Jemmy?"

"Right so," said I, "ain't what we expected."

"Two years gone, is it?" she replied. "Prob'ly spent on

Duncan Campbell's Floating Academy or I miss my guess.''

(She referred, reader, to the hulk, *Justitia*, which floats at Woolwich and served as a prison ship at that time; Duncan Campbell was its governor.)

''You may guess what you like,'' said Bunkins, all bluff and tough, ''but we're shy to do our business with any but your husband, since it's him we dealt with in the past.''

''He left me in proper charge to do all business for him—even your kind.''

''*Our* kind? Listen to her, Jemmy. Ain't she got a queer tongue on her?''

''I never heard the like,'' said I.

''And what kind might our business be, Mrs. B.?''

''You're as rum a pair of scamps as ever I seen.''

''Just supposin' you're not too far off the mark—just supposin', mind. Well, it might be that a pair of scamps such as you take us for might learn a new knuckle trade at the Academy, might learn burglarin' f'r instance. With such we're no longer dealin' in ticks and rings, but in roomsful of the best. So the question is, could you take a wagonload? Them up in Field Lane could, I've no doubt of it.''

''You got the wagonload now?'' she asked, leaning forward eagerly. All but licking her chaps she was. ''I'll give you a better price than them on Field Lane. I'll give you a better price than George ever would.''

Then did Bunkins quite literally back away, bumping into me who was behind him in his movement. ''That's as may be,'' said he, ''but still I'd feel easier dealin' with him. Where is the old cod? When'll he be back?''

She sighed, principally, it seemed, from exasperation. ''When'll he be back?'' said she. ''Well, that ain't easy to say. He was called back to Warwick, for his father was near to death. That was over two weeks past. Just yesterday I received a letter from him sayin' that his father was takin' a turn somewhat for the better but was still in danger of death, so that he could not but stay on longer. How long, he could not say. In the meantime, said he''—and here her voice rose to an imperious shrillness—''I was to go on conducting business in the manner he had taught me, for he had all faith in my good sense and judgment.''

''His father?'' queried Bunkins. ''How old must he be? George is near sixty, ain't he?''

''Sixty-one to be exact, and his father's fourscore years and something. It ain't rare for a man to live long outside London. He's got property. Set George up in business here, he did.''

''Well, I suppose it's right with him, should be right with me. Tell you what, I'll visit, or Jemmy will, and tip you when we be comin' by. It'll be long past midnight, sure.''

''Just tell me the when of it, and there'll be a man or two to help you unload. You can pull around the back where you'll not be seen by the hornies.''

''Fair enough, but Mrs. Bradbury, I warn you, if you cut us on the price, we'll load up again and be off to Field Lane.''

''Have no fear of it, chum. You'll come away with a smile on your mug.''

With that, and without goodbye, we did leave her. Outside, in Bedford Street, Bunkins said naught till we were well away from the pawnshop. Indeed he may have kept silent longer, for it was I spoke first.

''Tell me what you're thinking, Jimmie B.''

''I'm thinkin' she murdered him,'' he whispered.

''Truly? She told a good story, and she's a mite small to do the deed herself.''

We rounded the corner onto Maiden Lane, and he pulled me into a recessed doorway, where we might talk without fear of a listener. I had never known him to be quite so cautious before. It was a mark of the seriousness with which he took the matter. Only then did he speak, and then not much above a whisper.

''I'm with you there,'' said he. ''She *is* too small. She must needs have someone help her, or do the job for her.

I can't see such a woman as that usin' a knife or a dagger in such a manner as killed him, much less sawin' off his head. And as for the tale she told, it's a tale like any other— might be true, more likely not.''

"Something in its favor," I suggested, "is its temporary nature. She cannot keep him there in Warwick forever. He must return someday soon."

"True enough," said Bunkins. "Could be she has a buyer for the shop. It's an easy matter to write his name on a bill of sale and make it look like he wrote it hisself."

"Can you say with certainty it is Bradbury's head you viewed at Mr. Donnelly's?"

"Not sure certain, no."

"Well, nevertheless, I think you should go to Sir John with your suspicions and your uncertainties. Let him decide what is to be done."

He gave that a moment's thought, then shook his head in an emphatic negative. "Naw," said he. "I ain't ready yet. Let me nose around a bit more. It might be if I keep an eye on the shop, I'll be able to figure out just who it is was in on it with her. Now don't that make sense?"

I admitted that it did, particularly in that it was him who had put the name Bradbury to the head in the first place. It seemed he had every right to withhold his suspicions until they became something more. And so we parted at that—he off to his afternoon lessons from Mr. Burnham, and I to Bow Street. Though I could not say that I was entirely satisfied, I was at least prepared to admit that this was Bunkins's matter, and up to a point he had the right to handle it as he would.

Days passed. The week went. Lord Laningham would be buried with due pomp on Monday. Since Sir John heard nothing from Lady Laningham in the days leading up to the funeral, he assumed quite rightly that with her silence she had declined his request for an autopsy. Commenting upon this, he slyly revealed a possibility he had not earlier made clear, one I had not so much as considered.

I, who had seen the funeral procession while out on my morning errands, mentioned it to him as he left his court that day.

He nodded slowly, signaling his understanding. "And with him will be buried our chance to have a look inside him, whatever that might yield."

"As you say, Sir John. It would take an unusual circumstance to dig him up again."

"Unusual indeed," said he, "since all seem to be against it." Then did he add: "You know, Jeremy, Lady Laningham assumed I suspicioned her nephew and Lord Laningham's heir, Arthur Paltrow. I suggested that the server, who to this day has not come forward, might also have had the opportunity to alter the contents of the bottle of wine."

"I do remember, yes sir," said I, "but I have given some thought to it, and I must say to you that when Lord Laningham hailed the server and sent him off to bring the bottle of wine from his table, he seemed to choose the fellow quite at random. He took the one who was nearest at hand."

"I had thought as much," said he, "and would not have mentioned it to her at all, save for the troubling fact that so far none has admitted he was the one delivered the bottle to Lord Laningham. There is, however, yet another candidate for suspicion. Can you name the person?"

He had taken me by surprise. In truth I had given little consideration to the matter. I had had no reason to think beyond what had come out in his conversation with Lady Laningham. Why should I have? I became a bit flustered and could only stutter out my reply: "Why no, Sir John, I . . . I . . . I could not say."

"Simply consider," said he, "who would have the greater opportunity for poisoning the bottle—if indeed there were poison in it. Why, that would be Lady Laningham herself. She had access to the cellar, might even have chosen the bottles for the occasion. I, of course, refrained from mentioning this to her, for I wished to gain from her permission for an autopsy. The fact that it was never given, by the bye, counts against her.''

''But do you truly hold her suspect? What would be her motive for such an act?''

''Oh, perhaps she had a lover.''

''She is over threescore years.''

''Such prodigies of passion are known even among those of greater years. He was a tiresome old fool, or so I hear—perhaps she simply wished to be rid of him. But to address your first question, do I truly hold her suspect? The answer is no.''

''No?''

''No, she seemed to behave as one might when the possibility of poison is suggested. We must keep firmly in mind that it is merely a possibility that has been discussed. As for her silent 'no' which was given our request for an autopsy, I daresay that had to do with matters of propriety, respect for the dead, et cetera, rather than any fear of discovery. I do not hold her suspect. I hold none suspect until poison be proven.''

''You've given me much to think about, sir,'' said I.

''You must always think, Jeremy. Always consider all the possibilities.'' He sighed. ''Well, in any case, we shall have the opportunity to see them all again tomorrow evening.''

''We shall? I . . . hadn't known.''

''Yes, Arthur Paltrow has insisted that the concert be given with the same program at the Crown and Anchor as a memorial to his uncle. No doubt he will have a speech to make. I doubt we shall see him drop dead in the course of it, however.''

''Perhaps the missing server will come forward and identify himself.''

''Perhaps,'' said Sir John. ''We shall see.''

Saturday was the day of the choir rehearsal which Annie had so dreaded. She dreaded it no longer, for she had been drilled in her part—music and text—by Mr. Burnham. It was late afternoon but growing dark when she left Lady Fielding in the kitchen with instructions on when the roast of mutton ought be taken from the oven. There was naught to fear, for Annie had prepared dinner but for the full roasting.

Because it was still light when she departed, it was judged safe for her to find her way to the Crown and Anchor alone. Yet I had been put on notice that in two hours' time I was to follow her and conduct her back through the darkened streets. I passed the time reading, and at the appointed hour set out for the tavern to bring her along. I did note that when I passed through the kitchen the roast smelled right savory and ready to eat, but that Lady Fielding was nowhere to be seen.

I waited at the Crown and Anchor with a small crowd of other men and boys who had been sent, as I was, to see the ladies home. And waited indeed still longer than I had expected, for there were continuous stops, starts, and repetitions as the choirmaster drilled them all in every part over and over again. In truth I could not distinguish Annie's voice from the rest of her sister sopranos, yet they did all sound good to me; the choirmaster, however, seemed to be satisfied with nothing less than perfection. As it was, he kept them all near an hour beyond what was expected.

Annie and I were resigned to cold mutton as we marched back to Bow Street. That seemed to bother her not in the least, however, for she hummed and sang her favorite parts of the *Ode* as we went and was in a most happy mood.

"Did we not sound glorious, Jeremy?" she burst forth at one point. (It seemed to me that even her diction had improved.)

"Indeed so many voices together do make a powerful sound."

"And I sang well," said she, "well as any. Did you notice the choirmaster spoke to me as I come down off the stage?"

"What was it he said?" For I had noticed and I was curious.

"He praised me for my preparation, said he wished all had worked as hard. It's Mr. Burnham did all that for me— just a couple of hours every day is all it took. Ain't he a good teacher? I mean, *isn't* he?"

She got from me the hearty agreement that she expected and that he most certainly deserved. Yet she paid it little mind as she rushed on.

"And do you know, Jeremy, he has promised to attend the concert tomorrow evening, that he might hear the results of his labors with me. He must sit at our table, of course!"

I agreed that he must, but thought as I did so that the matter of his complexion might indeed cause the rest there some surprise. But again I reasoned with myself that it should not.

The roast was near an hour overdone, yet not quite ruined, for the fire I'd built and fed had burned to embers by the time Lady Fielding had returned, fearing the worst and full of apologies. She had been called out of a sudden to the Magdalene Home by an emergency: a new girl at the Home had got into a fracas, drawn a razor which she had concealed upon entering, and slashed two of the other girls before she was overcome by the rest. The news had so upset Lady Fielding that she flew out of Number 4 Bow Street without thinking to pull the mutton from the stove, or even inform me that she was leaving.

Sir John was most understanding, but suggested that it might be proper to send a constable to the Home to bring the girl in. "She should be charged with assault, Kate," said he.

"Too late, Jack," said she. "We have already expelled her from the premises—without her razor, of course."

"And the two girls she cut?"

"Taken care of nicely by Mr. Donnelly."

This conversation, which took place at the dinner table, was interrupted by Annie's serving of the roast. She had done all that could be done with it, cutting away the charred parts, serving it forth sliced and chunked with a bit of brown sauce. Though it quite fell off the bone, there was flavor left in it, and it had the smell of a good roast still.

"Why, this is not bad, not bad at all," said Sir John as he tasted it. "I confess that mutton is a meat I never much liked unless it be cooked clear through—overcooked, some might say. Let us all be glad the meal was saved and pray for the welfare of that girl sent out into the cold."

"Jack, do you think . . . ?"

"You did what you had to do, Kate."

There was a commotion at the door when Mr. Burnham sought entry to the ballroom of the Crown and Anchor. I had half expected something of the sort, and so had seated myself at our table in such a way as to have the entrance within view. When first I spied him I was up from my chair, hurrying over to conduct him to our party. By the time I reached him he was engaged in a wrangle with the ticket taker, one that might have quickly grown to something nastier, for Mr. Burnham was a man who knew his rights.

"You have my ticket, sir," said he, as I arrived. "It is not counterfeit. It was bought and paid for, at a pretty price I might add, and now I *demand* entry."

"Well, if you'd just wait till I—"

"Am I unsuitably dressed?" Aside from an earl or a duke, there was probably no better-dressed man in the room.

"No, no, it ain't that, but if you'd just wait for the inn-keeper to come. Maybe he'd—"

I tugged at the fellow's sleeve, and with all the authority I could muster I sought to intimidate him.

"See here," said I, "what is the difficulty?"

He took in my erect bearing, my steady gaze, and my grand bottle-green coat and was about to answer me quite respectfully, when Mr. Burnham let forth a mighty bellow.

"Or is it my color?"

I waved a plea of silence to him and addressed the ticket taker once again: "I am here," said I, "to conduct this gentleman to the table of Sir John Fielding, where he is expected. This I propose to do. You may summon the inn-keeper, if that is your wish. When he arrives, you may direct him to our table. Now, if you will, Mr. Burnham, come right this way, sir."

Reluctantly, the ticket taker stepped aside, and Mr. Burn-ham passed him without so much as a sidelong glance. Those at tables nearest the door had heard most of what had been said; all had certainly heard that final, exasperated shout of his. Now had they the opportunity to gape at him whose presence had occasioned the disturbance, and gape they did. As I led the way, I read amusement in some faces, disapproval in others. There seemed to be none who would simply look and casually turn away.

I felt a strong hand upon my shoulder and half turned as I progressed to find Mr. Burnham smiling broadly in ap-proval.

"Well done, young Mr. Proctor," said he. "Though I do never accept an affront, I am always pleased to find an ally. And you were, I thought, most impressive."

I grinned my thanks and beckoned him onward. We reached the table where Sir John presided. All turned to us, save the president, who had not yet noted our arrival; nev-ertheless, it was his attention I called for, and to him I introduced Mr. Burnham first. I took him round the table, presenting him, one by one, to those who sat at it. Lady Fielding's eyes near popped from her head when first she saw him, but she gained control of herself and murmured that Annie had told us much about him. To Messrs. Don-nelly, Goldsmith, and Humber I introduced him—not one flinched at grasping his hand—and lastly at Annie I waved, saying that of course he knew her well. And of course he did.

Sir John brought Mr. Burnham back to him and urged him to take the place next him at his right. I found a seat beside Annie across the table from them, and we listened happily as the two began a proper conversation, something regarding Annie and her progress. But after a bit of talk, Sir John broke off the discussion and rubbed his chin in thought for a moment.

"May I ask you, sir," said he, "where are you from?" The table fell silent.

"Where would you take me to be from?" countered Mr. Burnham.

"Well, sir, because of my blindness, I draw additionally upon what my other four senses provide. My sense of hearing gives me much. I know many men by the sound of their voices, and those whom I do not know, I can nearly always place as to origin by their mode of speech. Yours, I would say, eludes me somewhat. There seems to be something of the Welsh manner in it. Am I correct in that?"

"My father hailed from Shropshire nigh on to the Welsh border."

"Perhaps that accounts for it then. Did he speak Welsh? Do you?"

"He knew a few words, but I none at all."

"You were not born, then, in that locality?"

"No sir, I was not."

"Then you have me, I fear. Where were you born? Where did you grow to manhood?"

"In Jamaica, sir, across the sea. And I fear that the advantage I hold over you here is quite unfair. If you had your sight, you would know me in an instant for what I am—half English and half African, a mulatto, as they say."

"Why, then I compliment you, sir, for your diction could not be improved. And I compliment you, as well, for having taught me something."

"And what is that, Sir John?"

"You have taught me a new manner of English speech. There is a lilt to it, something musical, an up-and-down quality in the Welsh manner—yet different."

"In truth," said Mr. Burnham, "I have done what I can

to speak more in the London style. I should be happy to lose my island accent.''

''Do not, sir,'' Sir John charged him. ''It is pleasant to hear and a great relief from the usual jawing I hear about me.''

Though said gruffly, it was meant friendly, as Mr. Burnham instantly perceived, and he burst out laughing. Sir John joined him in chorus, grasping his arm in friendship. The two were laughing still when the servers descended upon us, slamming down our dinner plates on the table. All about us came the same bang-bang-bang, the clatter of knives and forks, and the roar of conversation dulled to a hum as the hundreds in the room settled down to the serious matter of beef, pudding, and dripping. We at our table broke off into our separate conversations. Annie, beside me, nibbled at her food, then pushed it aside in my direction, declaring it was mine for the eating. She complained to Mr. Donnelly, on her other side, that she felt ill. ''Perfectly normal,'' he assured her. ''You are suffering a sort of fright I myself have seen in my Navy service. Sailors can eat little before a great battle.'' Yet she seemed to take little encouragement from such talk. She left us early, leaving to go backstage with the chorus. All wished her well, Mr. Burnham most heartily of us all.

It seemed no time before we had supped and drunk our fill, and the same servers were back to collect the plates they had hurriedly put before us. The musicians began to assemble upon the stage. It was then that I was surprised by a summons from Sir John. I was up and off to his side in less than a moment.

''Jeremy,'' said he to me, ''I should like you to convey me across the room to the Laningham table before the program begins. I must pay my respects to Lady Laningham, and I wish to meet the heir.''

And so it was done, though no easy matter with servers milling about in the narrow spaces between the tables. Nevertheless, with Sir John clasping tight to my shoulder with one hand, we two made it without collision as I chanted, "Make way, make way please for Sir John Fielding."

Thus we arrived. I placed him before Lady Laningham; all done up in black she was, though in a different dress and looking ever so modish. Perhaps, I thought, she truly had found someone to offer her physical consolation. Yet she met Sir John quite soberly, and in response to his observation that Lord Laningham's funeral had taken place— "a grand ceremony, as I have heard"—she muttered something about "a missed opportunity." Then she added quite distinctly: "I wish now that I had acceded to your request."

"There is now no likely possibility—" he began.

Yet before he could finish, she bent to him and whispered in his ear. She seemed most passionately angry.

So fascinated was I by this, so intent was I in getting some hint of what was said, that I at first failed to notice the gentleman who had risen from the far side of her table and come round with the clear intention of making Sir John's acquaintance. He stood behind Lady Laningham awaiting his chance; then, when she had done, he rushed forward to introduce himself.

"You, I believe, are Sir John Fielding, are you not?"

Lady Laningham turned, scowling, to the intruder, who was not in truth a terribly impressive figure; of less than average height he was, all flushed and eager in his manner.

For his part, Sir John recoiled slightly at the suddenness of the approach. He withheld his hand.

Yet not to be deterred, the fellow grasped it and pumped it energetically as he said, "I am Arthur Paltrow, and I have hoped to meet you ever since I came to London. I could not wait for my dear aunt to present me to you."

"Ah," said Sir John, "Lord Laningham's heir, of course. But hoped to meet me? Why is that, sir—or need I now address you as m'lord?"

"Not yet, no, no, but it should be obvious. Your fame— that of the Bow Street Runners—has spread even to our little corner of England."

"Gratifying, I'm sure," said Sir John, "but let me express my condolences to you upon the death of your uncle."

Then did Mr. Paltrow immediately bow his head and assume a most solemn manner. "Ah yes," said he with a sigh, "a great man he was, ever an inspiration to me."

"You were close to him, then?"

"As close as circumstances permitted. He was ever in London, and I with my little family, off in the country. I should like to introduce them to you, if I may."

With that and not a word to Lady Laningham, he swept Sir John away. She, having thus been ignored, turned to me in anger. Whether it was that she wished me to do something about the snub she had been given, or in some perverse way blamed me for it, I could not say, for she said nothing. She seated herself with a great thump and turned away from us all.

I trailed along in time to hear Mr. Paltrow's wife, Pamela, and two daughters, Felicity and Charity, offered in introduction to Sir John. They were plump females all; the two girls, only a bit older than myself, were as unlike their father as any could be, except for a certain same eagerness in their eyes.

Mr. Paltrow sought to prolong things a bit, speaking in grand terms of the dinners and musical evenings he planned once he was "properly situated." He promised that Sir John would be invited to the very first of them.

"I shall look forward to it."

"Not more than I."

Just then the group was approached by one whom I recognized as the innkeeper of the Crown and Anchor. He greeted Sir John hastily, then addressed Mr. Arthur Paltrow, urging him to the stage that he might address the audience, as was his wish.

"The orchestra is ready, sir," said the innkeeper. "They await you."

"Then, Sir John, I must go," said Mr. Paltrow. "I'm indeed so happy to have met you at last."

"And I, you and your family," said Sir John with a polite bow. "Jeremy?"

He signaled that we were to return to our table. As we marched back, he muttered to me, "I shall not be drawn into their domestic squabbles! The idea of it!"

"What, sir, is the matter?" I called back to him.

"He intends to move his family directly into the Laningham residence, and now the present Lady Laningham wishes her husband dug up and cut up simply to take revenge by casting suspicion on the next Lord Laningham. Does she not understand that she lost her chance when she buried her husband?"

His voice had risen in indignation. As we pushed along toward our table, I noted heads turning in interest at what was said. He was not usually so careless about speaking of such matters in public.

Nevertheless, I asked, "Is that what she was whispering about?"

"Yes, it was," he hissed angrily.

We managed to seat ourselves just as Arthur Paltrow walked out upon the stage and took his place before the orchestra. I noted, with some surprise, that an empty chair had been placed at precisely the spot it had occupied the week before, and beside it lay his uncle's knobbed staff. Did Mr. Paltrow mean to remain and play his uncle's role that evening, capering and jumping about? Even to one as inexperienced and ignorant in the ways of the great world as I was then, that seemed to me to be in singularly bad taste. But whatever his intention, he waited until the audience had grown quiet, and only then did he speak forth.

"My name," said he, "is Arthur Paltrow. I come before you this evening as a representative of the late Lord Laningham's family."

(He did not, at least, introduce himself as the heir apparent to the title, though it was common knowledge by that time.)

"Speaking for the family," he continued, "I wish to assure you all, members of the Academy of Ancient Music and those of you who attend individual concerts, that our family will continue its patronage of the society and its concert programs in the future, just as it was done under my dear uncle. We are certain as can be that he would have had it so. And we would just as certainly want it so."

At that point Arthur Paltrow paused, and a scattering of applause was heard from the audience; the scattering took on force and volume until it thundered approval and thanks through the wide ballroom of the Crown and Anchor. He waited modestly, his head slightly bowed, until at last the applause subsided. Only then did he raise his head and look out upon the multitude.

"Thank you," said he with a nod. "The program this evening is a repetition of the one offered last Sunday. It consists solely of pieces by the late, lamented master Mr. George Frederick Handel. To wit: his Opus three concerti grossi numbers one and two, the choral work *Ode for St. Cecilia's Day,* with the Academy chorus, and that great favorite, the *Water Music.* The program is repeated because it was never completed. Interrupted it was, as you all must know, by Lord Laningham's tragic death on the very stage upon which I stand. Therefore this concert is performed as a memorial to him. Think of him, I beg you, as you listen to the strains of this beautiful music. You will note that here beside me are his chair and staff, so familiar to you all. They will remain here throughout the evening as a reminder to you all of Lord Laningham. Then they will be removed and put in some place of honor, yet to be determined. None but he will sit before the musicians on this stage.

"That is all, and again, I thank you."

So saying, he turned and walked slowly off the stage. Immediate applause followed him this time, swelling to an ovation even grander than the one he had received earlier. He had quite won them over.

Even Sir John, who had not taken part earlier, clapped loudly with the rest. Then did he turn to our table and shout over the applause: "A good speech! Would you not say so? Spoken with grace and humility—a good speech, by God!"

And all at the table did most heartily agree, turning to one another, nodding, each offering his separate comments in praise.

Then did the concertmaster stand, claiming the attention of the members of the orchestra, to whom he offered the downbeat. The concert was begun.

I am no connoisseur of music in the grand style, reader, though I have been since to more concerts, operas, and musical evenings than I can count (for the most part at the behest of my good wife, who is, I'm convinced, something of a connoisseur). Nevertheless I can tell you in truth that I have never heard such music, Handel in particular, played and sung better than it was that night. The two concerti grossi were better than I had remembered from the week before, perhaps because I had earlier been distracted by Lord Laningham's playful attempts at leading the orchestra. But the *Ode for St. Cecilia's Day,* with the entire choir onstage, was truly glorious; and this time, I do swear, I could hear dear Annie's voice giving strength to the entire section as it soared over the kettledrums and competed with the trumpets. And the *Water Music,* so often played, could not have been done with greater dignity and strength; it was, as I remember it now, music that suggested to me the perfectibility of man—or at least the hope of it.

With great applause and shouts of "Bravo!" and "Bravissimo!" the audience expressed its intense pleasure at the performance. Mr. Alfred Humber, who was a member of the Academy of Ancient Music and a faithful attendant at the concerts, had no hesitation at calling this one quite the best he had ever known. Though he, Mr. Donnelly, and Mr.

Goldsmith left directly when the program was done, the rest of us remained. Mr. Burnham offered lavish congratulations, and Annie gracefully returned them to him, saying that she owed all to him; then did he take his leave from us, thanking Sir John and Lady Fielding for having him at their table, winning a warm farewell from Sir John.

As we four started for the door, the innkeeper appeared and called Sir John aside. I might have sidled along to listen in, for I had keen interest in the matter of the missing server, but just then Lady Fielding caught us both, Annie and me, and demanded to know why we had not told her that Mr. Burnham was a black man.

"But my lady," said Annie, "he isn't black, he's brown."

"Don't be impertinent, young lady."

Then did I hasten to say, "I—we, that is—had not thought it would matter. It did not to us."

"Well," said she, somewhat nonplussed, "of course in his case it didn't . . . really . . . matter. But I do think I should have been forewarned. I'm afraid I gawked a bit when you brought him to the table, Jeremy."

"Oh, really?" said I. "I had not noticed." (Though certainly I had.)

"I hope he did not," said she, quite sincerely. "When you left the table with Sir John, I had quite a pleasant conversation with him—about his homeland and such. His father has made quite a young gentleman of him. Yet Mr. Burnham will not deny his mother. He says he misses them both greatly—and equally."

"And he's such a good teacher, mum," put in Annie.

"Oh, I have no doubt of it. Even coached you on the Cecilia ode, did he?"

"Taught it to me, music and words—though words he calls 'text.' "

"Playing it upon the harpsichord, no less. Such an accomplished young man." She sighed. "But both of you, please, do give me a bit of advance notice in the future, won't you?''

Sir John then broke away from the innkeeper and signaled his readiness to depart. We were among the last. The Laningham party had left long before by some exit known to them, avoiding the crowd. I had noticed how rigidly apart from the rest Lady Laningham conducted herself as they moved away from their table. Had she truly been as badly used by Mr. Paltrow as she had claimed?

As for ourselves, we reached the street to find the captain of the Bow Street Runners, Mr. Benjamin Bailey, awaiting us that he might see us back to Number 4. Though Sir John had not requested it, he seemed gratified to find the tall, imposing figure there at the door to the Crown and Anchor, though not so happy to hear the news he had to impart. It seemed that one of Constable Perkins's snitches had passed on the word that Jonah Slade (he who had assaulted Constable Cowley with a knife) had managed to slip out of London.

''And where has he gone to?'' asked the magistrate.

''To Ireland, said the snitch.''

''Ireland, is it? From what I've heard of Slade, he's pure Londoner and should stick out like a zebra in a herd of horses. We shall notify the Castle in Dublin to keep a watch for him. If not there, he should turn up in Cork. Such as him cannot live outside cities.''

''I'll just walk on ahead a bit,'' said Mr. Bailey, ''and clear the way for you.'' He hesitated. ''We should be glad, Sir John, bein' quit of one such as Jonah Slade. The search for him has caused no little trouble and time.''

''Right you are, Mr. Bailey. Still and all, I do hate to see one such as him get away from us here. Others of his ilk may be encouraged to think they can do the same. We must put fear into them.''

''As you say, Sir John.''

Then did Benjamin Bailey march off at an easy pace, and we four following, Sir John and I together, and the women close behind. Annie twittered her excitement at being part of the evening's triumphant performance. She thanked Lady Fielding effusively for having sent her up to the stage the week before. And on and on . . . never been so happy in her life, et cetera.

Sir John moved us ahead of them a few paces, and pulled me close.

"What thought you, Jeremy, of that fellow Paltrow, soon to be Lord Laningham?"

"Well, sir," said I, "to be frank, I thought twice of him. When he rushed to you to introduce himself, he seemed altogether too eager to make a good impression. Quite unsure of himself he was. I thought there was little noble in him."

"Truly said, Jeremy."

"But then," I continued, "I thought, as you, that the speech he gave in introduction to the concert and in memory of his uncle was meet and fit in every way. I could scarce believe the man you had just met had given it. Even his bearing had altered."

"Yes, well, it sometimes is the case that men show their true mettle before the public, rather than in private conversation. In any case, neither of the two men you describe—and I concur in your estimates—would seem likely to commit murder. Lady Laningham, however, presents us with a greater possibility than I had perhaps earlier realized. She has a good deal of venom in her."

"She was quite modishly dressed, even for one in mourning."

"I'd like to know when she ordered up her widow's weeds—perhaps a little early? We might make inquiries of her dressmaker if we can discover the shop that serves her." We walked on a bit. Then did he ask: "Rouged and powdered, was she?"

"Discreetly so, yet I thought a bit improperly under the circumstances."

"Oh, indeed. Could she have a lover? Who would know?

Why, Mr. Goldsmith, of course. He is a great font of tittle-
tattle, it would seem from our own experience. By the bye,
Jeremy, you must mention nothing of this conversation or
any other to him, even if he should specifically inquire—
specially not then.''

"I noticed you had little to say to him at table," said I.

"True. I would not cut him, for he is Mr. Donnelly's
friend, and has been a guest in our home, and he is in many
ways a good man. Yet he is one of those with whom one
cannot speak freely.''

The women had fallen somewhat behind. Mr. Bailey had
halted to allow them to catch us up. When we resumed, it
was at a slower pace. The night was mild for January, yet
as ever on a winter night in London, there was a damp chill
about us. And our breath clouded out before us as we
walked the empty street. Sir John sent out a great billow
in a deep sigh.

"What is it, sir?'' I asked.

"Well, I have been thinking on it, Jeremy, listening to
myself, and I tell you true, I am quite ready to give up this
notion of poisoning. It was, after all, a mere fancy, a maggot at my brain. Mr. Goldsmith may indeed be right. Perhaps I am needlessly suspicious. Here I am, taking Mr.
Paltrow's measure, asking myself if such a man could commit murder, and I look with doubts upon an old woman's
efforts to make herself look pretty and perhaps a little
younger—could she have a lover? I ask. All this, and the
matter of poison, is pure supposition on my part. It has not
been proven. It is not now likely to be proven.''

"And the missing server?'' I put in at that point. I had
great faith in Sir John's suspicions and liked not to see him
surrender them without a fight.

"That was the thinnest straw at which I grasped, a mere
hypothesis. You yourself said Lord Laningham hailed the
server at random.''

"He seemed to.''

"Well, even that straw has crumbled to dust. The miss-

ing boy turned up today, I was told by the innkeeper, and
he had been called away by word of an illness at home. He
had not even remained to see Laningham's collapse. His
memory of the incident was dim, but he remembered col-
lecting the bottle at the table, opening it, then pouring a
glass for the remaining gentleman at the table before bringing it to the stage.''

"For Mr. Paltrow, exactly as Lady Laningham had
said.''

"Quite right. The innkeeper said he would send the boy
round for questioning if I liked, but he vouches for him.
So you see? There is nothing, less than nothing. What was
it to which Mr. Donnelly attributed the cause of death?
Circulatory failure—the heart stopped beating. I am now
prepared to leave it at that. Let that be an end to it.''

Yet, reader, it was not to be so.

The important events following Monday's funeral took
place some distance from Number 4 Bow Street. On Tues-
day, in a solicitor's office in Charing Cross Road, Lord
Laningham's will was read. Present were Lady Laningham,
Mr. Paltrow, and his wife, Pamela. Aside from a lump sum
of one thousand pounds to the Academy of Ancient Music,
individual gifts to each of the servants, and something near
a hundred thousand in stocks, rents, and cash which went
to Lady Laningham, all the rest, valued at near half a mil-
lion, went to Arthur Paltrow, his nephew and heir. With it,
and considered in the valuation, were estates and houses in
England, and properties in the colony of Virginia—and of
course, in all this came the title, Earl of Laningham.

The new Lord Laningham, that very afternoon, took possession of the great house in St. James Square, moving in
his little family, bag and baggage. He did not demand that
his aunt move out, but requested that while she searched
for suitable accommodations for herself she remain *as a
guest* in her apartment of rooms on the first floor of the
house. There followed a bitter row between them. Though

it took place in the library behind closed doors, the shouting and screaming was heard by the servants, who placed its duration at better than a quarter of an hour. Then did Lady Laningham leave the library in great fury and go straight to her rooms. Hours passed. Her dinner was brought to her early on a tray at her request. Some time after that, as was her custom, she called for her tonic.

At about that time we at Bow Street were just eating our dinner. Annie had saved mutton enough from Saturday's burnt roast to make a good stew, flavored with onions, garlic, and that favorite spice of hers, paprika. Though it was but a humble meal, Sir John pulled out a bottle of claret from his small store and had me open it. Right there in the kitchen we toasted Annie and the grand success she—and the rest of the choir, of course—had enjoyed the night before. Annie did declare that she was the happiest girl in all London—and quite the luckiest. We ate our fill and finished the wine, and as Annie and I collected the dishes for washing, Lady Fielding and Sir John sat back in their chairs, well pleased with the evening.

"You know, Kate," said he, "if I were a man with the tobacco habit, I should light up a pipe just now."

"Not in my house you would not!"

"Now, my girl," he teased, "I said merely *if* I were such a man."

Both laughed at that, and were still laughing when from below came a rising thunder of footsteps on the stairs—at least two were there. Then an urgent banging upon the door. I was nearest. Sir John nodded to open it up.

It was Mr. Baker, the night constable and gaoler, together with a man whom I'd never seen before.

"Sir John," said Mr. Baker, "this here footman—"

"From the Laningham house, sir. Something terrible has—I mean to say, Lady Laningham, *old* Lady Laningham, that is, she drunk her tonic and got sick, pukin' and gaggin' something terrible. 'I'm poisoned,' she says, and calls out for you. Oh, do please come, sir. She's a good mistress and she's terrible sick."

SIX

*In Which Letters
Are Sent and a
Discovery Is Made*

We arrived separately. Sir John, who had luckily encountered Constable Bailey on his way out of Number 4 Bow Street, enlisted him in the expedition, and together they rode in a hackney coach with instructions to the driver to follow the footman, who led the way on horseback. I had been sent to fetch Mr. Donnelly from his surgery, if he be there, and take him forthwith to the Laningham residence in St. James Square. Though I ran to my destination in Drury Lane and found him in his rooms at the rear, the time it took for him to organize his departure and us both to make our journey by hackney to St. James Square put our arrival at least a quarter of an hour following that of Sir John and Mr. Bailey. Much had happened in that time. Since I was not present, I cannot offer it to you as a witness might. What follows, pieced together from what I later heard from Sir John and Mr. Bailey, is an account of what happened in that period of time. Though it be hearsay, because of its sources I trust in its accuracy.

Sir John and Mr. Bailey were admitted to the great house without delay or question by a very worried butler, a man

who later became known to them as Mr. Poole. Inside, filling the large entrance hall, what seemed to be the entire
staff of servants—a considerable number—were milling
about, talking distractedly among themselves in small
groups. Upon Sir John's appearance, the hum of worried
conversation did immediately cease. All turned toward him
as one expected, one whose arrival was hoped for.

So that there be no doubt of it, the butler announced to
the room at large: "He is here." None came forward. All
simply waited in silence.

"Where is she now?" asked Sir John. "That is, Lady
Laningham, of course."

"Up these stairs here, sir." Then, aware of Sir John's
blindness, perhaps for the first time: "But of course. My
apologies, sir. Here, let me take you there." With that, he
grasped Sir John's arm at the elbow.

Sir John shook loose. "I have my own ways of dealing
with my condition. You lead the way. Constable Bailey will
follow. I shall grasp onto him."

"As you wish, sir."

Thus they proceeded. And as they ascended the wide
staircase, Sir John put a number of questions to the butler.

"What is her condition?"

"Very grave, I fear, sir."

"When did the attack come upon her?"

"About an hour past."

"And it was with the drinking of her tonic?"

"That is my understanding, sir. It is a usual thing with
her, sir—her tonic each night. It is, in truth, mostly gin,
sweetened and darkened with sweet spirits. It puts her to
sleep, and that is why she takes it."

"Who is it prepares it?"

"That is done in the kitchen, sir. It would be the cook
or one of her staff. Her maid carries it from the kitchen to
her. It was she who was with her when the attack came
upon her, and she to whom she made her declaration."

"That she had been poisoned?"

"Yes sir, and called for you."

"I am grateful to the maid, to you, and the footman who brought me," said Sir John. "But now, tell me, who is with Lady Laningham now?"

"The new Lord Laningham, as he wishes now to be addressed, his lady wife, and Dr. Diller."

"Ah, a medico. Is he known in the house?"

"He treated the late Lord Laningham. He was sent for, not by name, by the new master, who simply ordered that a doctor be brought."

By that time they had reached the first floor and now stood before the door to Lady Laningham's chambers. Sir John, realizing this, continued in a low tone. "What is your name, sir?"

"Humphrey Poole, sir."

"Then, Mr. Poole, I have a request. I would like you to go now and in some suitable private place, perhaps belowstairs would be best, assemble the maid, the cook or the member of her staff who prepared the tonic, and any other of the servants who you think might have something relevant to contribute on the matter. I shall let you be the judge on that—but be a lenient one. I am here to learn all I can of this. If one of the staff has something to say, I wish to hear it."

"It will be my great pleasure to do so, sir."

"One more thing. I myself sent for a doctor, one whom I trust, named Gabriel Donnelly. He should be arriving in the company of a lad named Proctor. If they should arrive while I am engaged in interviewing the members of the servant staff, send the lad to me. But Mr. Donnelly must in any case be taken to see Lady Laningham, no matter her condition and no matter if his access to her must be forced by me or Constable Bailey here. Is that understood?"

"Completely, sir."

"Go, then. Now, Mr. Bailey, give a stout knock upon the door, then step aside. I wish mine to be the first face seen when the door is opened."

And so, as Mr. Poole hurried away to the stairs, Mr. Bailey rapped stoutly upon the door. There was a pause of some long moments' duration. Mr. Bailey was about to knock again, when he heard footsteps beyond and stepped back quickly as Sir John had directed.

The door came open. Arthur Paltrow, now Lord Laningham, appeared, speaking harshly before he had properly taken a look at who waited in the hall: "I thought I said—" Then did he recognize Sir John. "You!" said he. "What are you doing here?"

At this point, reader, the accounts of my two informants differ. Sir John said merely that Lord Laningham sounded surprised. Benjamin Bailey, who had the advantage of sight and a good view of him, said that the man was for a moment struck dumb, his mouth agape, his eyes wide. "But more," Mr. Bailey later told me, "he looked like he would at that moment rather see the Devil hisself waiting there than Sir John Fielding."

Then did the Magistrate of the Bow Street Court say, with great assurance: "I am here because I was sent for."

"Well . . . well . . ." Lord Laningham thus dithered until he found the power of speech. "Sent for by whom?"

"By your aunt."

"But she is dead, only minutes ago."

"All the more reason for me to be here," said Sir John. "But the fact is, when first she suffered the attack, which you now tell me was fatal, she specifically requested my presence. I need not prove that to you. My presence here is proof enough. Now, if you will conduct me to where her corpus lies, I should like to view it."

"But how can you? You're . . ."

"I mean that only in the figurative sense. Constable Bailey here will serve as my eyes. I understand there has been a physician in attendance. I wish also to speak with him." And over his shoulder: "Come along, Mr. Bailey."

Sir John stepped forward, and Lord Laningham had no choice but to step aside. Once past the door, Sir John grasped the constable by the arm and allowed him to steer him along as they followed the new master of the house through a sitting room and another door into the lady's bedroom. Sir John said later that the smells of illness and death permeated the place. Mr. Bailey informed him that the body had been laid out upon the bed, covered completely by a sheet. The physician, Dr. Diller, stood by the bed, looking curiously at the two imposing figures who had entered. The present Lady Laningham stood apart, her hands clasped before her, an expression of consternation upon her face.

"Dr. Diller," said Sir John, "you are here?"

"I am, yes," said the physician.

"I am Sir John Fielding, Magistrate of the Bow Street Court. I am come because I was bidden to come by Lady Laningham in the first throes of her attack. She has passed, has she?"

"Only minutes ago."

"And when did you arrive?"

"But half an hour past. I was summoned by one of the servants. I dwell not far from here."

"Would you be so kind as to pull back the sheet so that Constable Bailey here might describe to me the appearance of the corpus?"

"Well . . . I . . ." Dr. Diller looked to Lord Laningham, who gave a sharp nod of assent. "Certainly," said the physician.

He threw back the sheet to reveal a figure—appearing somewhat withered, as Mr. Bailey pictured her—in a soiled nightdress. Two crown pieces rested upon her eyes. A piece of silk was looped under her jaw and tied atop her head, thus holding her mouth shut; this gave her shrunken face a tight-lipped, disapproving expression in death. All this Mr. Bailey dutifully described to his chief.

"Dr. Diller," said Sir John, "was it necessary to secure her jaw with the band of silk?"

"In this case, yes, it was. So violent were her spasms of vomiting that she had dislocated her jaw."

"Really!"

"Indeed I had to break her jaw, or she would have choked to death."

"Yet she died in any case. To what do you attribute her death?"

"Extreme indigestion," said he, with a certain authoritative finality.

"Oh? Only that?"

Again the medico threw an uneasy glance at Lord Laningham. Mr. Bailey whispered in Sir John's ear, informing him of this.

"I wonder," said Sir John, turning in the general direction of Lord and Lady Laningham, "if I might continue my interview with Dr. Diller in private?"

"Why, I . . . I . . . why, yes, I suppose you may. Pamela?"

Together, the two made for the door. Yet Sir John had not quite done with them.

"I would also ask," said Sir John, calling after, "that when all have left this room, it be locked and sealed. The corpus of this woman is not to be disturbed in any way. The customary washing of the body is to be forgone. No dressing her in clean clothing. She is not to be touched. That is my order as magistrate. Do I make myself clear?"

"Certainly, certainly," said Lord Laningham, "very clear. It will be done just as you say. You may depend upon it." He was once again that eager-to-please fellow we had met at the Crown and Anchor.

"Thank you, then, and if I see no more of you this evening, good night to you both." He waited then until he heard the sitting room door to the hall close before he resumed his conversation with the doctor. "Were you aware, Dr. Diller, that the late Lord Laningham died but a week ago before hundreds in the Crown and Anchor in a manner much like his wife died tonight?"

"Of course I heard of his death. He had been in my care before on a number of occasions. He was not a well man, though he pretended otherwise. I called upon his lady as soon as she was able to accept visitors and discussed the matter of his dying with her. From what she told me, I gathered he had died of an apoplectic seizure."

"Yet she, you feel, died of acute indigestion?"

"Well, there were differences, as I understood them. For one thing, she vomited copiously."

"*He* vomited copiously."

"He spoke a few dying words to her. She could not speak."

"Not indeed with a broken jaw. But as I believe I told you, at the onset of the attack she called for me."

"Ah yes." He hesitated. "The present Lord Laningham seemed to know nothing of that. We were all quite surprised when you and the constable here made your appearance."

"I've no doubt of it," said Sir John. "She said it to her maid. She also said—and I charge you to say *nothing* of this to *anyone*—that she had been poisoned."

At that Dr. Diller was quite taken aback. "*Poisoned!* Why . . . what . . ."

As he grasped unsuccessfully for words, a loud knock sounded upon the door in the sitting room.

"Mr. Bailey, attend to that, will you? If it is Mr. Donnelly and Jeremy, show them in at once." As the constable marched off to do Sir John's bidding, the magistrate returned his attention to the medico: "Do you know Mr. Donnelly, sir?"

"I have not met him, no, but I understand he is medical advisor to the new coroner."

"That is correct. I knew not that you would be here in attendance, and so I sent my young assistant to summon him—Ah, I hear their voices. Both have arrived. Mr. Donnelly happened to be at the Crown and Anchor on that fateful Sunday and did all that anyone could to assist the late Lord Laningham in his last hour. I should like you and Mr. Donnelly to compare your observations on the two deaths. Bear in mind, too, what the late Lady Laningham said to her maid: 'I have been poisoned.' I should like both of you to consider that possibility.''

At that point, or perhaps a moment or two earlier, Mr. Donnelly and I entered the late lady's bedroom. We had been swiftly ushered to the sitting room door by the butler, who had assured us that Sir John Fielding was yet inside and awaited our arrival. Upon our entrance into the bedroom, Sir John introduced the two medicos as I stared dumbly at the body on the bed. I hardly recognized the woman. She seemed but a shriveled thing as she lay unmoving with coins upon her eyes. Her hollow cheeks were without powder, her thin lips without rouge. I did not have to be told that she was dead.

As I waited, Sir John explained to Mr. Donnelly what he had in mind, ''a consultation over the dead, as it were.'' Both physicians were agreeable, and so we prepared to go—just where, I knew not at that moment.

Yet the first question asked by Mr. Donnelly was this: ''Where is the vomit? It must be saved.''

''It is here, right enough,'' said Sir John. ''The place reeks of it.''

''No, it is not,'' said Dr. Diller. ''The smell lingers, as such odors will, but Lord Laningham had the maid working quite feverishly to clean it up during my first minutes here with the woman. He said he would not have that stink in the house—which, under the circumstances, I thought rather insensitive of him.''

''Damn!'' said Mr. Donnelly. ''I hoped to have some of it to bring to a chemist for analysis.''

''There may be a bit on the rug, or perhaps on the bed, most of it bile, I should suppose.''

''Let us find what we can,'' said Mr. Donnelly.

''Gentlemen,'' said Sir John, ''I leave you to the search. Mr. Bailey, you may go about your duties.''

• • •

Mr. Poole, the butler, had established Sir John below the stairs in a kind of common room or parlor kept for the servants just beyond the big kitchen. The room and its furnishings were much like those I had first seen belowstairs in the Goodhope residence. At a corner table, one probably used to play cards, Sir John had seated himself; I stood just to his rear. His witnesses came and went, occupying the chair just opposite his at the square table. Thus it was that he might speak in a low voice, achieving some degree of confidentiality and intimacy with them.

The first to whom Sir John spoke was the cook. He was particularly interested in the preparation of Lady Laningham's tonic.

"A 'tonic' is what she called it, sir," said the cook, "but in truth it was naught but a flask of lightning with a quarter of sweet peach brandy for taste. It was a good stiff drink to put her under for the night, was all it was, and it always seemed to do the work for her."

"How long had it been her habit to take this tonic, so called, before bed?" asked Sir John. "Perhaps since the death of the late Lord Laningham?"

"Oh no sir, much earlier, sir. Years it's been. Some months past there was talk of it at table amongst us belowstairs. And there was general agreement she started with her tonics when the late Lord Laningham, God rest his soul, become incapable and the two started sleeping separate."

"I see. How long after taking her dinner did she call for her tonic?"

"Well, she ate early this evening, she did, though not much. Maggie, that's her maid, brought back her tray only half ate. Then, it wasn't long, maybe an hour, she come back and said the lady would like her tonic now. Couldn't have picked a worser time."

"Oh? How was that?"

"Well, just as she come down, so did the new Lord and Lady Laningham. They wanted to be showed all about the kitchen, askin' questions and all. I'd got the sweet brandy in but not the gin, and here's the new lady wantin' to see the size of the oven, askin' how many I could serve from it. She had questions about sauces and desserts, all manner of things. I had to get them out of the kitchen before I could add the gin, give it a stir, and hand it over to Maggie. Her tonic ain't hard to make, but she wants the portions right—or wanted them, poor thing. And at the end I just weren't sure I'd measured out the quarter brandy exact, what with one thing and another.''

''I understand. And all the time Lord and Lady Laningham were there, distracting you from the preparation of the tonic. You said that questions were asked by Lady Laningham. Did the lord participate? Did he also have questions?''

''No sir, he seemed to think this was women's things. He wandered around a bit, looked in cupboards and such like.''

''Who else was in the kitchen at that time?'' asked Sir John.

''Then? Wasn't anyone, as I can recall. My slaveys was off havin' a nip before the pots and pans come due for a wash. All the rest had ate early.''

''But surely the maid was there—Maggie?''

''Part of the time she was,'' said the cook. ''She went off somewheres, though.''

Having exhausted his store of questions, Sir John excused the cook and called to Mr. Poole that he would like now to talk with Lady Laningham's maid. She was brought to him in a state of near collapse, supported by the butler, weeping true and bitter tears. She, not Sir John, asked the first question.

''Is it true what I heard, sir? That the good lady's gone?''

''I fear it is,'' said he gently.

She sobbed and wiped at her tears, yet then delivered this tribute: ''She was a good mistress, sir, and I tell you that true, for none knew her better than me. Oh, she had her spells, maybe whole days when she was out of sorts, and course she'd speak rude to me now and again. But you know what, sir? She would then 'pologize to me. 'I'm sorry, Maggie,' she would say, or, 'Forgive me, Maggie.' I worked in great houses before, and there ain't one of your great ladies I ever heard of who would do that. Usually maids is just to wipe their feet on.''

''Was she out of sorts this evening?''

''Oh, she was, sir, something terrible. First thing she did when she came back from the lawyer's office was to bring all us servants together and read to us what each of us was left by Lord Laningham. It was a year's wages for one and all. Then, just as she was finishing that, all moved and teary she was, telling us she would take as many of us as she could to her new place, that we were a fine staff and none could want better—just as she was saying that, a knock comes upon the door, and in walks the new lord, and he declares, 'I'm takin' possession of this house.' He's followed not just by his family but by all manner of porters and such bearin' their baggage. Well, our Lady Laningham, she didn't say nothing, but I could tell she was just in a fury. So as long as the serving staff was together, he decides to give a speech as well. It was in the nature of a threat, it was. He said that all who hoped to stay on had better impress him well and proper in the next few days, for he would be looking like a judge upon us. 'Many are called, but few are chosen,' says he. Usin' Scripture to his own ends in that way, I call right disgraceful.''

''Indeed, Maggie, it does seem so,'' said Sir John. ''But through all this your mistress had nothing to say? She kept her silence to him?''

''Oh, she gave him plenty, she did, though not a word in front of the servants. No, she waited, she did, until well into the afternoon, thought things through, then sent word by me that she would meet with him in the study, which is at the front of the house.''

''And how did he take this summons?''

"Oh, he was eager for it, he was. Just like a bantam cock ready for a fight, couldn't get down there fast enough. Well, there was a row, there was. I couldn't say who got the best of it. I can tell you, though, that she matched him, shout for shout and curse for curse. Really, I'd no idea she knew such language."

"Precisely what was said?" he asked.

"Well, I can't say exact, for the door was shut, and I daren't stand too near so that it might seem I was eavesdroppin'. And wouldn't you know, no more than halfway through, this puffer-ball who now calls herself Lady Laningham comes down the stairs very suspicious of me and demands that I take her on a tour of the first and second floors. I'd no choice, of course, so off we went." She hesitated, then offered: "I did hear your name."

"My name? Really? By whom?"

"By Lady Laningham. Shouted it out, she did—'Sir John Fielding!' Like it was a proper name to conjure with. Then was I forced to go off with the other one."

"Hmmm." He mused for near a minute before offering another question. And when at last he did, she seemed well prepared for it. "You said she seemed out of sorts when you saw her next?"

"Out of sorts, yes, for she'd been given a 'terrible insult'—that was what she called it. 'Maggie,' said she, 'I've been made a prisoner in my own house.' And she went on to tell that he told her to keep to her chambers so long as she was in this house, and she was to take her meals there. 'That,' he said, 'should give you a proper in-cen-ta-tive for moving out soon as possible.' As if she'd want to sit down at table with such as them!"

Maggie paused then rather dramatically, and I believe Sir John was about to put to her another question, when she resumed in a great torrent: "But sir, she wasn't beat, not by much she wasn't. She had a plan, I know she did, for she said as much to me, and you were part of it, for she began then and there to decide when she would visit you next morning. She asked me, did I know when it was you held your court. Oh yes sir, you was part of her plan. And when she drank her tonic I brought her—''

''Not quite yet,'' said Sir John, interrupting. ''Tell me first about her dinner. She ate early, I'm told.''

''About six, which is early for her. If she'd waited a bit she might've had more of an appetite. Left a good half on it untouched, she did. I returned the tray and came back to her. And it was not long before she sent me down for her tonic—p'rhaps seven, p'rhaps a bit after. She said tomorrow would be a big day for her, and she would need her sleep. Usually when she takes her tonic she's asleep about an hour later, you see.''

''The present Lord and Lady Laningham were in the kitchen during cook's preparation of the potion, were they not?''

''Yes sir, they came down right after me.''

''Followed you, did they?''

''In a manner of speaking, I suppose.''

''But you did not remain in the kitchen, did you?''

''Uh, no sir, I did not.''

''Why was that?''

''I went to my little room here belowstairs—right down the hall it is. I . . . well, if you must know, sir, I had a call of nature.''

''Forgive the question. Let us say, then, that after an interval of time, you returned to the kitchen. Was the tonic ready for you then?''

''Not quite, but the new master and his mistress was just leaving. Cook finished up with it. I took it up to my lady, and she had a sip of it, and she complained right off. 'This tastes nasty,' she said. Yet she continued to sip at it, which was her way, you see, as I helped her dress for bed. She might take upwards of an hour to drink it all.''

''But not this evening,'' put in Sir John.

''No sir, once in her nightdress, she took a great gulp of it—then it wasn't long till she began to talk of stomach cramps. Then, of a sudden, she made a rush for the water closet, me with her, where she did vomit her dinner. That was when she said to me, 'I've been poisoned. Send for Sir John.' I got her into bed, where she began once more to vomit all manner of ugly matter, blood and bile and who could tell what more. But there came a break in it, which didn't last long, yet it gave me time enough to run to Mr. Poole and ask him to send for you. I was just returning when the new master shouts down from the first floor, 'Get a doctor for my aunt!' Mr. Poole says he will attend to it. Then, when I got back to her bedroom, I find them both there, looking over my lady there in bed. Her eyes were wide with fear. He says to me, 'How dare you leave her unattended.' I told him I was doing my lady's bidding. And he said, 'Now, you must do mine and clean up this foul-smelling mess.' Then the doctor came, and I was still cleaning. When I got up all that could be got up, I was sent out of the room. I knew Lady Laningham would die. She was still retching when I left.''

''You paint quite a picture, Maggie,'' said Sir John. ''I have but one more question for you. And it is this: What happened to the glass containing Lady Laningham's tonic? She had not finished it, had she?''

''Oh no sir, not near. Why, the truth of it is, I don't rightly know what happened to it. When last I looked, the glass was on her dressing table, but it wasn't there when I came back to the room and started cleaning up. I'm sure of that.''

''Thank you, then. That will be all.'' As Maggie rose from her chair to leave, Sir John called out to the butler: ''Mr. Poole, have you someone else for me to talk to? I left that matter up to you.''

The butler, who was nearer to Sir John than he realized, waited until the maid was on her way to her room, before he stepped forward and said, ''Only myself, Sir John.''

''Ah, so, then sit yourself down and let us discuss the matter. But, Jeremy?''

I leaned over to him. "Yes, sir?"

"While I talk with Mr. Poole, I wish you to find your way back to that room which was the scene of this awful calamity and search it for that missing glass."

The butler gave me explicit directions, and I had no difficulty making my return. Entering, as we had before, through the sitting room, I heard the voices of the two medicos in the next room, raised not in argument but friendly agreement. Their voices ceased, however, when I closed the door—not loudly but audibly—behind me. I found the two men awaiting my entrance, apparently relieved to see me and not another.

"Ah, Jeremy," said Mr. Donnelly, "what brings you up here?"

"A search," said I, "for the glass of spirits which began this fatal episode."

"I hope yours proves more fruitful than ours," said he. "Scrapings from her nightdress and a lump or two from the carpet were all that we came up with. They should not be of much use to the chemist, I fear."

"Yet we found common cause between us," declared Dr. Diller. "And we are prepared to press our case, are we not, sir?"

"Indeed," said Mr. Donnelly. "Oh, indeed, sir."

And as each of the two physicians congratulated the other on his findings, I snatched up a candelabrum and did the work I was sent to do, searching every surface in both rooms and in the water closet, as well. I looked under the dressing table and under the bed. I expected to find nothing—not perhaps the best spirit in which to conduct a search—and nothing was what I found. By the time I had done, the two were packing their bags, making ready to go.

"Shall we leave candles burning in here?" asked Mr. Donnelly.

"I think not," said his colleague. "The magistrate stipulated that the room be locked and sealed."

"In that case . . ."

We went about blowing out the lights until I, holding the candelabrum, led the way out, leaving the room in darkness but for the embers in the fireplace.

"Poor old girl," said Dr. Diller, not without feeling. "I hope she rests peacefully."

Then we descended the winding staircase. In the great entrance hall we found Sir John and the butler awaiting us. The rest of the servants had quite disappeared, gone no doubt below to discuss the unsettling events of that evening.

"We are ready, then?" asked Sir John.

"Completely," said Mr. Donnelly.

"Jeremy, as well?"

"I am, Sir John. I found no glass, nothing at all that would be of help."

"Then, Mr. Poole," said he, turning to the butler, "I thank you for your help and for your information. You will lock and seal her chambers, as I asked?"

"Candle wax will do, will it not?"

"That will do quite well."

Then out into the night. Dr. Diller left us on the walkway, suggesting we might easily find a hackney at the far end of the square, or certainly along Pall Mall; he himself dwelt in the other direction. He started off with an assurance to Sir John that he would have a letter from him in the morning.

Sir John waited until the medico was past hearing, then muttered to Mr. Donnelly: "Letter? What sort of letter does he mean?"

"A letter to you supporting the need for an autopsy of Lady Laningham. That, together with my own to Mr. Trezavant, should give sufficient weight to the one you shall undoubtedly write in the morning requesting such an autopsy."

We set out in the direction of Pall Mall. I noted that Sir John, whose hand clasped my arm at the elbow, was shaking a bit. Surely not from the cold; he wore his warm cape, and in general stood against the wind and chill better than most men. Then did I realize that he was laughing silently, chuckling to himself as if at a great joke.

The shaking ceased. "You've thought of everything, have you, Mr. Donnelly?" said he.

"I've tried to," said the medico. "Your request for an autopsy of the late Lord Laningham went for naught. Mine, had you solicited one such from me, would have carried little weight. However, another in this instance from so eminent a physician as Isaac Diller could hardly be ignored."

"Is he truly so eminent?"

"The fellow has treated members of the Royal Family, though not the King himself. His fees are so high that none less than the nobility can afford them. He lives, if you will, but a few houses up from the Laningham residence in St. James Square in a place nearly as grand."

"Yet he believed the poor woman had died of acute indigestion."

"No longer. In a spirit of great collegiality we compared our observations of the deaths of the Laninghams, man and wife, remarkable similarities, et cetera. I urged him toward the proper conclusions, and he drew them. I then timidly suggested that only an autopsy would reveal the truth, and he was for it absolutely. No doubt at this moment he believes the idea was his own."

"And the letter?"

"My idea completely. I said that you would hope for one but were too shy to ask."

"Shy? Hah! Thought him too great a blockhead—that would be closer to the mark. Acute indigestion indeed!"

"That, Dr. Diller said, was urged upon him by the present Lord Laningham. He insists he had his doubts—'only a preliminary finding,' said he." Mr. Donnelly hesitated, then gathering his courage, proceeded: "You know, Sir John, you are sometimes a bit too gruff with such fellows as Diller. Blockheads they may be—and I have yet to meet a doctor in London who knew as much as a seasoned Navy surgeon—but they can be useful. As my dear old mother used to say, you can catch more flies with honey than you can with vinegar.''

Sir John snorted. ''God help us—you Irish!''

Next morning the letter to Mr. Trezavant was written. It was much the same as the last letter to him, yet Sir John did not neglect to quote Lady Laningham's declaration—''I have been poisoned''—or to say specifically that he had been summoned by her, only to find her dead upon his arrival. He explained Mr. Donnelly's presence at the scene, but noted that at the time of her death, ''that esteemed physician, Dr. Isaac Diller, was in attendance. From him and from Mr. Donnelly many interesting questions arose, questions that can only be answered by a full and proper autopsy of the corpus.''

I put the letter before him, dipped the pen, and placed it in his hand in the proper spot upon the page. He put upon it his uniquely impressive scrawl.

''Now, Jeremy,'' said he, ''I should like you to hasten to Mr. Donnelly's surgery and get from him the promised letter. I trust we shall not have to wait too long on Dr. Diller's missive.''

Yet I lingered.

''What is it, lad?'' he asked.

''Well, sir,'' I asked a bit timidly, ''if it would not be too forward to ask, I was wondering if I might know what it was the butler had to say to you.''

''You may know, yes, but I shall impart it first with a caution. It is this: When we enter upon an investigation of this sort, we must always do so with an open mind. We are, at this point, only gathering facts. When we reach our conclusions too early, then we are inclined to seize upon those facts which support our conclusions, and ignore, or even reject, those which do not. And you can see, I'm sure, the dangerous fallacy in proceeding in such a way as that.''

''Well, yes sir, I suppose I can.''

"That said, I'll tell you now that the butler had placed himself in the alcove near the door in such a way that he heard near all that was said between Lord Laningham and his aunt during that fierce quarrel in the library. He merely confirmed what I had guessed from the maid's information that my name was shouted out by her mistress. To wit: that after hearing that she was no longer to have the run of the house that had been her home for thirty years or more, she informed him that I—Sir John Fielding, as she shouted it out—suspected poisoning in the death of the late Lord Laningham, that I had urged her earlier to allow an autopsy upon his body, and that now she intended to give it. This was the threat she had whispered to me that evening before at the Crown and Anchor. Now, you have heard thus far, and that is the crux of it. What say you to that?"

"Why," said I passionately, "that in so saying, she offered to him her death warrant, that so frightened was he of what an autopsy might reveal that he prevented her from giving permission to dig up her husband by poisoning her. He had the opportunity with that visit to the kitchen."

"That is what one might suppose, but let me offer some arguments against that conclusion. First of all, Mr. Poole admitted upon my questioning that Lord Laningham took her threat with equanimity, if not indifference. That may have been bravado on his part—or superior knowledge. It is doubtful that the body could have been exhumed without his permission when he passed from heir apparent and assumed the noble title—she had overestimated her strength in the matter. You speak readily of poisoning, Jeremy, yet so far it has not been proven. So far it is merely my suspicion, my fancy. It's true she said when taken ill, 'I have been poisoned,' but I put that thought in her mind, did I not? Of course I did, for in her next breath she called for me. And finally, if poisoning it be in the case of the late Lord Laningham, as well, then how do you explain the fact—given separately from two sources—that Arthur Paltrow, while still the heir apparent, drank from the same bottle of wine as his uncle, and did so without ill effect? I should like to have an interview with him, but such would have to wait until poisoning be proven.''

''And that,'' said I, ''cannot be done without an autopsy.''

He nodded. ''Thus we proceed one step at a time. Now off with you, Jeremy. We cannot take that next step until we have those letters in hand.''

Needing no further urging, I took my leave of him and made my way swiftly to Mr. Donnelly's surgery in Drury Lane. It was still quite early in the day—so early, in fact, that when the good doctor answered my insistent knock upon his door, he had lather upon his face and his razor in his hand. There were as yet, needless to say, no patients assembled in his waiting room. He led the way back to his quarters in the rear. He resumed his place before mirror and washbasin and lathered anew.

''The letter to Mr. Trezavant wants only a final paragraph and my signature,'' said he. ''You may read it if you like, Jeremy.''

I took the permission given as an invitation and picked it up from his writing desk. Mr. Donnelly wrote a rather florid hand, full of decorative curls and flourishes. The content of it, too, seemed rather florid. He stressed the fortunate coincidence which had brought him together with Dr. Isaac Diller at the unfortunate death of Lady Laningham. Describing how these two men of medicine had compared observations on the deaths, but eight days apart, of Lord and Lady Laningham, he declared that they had discovered a number of startling similarities. Rather subtly, he gave all credit to the senior medico and suggested that the matters he had raised prompted him, Mr. Donnelly, to urge that an autopsy be performed upon the corpus of the late Lady Laningham. He knew it might indeed be considered an extreme request by Mr. Trezavant, yet since he had been led to it by so eminent a physician as Dr. Isaac Diller, he felt it only right to make it.

There the letter ended. I replaced it upon the writing desk. Mr. Donnelly noted my action in his mirror. He turned and gave me a sharp look.

"Well, then, Jeremy, what do you think of it?"

"A good letter," said I. "There is much honey in it. I believe you shall catch your fly."

"What . . . I . . ." Then he laughed. "Ah yes, of course, honey and vinegar. Surprised you remembered that. But it's true, don't you think?"

"Mr. Donnelly, I've not had enough experience of the world to know." He always seemed to overestimate me in such ways.

"Ah, well," said he, "no matter. Do you believe it needs something more—a closing paragraph in summary or some such?"

"No, I believe it to be fine just as it is. You must have worked long and hard on it to create such phrases."

"Not a bit of it. They come to me quite natural. The Irish call it 'blarney,' and I've a good store of it. In point of fact, Jeremy, I've been up for hours, even been to the chemist with those paltry samples of m'lady's vomit. There, by the bye, I received a bit of a disappointment."

"They were insufficient for any sort of test, as you assumed?" said I.

"Nay, more. I learned to my surprise that there is no known test for separating and identifying the poison I most strongly suspect was employed in both instances."

"And what was that, sir?"

"Arsenic, Jeremy—common enough, has all manner of uses."

"Among them," said I, remembering what I had learned from Mr. Bilbo, "poisoning rats."

"Ah! You know that, do you? Quite right you are—and with the right dosage it can be just as effective when used upon men and women."

"Does that mean, sir, that an autopsy would be of no use?"

"Certainly not. Arsenic and other strong poisons, as well, leave their tracks in the body. It will be up to us to find them."

That was said in such a way that it seemed to beg clarification.

"*Us,* sir?" said I. "Will you require help?" I was eager to provide assistance if such be needed.

He had by then done with his shaving and was toweling patches of lather from his face. He looked at me sharply, as if he had perceived the purpose of my question. "Will I require help? No, let us say, rather, that I have had it thrust upon me. In winning the help of that fellow Diller, I left the way open for him to take part in the autopsy. He is eager for the chance."

"Then he will no doubt do all he can to see that the autopsy takes place."

"And I must do no less," said Mr. Donnelly, going to his desk. "Here, I shall sign this thing so you may take it away." He took up the quill, dipped it, then paused a moment in thought. "How does one end such a lickspittling letter as this one?"

" 'Your humble and obedient servant,' I suppose," said I. It was the line chosen most often by Sir John to conclude his letters. "Such forms mean little."

"Yes, that should do. Though in truth, as I glance now at some of the phrases, they seem more to have been authored by some educated slave, rather than a servant, much less a doctor of medicine," said he. Then, with a sigh—"Ah, well"—he bent to his task, dashed off some phrase in conclusion, and signed his name. "All in a good cause."

So it was that I took the letter sealed and addressed to Mr. Trezavant back to Number 4 Bow Street. There I discovered that in my absence the promised missive from Dr. Diller had arrived by messenger. I was instructed by Sir John to deliver all three letters to the coroner and wait for a reply.

Arthur, the respectful butler, greeted me at the door of

the grand house in Little Jermyn Street, bade me wait just inside the door, then set off up the long hall to communicate my arrival to his master. It took no more than a pair of minutes for him to return and invite me to follow him. When ushered into that same room in which I had earlier met Mr. Trezavant, I found another man present, a gnarled, gnomish sort of old fellow. He was seated behind the large desk next Mr. Trezavant. The two men seemed to have been occupied in the examination of a great pile of ledgers. The old gentleman offered me an annoyed stare, no more. Mr. Trezavant, the very soul of formality, struggled out of his chair. Erect, he seemed near as wide as the desk.

"I presume you have a letter for me, young man."

"In fact, sir, I have three."

Having said that, I offered them to him. He took them and continued to hold them out, weighing them in his hand, more or less.

"Three, is it? And what do these letters concern? I take it you must know, since you took them in dictation."

"Only one of them, sir, and that be the one from Sir John Fielding. The other two are from your medical advisor, Mr. Gabriel Donnelly, and Dr. Isaac Diller of St. James Square. I am certain that Sir John's letter and Dr. Diller's have to do with the death of Lady Laningham the evening past. As for Mr. Donnelly's, I think it likely that that, too, is its subject." Then said I, lying most glibly, "Of that, however, I cannot be sure, for it is addressed to you and sealed, and I did not see its contents."

"I did not know Lady Laningham was ill," said Mr. Trezavant.

"She died very suddenly, sir. There is some question as to what caused her death."

"Is this, then, another request for an autopsy, so called?"

"It is, sir," said I. "Sir John has instructed me to wait for a reply."

"Well, in this instance, young man, I must disappoint you and your master. As you can see, I am deep in matters of business here. Sir John shall have his reply—written, if it must be so—before the end of the day. There are three letters to read, consideration to be given, and perhaps advice to be sought. Rest assured, however, that I shall not take lightly any cause to which Dr. Diller has lent his name and his energies.''

I stood awkwardly, wondering what I was to do. I was hardly in a position to insist, yet thought perhaps he might yet be persuaded were he to know more of the facts.

''You . . . you . . . should know, sir,'' I stammered forth, ''that Dr. Diller was in attendance at the time of her death.''

''All the more reason to give the matter close consideration,'' said he calmly. ''Good day to you, young man. Arthur? Show him out with our good wishes.''

The butler, who on this occasion had not absented himself from the room, opened the door behind me. I had no choice but to bow and wish Mr. Trezavant a good day in return. Even quicker than we had come, the butler and I paced the distance down the hall to the front door. It was opened for me, and through that portal I exited.

''Good wishes to you, young sir!'' the butler called after me.

Yet I, sulking a bit, gave him nothing in return, not even a wave. I felt ill used. While on my previous visit I had been treated with excessive courtesy, on this occasion I had received it in the minimum. Much later I discovered that the old man who seemed resentful of my intrusion was Mr. Trezavant's partner in business. Whenever he was present, I would be treated similarly.

There was naught to do but tell Sir John that I had failed to coax a reply from Mr. Trezavant. Yet he took it lightly and seemed satisfied with the promise that he would have a reply before the day was out. Having nothing more for me to attend to, he bade me go up and study the *Institutes of the Law of England,* if that were my wish—and indeed it was my wish.

What he had told me was true. The great work was indeed well written. Sir Edward Coke's sentences marched across the page in stately, though somewhat archaic fashion. Yet the matter with which they dealt was often so complex that it challenged my understanding. I had made it my habit to read through it very slowly, noting passages on a sheet of paper to which I might return for further study. Thus in near a month I had penetrated no more than fifty pages into the first of the four volumes. Yet I was determined that nothing should dissuade me from my task, nor from my ambition, which was the law.

Thus I read and reread through the rest of the morning, a session of study that lasted two hours or near three. It ended with Annie's arrival from her schooling with Mr. Burnham. It was her habit to offer me an enthusiastic report on all that she had learned that day—and in truth she seemed to be learning quickly and well under his tutelage. And so, as I heard her footsteps upon the stairs I reluctantly marked my place in the book and closed it. She came bursting through the door in her usual manner, her cheeks aglow from the chill January wind, and dropped her books—Shakespeare and a primer—upon the kitchen table.

"Well," said I to her, "what have you to tell?"

"Oh, much," said she, "but that can wait. Jimmie B. walked the way here with me. He waits below in the street."

"In the street? Why did he not come up with you?"

"A good question. I did what I could to persuade him, but he would have none of it."

"Ah, what does it matter?" said I, grabbing my hat. "I shall see what it is brought him here."

"He says it's important."

Then down the stairs and out the door I went to Bow Street. There Bunkins waited, leaning against a streetlamp, hands thrust deep into his pockets, his coat collar turned up about his muffler. In short, he appeared quite uncomfortably cold.

"Hullo, Jimmie B., what have you for me?"

"I've a surprise should give you a rise."

"Indeed I can't wait till I'm told, but come in, come in, out of the cold." I beckoned toward the door.

Yet Bunkins shook his head. "Nah," said he, "let's take a walk and have our talk."

Unable to think of proper rhymes to express myself, I burst out in frustrated prose: "Jimmie B., why is it you will seldom come up and visit? What have you against our little home?" Then I added, "Ain't it grand enough for you?"— which I knew was not true.

"It ain't that," said he, "it ain't where you live. It's what I have to go through to get there—past the gaoler and the Beak Runners, past that terrible strong room with its iron bars. Something in me left over from when I was a scamp and a proper village hustler, well, it just turns me cold at the thought of shovin' my trunk by those poor cods behind those iron bars. I must be feared of bein' grabbed and locked up for my past sins. I got a dream about that comes often in my sleep. Same one over and over again."

Regarding him closely, I saw that he was most serious about the matter, for it distressed him to tell it. I could do naught but shrug and say, "As you will, then," as I fell into step with him. I noted that we proceeded in the direction of Bedford Street and George Bradbury's pawnshop, which did not much surprise me. As was often so with Bunkins when he had some bit of information to impart, he said little along the way, choosing, rather, to pick the time and place to make his revelation. And so we walked in near silence as we cut across Covent Garden, where the wind whipped across the open space. It was colder at that hour than it had been earlier when I made my journey to Mr. Trezavant's residence on Little Jermyn Street. Perhaps a storm was coming. Perhaps there would be snow by morning. Only once did Bunkins complain against the cold, but that in such curses and obscenity that they need not be quoted here.

"You've a cape," I responded a bit sullenly (for I felt the nasty chill as keenly as he did). "Why don't you wear it?"

"Aw, I feel a fop when I do. Wouldn't look right where we're going."

When indeed we did turn down Bedford Street, I assumed we were to pay another visit to the pawnshop. Yet as it developed, I assumed wrongly, for he led me to a grogshop directly across the street from it.

"In here," said he—and only that.

The place was dark and murky with tobacco smoke, as such places are even in the daytime. A single lamp burned over the bar. Greater light issued from the fireplace, where a warm fire blazed. Though I had expected (and hoped) that we would crowd in with those on the benches round the fire, Bunkins led me to a table next to the rattling windows. I thought he could have chosen better. Spitting on his fingers, he wiped more or less clean a panel of glass so that he might better view the pawnshop.

"You do the same," said he.

I managed as well as I could and was gratified that the place I had smeared clean did not immediately frost over from the cold inside the dive. Oh, indeed it was a proper dive, as ill kept and filthy as any on the street. And the serving girl who approached as plump and ill favored as any of her occupation in London. When she inquired our pleasure, I had difficulty making out her words, as she had lost many of her teeth in the front of her mouth. Yet Bunkins understood her and called for grog. I asked for coffee.

"You only get that with a flash of lightning here, dearie."

"Then I'll have the gin on the side."

"That's two cups to wash," said she.

"When did you start washin' them?" Bunkins sneered.

She took offense at that. "You been here every day," said she to him. "You seen me workin' away behind the bar."

"Only in fun, m'sweet." (Said with a wink.)

Mollified somewhat, she rumbled corpulently back to the bar.

"Been here every day, have you?" I asked Bunkins.

"I have," said he. Turned to the window, he spoke, his eye fixed upon the patch he had cleaned for viewing. "Been keeping close watch upon Bradbury's shop across the way. Now, there's not many come into such a place. So it's easy to note when one comes in often or stays long. And I noticed two in particular. One's a tall fellow who comes and goes, not like he belongs exactly, though something tells me he dorses there. He—"

I reached over and touched his arm as the serving girl returned. He glanced over in her direction and nodded to me. He fished fourpence from his pocket and dropped them on the table. She, in turn, lined up the drinks and scooped up the coins. Without a word, she went back to her place by the bar and near the fireplace.

"You going to drink that?" Bunkins asked, pointing at the cup of gin before me.

"No," said I, "it would only put me in trouble."

He reached over for the cup and downed the gin in two gulps. Meanwhile did I sip at the coffee. It was vile stuff but strong and hot, welcome on such a day.

Bunkins returned to the window and resumed where he had left off: "Like I said, the tall fellow just comes and goes, and he don't stay away long. When Mrs. Bradbury goes off by herself to do errands and buying and such, he looks after the shop while she's gone."

"I understand," said I. "But you said there were two."

"Indeed there is, chum, and that other one comes regular as the clock on the wall, just about this time every day."

"Well, who is he?"

"I'll not say, not now. Let's just wait until he comes, and see if you recognize him. You'll know the cod. Oh yes, indeed you will."

Bunkins would say no more. We waited, our eyes fixed

to the two spaces we had made for watching. Bunkins had said I would know the fellow, implied he was an acquaintance—a friend? Quite baffled, I tried to guess who or what he might be. One of the Bow Street Runners, perhaps? Surely not. I had at least a nodding acquaintance with one and all. And while some had their faults, none would consort with a murderess. None would, according to Bunkins's suspicion, take part in murder.

"Here he is now," said Bunkins.

I leaned over so as to see better, and my eyes were drawn most immediate to a figure strutting down Bedford Street as if it were his place alone. Did I know him? Yes, I did. You might call him an acquaintance, though never, never a friend. He was none other than him I had fought, his knife against my club, in an alley quite near to this place just off this very street, not much more than two months past.

"Why," I whispered, amazed, "it's Carver."

"So it is, chum, Jackie Carver."

"He's made a remarkable recovery."

"He has for sure certain."

I watched him walk up to the pawnshop, throw open the door, and enter it—again with that bold sense of proprietorship. He quite disappeared inside. It was my guess he had walked past the curtain into the rear of the shop. I turned to Bunkins.

"He's the other visitor? The second one?"

"Oh, that one, he's more than a visitor. You saw how he walked into the place. When he goes inside, he goes to stay. I sat here Sunday, which Mr. Burnham gives me free. I watched him go in about this time that day and he never come out. She slipped down and locked the door, and he stayed I never knew how long—three hours, at least. That's how long I waited. There's your murderer, chum."

I gave that but a moment's consideration. "I think you're right, Jimmie B."

"Course I am. He woulda killed him while the old man was sleepin'."

"That's his way," said I. Then did I add most solemnly, "You must tell Sir John."

"I ain't sure I'm ready to do that just yet. I'd like to know more."

"If you don't tell him, then I shall."

Bunkins, his face screwed in torment, slammed his fist down upon the table. "Damn! I was 'feared you'd say that!"

SEVEN

In Which Permission Is Granted and an Autopsy Is Done

We were out tramping the streets once again. Bunkins might have been content to pass an hour or more drinking grog in that primitive setting—he liked far too well spending his time so—yet I had reminded him that he must soon return for his afternoon lessons with Mr. Burnham. With a sigh, he had then agreed he must leave. He, warmed by the grog, and I, by the coffee, held out better against the chill than we had on our way to Bedford Street. He was, in any case, capable of more than cursing the cold. We prepared our course of action.

Though he argued that all we had at that moment were suspicions, we agreed that our suspicions were strong. Sir John, I declared, would know just what must be done to turn suspicion to proper evidence. Could he say with certainty that the head in the jar once sat atop the body of George Bradbury? No, he could not—but Bradbury's absence from his shop was indeed cause for question. Were we certain that Jackie Carver had dispatched him? No, we were not—yet both Bunkins and I thought him capable of it, specially if it be done in any way for gain. Then did a terrible thought come to me.

"Jimmie B.," said I, "you must in no wise let a word escape to Sir John of my battle with Carver."

"But why not?" said he. "You beat him fair and square—better than fair, for he had a knife and you had only the club given you by Mr. Perkins."

"True enough, yet to hear that of me might prejudice him against the entire matter. He might think that I bore animosity against Carver still."

"Well, you do, don't you?"

"Not sufficient to name him a murderer."

"He would've done murder to you that partic'lar night. I know it, and you know it, too. And all he'd have got from it was a coat. Who can say what he's after this time?"

"Even so, you must leave me out of it. If you were to tell the whole story, Mr. Perkins would suffer, as well."

"What am I supposed to say, then?"

"Say only that you knew his evil reputation from your own days beyond the law. Tell Sir John that he often threatened with his knife and once did so to you. That much is the truth, is it not?"

"It is, right enough."

"Then tell him that."

We had by then reached the corner of Bedford and Chandos Streets, which was our usual parting place. We had stopped, each facing the other, glancing round us at the unusually sparse crowd at this junction, no doubt depleted somewhat by the fierce cold. Bunkins hopped on one foot and then the other, his chin buried deep in his muffler. Though he said nothing, it seemed certain that there was something he wished to address. At last he spoke.

"Listen, chum Jeremy, like I said when we started out, I ain't real pleased to go back there where the Beak keeps his office. The gaoler don't like me, and I don't like him. Seems to me he'd like to pop me in his strong room just for a joke." He paused a moment, then rushed on: "You couldn't fix it so Sir John could come over and visit Mr. Bilbo, could you? Then I could take him aside before he goes and tell him all about this Bradbury business.''

''I don't see how I could do that, Jimmie B. He has duties at court.''

''I didn't really think that would work. Well, maybe you ought to tell him, 'stead of me.''

''He'd want you there to ask questions of you. I'm sure of that.''

''I s'pose he would.''

Then did a thought occur to me: ''If you were to come between half past three and half past four, that's when Mr. Fuller usually takes the prisoners off to the Fleet. There's customarily nobody about except Sir John and Mr. Marsden. But I'll be there to take you right to the Beak, just in case Mr. Fuller happens to be about.'' I forced a smile. ''Done?''

Reluctantly, he bobbed his chin in the muffler. ''Done,'' said he.

Then, with not a word more, he turned and hurried off in the direction of the Strand, which would take him on his route home.

On my return to Number 4 Bow Street I was seized upon by Annie, who told me that the potatoes she had saved for the evening dinner had gone rotten on her. She had meat enough, but it might be good to have a few more carrots and turnips for next day's stew. Since I was bound by Lady Fielding's contract with her to do all the buying that need be done, I went off dutifully to Covent Garden to purchase all that she required. Annie, of course, remained safe and snug in the kitchen, tending to her studies.

It was something of a problem, of course, keeping a proper store of vegetables in store in the winter. And it was even more of a problem buying wisely, for the sellers would do what they could to pass frozen for fresh to the unwitting purchaser. I had become wise in their ways and went from stall to stall, testing and squeezing beneath the sailcloth blankets they had tossed over their wares. As a result, my visit to the Garden took far longer than usual.

I found, looking at the clock that ticked upon the wall opposite the strong room, that near an hour had elapsed since my departure. Mr. Fuller was then pulling on his greatcoat, making ready to conduct two prisoners off to the Fleet.

"Cold out there, ain't it, Jeremy?" he inquired.

"A good deal colder than this morning—colder and colder by the minute, it seems."

"That's as I s'posed. I thought to get these two cods off to their new home before it gets much worse."

Then did I hear Sir John's deep rumble from nearby: "Oh, Jeremy, come here, lad, if you will."

He was, as I suspected, in Mr. Marsden's alcove. Magistrate and clerk had evidently been in conference for some time, for both were seated in relaxed postures. Mr.. Marsden puffed upon his pipe. I eased down the canvas bag full of vegetables which had grown heavy in my hand.

"Yes sir," said I. Then adding, to account for my absence: "I was off buying in the Garden."

"Admirable," said he, "for we must needs eat. I have news in which I believe you will take some interest."

"Oh? And what is that?"

"Mr. Trezavant was as good as his word. His response to that great packet of letters you delivered him this morning came just before I began my court session. Mr. Marsden read it me, and I'm happy to say he has given permission to perform an autopsy on Lady Laningham. The corpus is now in transit to Mr. Donnelly's surgery."

"But that is wonderful news, Sir John!"

"Good news, certainly. To call it wonderful may be a bit much. Remember, Jeremy, one step at a time."

"Yes sir."

"The footman who delivered the letter to me inquired the address of Mr. Donnelly. I'd no idea of it. Luckily, Mr. Marsden had it filed away. Otherwise, we should have had to ask him to leave it for you to deliver. Where were you, by the bye? We sought you upstairs, but Annie said you'd gone out."

"With Jimmie Bunkins, sir. He has a matter of importance he would like to discuss with you."

"Is he in trouble?" asked Sir John.

Just as I opened my mouth to assure him otherwise, the voice of Mr. Fuller bleated forth from around the corner. "You can be sure of it! Once a thief, always a thief!"

"Careful there, Mr. Fuller. That may be traditional wisdom," said Sir John, "but it lacks something in charity."

"As you say, Sir John." He grumbled it like a sullen old man.

"Now, I must ask you again, Jeremy, hoping for no interruption this time, is he in trouble?"

"No sir, quite the contrary. He has been investigating a matter and wishes to put his suspicions before you."

"They are suspicions only? What matter does he investigate?"

"The matter is murder."

"Ah, well, murder, is it? Even suspicions of murder are of interest to me."

"He will visit you this afternoon."

"I await his report with interest."

"I'll bring him to your chambers soon as ever he comes."

"Fine, if that is where I be. Oh, but one thing more, Jeremy. A fellow from the post letter office dropped by to say there was a letter for me arrived from Lichfield, no doubt something to do with your fellow Roundtree. He, by the bye, has not yet had the grace to take advantage of Kate's kind offer. He has not surrendered himself after—how many days?"

"It's been a week, Sir John," said I, mumbling in embarrassment.

"Why the fellow from the post did not simply drop it off, I don't quite understand. He said he had all manner of letters and such for Mr. Garrick at the Drury Lane. Couldn't

be bothered with mine. You see how little the law is respected in London, lad? In any case, do go off and get it
for me, will you? It may bear information that will help
you find the fellow at last."

Thus it was that after I had delivered my sack of potatoes, carrots, and turnips to Annie on the floor above, I set
off in haste for the post letter office, aware that if I did not
hurry, I might not be able to keep my promise to Bunkins.

As it happened, I did not. Delayed as I was by an incom-
petent clerk (no doubt a paid appointment, as are so many
today), I did not return until nigh on four o'clock. Bunkins
had arrived only a few minutes before me and had been
forced to endure Mr. Fuller's glare of contempt while Mr.
Marsden led the way to Sir John's chambers. Had he been
alone, he might have waited for me, yet as it happened, he
was not. Mr. Burnham had accompanied him, and was just
seating himself beside Bunkins and opposite Sir John as I
entered the room.

This, as I later learned from Bunkins, is how he became
involved in the matter:

Bunkins was late for his afternoon lessons. Though it had
been a near matter a number of times before, he had never
previously violated the hour and minute set by Mr. Burnham. This was because, first of all, Mr. Burnham was quite
insistent that instruction begin precisely at the appointed
hour; he declared it to be "part and parcel of the process
of education." Secondly, Bunkins respected the times set
by Mr. Burnham because he respected Mr. Burnham; he
had learned well from him, while every other tutor he had
had made him feel like some dull-headed dolt. Jimmie Bunkins wished, in short, to please him, yet he had indeed been
late, and not only that, he had also come back with spirits
on his breath. Mr. Burnham demanded an explanation, else
he would put the entire matter before Mr. Bilbo.

Having no choice, Bunkins told him the entire story,
from our first glimpse of the human head in St. Andrew's

Churchyard to his activities with me that very day. All that was left out, I was gratified to hear, was my own earlier experience with Jackie Carver—Bunkins kept my secret. Mr. Burnham was fascinated. He asked, rather than demanded, to go along with his pupil to Number 4 Bow Street, for he was eager to know just how Sir John Fielding might deal with this information. Under the circumstances, Bunkins felt he could not but give his assent. And so, after hurrying through the matter for study that afternoon, the two set off together and arrived just before me.

Once I had identified myself to Sir John, I, too, took a place before him and listened as my chum began to spin his tale. He told it well. No doubt having recited it once to Mr. Burnham had given him the opportunity to edit and shape it somewhat. However, his prime listener did put to him some questions along the way. The first few of them came not long after Bunkins had begun. He had told of our journey to St. Andrew's Churchyard to view the head which had been there stuck on a pole. At this point Sir John raised his hand to halt the narrative.

"Pardon me for interrupting," said he, "but this gruesome object, you say, had attracted quite a crowd. I heard of the matter, of course, and as I understood it, Mr. Saunders Welch, the magistrate, had offered a reward to him who might identify the . . . well, the owner of the head. Is that correct, Bunkins?"

"It is, sir, yes. That's why all of them was out there lookin' at it."

"And was it not found in the Fleet sewer, near Holbourn Bridge?"

"That's as I heard it, sir."

"Then should you not be telling your story to Mr. Welch? He has claimed a good deal of outer London as his territory, more or less. And since I believe it not the business of magistrates to compete, I respect that claim. Now both Holbourn and St. Andrew's fall roughly on his side of the line—if indeed there be a line. Thus I repeat, should he not be told what you are telling me?''

Yet Bunkins knew well enough already what Sir John had explained—knew it from his days of thieving—and he had a notion of just how jurisdictional interests might, in some matters, overlap.

''I understand, Sir John, but I think you should hear me out, for there's part of this comes right close here to Bow Street.''

''Then,'' said the Magistrate of the Bow Street Court, ''by all means continue.''

And indeed that is what Bunkins did, telling of his visit to Mr. Donnelly's surgery, that he might have another look at the head; and of how, by means of the surgeon's advice regarding the depredations of polluted water and putrefaction upon the object, he managed to make out the features of one who might once have been George Bradbury, the owner of a pawnshop in Bedford Street. And there did Sir John stop him again.

''Bedford Street, you say?''

''Yes sir.''

''That is right close to home indeed. How well did you know this man Bradbury? Surely you are not in the habit of carrying off objects from Mr. Bilbo's residence and pawning them?''

In spite of the seriousness of the matter, Bunkins laughed quite heartily at the notion. Yet once he had got himself in control, he responded soberly: ''Oh no, sir. I am as well provided for as ever a fellow could be. And besides, that would be thieving, and I have left all that behind me. But it was during my days on the scamp—I mean, when I was a thief—that I saw George Bradbury often. May God forgive me for snitchin' if the man still lives, but the truth of it is I knew him as a fence for objects I had stole. Now, I gave all that up when Mr. Bilbo took me in, and that's going on three years past, so I had not seen him all that time except for once I chanced to spy him in the street not so long ago.''

"Might you be more exact about when it was you saw him?''

"I'd put it about a month past, sir, p'rhaps a few days more.''

"You said *if* the man still lives but a moment ago. I infer from that that your identification of the bodiless head was less than absolute and positive.''

"No sir, I can't say for sure certain it was old man Bradbury bobbin' around in that jar. That's why Jeremy and me went off from the doctor's to Bradbury's shop in Bedford Street.''

"Oh you did, did you? Both of you? Well, I should like to hear about that.''

Sir John's wish was no sooner expressed than it was granted. Bunkins told colorfully of our visit to the pawnshop—a bit too colorfully, it seemed to me. It would have sufficed to say that I accompanied him into the place, but to say, as he did, that I had ''come in all shifty and grimy, lookin' the very picture of a village hustler'' seemed to me more than was called for. In fact, it drew laughter from the magistrate.

"Grimy, is it? Is this true, Jeremy? I have been assured by Kate that you always present a good appearance.'' (Much mock concern in this.)

In my defense I offered the truth. "I had just done cleaning the kitchen fireplace, Sir John. Bunkins helped. He was none too clean himself.''

"Well and good. Continue, Mr. Bunkins.''

That he did, telling first of Mrs. Bradbury's hasty accounting for her husband's absence (''She seemed to be making it up as she went along''), and then of her keen interest in the loot from the putative burglary which we were to cart in some future midnight.

"Was it made clear to her that these would be stolen goods?'' asked Sir John.

"Oh, it was, for sure certain."

"Worth noting," said he. "Proceed."

"Well, sir, this woman who says she's Mrs. Bradbury—he weren't married when I knew him before—she's just a small thing, she is. Why, she didn't near fill out the dress she was wearin'. I didn't see how such a woman as her could kill a man and cut off his head, and do God only knows what else with the rest of him. She'd need help from a man, now wouldn't she?"

"In the ordinary course of things, one would expect that, yes."

"Exactly what I was thinkin' at the time," Bunkins declared. "That's why I decided to set up across from Bradbury's pawnshop at odd hours of the day and see who came by—and stayed. And that is what I done."

"And you picked out a candidate?"

"I did—one who is known hereabouts as Jackie Carver. I think it ain't his real name exactly, more of a name he made up for himself like a threat, for he is right handy with a knife. He's known for it around the Garden."

"And has he killed before?"

"There's talk. And he's always threatenin' with his knife. He threatened me once over a ring he took from me and sent me runnin' for my life."

"This would have been some time past?"

"Yes sir, when I was a thief."

"Well, if he be also a thief," said Sir John, "then he would naturally seek out a fence for his stolen goods. This alone would not make him a murderer."

"No sir, true enough, but this one is not just a thief but a pimp, as well, and he don't just visit the shop, he goes to stay—hours at a time—so I discovered."

"You're suggesting, Mr. Bunkins, that this fellow Carver, if that be his name, has some hold over this woman, this Mrs. Bradbury?"

"She might be one of his old molls."

"She might indeed. I see your point." Sir John remained

silent for a good long moment as he considered what he had heard. When he spoke again, it came in the nature of a summing up: "I admire the work you have done in this, Jimmie Bunkins. When Jeremy told me that you wished to present suspicions of murder, I did not, in all truth, expect much. Yet what you've given me here are very thoroughly investigated suspicions. I like it especially that you refuse to claim positive identification of the head. All your subsequent actions proceeded quite logically from that, and I respect what you offer as *logical* suspicions." Again he paused.

Bunkins, smiling broadly at such praise, gave a heartfelt thank-you to the magistrate, adding, "It makes me happy to hear you say so, sir."

"However," said Sir John, taking up where he had left off, "they remain suspicions, no matter how logical, no matter how well investigated. You were correct in supposing I would have an interest in this, for while it is true that Mr. Saunders Welch had an interest in the identification of the head, we have a greater interest here at Bow Street because of the questions that you have raised regarding the whereabouts of George Bradbury. The problem for me now, and indeed it is my problem and no longer yours, is how best to proceed."

"You could arrest 'em, sir, the both of them, and make them sweat."

"I could not, in all truth, do that, for there is not yet sufficient evidence against either of them—certainly not against Carver—to charge them with murder. I could detain them for questioning, however, and I may do that. But if I am to proceed as logically as you have, young sir, then the next step would be to write to the local magistrate and ask for confirmation of her account of her husband's absence. She said Mr. Bradbury was in Warwick?"

"Yes sir."

"Well, that I fear will mean a bit of waiting. Nevertheless, in the interest of proper procedure, that is what must be done.''

"May I make a suggestion, Sir John?''

It was Mr. Burnham who had spoken up. He had listened intently throughout the dialogue between his pupil and the magistrate, occasionally nodding, chuckling to himself once or twice when appropriate. In no wise had he attempted to draw attention from Bunkins to himself. He had been the very soul of tact.

"Mr. Burnham, is it? Why,'' said Sir John, "of course you may. You had been so quiet I had near forgot you were here with us.''

"I came,'' said the tutor, "out of pride in my pupil and his activities in your behalf. I wished to be certain that he would tell the story to you in the same detail I had heard it from him.''

"May I interrupt?'' Sir John inclined his head in Bunkins's direction. "Are we four the only ones who know all that you have told me?''

"Just us four,'' said Bunkins, "but like I said, the surgeon knew I had a good idea who belonged to that head he had in his cupboard.''

"I'm content with that,'' said Sir John, "but let us keep it so—just us four.'' Then: "By all means, go on, Mr. Burnham, and pardon my intrusion.''

"Certainly, sir. As I said, I wished him to tell the story in all its detail—and as I recall from its earlier telling, he did that. Only one thing I recall, and that was speculation on his part. He mentioned to me in passing that if George Bradbury *were* dead—that is, murdered—then his murderers would seek to sell his shop, for they could not forever maintain that he had gone home to comfort his dying father. That made remarkable good sense to me, sir, for it struck me that murderers are not the sort to be content very long as shopkeepers—certainly not the pair he has described.''

"I grant all that,'' said the magistrate.

"Hence, my suggestion. What would you say if I were

to go direct to the shop and inquire of Mrs. Bradbury if the shop is for sale?''

''In just such a way? If they had not put it about, then they would be suspicious.''

''I would wager they *have* put it about. I would say to them I heard it mentioned at Mr. Bilbo's gaming establishment. Such things are discussed there. And if they become suspicious, what of it? It would merely, as Mr. Bunkins puts it, 'make them sweat.' ''

''But come now, Mr. Burnham,'' objected Sir John, ''would they believe—forgive me for saying so—but would they believe that a black man would have the wherewithal to purchase a pawnshop?''

''Sir,'' said he, ''I doubt not that I *do* have sufficient funds to buy such a dingy little place, complete with its store of castoffs. When I claimed my freedom, my father settled upon me a considerable sum of money. Not, however, that I would ever truly consider investing it in such a disrespectable business. No, my thought was this: I shall let them know that I know of their trade in stolen goods, and give them the impression that I am eager to continue it. In this way, my color should help convince them that I am earnest in the matter, for it has been my observation, sir, that Londoners are ever ready to believe that a black man has evil intentions.''

Though said with a smile, Mr. Burnham's last remark was meant in all seriousness and evoked no laughter among us. Bunkins and I exchanged uneasy glances. Sir John coughed, cleared his throat, and gave permission to the tutor to pursue his plan. With that, Mr. Burnham stood and took his leave, promising to return as soon as he was able.

The three of us did take a moment to listen to his footsteps as he made his way down the hall toward the door to Bow Street. Sir John then roused himself from his brief torpor and bade me go to Mr. Marsden and draw from his list the name of the magistrate who served the town of Warwick. That I did without delay. I returned to find Bunkins spinning the tale of Mr. Burnham's emancipation. Knowing that it would take a bit of telling, I resumed my seat in the chair beside Bunkins. Sir John gave him his complete attention till it was done, only nodding from time to time to indicate his continued interest and comprehension.

Only then did he venture a comment. "A remarkable story," said he. "It bespeaks a great yearning for freedom on the part of the son and great generosity on the part of the father. The two must have had a very strong sense of family between them."

"And still do," said Bunkins, "for they write letters, one after the other. Mr. Burnham's great regret is that his mother can't write him. He misses her, he says, and hopes she knows it."

"Remarkable," said Sir John, "though certainly not unique, considering the institution from which Mr. Burnham has emerged. There may be a number of such stories from Jamaica and the North American colonies. I doubt not that we shall all come to regret that slavery was permitted." Then did he turn to me: "But Jeremy, you're back, are you?"

"I am," said I, "with the name of the Warwick magistrate. I would remind you, however, that I have here in my pocket the letter from the Lichfield magistrate. Would you want that read to you?"

"No, one thing at a time, and this matter of George Bradbury must take precedence at the moment. Here is the inkwell and the pen." He opened the drawer, felt about in it, and brought out a sheaf of clean sheets for writing. "Why do you not bring your chair round to your usual place and we shall indite a letter together to Warwick."

"Together, sir?" He had never sought my help before in composing such letters.

"I fear I am sometimes a bit too blunt to my fellow magistrates. I shall depend on you in this instance to prevent me from causing undue alarm to the recipient. I recall that once some years ago I put a simple inquiry out as to the whereabouts of a fellow, and the magistrate, misinterpreting the urgency of the situation, immediately put the poor fellow under arrest. If George Bradbury lives, I do not wish to have him locked up.''

And so we began the task. As I suspected, Sir John needed no help from me in putting together this letter or any other. Yet after each paragraph he questioned me as to the appropriateness of its wording, and once did defer to me on the construction of a sentence. As I look back upon this, reader, it seems to me that his intention in this exercise was to elevate me in the eyes of my friend. Bunkins, for his part, looked on and listened in great fascination.

As completed, there was little to be read into this communication. It was a simple request for information on George Bradbury. Had he lately returned to Warwick to attend his ailing father? Was he still there? If not, when did he leave? And so on. There was naught to cause so much as a raised eyebrow. The letter was read back to him and approved. With my help, he affixed his signature. His seal was applied, and Bunkins offered to post it on his return to St. James Street. There was then little to be done but await Mr. Burnham's return—and that was but minutes away.

We heard his hurrying footsteps—all but running he was—ere he presented himself at the open door to Sir John's chambers. Bunkins and I were there to greet him, yet he burst past us, beckoning us to follow, and made straight for Sir John.

"A most astonishing development," he announced loudly. "I was greeted at the shop on Bedford Street by one who claimed to be George Bradbury!"

Naturally, because of all he had heard, Mr. Burnham was dubious. He had entered with his story prepared, expecting to be greeted by Mrs. Bradbury, but through the curtain came a man who he knew, from Bunkins's description, could not be my old adversary, Jackie Carver. "He was a tall, thin man,'' said the tutor, ''of about thirty years, nothing at all remarkable about him, except that he wore beneath his coat a waistcoat of a plaid of the kind one sees on Scotsmen—quite colorful—yet he was no Scotsman. In most respects he seemed to talk as any Londoner of the working class.''

''That weren't George Bradbury!'' crowed Bunkins. ''He's an old fella, twice that age. He may be thin but he ain't tall, no bigger than me. He—'' And then did he fall silent of a sudden, as if a thought had just occurred to him.

''Nevertheless,'' said Mr. Burnham, ''that is how he identified himself to me. I said to him, 'I should like to talk to the owner of this shop.' He responded: 'You can talk to me.' 'Are you George Bradbury?' I asked. 'Yes, I am,' said he.

''Now, doubtful though I may have been,'' continued Mr. Burnham, ''I decided to proceed with my plan and informed him that I had heard that his shop was up for sale. 'It might be,' said he, 'but that would depend upon the offer.' I then told him that the offer would depend upon how much queer trade was done out the back door and how many such suppliers he had. He took this in, considered it a moment, and said, 'I must talk about it to Mrs. Bradbury.' Note he did not say 'to my wife,' as one might commonly say. In any case, he asked that I come by next day in the morning. I bade him good day and opened the door to go, then did he call after me, asking where it was that I had heard the shop was up for sale. I had my answer ready, of course, and told him I had heard the matter discussed at Mr. Bilbo's gaming establishment. 'Do you frequent such places?' he asked, all surprised. 'I do when it pleases me,' said I, and with that I left him.''

''Very intriguing,'' said Sir John. ''He did actually say that he was George Bradbury?''

''He confirmed it plain as you just spoke the name. 'Yes, I am,' said he.''

"Have we any idea just who this impostor might be?" asked Sir John.

At that I looked at Bunkins, for I then remembered well that he had mentioned just such a tall man to me and realized for the first time that he had been dropped from his report to Sir John. (I also reflected uneasily that I might know the man quite well myself.) Jimmie Bunkins blushed in embarrassment. If I remembered the tall man, then so did he. I saw him struggle valiantly with himself until at last the better Bunkins triumphed. He admitted his omission.

"Sir," said he, "I think I may know the cod—or at least I spied him a few times before, while watchin' the shop. He seemed to come by certain times so Mrs. Bradbury could go out doin' her daily buyin' and such. He'd watch the store for her. I should've said something about him. I guess I just forgot—or maybe didn't think him important enough to mention."

"Well," said Sir John, "now you have mentioned him. And now we know there may be three conspirators involved. It is all the more important to get that letter off to Warwick. But Mr. Burnham?"

"Yes, sir?"

"I think it best that you do not accept the invitation extended you to return tomorrow. We have planted our seed. Let us stand back awhile and see if it grows."

After the two had left for the great house in St. James Street, Sir John returned to confer with Mr. Marsden; it was the report to the Lord Chief Justice which occupied them and would continue to do so until the month's end. I might have held him and would have done had I been more certain in my own mind just what course I ought to take.

In truth, I was all in turmoil. Unlike Bunkins, who had merely to admit an error of neglect, I had to wrestle with myself over another's guilt—or probable guilt—or perhaps only possible guilt. Was it up to me to weigh this? Most likely it was not. The sensible thing would be to go to Sir John with my suspicions. Let him give what importance he would to it—then the matter would be out of my hands for good.

My problem had been caused by Mr. Burnham. His description of the man who had falsely presented himself as George Bradbury included a detail of dress which had sounded in my mind as a resonant, echoing chord of music. He had mentioned that the fellow wore a plaid waistcoat in the Scottish style. While there were many tall, thin men round and about Covent Garden, there was but one I knew of who wore such a waistcoat, and that one was Thomas Roundtree.

Why not tell Sir John this? It was not so much because of any affection I had for Roundtree personally; though it was true he was likable enough, he had deceived and embarrassed me, and I held that against him. No, I hesitated because of his daughter, Clarissa, whom I liked and pitied. Her faith in her foolish father, while misplaced and naive, was in itself admirable. If I were to suggest to the magistrate that Roundtree was the third of conspirators, as they had been dubbed, it would only cause her further pain and grief. And it might indeed have the direst of consequences for him. Perhaps his involvement was quite innocent. Perhaps he merely tended shop for Mrs. Bradbury.

What was I to do? Procrastination seemed the safest, if not the wisest, course. I would do nothing for the present and await a time when the information was most pertinent, even essential, before voicing my suspicions. Perhaps the letter from the Lichfield magistrate would force my hand. It was there in my coat pocket still. That I had it seemed to have slipped Sir John's mind for the present. It would have to be read to him, of course, but perhaps I might pick the right moment.

That moment came at the dinner table. Annie had once again presented us with a meal which, in any other household, would have seemed altogether exceptional. Yet we, spoiled by our cook, took it as the usual and our due. What she called stew was distinguished from what was customarily called by that name by virtue of its flavor—or flavors, really, for with onions, garlic, her favorite paprika, and one could only guess what other rare spices from her cabinet, there was no telling what combination of tastes might come. In short, we had all eaten well. And in that period of happy relaxation during which we sat at table, belching our satisfaction, Lady Fielding happened to mention that with the new year had come the burden of writing a great many begging letters to the great and the rich that the Magdalene Home might continue its operation for another twelve-month.

"I was wondering, Jack," said she, "if you might loan me Jeremy's services as a letter writer."

"Oh, well, I—"

Yet she plunged on: "I thought I might draw up a list of recipients and an exemplar that he might duplicate. That would leave me free to tend to day-to-day matters at the Home, which are quite enough to fill my day, please believe me."

"Oh, I believe you, Kate. It is only that Mr. Marsden's time has been fully taken with this damned report to the Lord Chief Justice as scribe and reader." He hesitated. "Uh, how many letters of the sort do you wish written?"

"About fifty, perhaps more. He would write them, and I would sign."

"That is a great number, certainly. Well, by all means draw up your list and draft your exemplar. Jeremy will get to them when and as he can. Right, lad?"

"Right, sir. But Sir John?" said I, drawing the Lichfield letter from my pocket; this seemed an opportune occasion. "I am reminded of the letter which arrived today from Lichfield. I have it here."

"Ah, of course," said he. "With this Bradbury matter, it had quite got past me. If you have it, then read it, by all means. There can be naught in it to offend feminine ears."

Annie made a face at that. I broke the seal, opened the letter, and began to read aloud. "Dear Honored Colleague," it began, then went quickly to the matter.

" 'Having only returned from Yorkshire in attendance of a suit dealing with family property there, I came late to your letter inquiring into the present whereabouts and past of one Thomas Roundtree. In my capacity as Magistrate of the Town of Lichfield, I had come to know the fellow well. He was frequently brought before me for drunkenness and the disturbing of the peace. Also charges of petty thievery were brought against him on a few occasions, though none were proven. He was a fair carpenter, and in homes in which he worked, items of value sometimes went missing. Mr. Roundtree left Lichfield something over a year ago, some said to London, and I was glad to be rid of him.

" 'The circumstances of his departure were as follows: Mr. Roundtree had him a wife, a woman of good family named Sarah Gladden. He had seduced her and put her with child. Considering her condition, the family allowed the two to be married, though they were in no wise keen to welcome him as a son-in-law. The child was born, a daughter, Clarissa, and the little family had a difficult time of it, what with Roundtree's drinking and general inability to earn sufficient. Yet also, sadly, did the fortunes of the Gladdens decline. Mr. Gladden died five or six years after his daughter's unfortunate marriage, leaving his wife and an unmarried daughter, Esther, the sister of Sarah, only the bookshop from which he had managed to draw a living for the three of them and make occasional gifts of money to Sarah when the rent had to be paid. The two women attempted to run the shop themselves. Neither had a head for business, and it was only a few years before the shop was lost to creditors. At about the same time, Miss Esther Gladden fell ill with consumption and died swiftly; the mother was taken in by her people in Cambridgeshire. This left Sarah Roundtree altogether dependent upon Thomas Roundtree—and he proved undependable as earlier. She, too, fell ill with consumption, which she may have contracted while nursing her sister; it took a year or two, but she did also die, leaving her daughter, Clarissa, then ten years old, in the sole care of her husband. He kept the child a few months until reports of her neglect brought a visit from the vicar. From the condition of their rooms and the poor health of the girl, Mr. Roundtree was judged to be an unfit parent. Clarissa Roundtree was taken from him and put in the parish poorhouse. It was then that her father left Lichfield, declaring that he would make his fortune, prove himself fit, and return to buy her out of the poorhouse.

" 'He did return two months past, though with no fortune in evidence. He told them at the parish office he wished only to visit his daughter. In fact, there were two visits, and on the second of them, he did spirit her away dressed in the clothes of a boy. It was my assumption that he took her away to London. Lacking the resources to have them followed, I could only hope that some hint of their location might come, as it has now come from you. Find Thomas Roundtree, and you will find Clarissa.

" 'This brings me to an urgent request which I would put to you. Just as Thomas Roundtree has made himself a fugitive, so has Clarissa Roundtree made herself a fugitive from the parish poorhouse. She should be returned to us for her own welfare. If she remains in London, as I believe that is where she is now, she will soon fall into degradation and crime, as you must certainly know. It is my hope that when you find her, for I am sure you shall, you will notify me. When I hear from you that she is in your care, I shall have someone sent from the parish office to bring her back. Thomas Roundtree is no doubt guilty of abduction, as well, but him I shall leave to you.

" 'Hoping that this does not put upon you too great a burden, I remain your humble and obedient servant, William Bladgett, Esquire, Magistrate of Lichfield.' "

When I had finished the reading of the letter, I looked up for the first time and saw that both Annie and Lady

Fielding had been moved to tears. Annie's eyes glistened; Lady Fielding wiped at the tears on her cheeks. Sir John's head was bowed.

"Ah," said he, "what a lot of human misery is there in the pages of that letter."

In truth, reader, my own eyes were damp, and on more than one occasion I had to clear my throat to continue reading.

Lady Fielding produced a handkerchief and blew her nose, then passed it to Annie. Then said she, with great feeling, "What are we to do, Jack?"

"Why, we must do as he requests. He is entirely correct. If that girl stays in London, she will only come to harm."

"But to return her to the parish poorhouse! Do you know what those places are?"

He sighed a great sigh. "I have heard, of course I have. Yet what other course have we to offer?"

"Why, I would gladly make a place for her in the Magdalene Home for Penitent Prostitutes. She's such a bright girl. She could learn a trade there."

"But Kate," said Sir John, "she is neither penitent—for she is by your own report willful and must certainly have collaborated in her escape from the poorhouse—nor is she yet, thank God, a prostitute, though some as young as she do follow that dismal calling."

"I know, but would it not be good to rescue her *before* she is forced out onto the streets?"

"You take too much upon yourself. You cannot hope to save every child in London who needs saving. There must be hundreds, perhaps thousands."

"Oh, that's true, but . . ."

"Perhaps you could find some place for her in service," offered Annie. "She's a bit young, but I was not much older when I began."

Then followed a discussion of Clarissa's age. Was she only eleven? Perhaps twelve? If the latter, she might indeed be offered in service. Lady Fielding gave it as her opinion that the girl would pass for thirteen or fourteen, for she was tall and spoke well.

"But you reckon without her wishes," said I to them. "She seems determined to stay with her father. How do we know that if you found a place for her in one of the houses in St. James Street or Bloomsbury Square, she would be any more likely to stay than she was in the parish poorhouse? She might simply run away again."

"Jeremy is right," sighed Lady Fielding. "She does truly love that foolish, reprobate father of hers."

Now, I realized, was when I might—and probably should—tell Sir John of my suspicions regarding Roundtree. Yet I did not. Instead, I said something that surprised even me.

"I think they plan to emigrate to the North American colonies. Why not simply let them go?"

"What makes you think that?" asked Sir John.

"Something that was said—or rather, not said—by her the last time I talked with her."

"How would he raise the passage?"

"I know not," said I. Then, improvising: "Perhaps he has indentured himself. Perhaps he has indentured them both."

"It's possible. There are always ways of getting there. And those who wish to run away always run west, it seems."

At that, discussion seemed to subside. There was a period of silence there at the table. At last it was broken by Lady Fielding, who looked sharply at me.

"When did you last see her, Jeremy?" she asked.

"That was when I delivered the cape you found for her—a few days ago it was."

"Yes, and I resolved then to keep a close watch upon her. But the day-to-day intervened. Things keep getting in the way of our best intentions. Let me go tomorrow and visit her again. I know not what, if anything, we shall say of all this, but let us at least talk with her again." She reached over and touched her husband's arm. "That will do, will it, Jack?"

"Don't frighten her away. That is all I ask. I feel bound somewhat by that man Bladgett's request."

"We'll be careful what we say, I promise."

That is how it was left. The evening took its course. Lady Fielding retired to their bedroom with the declared intention of beginning work on the list of prospective donors to the Magdalene Home. Sir John followed to sit, as he so often did, in the dark little room beside theirs which he called his study; he would be giving serious consideration to one thing or another—perhaps to that which we had so earnestly discussed, perhaps to the Laningham puzzle, or perhaps again on what were to me the more mundane matters of the administration of his office.

As was my usual, I did the washing up after dinner, while Annie pored over her books by candlelight. She droned quietly through her primer with little difficulty—already she had read it a few times under Mr. Burnham's guidance—and then took up one from our lot of Shakespeare plays which she had been carrying about with her, *Hamlet* I believe it was. This she read louder, spelling out words to me that I might pronounce them and as often as not explain their meaning. I was past minding such interruptions; they lightened the work of scrubbing and scouring. When I had done, I joined her at the table.

Then, catching us by surprise, came the sound of footsteps upon the staircase. They mounted in a steady, plodding rhythm; there was no urgency to be heard in them. Annie and I looked at each other and shrugged. She rose from her chair at the table and was there for the anticipated knock. When it came, she threw open the door, revealing Mr. Donnelly, who looked slightly disheveled and certainly tired.

He greeted us both, smiled wanly, and asked if he might speak with Sir John. "The autopsy is done," said he, "and the body is on its way back to the great house in St. James

Square. I have a brief report to present to Sir John.''

"I am here," came that deep voice from behind us. Sir John descended the stairs and, in his manner, took charge. "Do you wish to do this in private?''

"Not necessary, sir. What I have to say can be put briefly—and I must be back to my surgery so that I may write it out.''

"Then let us hear what you have to say.''

"Absent any certain test for arsenic, which is the poison I suspect—''

"You do suspect poison, then?''

"I do now, for there were lesions and ulcers all through her digestive tract. To put it more descriptively, her esophagus and stomach lining had been burned raw, and there was much damage to her kidneys, as well.''

"That, I take it, would be consistent with a death by poisoning?''

"Completely consistent.''

"And you suspect arsenic was used?''

"I do, yes.''

"And why that, in particular?''

"Because it is readily available, and because now that I have had a chance to do a bit of studying, I find that its effect is completely consistent with the violent symptoms displayed by Lord and Lady Laningham—heavy vomiting, the vomiting of blood, and diarrhea with blood in the case of Lady Laningham. It may have been so with Lord Laningham as well. I had no opportunity to examine him at the time of his death.''

"And you intend to put all this in your report?''

"Yes, and in my testimony, as well—as you shall hear. Mr. Trezavant has scheduled a coroner's inquest into the death of Lady Laningham tomorrow at ten. He has asked, since you evidently offered to acquaint him with the procedures, that you be by his side to instruct him. And to facilitate that, he would like to hold the inquest in your courtroom. Unless he hears from you to the contrary, he will, he told me, be here promptly at ten.''

Sir John remained silent for a moment. ''Well,'' said he, ''it is true that in some foolish fit of generosity I offered to help him through his first formal inquests. That, I suppose, is the price that I must pay for him calling an inquest at all. I shall do my duty, seeing that he does his.''

''I shall see you at ten tomorrow then, Sir John.''

''Ten it is. Is there anything that you have not said that you wish to add?''

Thinking on that but a moment, Mr. Donnelly said: ''Only this: Whatever misgivings I may have had about the shortcomings of the medical knowledge of Dr. Isaac Diller, who with me performed the autopsy, were insufficient ten times over. The fellow knows nothing of the inner workings of the human body. I do not believe he had ever until now seen inside one.''

''And will Dr. Diller be present to give evidence tomorrow?''

''Why, of course, Sir John. Need you ask?''

EIGHT

*In Which We Receive
a Guest and an
Inquest Is Held*

Because Lady Fielding saw the need to complete not only the list of prospective donors but also the model letter from which I was to write to each, we were somewhat late in setting off on our return visit to Half-Moon Passage. In truth, I felt somewhat ambivalent about making the trip with her. I realized, of course, that she could not comfortably make the trip alone, and I certainly saw the need for communication of some sort with the girl; nevertheless, I should have liked to have the opportunity to witness Mr. Trezavant's inquest into the death of Lady Laningham; almost, I admit, would I have preferred it.

At last she did sweep into the room, dressed for the day, the completed list and exemplar in hand. She dropped the sheaf of papers down upon the kitchen table and blurted the briefest of instructions: "Write the letters complete but for my signature."

"Yes, mum."

"Now, Jeremy, let us be off to that den of iniquity."

I trailed in her wake. Once under way at such urgent moments as this one, she seemed to cut through space like some proud, swift ship through water. There was no stopping her; only a fool would try.

And thus did she fly down the stairs at a perilous speed and sail down the long hall to the door, and out onto Bow Street.

"Jeremy," she cried, as I caught up with her, "you must find us a hackney, for after I have made my visit to this girl, Clarissa, I will be off to the Magdalene. Make it clear to the driver that he must wait for me."

What might have been an impossible task an hour or two earlier proved no trouble at all now that the morning was somewhat advanced. Standing idle the coach was, and the driver beside it. When I put to him Lady Fielding's requirements, he made clear his own.

"I charges extra for waiting," said he.

"Fair enough," said I, "but how much?"

"A penny for a short time and tuppence for a long one."

"And who's to judge whether it be short or long?"

"Why, I am, of course."

There was no arguing that, and after all, the fellow *was* available, so I beckoned him forward to where Lady Fielding waited at Number 4, while I ran on ahead to her.

The streets surrounding Covent Garden were so crowded and narrow that our trip to Half-Moon Passage in the hackney could then likely have been made much faster afoot. Nevertheless, it was another chill morning, and we rode warmer than we could have walked. Expecting further instructions from her regarding the task she had put me to, I was surprised to receive none. Insofar as I remember, Lady Fielding said nothing the entire length of our journey. I supposed that she was thinking ahead to what might and might not be said to Clarissa Roundtree. I had wondered about that myself.

Half-Moon Passage was at its far end—near to the Strand—little more than a walkway. Since he could not drive us through and turning round was near impossible, the driver halted at Bedford Street, banged on the roof of the coach, and shouted down to us that he would wait here and we must go the rest of the way on foot. That we did, though Lady Fielding was set grumbling that we had no assurance the hackney would be there when we returned. I calmed her as best I could, pointing out that the driver had not yet been paid and would likely wait till afternoon, if need be, to get his money. Thus we came to the ramshackle lodging house, now quite familiar to me, went through its littered and foul-smelling courtyard, up its rickety stairs, and down its shadowy hall, then finally to the door of the Roundtree room.

"Give it a good stout knock, Jeremy," said she.

I tried, but with the first blow delivered by my doubled fist the door flew open. Lady Fielding looked at me curiously, a question in her eyes. I thought perhaps Clarissa was out on some errand. Nevertheless, I was sufficiently wary that I preceded Lady Fielding through the door, stepping just inside the room to survey it. What I saw quite shocked me.

Off to the left, on which side stood the bed, Clarissa Roundtree lay on her long, low trundle bed before the fireplace, wherein a bright fire blazed. A woman tending her had turned at our intrusion and wore upon her face a look of consternation and alarm.

Lady Fielding pushed past me and went swiftly to them. I followed, quite bewildered at this sudden turn. We looked down upon Clarissa. Her face was sickly pale and her eyes were closed; she shivered beneath a blanket and the cape, which had been thrown over her. I could not tell if she was conscious.

"How long has she been so?" asked Lady Fielding.

"It come on her gradual two days past," said the woman who knelt beside the girl. "She got worse, coughin' and the like, yesterday. Only today has she been so bad. She shivers and then she sweats. She's terrible sick."

"Oh, I can see that. What has she? Has a doctor seen her?"

"No, mum, we ain't got a doctor here, but it seem like some sort of ague to me."

The woman looked familiar to me—in her twenties, blunt and square in her frock, with something of the farm girl about her. Could she have been the "nekkid woman" I glimpsed who had propelled the whoremonger out into the hall? She looked strong enough and capable of it.

"Well, my girl," said Lady Fielding, as she took charge of matters, "I believe we must take Clarissa with us if she's to get well."

It seemed to me that she spoke no more than the plain truth. The girl on the pallet bed looked nearer to death than to life.

"I don't know as I can let you do that, mum," said the woman, courteous even in her obstinacy.

Lady Fielding knelt beside her, yet gave her attention to Clarissa. She placed her palm to the girl's forehead.

"Good God," said she, "the child is burning with fever!"

"I know," wailed her putative nurse. "There ain't nothin' I can do to bring it down!"

"Bless you, you've tried, haven't you? But don't you see? She must see a doctor, and we have for her the best doctor in London."

"Truly so? But where'll you be takin' her to?"

"To Bow Street."

"To the court? She ain't done nothin'."

"No, no, no, not to the court—up above it, where we live."

"Ah, you're the lady come visited her, gave her the cape and all."

"Yes, I am. I should have introduced myself. I am Lady Katherine Fielding. My husband is Magistrate of the Bow Street Court."

"The Blind Beak?"

"So they call him."

"Well . . ." The woman hesitated in an anguish of indecision. "She spoke well of you, and she is terrible sick, so I . . . I . . . suppose you takin' her out of here is for the best. But what'll I tell her pa?"

"Tell him we took her to save her life. If he loves her as much as she loves him, then he will understand." She waited an instant—only long enough to get an assenting nod—then said, "Let us bundle her up. We have a hackney, but she must be kept warm on the journey. Jeremy? We shall need your help."

I gave a good deal of it. Once the two women had wrapped Clarissa's nearly lifeless form in the blanket and cape that covered her, I knelt down and lifted her bodily from her narrow bed. Once on my feet, I hefted her weight and judged her to be not all that much heavier than a good-sized sack of potatoes, something less than a hundred-weight, I should have supposed. As I made my way to the open door, Lady Fielding remained behind a moment.

"You're a good sort, I can tell," said she in a low voice. "If you ever decide to reform your life and learn a respectable trade, you have only to see me at the Magdalene Home. We'll find room for you."

What the woman responded I know not, for I was through the door by the time her answer came and down the hall a bit when Lady Fielding emerged and hurried after me. As I hit the chill of the outside air and started down the steps, Clarissa roused slightly from her stuporous state. Her eyelids fluttered, yet she shivered more violently and breathed with exertion, wheezing as some old man might as she inhaled. Her lips moved. She sought to speak. I inclined my ear to her that I might hear her better.

"Where . . . we going?"

I thought to say something reassuring. "Where you might be made well."

Lady Fielding came up behind, asking what Clarissa had said. Having been informed, she kept up a steady stream of encouragement to the girl through the courtyard and back down Half-Moon Passage as we made our return to the waiting hackney coach. I know not whether Clarissa truly understood, yet she seemed to take heart somehow as she bumped along in my arms.

Those who passed us by seemed to give us a wide berth. They shrank back, stared, muttered to one another. There was then in London even greater fear than today of sickness of any sort. Therefore I was not much surprised when, upon our arrival at the hackney, the driver protested strongly against accepting Clarissa in her state as a passenger. Yet I was somewhat taken aback by the fierceness with which Lady Fielding met his protests. She threatened him with the power of the magistrate; she threatened him with the Bow Street Runners; she assured him that it was more than likely he would never again be permitted to drive a hackney coach in Westminster or the City if he did not return us now— and quickly—to Number 4 Bow Street.

Cowed, intimidated, all but brought to his knees (speaking figuratively, of course), the poor fellow gave in with a single question.

"She ain't got the plague or some such horrible disease, has she?"

"Certainly she has not!" said Lady Fielding most emphatically.

(I found myself wondering just how she could be so sure.)

"Awright, then," said the driver, "put her aboard, and let's get it over with."

That was easier said than done. Coach doors are none too wide, and to work Clarissa and myself through one could not be accomplished without a struggle and a bit of bumping. Still, it was done, and when I had the girl upright on the facing seat, I found her eyes open and her mouth twisted in a smile; she seemed to be coughing—but then, only then, did I realize that she was laughing at me.

"Well, Miss Pooh, I'm glad to see you're not so ill that you can't have a bit of fun at my expense. I apologize for the bumps. I did the best I could."

Then did Lady Fielding enter the coach, pull the door shut, and take a seat beside her.

"What's this? What's this? Having a conversation, are you? You shouldn't tire her if she's awake. Here, child, lean on me. It won't be long until we have you warm, and in a proper bed." Then did she halt, quite suddenly aghast. "Oh, but Jeremy! Where shall we put her?"

The answer to that, as I had foreseen, was in my bed. Sir John and Lady Fielding's was out of the question. Annie's, which was wide enough, could not be shared with one so ill. Mine alone would do, and so I offered it, volunteering to sleep in the kitchen on a pallet before the fireplace. My offer was accepted.

Getting her out of the coach was not near so difficult as getting her in. Lady Fielding aided, and Clarissa, now fully conscious, was also able to be of some help. Nevertheless, it was I who carried her into Number 4 and would have taken her alone all the way upstairs were it not for the help of Mr. Fuller, which was offered along the way. He and I ascended quite slowly, careful of the load we carried between us. Such concentration called for quiet, and in our silence above I heard voices rise from the courtroom below. One of them I recognized as Mr. Donnelly's. I knew that I must fetch him from the inquest ere he left for his surgery.

Thus it was that when at last we eased her down upon my bed high in the little room above them all, I left Lady Fielding to arrange things properly and returned downstairs with Mr. Fuller. There I entered the courtroom and stood by the door, searching the room for Mr. Donnelly.

He was not hard to locate—except he had his back to me. Standing before Mr. Trezavant, he was just concluding his testimony: ". . . and so, in summary, I would say that the ulcerated areas of her esophagus and stomach, the blisters upon her tongue, and the damage to her kidneys are of the sort that one might indeed expect to find in a case of arsenic poisoning." (Perhaps there was more and greater detail, reader, but having no medical knowledge to speak of, I commit here to paper only that which I can recall with some degree of exactitude.) Having made his statement, he kept his silence as Mr. Trezavant took a moment to confer with Sir John, who sat beside him at the table.

Concluding, Mr. Trezavant dismissed Mr. Donnelly and summoned Dr. Isaac Diller. As Mr. Donnelly turned round to take his seat once again among the witnesses, I waved at him, caught his attention, and beckoned him to the door. He came, frowning.

"What is it, Jeremy? Can't it wait?"

"I don't think so, sir. Lady Fielding has brought in a patient, a girl of about twelve. Could you look at her? She seems quite ill—fever, difficulty breathing, all of that."

"Well . . . all right. Just let me get my bag."

As he went to fetch it, I surveyed the room once more and noted that among those witnesses present were Arthur Paltrow, the new Lord Laningham, and Maggie, the deceased lady's maid. The coroner's jury was in no wise impressive; most had probably been bribed off the streets to take part in the proceedings. As Mr. Donnelly returned, bag and hat in hand, Mr. Diller began to hold forth in rotund tones upon his qualifications and honors. From the sound of him he would be at it ten minutes or more before getting on to the true subject of the inquiry.

Mr. Donnelly simply nodded to me, and we exited the courtroom. I led him up the stairs, explaining as I went that the girl had been put in my bed up on the top floor.

"That may not have been wise," said he. "We know not what manner of contagion she may carry."

"Nevertheless, sir, that is where she is."

"You say she's but twelve years old?"

"Eleven or twelve, sir."

"Is that not a bit young for one in the Magdalene Home?"

"Oh, she's not one from the Home," said I.

"Then how did she come to be brought here by Lady Fielding?"

I hesitated. "It's rather a long story, sir."

"All right, later perhaps."

Not another word passed between us until we reached my room. Lady Fielding was there bending over Clarissa, giving her close attention. On top of the wrappings the girl had worn on her trip to Number 4 Bow Street were now the two blankets under which I slept.

"I've stopped the chill," said Lady Fielding, "but now she seems a bit too warm."

A few drops of perspiration stood out on Clarissa's brow.

"It's a fever of some sort, right enough," said the medico, putting a hand to her head. Then to Clarissa: "Can you speak?"

She nodded. "A little," she said with a bit of difficulty. Her breathing was shallow and labored.

He sat upon the bed and pulled back the mountain of covers over her upper half and unbuttoned the frock she wore beneath it all.

"She coughed up some nasty stuff," said Lady Fielding. "I wiped it from her face with my handkerchief."

"Is there blood in it?"

"No, see for yourself."

She opened the handkerchief and displayed a slimy mess of gray-yellow. Mr. Donnelly gave it a brief look, then returned his attention to Clarissa. He spread her frock wide upon her flat chest; she had not even the beginnings of a woman's breasts. Putting his hand gently upon one side and then the other, he studied her face.

"Do you feel pain here in your chest?"

"Hurts . . ." She panted. "To breathe . . . right side . . . difficult . . . to breathe."

With that, he opened his bag and pulled from it something quite like a small ear trumpet. Then did he place the horn end upon the left side of her chest and put his ear to listen at the other end. After listening to the right side in this manner, he repeated the exercise, though first thumping soundly with his middle finger upon the place he listened. Then he threw back the covers and sat back. Glancing first at me and after at Lady Fielding, he then addressed Clarissa direct.

"My girl," said he, "you have pneumonia. It is not so much a disease as it is a condition, an infection of the lungs. Luckily for you, only one lung is affected, the right. It no doubt began as a cold, a catarrh. Did you have a discharge from the nose and coughing for a few days before your chest began to hurt and your breathing was impaired?"

Clarissa nodded.

"Well, then, that infection descended and settled in your right lung, filling it with fluid, mucus, and such. So long as that infection is there and that mucus, you will have trouble breathing.

"Now"—and here he addressed Lady Fielding and me— "as for treatment, here is what you must do. She must have liquids—water and clear broth, as much water as you can get her to take—for the fever has dried her out. I shall give you some quinine bark with which to make a strong tea. It works well with the ague to bring down fever and may well help her. You can get more of it at a chemist's shop. I'll come back this evening to see how she fares, and in the meantime, I'll consult my books to see if anything more may be done for her. The important thing now is to bring down her fever."

Now to Clarissa: "You heard all that, my girl?"

Again, she nodded.

"Then I'll expect you to cooperate. You must drink water, and the tea will taste quite disgusting, but you must drink that, too. Cough up as much of that mucus as you can. You must get it out of you. You'll have a cloth for that. You'll see to it, Jeremy?"

And so, having attended to her, he dropped into his bag the device with which he had listened to her lungs and rose to go. He invited me down to the kitchen that I might receive instructions in brewing the tea.

Once there and once so informed, I listened as he expounded further upon the case. "I expect," said he, "that it is to you and Annie that most of the nursing will fall, so a few more words to you on the care of the patient. You have no fireplace in the room, and she must be kept warm during the night. Another blanket, if necessary—but a charcoal brazier would be better. Haven't I seen one about somewhere?"

"Downstairs, sir, for the Runners."

"Filch it, borrow it, whatever you must do. Bring water up to Lady Fielding now, and then begin on the tea, which should be administered to her twice daily. And by the bye, you're all very fortunate."

"Fortunate? How is that, sir?"

"It's a risky matter to bring anyone into your home with an illness that has not been diagnosed. Fortunately for you pneumonia, though serious, is not terribly contagious. More than likely it developed, as I said, from a catarrh. All of you here are well fed and strong. You should be able to fight off a catarrh without difficulty. That girl upstairs, on the other hand, seemed ill fed and underweight, easy prey to illness like so many children in this district. What is her name, by the bye?"

"Clarissa," said I, "Clarissa Roundtree."

"Rather a fancified name for one in such modest circumstances. She seemed to speak well, too, the little I heard from her. Something fine about her. Yes, I do wish to hear her story, but just now I must get myself downstairs and learn the outcome of this inquest."

"Yet it seems certain, does it not?"

"Nothing is certain, particularly not when dealing with such . . . well, never mind. I shall see you this evening, no doubt."

So did he bid me good day and left by way of the stairs for the courtroom. For my part, I made hastily to follow his instructions regarding the patient. I filled a pitcher with water and set beside it a cup to take upstairs. Then remembering what had been said in the sickroom, I pulled an unused cloth from the drawer which contained my supply of cleaning rags. All this then I took in hand as I trudged up above.

"Ah, there you are, Jeremy," said Lady Fielding by way of greeting.

"Here is the cloth to trap her mucus."

She held it up and looked at it rather critically. "It could be cleaner," said she.

"But its purpose is to be soiled," I argued.

"I suppose you're right."

"And here," said I, "is water and a drinking cup. Mr. Donnelly said she is to be given as much as she will take."

"Of course! I know! I heard him plain!"

She was right. What could I say? I cast a glance about me, and it fell upon Clarissa. In spite of her difficulties, there seemed to be a look of amusement in her eyes at my speechlessness—quite the same look I'd got from her in the hackney. There was mockery in that girl.

"Well," said I at last, "I'll go down and see to the tea." Then did I turn to go.

"Jeremy," Lady Fielding called after me, "forgive me for speaking sharp at you. You're a good lad, none better."

My hurt feelings thus mended, I returned to the kitchen.

There was much up and down the stairs that day. After the quinine tea was delivered, Annie arrived and heard my account of our morning's activities, then went up to the sickroom to visit the patient and receive her orders from Lady Fielding. I took that opportunity to fly down the stairs to discover what I could of the outcome of the inquest.

To my surprise, the proceedings had only just ended. I caught sight of Mr. Donnelly disappearing out the door of the courtroom, with Dr. Diller close behind. Both of them, I supposed, had patients to see at this late hour. Those who had served as the coroner's jury milled about, seemingly reluctant to leave. I sought Sir John and saw him turning away from Mr. Trezavant, who was obviously taking his leave. Sir John, it seemed to me, looked none too happy. I approached him cautiously, for once his back was turned, the look upon his face had gone from displeasure to plain exasperation. Yet approach him I did.

"Sir?"

"Who is that? Jeremy? Were you here through this . . . this . . ." He hesitated. "Is that fellow Trezavant anywhere within earshot?"

"No, Sir John, he's out the door as we speak."

"Then I shall say it—this travesty of a proper inquest. In all truth, I wish to stay on good terms with him, for it does no good to have a magistrate and a coroner at odds. But dear God, he does make it difficult for me to maintain a good opinion of him."

"Uh, no sir, I was not present." Though I dreaded asking the question, I felt I must: "What was the finding?"

"Death by natural causes."

"What?" I was truly astonished. "Did he direct the verdict?"

"Oh no, though he may as well have done."

Sir John disclosed that Mr. Donnelly had been unwise enough to use in his testimony the clinical term "ulceration" in describing the raw burns in the throat and stomach of Lady Laningham. When Dr. Diller testified immediately afterward, he, too, used that term. Mr. Trezavant asked him to define it, which the doctor did right enough as "an erosive condition in the skin, a burning," then went on to explain that in this instance the condition existed in the inner skin—the stomach lining and the walls of the esophagus. Then did the coroner inquire in all apparent innocence if this condition in the inwards did not sometimes occur from natural causes as a kind of disease of the stomach; Dr. Diller agreed that it sometimes did. And the penultimate question: "Was not your original opinion on the cause of

Lady Laningham's death acute indigestion?'' The reply:
"Yes, originally, but—'' "Would not ulcers of the sort that
you and Mr. Donnelly described cause acute indigestion?"
"Of course, but—''

The coroner's jury was never permitted to hear the doctor's objections. What they heard instead was a long disquisition from Mr. Trezavant on death by poisoning, which
he said was very rare, and death from ulcers "of the sort
described by our two medical witnesses,'' which was much
more common. In this summing-up, he touched upon the
information given by the maid that Lady Laningham had
declared, "I've been poisoned,'' and had asked that Sir
John Fielding be sent for. "But the magistrate himself has
appeared before you, and in his testimony conceded that he
may have put the notion of poison in her mind in an earlier
conversation in which he suggested the possibility—the
possibility—of poison in the death of her husband.'' Mr.
Trezavant pointed out that by Mr. Donnelly's testimony, no
chemical test existed to prove the presence of a poison of
the kind he suspected in her body. It was only by means
of its effect upon the body, chiefly the ulcers upon the lining of the stomach, that he believed that poison had caused
her death. Yet we have heard from Dr. Diller that ulcers of
this kind may come also from a sickness of the body. The
question is: Were these ulcers caused by poison, as Mr.
Donnelly has strongly suggested, or did they exist before
the attack that caused her death? If the former, then your
verdict must be 'willful murder by person or persons unknown.' If the latter, then it would be 'death by natural
causes.' It is up to you, gentlemen of the jury, and only to
you, to make the decision.''

(I readily confess, reader, that Sir John's account of the
proceedings was not so detailed, nor as complete, as what
I have just given. What he said there in the courtroom was
augmented by his later remarks and those of Mr. Donnelly.
Sir John did, however, conclude as follows:)

"Then, Jeremy, he allowed the jury to confer amongst

themselves right there before us. They argued the matter and argued it some more, throwing out questions from time to time to Mr. Trezavant, which he answered to suit his purpose. Their so-called deliberations were like unto some dispute in Bedlam and made just so much sense. I became so annoyed with the jury that I left the room to confer with Mr. Donnelly. We were both mightily disgusted. After near an hour, Trezavant himself concluded they had talked it through quite enough and demanded a verdict. He got the one he wanted.

"Death by natural causes," said I.

"Indeed," said Sir John. "He had bewildered them completely with his talk of—"

Seeing the approach of one quite unexpected, I touched his arm to halt the swift flow of his speech.

He responded in a whisper: "What is it, lad?"

"Lord Laningham comes—Mr. Paltrow."

Before he could quite compose himself, the putative nobleman was upon us, his face fixed in a frown.

"Sir John, I wonder might I have a word with you?"

"You may, of course. I take it, from the sound of your voice, that you are Lord Laningham."

"I am indeed. Forgive me for not announcing myself. I quite forgot your affliction."

"I often do myself. Why not in the room in back which serves as my chambers?" said Sir John to him—and then to me: "Jeremy, come along, will you? I would have you search out the records on the Goodhope affair. You recall it, I'm sure."

This was a very pointed instruction to me to accompany them that I might study Lord Laningham's reactions during whatever conversation they might have between them. The mention of the Goodhope affair lent a certain spice to the invitation. Whatever his petitioner had in mind, Sir John clearly meant to use the occasion for purposes of interrogation.

"Just follow me, then, Lord Laningham. I know the way

quite well. Within these four walls I get along as one with two good eyes.''

So saying, he led the way confidently and without mishap. I trailed along behind both. Not a word passed between them until they—and I—were settled within the room in the rear to which he had referred. I had a moment to study Lord Laningham, and I noticed a peculiar darkness about his eyes. Had they been so when I saw him first at the Crown and Anchor? I had not noticed then.

As I pulled down a box of records at random and began shuffling through them, Sir John leaned forward across his desk, saying nothing, as he might if staring long and hard at another through the black silk band which covered his blind eyes; he had said to me more than once that silence was often a potent weapon in such situations as this. He upon whom Sir John had fixed his attention shifted uneasily in his chair, and after a long, uncomfortable moment, spoke up at last.

''Perhaps,'' said he, ''this is not the best moment to talk.''

''On the contrary,'' said Sir John, ''it is as good as any other and better than most. In about half an hour's time I must sit at my court. I trust what you have to say will not take so long.''

''Oh, no, not nearly so long.''

Sir John simply waited.

''I was shot at,'' began Lord Laningham.

Again, response was slow in coming. Then, finally: ''Describe the occasion.''

''Uh, yes, of course. I was sitting in my study at my desk yesterevening, putting my papers in order. The room is at the front of the house, just to the left as you come in the door. It was quite late, past midnight, and the servants had all retired for the night. Probably unwisely, I had left open the curtains and, with candles on the desk to light my work, I must have been quite visible from the street. Quite without warning—I heard no one about—a shot broke through the glass, passed but a foot away from where I sat, and buried itself in the wall.''

''And what did you do then?''

''Why, I threw myself down to the floor behind the desk, lest another shot follow the first.''

''Did one?''

''No. A moment afterward I heard someone scurrying away outside, and I thought it safe to crawl on the floor to a place where I might pull the curtains closed without being seen. The curtains are of thick stuff, and once closed, they made me quite invisible to the street outside. I thought it then safe for me to rise, and so I went out into the hall, where I gave out a 'Halloo,' hoping that the shot had roused one of the servants; yet I neither saw nor heard any about. And so I unlocked the door to the street and peered outside. I saw no one. Slowly then, and very watchfully, I ventured forth as far as the walkway. At the high end of the square I saw nothing, no one. Yet at the near end, I perceived a figure—not clearly, for there was a mist about—hurrying off toward Pall Mall. It was too far to give him chase, and of course I could not be absolutely certain that he was the one who shot through the window at me, and so I had no choice but to return to the house.''

(It should be said, reader, that as I listened to his tale, it seemed to me that it was told altogether too smoothly. He told it not so much as a man who had had a frightening experience as one who had written it down and memorized it. There were even accompanying gestures: he cupped a hand to his mouth for his ''Halloo''; he mimed his exit from the house, holding two pistols, a determined look upon his face. That I thought quite queer. The gestures were lost on Sir John, and he could not have meant them for me, for he gave me not a glance as I continued shuffling papers.)

''And then what?'' asked Sir John, rather severely.

''Why . . . why . . . I don't know,'' said he. ''Let me

think.'' Must he now truly consult his memory, or had he been suddenly forced to improvise?

"Did any of the servant staff present themselves upon your return?"

"What? No, no." He hesitated. "Well, as I recall, I returned to my study, drank two brandies, and went at last to my bed. I was, well, as you may imagine, quite . . . quite disturbed by what had happened."

"Of course." Only then did the magistrate alter his reserved, rather cold manner. As if to signal the change, he leaned back in his chair and rested his chin upon his palm in a rather casual manner. "Tell me, Lord Laningham, have you any idea who may have perpetrated this attack, and for what reason?"

"In a way I have, yes," said he, suddenly fluent once again. "When the late Lord Laningham welcomed me to London, he sat me down in that very same study and talked to me as his heir. He seemed to sense that he had not long to live, though not even he could have known that his death would be so near, so ghastly, and so tragically public."

Before he could continue, Sir John held up his hand to halt him. "If I may interrupt," said he, "when did this conversation take place?"

"When first we came to London."

"And when was that?"

"About—oh, when was it? I think, yes, about six months ago—no, not so long. At the end of August it was."

"Very well, continue please."

"Let me see, where was I?"

" ' . . . so near, so ghastly, and so tragically public,' " said Sir John, prompting him as one might a player in rehearsal.

"Ah yes. He was very generous to me at this meeting. In fact, he advanced me a sum of cash and presented me with a letter of recommendation to his bank. Then did he tell me that while I might look forward to bearing the Laningham title, with it came a burden of danger. He explained that earlier in the year he had received an unsigned letter, detailing wrongs that had been done the correspondent's family by the Laninghams over a period of two generations—lands seized, a business ruined, all of that. The letter concluded with a most appalling threat of revenge. The unknown correspondent swore that in repayment for these wrongs, he would eradicate the entire Laningham line. Well, the late lord knew nothing of these purported wrongs. He'd heard nothing of them from his father and had too high an opinion of him to believe there was substance to them. And so he refused to take them or the threat of revenge at all seriously. He destroyed the letter and said nothing of it to anyone.

"All this took place on the family's estate near Laningham in the summer or perhaps late spring. It was there he had received the letter. One day, however, he was out riding alone in the fields along the woods when a shot rang forth from some distance away. The ball passed close and bedded in a tree nearby, so that it set the horse to rearing and jumping about. It had come from a musket, yet he knew not whence. Being unarmed and not wishing to give him who had shot the time to reload, he turned back and rode home fast as he could. He never again rode out alone or unarmed. He then received another letter, which congratulated him on his good fortune in escaping the bullet which was meant for him, yet renewing the threat in a most explicit manner: 'I shall follow you wherever you go,' said the correspondent."

"And this letter, too, was destroyed?" Sir John interjected.

"Why, yes, my uncle said that he had no wish to frighten Lady Laningham."

"Perhaps he should have frightened her, since the fellow seems to have taken his revenge upon her, as well."

"You believe then that she was murdered? Poisoned?"

"With all my heart," said Sir John, with just the hint of a smile.

"Well, then," said the other, "you must also believe that my uncle was the victim of this anonymous letter writer."

"It would stand to reason, would it not?"

"Yes, of course—the similarity in the manner in which they died and all—of course it would. Yet I drank from the very bottle of wine from which he last drank. It was from his private stock and tasted no different from the others which we had drunk that night."

"That has been told me. No different, you say?"

"No," said Laningham with great certainty. "Could it perhaps have been that the food he ate that night was poisoned?"

"All things are possible."

"This is most—well, of course it is—it's most distressing."

"Yes, it should be, for it certainly means that you, too, are in danger. The shot through your window confirms that. Whenever you appear in the streets, you must fear the assassin's bullet. Each meal you eat will be suspect. You, perhaps your whole family, may fall victim to this revenger's design."

"What can I do?" he wailed.

"First of all, you must have a bodyguard of some sort. Many of our public men have such, ex-soldiers who are skilled with weapons to accompany them as they go out amongst the many. At the very least you should arm one of your servants, a footman perhaps, and have him trained for it. Let him go out and investigate should another shot be fired at night. As for an attempt upon your life by poisoning, well, a food taster perhaps, though that may be going a bit too far. I have talked with your cook. She seems altogether quite reliable, and I've no doubt she's been with the late lord and lady for many years. Inquire of the butler which of the servants has been on the staff for less than a year—and which of those traveled with the family to Laningham last spring when the first letter was received and the first attack made."

"Why, I shall hire a whole new staff," declared Lord Laningham.

"That might be unwise," said Sir John. "You have no way of knowing just who this secret plotter might be. You might unwittingly hire him."

"You're right, of course!"

"And do what you can to discover his identity. Do what your uncle failed to do. Examine the Laningham records. Perhaps some perceived injustice was indeed done in the past to some local family. Look for the recurrence of a name. Why should you suffer for the sins of a grandfather or a great-grandfather, eh?"

"Quite right, but . . . but all such documents are kept at the family estate."

"Then do so at your first trip there." Sir John paused long enough to give a great wise nod. "There, my lord, I have given you some practical steps to take in order to ensure your safety and that of your family. Take them, and you will feel much better, believe me. But now, if you will forgive me, I must prepare for my court session."

With that, Sir John rose to his feet, and Lord Laningham followed, though somewhat reluctantly—or so it seemed to me.

"I have but one further question for you," said the magistrate.

"Oh? And, uh, yes, well, what is that?"

"Why did you come to London?"

The simple and direct nature of the inquiry took the poor fellow completely off guard. After no end of hemming and hawing, he at last got it across that he had come at his uncle's invitation.

"Yet to bring your entire family for such a long stay. What was your purpose in that?"

"My daughters," said Lord Laningham, rather cryptically.

"I do not understand."

"They are both too young to be presented in society.

Felicity is but fourteen and Charity a year younger. Yet Pamela and I thought that they were of an age to be acquainted with . . . with the great world, as it were. They grew up rather simple country girls, I fear. We took them a number of times to Vauxhall Gardens before it closed for the season, and went often to the theater. We wanted them to see how proper ladies behave. Pamela has begun drilling them on matters of manners and courtesy.''

"All of this in anticipation of the title you have now inherited?''

''Uh, well, yes . . . yes indeed. It was as my uncle would have it. And . . .''

"And what?''

"We want the best for our daughters.''

"All parents do. But now, thank you, Lord Laningham, for reporting this dreadful attack. I shall have Mr. Bailey send one of our men round St. James Square after midnight for the foreseeable future. Beyond that, there is little I can do, except add to the advice I have already given that it would be wise to keep the curtains drawn after dark.''

"I had already thought of that. Yes, of course, that would be wise. But here, do accept this.''

Lord Laningham drew from his pocket something in the form of a letter. He placed it in Sir John's hand.

"What have you given me?'' Sir John asked it somewhat suspiciously.

"An invitation to a simple occasion at our residence. It will, or course, take place after my aunt's funeral, and in respect to it I have asked that the music be properly funereal.''

"Music? I do not understand.''

"You will. All is there in the invitation. I chose to deliver it myself that I might urge you to attend—and Lady Fielding, too, of course.''

"Well, I . . .''

"Just send a note of acceptance. And now, Sir John, with my thanks, I bid you good day.''

He turned and marched out the door, closing it tight behind him.

"Jeremy, come here and read to me this . . . this invitation."

I was already at his side. I took it from him and broke the seal. Opening it, I found the text so rich with flourishes and looping curves that it seemed at first quite illegible. Yet gradually it made itself plain to me.

"It's most artistically writ," said I, quite dubious.

"Well, do your best."

" 'To Sir John and Lady Fielding: Your attendance is humbly requested at the residence of Lord and Lady Laningham for dinner at eight and a musical entertainment to follow by Mr. John Christian Bach upon the fortepiano on Sunday evening next.' "

Sir John listened attentively, a smile growing wider upon his face. When I had done, he burst forth with a great bellow of laughter.

"Well, the fellow has nerve," said he. "I give him that. Quite an audacious move."

"What do you make of him, sir?"

"Oh, a great many things. I perceive, for one, a man so unsure of himself in ordinary discourse that he must write out the essentials of what he wishes to say and commit them to memory."

"Would you not say," I put it to him, "that this makes suspect what he has reported?"

"Not necessarily. He does certainly bumble about quite often when speaking impromptu, answering questions, and so on. He may have wished to organize well what he had to say—also to add a few decorous passages. As for the tale he told, such plots of revenge are possible and have been known, particularly in rural parts of the realm such as theirs. I'm sure there is a hole in the window of his study, yet I confess I would be more accepting of his information if he had been able to present those threatening letters his uncle had received. Let us say that I neither accept nor totally reject what he has told us.''

"He even acted it out with gestures as he told his story,'' said I.

"Did he?'' Sir John chuckled at that. "But tell me, Jeremy, was there anything more? Something I may have missed?''

"No . . . yet, perhaps one thing. I noticed a peculiar darkness about his eyes that I had not seen when I met him earlier.''

"Hmmm. What could have caused that? I wonder. Worry? Loss of sleep? Guilt? I shall give that some thought. Now, however, I must be off for my time on the bench.''

It was not until I had left him with Mr. Marsden that I realized I had said nothing to Sir John of the guest who had been installed in my bed. Then did I reflect that it might be just as well so. It had been Lady Fielding's decision to bring Clarissa in—though if consulted I would have agreed in it—and so it should probably be she who informed him of the girl's presence. Well enough, then.

The charcoal brazier stood by the door to Bow Street. It was there the Runners warmed their hands when they came in at night. That was when it would be missed, so it would be better taken in the daytime. It was naught but a large, round, and heavy iron pan—not flat, of course, but higher by a few inches at the circumference than at the center. It was then empty of coals, live or dead—Mr. Fuller must have taken care of that—and so was ready to be taken up the steps, carried by the handles that were attached on either side. It all could have been accomplished so easily but for the fact that just as I was making for the stairway, Mr. Fuller stepped out from his space, leading three prisoners to the courtroom, only one of whom was in hand irons. He looked at me curiously, and then a great frown knitted his features, making ugly a face that was none too handsome.

"Here, you, Jeremy, where you goin' with that?"

"Up to the sick girl. Mr. Donnelly said she was to be kept warm, and there's no fireplace in that room."

"Well, I s'pose it's all right if the doctor said so. You should ask, though."

"You're right, Mr. Fuller. I'm sorry."

Then up to the kitchen, where I shoveled some hot coals out of the fireplace and into the brazier and replaced them with fresh. I banked the fire so that it should burn well the rest of the day and provide hot coals at night when they would be needed. Then I struggled up the stairs with the brazier, now heavier than before.

Annie was there, sitting by the bed where the patient lay asleep. She put a finger to her lips to quiet me, but it was no easy matter being quiet with such a load. On a stool near the window I placed the brazier as noiselessly as possible. Still, there was a dull clang. No matter. Clarissa slept on. Then I opened the window just a bit. Of a sudden, Annie was beside me.

"Why do you open the window?" she scolded in a whisper. "She'll have a draft. 'Twill make her worse."

"The smoke must have someplace to go," said I, most confident. "If it don't, she'll choke in it."

Then did I point to how the smoke from the brazier, rising, was sucked out the window through the crack I'd made. She nodded, mollified, then gathered up her books.

"The girl is breathing better—what's her name? I've forgotten."

"Clarissa."

"Well, I must be off to Mr. Tolliver in the Garden to get some meat and a good bone for her broth, and some mutton for our dinner."

"I'm sorry, I had no time to—"

"I know that," she interrupted. Then: "Stay with her, will you? Lady Fielding's left for Magdalene. If the girl wakes, 'twould be best to have someone near." Annie nodded toward the bed. "She seems a good sort. Talked a little."

"Go on," said I. "Do what needs be done."

"I'll not be long," said she, "but then I must make the broth, and that takes a while."

With that and a wave, she went quietly from the room.

I settled down in the chair beside the bed and studied the patient. In truth, her condition did seem to have improved somewhat. Her breathing was a bit deeper and less labored. Though hardly rose-cheeked, she was no longer the same deathly white she had been when I carried her from the room in Half-Moon Passage. She neither sweated nor shivered. Yes, all that taken together meant a definite improvement.

I wondered if the brazier would truly warm the room. Perhaps Annie had been right. Perhaps the little I had opened the window would do the patient more harm than good. I turned and inspected window and brazier. Yes, the smoke was flowing outward just as I said it would. Then did I realize the door to the room stood open. I could not hope to warm the place with heat escaping down the stairs and out into the house. I rose quietly and tiptoed to the door and pulled it shut most silently. Yet when I returned to my chair, I found Clarissa's eyes open and fixed upon me.

"You . . . did not wake me," said she, quite reading my thoughts.

"How do you feel?"

"Better . . . I . . ."

And then she fell to coughing. She struggled up in bed, and I assisted her, thinking perhaps she knew best. She grasped at the rag I had brought and put it to her mouth just in time to deposit in it a great wad of phlegm. Panting from the exertion, she pointed to the drinking cup. I filled it and raised it to her lips. Though she did not drink as much as I had expected, she seemed to want greatly what she took. Then did she lie back down again, and breath by breath, settled into a more even rate of respiration. Though she smiled at me and seemed to wish conversation, I thought it best that she not speak. And so I launched into a monologue of a sort which, I hoped, would answer all her questions.

"You are with us at Number Four Bow Street," said I, in a manner merrier than I truly felt, for I thought to cheer her. "The handsome woman who brought you here you met before, of course. She is Lady Katherine Fielding, wife to Sir John Fielding, who is the Magistrate of the Bow Street Court, over which he presides on the ground floor. The young lady who attended you before me is Annie Oakum, who is the best cook in all London, as you will discover when you are able to eat proper meals. Though not just yet, for the doctor who attended you—the capable Irish fellow who is certainly the best physician in all London—he has condemned you to a diet of clear broth for the time being. And, ah yes, his name is Gabriel Donnelly. Me, of course, you know already from our pleasant conversations at your lodgings in Half-Moon Passage. Now this"—I waved a hand around me—"is my room. You are my guest here. You will note please your luxurious surroundings—the bed with which you have become so well acquainted, the chair, the stool. What more could one want? A bit small, I admit, and a bit cold in winter, yet you as my guest now enjoy the warmth of a charcoal brazier which I stole from below." I looked about me. "Have I missed anything? I think not."

"Books," said she in her weak voice.

"Ah yes, the books. I have a few, or perhaps quite a few, for many were left here in this room by Sir John's late brother, Henry, who was himself Magistrate of the Bow Street Court but is far better known as an author."

Then did an idea creep into my head. I knew that I could not keep up this foolish palaver indefinitely. Yet it was apparent from the way her eyes had brightened during it that she wished me in some way to continue. Perhaps . . .

"Miss Pooh," said I to her, "would you like me to read to you?"

She nodded her head in an emphatic affirmative.

Now, of course, the question was what I might read to the young patient. I passed my eye along my two shelves of books, pondering that question. Not all books are suitable to be read aloud. If I were to take down a volume of that in which I took the greatest pride, *Institutes of the Law of England,* I should probably bore the poor girl quite to death. No, give her something she could like. She was a reader of romances, so why not read to her the greatest romances? Feeling sure of my choice, I pulled down the first volume of *Tom Jones,* returned to the chair, and opened it beyond the dedication and introduction to Chapter Two, where the story does properly begin. It was there that I began reading.

" 'In that part of the western division of this kingdom which is commonly called Somersetshire, there lately lived, and perhaps lives still, a gentleman whose name was Allworthy . . .' "

So I continued to read through Book One and well beyond—near to the end of Book Two. Over an hour I read and much nearer two—perhaps more. The patient responded well to the treatment; most attentive she was. It was only I who, for some reason, failed in the end to respond to Squire Allworthy, Miss Bridget, Blifil, and the rest quite in the same way that I had at my first acquaintance with them. For I blush to admit it, reader, but eventually, as the room grew warmer and somewhat darker, my eyes blinked and drooped, and at last I fell asleep over the open book.

I was wakened, I suppose, by the sound of the door opening. Or was it the light of the candles shining in my eyes? In any case, I was wakened sudden by the entrance of Lady Fielding and Mr. Donnelly. She bore a three-candle holder;

but for the light they provided, my little room had gone completely dark.

"Jeremy! We were told you were reading to her," said Lady Fielding.

"I . . . I was. I must have fallen asleep."

"But look at the poor child. She's feverish again. Just see how she perspires! Oh, why could you not have kept a sharper watch over her?"

"Lady Fielding," said Mr. Donnelly, "there is naught he could have done to prevent it. And strange though it may seem, sweating is a hopeful sign. Though it is, of course, an indication that her body temperature rises, it may also be a sign that her illness approaches its crisis."

"Crisis? I do not understand."

"Simply put, she must get worse before she can get better."

"Ah, I see—or at least I think I do."

Clarissa did indeed seem worse—whether suddenly so, I could not say, for I had no way of knowing how long I had been asleep. My last memory of her, as my eyes blinked and I apologized for losing my place, was of a girl with a slight smile upon her face, one who, just as I, was finding it difficult to remain awake. Yet now indeed she sweated. The hair about her forehead was damp; beads of moisture stood out upon her brow; even her upper lip seemed wet.

"I will say, Jeremy, you've got the room good and warm," said Mr. Donnelly. "Go down now and prepare another quinine tea for her."

"Oh," said I, jumping to my feet, suddenly stricken, "but I can't."

"Can't? Why not?"

"I've not yet been to the chemist."

"Well, then, you must fly, for he'll not be open much longer. Go to the shop on Drury Lane near my surgery— just three doors down. Have you still that slip I gave you?"

"I have it in my pocket."

"Then go swiftly."

Go swiftly? Reader, I ran the distance, dodging and bumping through the streets crowded with those returning from their daily work. I knew the shop well, for I had passed it many times. And as Mr. Donnelly had warned, as I entered, the chemist did indeed seem to be preparing to close for the night. I presented the slip given me by the medico. The chemist nodded wisely, stroked his chin, and retired to the rear to search out the substance. He returned with a goodly quantity of the stuff in a vial. Quinine costed dear. It took near all the shillings and pence I had in my pocket to make the purchase.

"That's fivepence for the vial," said the chemist, as if to account for the price. "You bring that back, and I'll refund you the cost of it."

He corked the vial and handed it over. As I left the shop he waved me a goodbye, then followed me to the door to lock up. Indeed I had arrived just in time.

I saw no need to run back to Bow Street, though I did set a fast walking pace for my return. I had not gone far before I became aware of one beside me, matching me step for step. Was this some ruffian about to pounce on me? I tensed, making ready. He would be sorry if he did. I stole a glance at him and received a proper surprise.

"What was it you bought at the chemist?" asked Thomas Roundtree.

It took me a moment to recover my wits. At last I blurted, "Quinine."

"Quinine's for the ague. Has she got the ague?"

"No, since you ask, pneumonia is the problem."

His face darkened, yet he continued to keep pace with me. I considered running from him—but to what purpose?

"She's goin' to get well, ain't she? I know some died of it."

"We're tying to make her well. That's why we took her away."

"You took a lot on yourself doin' that. First I thought it

was just some trick of that blind judge to bring me in, but I got to admit the child is terrible sick.''

"Yes, she is," I agreed.

"She's all I got," he said. "I done things I never thought I'd do so her and me could be together. She's bright, just like her mother." Then he repeated: "She's all I got. I must have her back in five days. Some way or other, I'll get her in five days. That's when . . . well, never you mind about that."

"That's when your ship sails?"

"She tell you that?"

"No, I guessed it. Where else can you go but the colonies?"

"Five days," he said.

Then did he turn from me as I started up New Broad Court, which led to Bow Street. He said no farewell but simply walked on, shoulders high against the chill evening air. I stood at the corner and watched him shamble on. His clothes fit loosely upon him. Tall and thin, he looked for all the world like some poor scarecrow that had achieved the power of locomotion.

But yes, he had been wearing the same Scotch plaid waistcoat he had worn earlier, the same one Mr. Burnham had described. I saw it plain.

NINE

In Which the Patient's
Condition Improves, Though
Her Father's Does Not

It must have been well past midnight when Annie stole into the kitchen to waken me. I must have been but half asleep, for I was aware of her stealthy steps past the master's bedroom and down the last flight of stairs. He who sleeps cold sleeps light, and by the time Annie came for me, the fire before which I slept had dwindled to rosy coals, and the blankets provided by Lady Fielding scarce did to keep me warm. She found me rising and ready to spell her at Clarissa's bedside.

"Did you sleep?" she asked.

"A bit," said I.

"It's a wonder," said she. "It's gone so cold in here. Ain't getting any warmer up to the top of the stairs, either."

"I'll bring the last of the coals up with me."

"Stick a candle or two in your pocket, as well. There's only a nub burning up there now."

Annie provided a pan with which I might carry the coals collected from the fireplace. I proceeded most carefully up the stairs. It would not do to trip and scatter live coals about. Through the gloves I wore, I felt the warmth of the pan in my hands; I should not like to be forced to pick up coals even with gloved fingers. Yet thankfully, I reached the sickroom without incident.

I first fed the brazier from the pan, then lit the candle I had brought from the one which now seemed about to gutter out. Then and only then did I sit down in the chair at bedside and give my attention to the patient.

If anything, Clarissa's condition seemed to have worsened since last I looked upon her. That would have been when I brought the quinine tea to her. She had by then taken some of the broth Annie had made for her, and it may have strengthened her a bit, if only temporarily. I left before seeing the result of this second dose of quinine. From the look of her at this moment, it would seem that it had not had the desired effect upon her. She lay pale and sweating as before. The only change in her treatment suggested by Mr. Donnelly was the addition of cold, wet compresses to her feverish brow. I reached into the pan of water at her bedside—quite cold the water was—extracted the cloth, and wrung it out. With it I bathed her face and neck, and laid it flat across her forehead. That, it would seem, was all that I could do for her at the moment. Yet it was right that we should watch over her, Mr. Donnelly had said, for if she were taken with a coughing fit, she might need to be put upright in a sitting position to rid herself of phlegm; there was always the danger that she might choke upon it. We were also to watch for any unnatural change of color: a sudden blush of red was cause for concern; if she were to take on a purple hue, then I, Jeremy, was to be sent at once to rout him out of bed. But barring such events, she was simply to be kept warm and comfortable and allowed to sweat, that her body might fight the infection.

And so here I was at her bedside again. Lady Fielding had taken her turn after accounting for Clarissa's presence in our home to Sir John. He had taken it neither well nor ill, yet repeated his intention to send her back to Lichfield when she was well enough to travel; they may have talked more of it, though not in my presence. After dinner, Annie had taken over the sickbed watch, and at midnight, or probably a bit after, I had relieved her.

As I gazed down upon the girl, I recalled that curious brief meeting with her father some hours before. How different it had been from the first walk we had taken together. The man I saw last evening seemed haunted, desperate— and quite naturally so, for his daughter was deathly ill. And how was it that he had put it? "She's all I got," he had said, and of course it was true. Yet I found it difficult to imagine their relationship. How could she love him so? Why did she? He, a reprobate and a drunkard, one so neglectful of her that she had been taken from his care by the parish. What did she find to love in such a one? Except . . . and then was a truth revealed to me—*except* if she was all he had, then he was, in the same way, all *she* had. Putting myself in her place, remembering my own dear father, even had he Thomas Roundtree's faults, would I not then have loved him still?

Such thoughts as these made far more difficult and urgent the problem that the presence of Roundtree posed to me. He was, I was certain, the third man at the pawnshop. Not that his waistcoat alone proved it—but no, there was Mr. Burnham's description, as well, which matched Roundtree perfectly. There was also his refusal to surrender to Sir John even under the generous terms offered him by Lady Fielding; if he was involved in the murder of George Bradbury, the last thing he would wish would be to find himself at a magistrate's mercy—there might be questions, matters to be accounted for. In short, he had a guilty conscience. What was it he had said? "I done things I never thought I'd do . . ." Murder certainly might be one of them, for he had evidently been guilty of no more than theft before. Yet I had liked the man when first I met him, and pitied him when last I saw him. Was it possible to feel thus about one who might have been involved in murder? Yet such feelings stretched only so far. I had not been moved, had not even considered warning him away from his evil companions at the pawnshop. That surely told me where my true loyalties might lie.

They were with Sir John, of course—and with the law. Then why had I, until now, withheld from him my suspicions—certain though I might be, they were no more than that—regarding Thomas Roundtree? Why, of course it was because I liked and pitied the man; and even more, because I liked and pitied his child, the girl who now lay in the bed before me. I wished them well. In part, I hoped they might make their escape to the colonies, and I, like Lady Fielding, had no desire to see her sent back to Lichfield's parish poorhouse. And so I knew all too well that when I told Sir John what I suspected of Thomas Roundtree, I would surely feel a sense of having betrayed the two of them—yet tell him I must.

Thus did the night pass uneventful, but for two coughing fits which produced a great quantity of phlegm. I raised her, as I had been instructed, to help her expel the mess that bubbled up from her chest, but I cannot say that on either occasion did she regain consciousness. Once done, she simply sank back upon the pillow and gave herself fully to the battle against the sickness within her. I bathed her face and neck often and applied the damp cloth to her brow. For the most part, I watched and waited.

The room remained reasonably warm. On a couple of occasions, I rose and poked about the coals and added a few fresh from a box I had earlier brought. Having dozed off once previously, I was determined to keep awake during the entire length of my stay at her bedside. Yet it did indeed become difficult. At least earlier I had the words printed upon the page on which to concentrate, and ultimately they failed to keep sleep away. I feared that if I were to read to myself by candlelight I might soon begin nodding off as I had before when reading aloud. So now had I but my will to sustain me, and indeed my will performed wonders. Yet eventually I found I must walk about the room, rub my face, dig at my eyes, even pinch myself. Then, later, looking out the window, I saw the first faint glimmer of light in the orient. Deciding I had successfully endured the night through, I allowed myself to relax a bit. I sat down in the chair next the bed—and promptly fell asleep.

It could not have been for long, however, for as my eyes fluttered open, I perceived that there was not much more light in the room than there had been when they had fallen shut. Still, there was movement in the bed. Taking a moment to focus my exhausted eyes, rubbing them, looking again, I saw that Clarissa Roundtree sat up in bed, not coughing, or sweating, or talking in some hesitant, delirious manner. No, none of these.

In fact, she was smiling.

"I'm very much better," said she to me.

The word spread throughout the house. At Clarissa's assurance that she might spare my attention for a moment or two, I rushed downstairs to set the fire in the kitchen and start it. There I met Annie, who, without much skill, was attempting it herself. As I set things right in the fireplace, I told her, quite excited, of the patient's sudden improvement.

"Her color is better," said I. "Her forehead and cheeks were as cool to the touch as yours or mine would be. She has no fever."

"But it may come back," objected Annie, quite reasonably.

"Yet it may not," said I, "for Mr. Donnelly said she must get worse before she could get better. She has passed her crisis."

"I must tell Lady Fielding."

And up she went to knock on the door of the master's bedroom, leaving me striking flint against metal, blowing on the sparks to start a smoldering. By the time I had returned to the room at the top of the stairs, Lady Fielding was there, dressed in her nightgown and wrapper, fussing nicely over the girl. She looked up and smiled at me.

"It was just as Mr. Donnelly said it would be," said she.

"Why, of course," said I. "Is he not the best doctor in all London?"

And at that both of us did laugh most heartily, as if I had just told the grandest joke ever.

Indeed it was not long afterward that Clarissa was visited by the best doctor in all London himself. He arrived just as we were finishing a good breakfast of bread and bacon. He listened, quite pleased, at our tale of his patient's turn for the better, though he declined credit for himself.

"In cases such as these," said Mr. Donnelly, "the body heals itself. It is the physician's task to allow it to happen, merely."

Lady Fielding accompanied him to the sickroom. As the table was cleared and Sir John accepted a second cup of morning tea, he asked Annie rather pointedly if she did not suppose that he was somewhat in need of a good, close shave. Taking the hint, I went to fetch razor, strop, and soap while Annie put the kettle on the fire. It was just coming to a boil when doctor and nurse returned, smiling, to our company.

"It's as you said," Mr. Donnelly declared. "The fever is gone. There is some hint of color returned to her cheeks. She does, however, still have a good deal of congestion in her chest that she must be rid of ere we pronounce her well. Is that her broth there steaming on the table, Miss Annie?"

"It is, sir."

"Well, you might also bring her some bread with it. She's quite hungry, she says. I daresay she hasn't eaten a proper meal in some time. If she can take the bread, then give her a bit more with broth in the early afternoon. I'll come by in the early evening to look at her again. She may even be able to take some meat into her at dinner. We'll see about that then."

"And what about the quinine tea, sir?" I asked.

"Continue that, morning and evening. If her fever returns, give her an extra dose. I do not, by the bye, think it will return."

That said, he pulled on his Navy greatcoat and made ready to go, adding only that we were to keep a check on her and continue to keep the room warm. "It should not be necessary to keep a constant vigil over her."

And so saying, he left with a polite goodbye to all. Then, as I prepared Sir John for shaving, wetting a towel in hot water and applying it to his face, the women departed as well—Annie to deliver the breakfast tray to the patient above, and Lady Fielding to prepare for her day at the Magdalene Home for Penitent Prostitutes. Thus were Sir John and I left alone. I lathered him well and stropped his new razor, wondering if now might not be a good time to broach to him the matter of Thomas Roundtree. How might I manage it? Then did Sir John himself provide me with an opportunity of sorts.

"Jeremy," said he, "tell me what you think of this business."

"Sir?" said I, not quite sure what was meant.

"Oh, this girl who now occupies your bed—the fugitive's daughter, who is herself a fugitive. What think you of this whole nasty matter?"

"I think a great many things of it, sir," said I, pulling the razor across his cheek with a first swift stroke. "I think her quick and bright, and she has a winning way about her. I believe that had we left her where she was, sick as she was, she would have perished by now. Perhaps you might go up and visit her, make her acquaintance, and you could judge for yourself."

He waved the razor away from his face. "Did Kate tell you to say that?" he asked, rather crossly.

"Why, no sir."

"Well, she has said but little else since the girl arrived here. 'If you would but meet her, Jack, you would know what a fine girl she is,' says Kate to me—at least a dozen times. You spoke of her winning way. Well, she has certainly won my dear wife to her cause. Nevertheless, I see little else to do but send her—what is her name?''

''Clarissa.''

''Ah, yes, rather pretentious, bookish sort of name. Indeed, I see naught to do but send Miss Clarissa Roundtree back to Lichfield—when she is well enough to take such a journey, of course.''

''Of course.'' I hesitated, the razor poised. ''There is a complication to the matter, however—or there may be one—regarding her father.''

''Oh? And what is that?''

And then did I tell Sir John all as I shaved him; he, listening closely, giving no sign to interrupt or cut me off. I told him of the detail of the Scotch plaid waistcoat that Mr. Burnham had mentioned in his description of him he had met at the pawnshop, and how I remembered Roundtree had worn one such on the morning he escaped from me. And further, I told him of my strange meeting with the fugitive the night before, and that he was once again wearing a plaid waistcoat. I told him, as exactly as I could, just what was said between us. Sir John heard me out. By the time I had finished, I had shaved him clean without a nick or a scratch.

He rubbed his face carefully, then nodded in appreciation of my work. ''Of course,'' said he, ''there is more than one Scotch plaid waistcoat in the city of London.''

''Of course,'' said I, ''yet the other details of Mr. Burnham's description fitted Roundtree well.''

''Yet these are only suspicions.''

''Only suspicions,'' I agreed.

He remained silent for near a minute. Then: ''I have a question for you, Jeremy. Kate has said how much this girl loves her father, how tenaciously she defends him. Let us say that your suspicions of him prove out, and let us also say that our worst fears are also realized and George Bradbury has been murdered. Given all that, would you say it was likely that this child, Clarissa, would know anything of it?''

It was a question I had not considered, yet it was one to which I responded confidently and without hesitation.

''I would say, Sir John, that there is not the slightest possibility of it.''

''Hmmm,'' said he, as he often did, and scratched his head in thought. He rose from his chair then. ''I believe I shall take your advice, lad.''

That puzzled me somewhat. ''And what advice was that?''

''I believe I shall go upstairs and make the acquaintance of this Roundtree girl.''

He proceeded in a most deliberate way to the stairway, and in another moment was lost from my sight.

Sir John remained with her far longer than I expected. Annie returned with Clarissa's breakfast tray, dressed for her daily trip to Mr. Burnham's reading class. As she pulled on her cape and tied it, she asked me to find a book for her.

''A book?'' said I. ''Which book?''

''Any book, so long as it's not too long and not too hard. I'm past the point where I can learn anything from the primer, and much as I like to *see* Shakespeare, readin' him is quite another matter. Quite difficult he is.''

''I'll see what I can find for you.''

''Do that,'' said she. ''It fair puts me out of sorts to see one young as her upstairs readin' with such ease. I've naught against her, mind. It's just it hurts me to think how long I waited to learn what every child knows.''

''Not every child, Annie—far from it. You're doing well. Mr. Burnham himself says so.''

''Well, I'll feel better when I've read me a whole book— one like that *Tom Jones* she's readin', one with a good story.''

''I'll find something.''

Reassured, she bade me goodbye, jammed on her hat, and left.

Next came Lady Fielding. She tiptoed in, quite surprising me, as I did the washing-up (her usual manner being to move about the house in a great flurry and dash).

Moving up close to me, she whispered, "He's with her now."

"Pardon, m'lady?"

"Jack—Sir John—he's with Clarissa. I kept telling him if he but met the girl, he would understand what an exceptional child she is. Who would have guessed that he would finally pay some attention to what I told him? He so seldom does."

"Oh, not so," said I. "He values your counsel in all things."

"Do you think so, Jeremy?" said she, brightening a bit. "Oh, but he can be so stubborn. Yet, to be sure, he is as good a husband as a woman could want and much better than I deserve." She sighed, and before I could contradict her in some flattering manner, plunged on: "Be that as may be, I must now leave for the Magdalene Home. I shall try to get away from there a bit earlier than is my usual. I know I always say that, but this time perhaps I shall. Farewell, Jeremy. You heard what Mr. Donnelly said—check in on her from time to time and keep her room warm. Oh, and Jeremy, please do get to those begging letters of mine. Do as many as you can today, will you?"

Then did she grab up her cape and, assuring me she could find a hackney for herself, left the room in a much noisier manner than she had entered it.

At last, near half an hour after he had climbed the stairs, Sir John returned. I looked at him as he entered the kitchen, wondering if it would be proper to ask his opinion of Clarissa Roundtree. As it happened, there was no need to put the question to him.

"A charming young girl," said he to me, "a singular mixture of intelligence and wit, optimism and bitter experience. And for your information, Jeremy, I'm inclined to agree with your judgment: if her father is involved in something truly villainous, then she knows nothing of it. Either that, or she is a far greater actor than Garrick himself. True, she loves her father, though he may not be worthy of it—but that is no crime in a child, a virtue rather."

"May I ask, sir, what did you talk of that long while?"

"You may. We spoke of a number of things—my brother, Henry, for one. It seems that you began reading *Tom Jones* to her, and she has picked up where you left off. It may prove a bit risky for her—though perhaps not, judging from her experience. She wanted to hear all about Henry—what sort of man he was, what else he had written, all of that. We talked also of her experiences in the parish workhouse."

"You made it plain, then, that you had learned of her escape?"

"I suppose I did. I asked, and she answered. She has a quick mind. She would have perceived that if I knew she had been an inmate of the workhouse, then I also knew that she had escaped from it—with the help of her father."

"And what," I asked, "were her experiences in the workhouse?"

"Hmmm, well, they were sufficiently grim that I am prompted to reconsider my decision to send her back. *Reconsider,* that is—not yet have I changed my mind about it."

"I'm sure you will decide what is right, sir."

"Then you are sure of more than I am." With a great sigh, he did then turn away and start for the door. "I must get on with my day," said he. "She should not need as much looking after as earlier, though I must say you have all given her good care. I'll send for you if I need you, Jeremy."

He did not have need of me that whole day long. That meant that I was condemned to hours of copying out Lady

Fielding's begging letter to this lord and that earl, and to several duchesses, as well. I made intermittent visits to Clarissa, and each time found her better than when I had looked in on her last. Annie came and prepared the afternoon meal of broth and bread that Mr. Donnelly had ordered for her; I gave to her a copy of the book I had chosen for her from my store above, *The Governess*, by Sarah Fielding, the last sister of Henry and half sister to Sir John. She took it gratefully and seemed specially pleased that it was a work by a woman in the Fielding family. And then it was back to the tedious task of copying. Mr. Donnelly looked in on his patient before dinner and was well pleased by her continued recovery; he prescribed meat once a day for her, yet directed that quinine should be continued in a tea twice a day until the supply be exhausted. At day's end, all I had to show for my labor was twenty-one letters addressed to more or less distinguished personages waiting to be signed by Lady Fielding. I took greater care with the fire that night and slept the better for it.

The next two days looked to be quite as dull as that which preceded them. Yet they were not. There came first an incident which would have later consequences of a positive nature. Let us say that it began in the morning with a visit from Clarissa Roundtree. I was engaged once again in my dull work with pen and ink at the kitchen table. I had, I believe, managed to copy out only four letters when I heard a curious clopping upon the stairs. I frowned at that, for it could only mean that Clarissa was up and about; she and I were alone there in the upper floors. Fixing my face in an expression of stern reproach, I rose to meet her.

At her appearance—her cape tied over a wool nightgown donated her by Annie, shuffling along in a pair of my old shoes—I growled quite gruffly at her.

"You ought not to be out of bed," said I. "Go back upstairs."

"Oh, pooh," said she, "I am well enough to sit. I sit upstairs in that chair by the bed and read. I may as well be down here and have a bit of company. I'm quite starved for conversation.''

"Nevertheless, the doctor—''

"Mr. Donnelly said I could sit. Where I do that should be my choice. Besides, it's warmer here by the kitchen fire. That should aid my recovery, don't you think?''

"Well . . . I'll bring some coals up to replenish the brazier.''

"Oh, later. Right now, why not make a pot of tea? That, too, would aid my recovery, I'm sure. I'm starved for a cup of tea.''

"I thought you were starved for conversation.''

"All right, then, I *starve* for conversation, I *thirst* for tea.''

No doubt it was a bit warmer in the kitchen than it was up above. No doubt, too, she was a bit lonely with only Tom Jones and company to keep her amused. I could understand her wish for a cup of tea. In fact, I wanted one myself.

"Fair enough," said I, "we'll share a pot of tea, then up you go to bed.''

"Fair enough indeed,'' said she, and gave me the first proper smile I had got from her since she arrived in the kitchen.

She took a seat at the table, and I filled the kettle and put it on the fire. I got down the tea and fed the pot generously. There would be enough for second cups for both of us. Perhaps I, too, was hungry for company.

As we waited for the pot to boil, she inquired what I was doing there at the table, and I explained in some detail, showing her Lady Fielding's model letter and the copies I had made from it. Then, with the tea brewing, she did ask me to tell her more about what Lady Fielding referred to in her letter simply as the Magdalene Home. At that I hemmed and hawed, unable quite to describe who it was gained from this benefaction without being trapped into a discussion of prostitution, which I thought not a proper matter for conversation with one so young as she. I must have dropped a hint or two, however, for as I poured the tea, she looked at me first with a frown, and then a light of sudden understanding came into her eyes.

"Oh," said she, "you mean it's a place for whores who wish to go off the game, do you?"

"Well . . . uh, yes I do. They're taught trades and found work—decent work."

"That's indeed a worthy cause," said she, with a firm nod of approval. "I've known some whores and some of them quite all right, Bessie down the hall for one. But they were all ignorant women who could do naught else to support themselves." Her face darkened once again with a frown. "I think it's a terrible thing how women are kept down, given no education—don't you? Don't you truly think so?"

"Why, yes, yes I do," said I, in all honesty.

"If it had not been for my mother teaching me to read and write, I should be as incapable as the rest. She gave me my vocation. I did tell you, did I not, that I shall be an author?"

"Yes, you did mention—"

"Of romances principally, but I shall also write poetry of the sort that—"

Then she herself was interrupted—by a knock upon the door. I leapt to my feet to answer. She responded with a look of startled caution; it seemed she had come to distrust sudden knocks upon the door.

Mr. Fuller was there. He had come to inform me that Sir John wished me to go off to the post office to pick up a letter that had just come in. Taking no notice of our little tea party, he simply turned, having delivered his message, and marched back down the stairs.

I looked back to Clarissa and saw anxiety, even perhaps dread, writ plain upon her face.

"Would that be a letter from Lichfield?" she asked.

"No, I think not," said I, hoping to relieve her somewhat. "Sir John is expecting a letter from other parts." And that, of course, was no lie.

I ran off to fetch my hat and muffler. Returning, I found her changed—sipping her tea, affecting a most casual manner. She glanced up at me and smiled rather loftily, as one might at a departing servant.

"I must go," said I.

"Well, then, goodbye," said she.

"You must return now to the room above."

"Oh, pooh, do let me at least finish my cup of tea. It's rather good. Few men can brew tea—none in my experience."

I sighed. "Well . . . all right, but once done you must go upstairs."

"Once done, I shall."

Reluctantly, I left. It seemed to me as I trudged out into Bow Street and turned directly toward the post letter office that the missive that awaited me there was almost certainly one from the Warwick magistrate; Sir John had expected its arrival this day. Had Clarissa Roundtree known its particular nature and its importance in the matter of her father, she might well have wished it were a letter from Lichfield. While hurrying along, I wondered again at the strange concatenation of circumstances which had brought Thomas Roundtree to us, and with him his daughter. More than that, I wondered at their fate.

The letter was indeed the one expected by Sir John. Once I had it in my pocket, I hurried even faster back to Bow Street. I near burst with curiosity as to its contents. It occurred to me that it would suit me well if the Warwick magistrate reported that George Bradbury was there still, attending his ailing father. I rued the day that Bunkins had brought me to St. Andrew's Churchyard; I regretted taking him to Mr. Donnelly's surgery for a second look at that repulsive head floating in the jar of alcohol. All in all, I should easily have believed that this was all a great mistake—Bunkins had never claimed to have made an absolutely certain identification—were it not for the involvement of Jackie Carver. That one was a killer; I knew it well, for he would certainly have killed me some weeks past.

And so I came to Number 4 Bow Street, where I saw a small crowd filing out the door; many of their faces were familiar to me—layabouts and idle women of the streets who received their midday's entertainment at Sir John's court. Their exit told me that the day's session was done. Waiting impatiently until the crowd had dispersed, I entered, taking the inner door to the right which led down the long hall, past the strong room where prisoners were held, and beyond Mr. Marsden's place of business with its imposing files and high scrivener's writing table, directly to Sir John's private domain. His door stood half open; he was at the moment just seating himself at his desk. I knocked before I entered.

"Jeremy, is it?" He often amazed me with his preternatural feats of sightless recognition.

"Yes, Sir John, and I have the letter from Warwick with me."

"Come in, lad. Open it by all means and read it to me."

I needed no further encouragement. I strode into his chambers, broke the seal on the letter, and not even bothering to seat myself, began reading.

" 'To Sir John Fielding, Magistrate, Bow Street Court, Cities of London and Westminster. Dear Sir,' " I read.

" 'In response to your query as to the presence of George Bradbury in our city, I have made inquiries, the results of which I now put before you. He came here three weeks past when his father, William Bradbury, a man of some eighty years, still lingered at death's door. Indeed he did not linger long, for the day following his son's arrival he died. Old Mr. Bradbury, a man much liked and well honored here, was buried the next day with little ceremony. There was some general resentment at this haste, for it deprived many who would have liked the opportunity of paying last respects and attending the funeral. Nevertheless, George Bradbury, the only surviving member of the family, prevailed: the father was buried; the will was read; the son inherited all. The fortune that was passed on to him consisted for the most part of property—house and surrounding lands, fields which brought in good rents, et cetera. He posted notices all about the shire and auctioned off everything—with one exception. House, furniture, his father's personal effects, lands, and fields were put on the block and sold. George Bradbury wanted only cash. The single exception to which I referred was his father's horse, a mare big as any stallion, and white as snow. She would have brought a pretty price, yet the son wished to ride her back to London in triumph. He left as soon as his business here in Warwick was completed two weeks ago, perhaps more accurately ten to twelve days ago. He had no friends here to bid farewell, so the exact day of his departure is difficult to fix.

" 'You may have perceived from what I have written thus far that George Bradbury was no great favorite hereabouts. Indeed he was not. Before he left for London a score of years past, or near that, he had been party to a number of questionable business matters, and in fact had appeared before me twice. On one of these occasions I fixed a fine on him of ten guineas, which his father paid. It was shortly afterward that the son left for London with a goodly amount settled upon him by his father in order to start a business there. I, for one, did breathe a sigh of relief to be rid of him.

" 'I know not the specific reason for your inquiry, sir, though good sense prompts that he is late in his return to London. Frankly, if that is the case, then I am not surprised. When I heard of his plan to return alone on horseback, I warned him against it. Though it is no great distance from here to your great city, the roads between are known to be infested by highwaymen. The horse he would ride alone would have been considered a prize to such as them. He dismissed my caution and said he intended to go well armed. Yet these highway robbers have their tricks. He may have been caught in some ambuscade and now lies in some shallow grave in a wood between here and there. He carried a great bag of money with him—sovereigns, guineas, and shillings—the proceeds of the auction. If a highwayman got it, he might well retire as a country squire in some distant corner of the realm. That would then be the last we would know of the matter. I understand Mr. Bradbury had a wife. (You see? I already speak of him in the past tense.) He boasted of her youth, her beauty, and her wit in business. Do not hold out to her much hope that her husband lives. Perhaps she will not grieve overmuch for him. I know I shall not.

" 'If you require more than this, let me know, and I shall provide what I can, for I remain your humble and obedient servant, Matthew Tiverton, Magistrate, City of Warwick.' "

"Well, what do you think of that, Jeremy?" Sir John burst forth immediately I had finished.

"I think it a good letter, sir, though it be plain from it that Mr. Tiverton has little use for George Bradbury."

"Little use indeed. Yet for our purposes, the letter is not near so helpful as it might be. I do wish the magistrate had been able to be more specific as to Bradbury's day of departure. Even so, it is placed back far enough that there would have been time enough for the pawnbroker to arrive for his appointment with death here in London. And Mr. . . . what is his name? Tiverton?—he is quite right to say that our man took a great risk in riding off on his journey alone, no matter how well armed he might have been. If there were but some way to prove that Bradbury had arrived here . . . But at this point I know of none."

"Then what are we to do? Simply wait and watch and hope those you call the conspirators show themselves, make some mistake, or . . ."

"Nooo," said Sir John. "I think it time to take some

action. I have formed a plan, not a very complicated one by any means, nor one which will demand the services of many constables. It will, however, require the help of your friend Jimmie Bunkins.''

"Bunkins, sir?"

"Yes, Jeremy. I wonder would you be good enough to fetch him? What I have in mind might make it necessary that he start his afternoon lessons a bit late. You should make this clear to his tutor. I have no doubt Mr. Burnham will cooperate in this.''

"I'll go immediately,'' said I, already backing out of the room.

"Yes, please do. And tell him, if you will, that if he has any old or dirty clothes, he is to wear them.''

What a peculiar stipulation! I left Bow Street turning it round in my mind, trying to fix just what sort of activity he might have in mind for Bunkins that might require him to rough his clothes, perhaps dirty them. I could have asked Sir John, of course, and he might have told me—and then again, he might not. I decided it was best to have done as I did—simply to do as he asked and trust that all would soon be revealed.

I took my usual route to St. James Street, which led me along the Strand and on to Pall Mall. I had bare taken my turn onto that wide way when I heard the beat of a drum— or, as it turned out, two drummers beating together—and thought perhaps a parade was coming in my direction. And indeed it was a parade of sorts, but the drums were muffled and their rhythm was slow and solemn, a doleful, dreadful time; it was a funeral cortege come crawling along. Coaches pulled over and made room for the procession. Pedestrians along the way halted as the black-draped wagon bearing the coffin passed by; a few of the men around me had the courtesy to remove their hats from their heads, as I myself felt obliged to do.

"Who has died?'' I muttered to the man next to me.

"Lady Laningham," said he. "It was ruled natural causes, but some say not."

I gave not a word in response to that, but once the black coach containing the Paltrow family had passed by, I returned hat to head and hurried on. Though I did not count the coaches, the procession was an impressively long one. My glimpse of Lord Laningham's cortege a week before, though it gave no true comparison, did at least suggest that the number of mourners attending her had equaled his.

I thought it strange that I had had to ask who it was had died. Here was I, after all, quite close to the Laningham residence in St. James Square whence the procession had made its start. And it had been but day before yesterday that the inquest had been held. This was proof how completely the putative murder of Bradbury, Roundtree's suspected involvement in it, and Clarissa Roundtree's illness had driven all else from my mind. I found it of great interest, too, that the man to whom I had put my query—an ordinary man of business, perhaps a tradesman or a shopkeeper of the more prosperous sort—had given voice to a general doubt regarding the finding of the jury at the coroner's inquest. I was still thinking upon this when I turned up St. James Street and made my way to the Bilbo residence.

In the interest of brevity, let me advance my narrative swiftly to a time quite near midnight that same day. I stood in the shadows of the dive across from George Bradbury's pawnshop on Bedford Street in the company of Constable Brede. He, the most solitary of nature and least talkative of all the Bow Street Runners, had been silent as a post since we had taken our position five minutes before, nor had he spoken a word during our short walk from the livery stable at the corner of Half-Moon, just at the point where it narrows from a street to a tight passage.

Sir John's plan was simple enough. Since some days before Bunkins had, in my company, proposed to Mrs. Bradbury that she buy certain goods which he proposed to steal in a bold burglary of some great house, Sir John suggested to him that he and I return to her and inform her that the burglary would take place this very night. If she then proved as eager to accept stolen goods as she had on our first visit, we would return at midnight with a wagon covered over with sailcloth. Upon his arrival, Bunkins would inform her from which house the swag had been taken and demand a price from her—say, something on the order of a quarter of their value. They would come to an agreement, and he would then throw off the sailcloth to reveal not a great treasure of goods but two or three armed constables, who would then leap out and put all in sight under arrest.

That was how it was planned, and that—save for a few changes improvised by Bunkins and me—was how it proceeded. He and I knew full well that I could not show my face again in the shop, for fear that Jackie Carver might be about and would, of course, immediately recognize me as one from Bow Street; nor could I ride along with him on the wagon box at midnight for the very same reason. (There was an awkward moment when Sir John had asked which of us was the better at driving a wagon. I said I was completely incapable. Bunkins surprised me by boasting that he could handle a team of four, for the driver of Mr. Bilbo's coach had taught him well.) There were details to be attended to: I had to return to the livery stable to engage a wagon and team for later that night, and Sir John wished me to be present when he explained the plan to the Runners he had selected to implement it.

When he had done with that, and the constable had left his chambers, I revealed my ignorance of his method by asking how we might prove murder by arresting the three ''conspirators'' as receivers of stolen goods.

''We shall arrest them on the lesser charge, which can be easily proven,'' he had explained, ''so that we may question them on the greater one. The important thing is to interrogate them singly and convince them that we know all there is to know about the murder of George Bradbury, that we accept it as fact and know these three to be the perpetrators of this heinous crime. I shall have a great deal of time to work on them, and I shall do so quite mercilessly.'' Then did he leer fiendishly in a most theatrical manner. ''Oh, for a pair of thumbscrews!'' he exclaimed. ''Had I such, I could have confessions from them immediately—if not sooner.''

Could he be serious? Of course not. It was seldom he jested about such matters, though. That he would do so now suggested to me that he looked forward to the interviews as a game of wits and wills.

And so we waited, Mr. Brede and I. He may have been silent, yet there was noise aplenty from within the grogshop outside which we stood. No doubt he would have had to shout to make himself heard. Since Mr. Brede never shouted, he said nothing at all. No, not even when the team and wagon at last appeared. I had been watching the pawnshop for any sign of light or movement when I felt a nudge at my arm, looked up, and saw the constable pointing down Bedford Street. There it was, revealed in the dim streetlamps; Bunkins sat high upon the wagon box, and behind him, beneath the sailcloth, were Mr. Perkins and Mr. Bailey, well armed, ready to leap out and take charge.

Bunkins seemed to have a fair command of the two horses, a pair of old grays which looked not much healthier than the ghostly spavined nags which had pulled the Raker's wagon as he went out bringing in the dead. Still, they proved stubborn. The single difficult maneuver Bunkins had to execute was to turn team and wagon into the dark, narrow passage beside the pawnshop which led to its rear. No doubt he had managed such a turn before with a larger coach and a team of four. Yet Mr. Bilbo's horses were younger, better fed, and well trained to their task; no doubt, too, Mr. Bilbo's driver had sat beside Bunkins and given him instruction through all difficult circumstances. In any case, whether the fault was Bunkins's or no, the horses balked at the entrance to the passage. After a good deal of urging, which he alternated with a bit of pleading, Bunkins gave up, climbed down from his seat, taking the oil lamp with him, and after some tugging and pulling, managed to lead the horses down the passage, hallooing as he went. A light came on above the pawnshop.

Mr. Brede signaled that he would now go across the street and cover the passage, should anyone be foolish enough to try to escape by running from the back of the shop to the street. We had agreed that I would cover the front door, the least likely escape exit, since I was no constable and was unarmed but for the club such as all the Beak Runners carry. The rest had pistols by their sides; Mr. Brede had a cutlass, as well. I, who had also crossed the street, was at the door but in a spot to one side of it where I could not be seen. I nodded to the constable across the space that separated us, no more than twenty feet. He nodded in return. We waited.

On any night except one like this, chill and damp, dark and foggy, Bedford Street might well be crowded with footloose drunken men who, should they see a constable in wait, would think it great sport to shout out a warning to the malefactor. Yet not tonight. I looked the street up and down and saw no one. All of the roisterers and merrymakers were inside the grogshops and dives up and down the street, seeking to warm themselves inside and out. I found myself wishing that Roundtree was among them.

Though we saw no one, within two or three minutes we began to hear voices from behind the shop. Indistinct they may have been; nevertheless one I made out to be Bunkins's, and the other—higher, whining one moment and hectoring the next—could only be that of Mrs. Bradbury. The two went on haggling in a most quarrelsome manner, until at last there was a pause of nearly a minute—then shouts, footsteps, a shot! The constables had made their appearance!

My club was out and in my hand. A tall figure came

running out the passage. Mr. Brede, just as tall and a good deal wider, caught him and wrestled him to the ground. It had to be Roundtree—and it was. At the same time, I heard a flurry of movement from within the shop. One of them was at the door, fumbling at the key in the lock. It had to be—yes, it was—Jackie Carver. I leapt aside as the door flew open. Once through the door, he started to run, and I might have missed him had he not turned in my direction. I jumped forward and hit him a stout blow with my club upon the back of the knee. I'd hoped to knock him down with it, but though it staggered him, it did not fell him. He regained his balance, turned, and faced me; in his hand glinted that object in which he placed such faith—his knife. I closed the distance between us. And then came a sudden look of recognition in his face, and from his lips issued a great howl of dismay.

"You!"

I expected him to leap at me, knife first. Instead did he turn and run. I had set myself for his charge, and it took me a moment to react properly—a moment too long, as it developed. For the shot that had been fired in the rear of the pawnshop turned out a great crowd from the grogshop across the street. There they were, still pouring forth from the entrance, yet they parted, making an avenue of escape for Jackie Carver. Nevertheless, a moment later—that moment too long—when I reached the crowd, that avenue was closed to me. I was pushed back by half a score of hands. He was one of their own, and they would permit no pursuit of him. I stood a moment, quite boiling with anger, slapping the club in an angry rhythm into the palm of my left hand. Then did I raise it above my head in a most threatening manner and make ready to charge, thinking I might beat my way through them. But behind me at that moment came a voice I knew well as that of Constable Perkins.

"Back off, Jeremy," he shouted. "If you don't, we'll have a riot on our hands. There be but four of us—and that ain't enough."

TEN

*In Which I Succeed
in My Interrogation
of Roundtree*

Bunkins told me that the business in the yard behind the pawnshop had gone queer right from the start. "First of all," he explained, "I led the team too deep into the yard, which was goodsized. Mrs. B. and Jackie Carver and the tall, skinny one came out fast, like they'd been up and waitin' on me. Only just the blowen come forward to deal with me. The two joes stood back by the house. So we did our haggle, Mrs. B. and me, and we settled on a good price, quarter-value it was, and I made to start untyin' the ropes and called for some help. Only thing was, first of all, I thought she settled too quick, and she starts crowdin' in on me to see right off what I got in the wagon, while the others continue to hang back. I began to think they had in mind to rob me of the goods, the horses and wagon and all, maybe murder me and cut me up into pieces, like they done to old Bradbury. I was damn happy it was constables in the wagon and not eatin' silver, gold plates, and paintings, and such.

"Anyways, I got the ropes undone on one side at the end and started to work on t'other when Mrs. B. walks over bold as brass, pulls up the sailcloth to look inside, and comes face-to-face with Constable Bailey. She lets out a scream, and Mr. Bailey rises up, pistol in hand, and jumps clear of the wagon. But instead of going after the two joes, which he probably didn't know where they were and maybe couldn't see them 'cause they was in the shadows of the house, he starts chasin' her around the yard. Then I got the other rope untied, which set the sailcloth free on Constable Perkins's side. He riz up and saw the situation immediate, saw the joes shovin' their trunks on out of there. And so what did he do? He fires his pistol—not at either one of them but up in the air, so's to let you know they was comin'. And I guess you know the rest.''

We walked together, leading the team back to the livery stable. It was such a short distance that there seemed no point to mounting to the wagon box once we were through the passage. They followed most compliantly, for they seemed to know that they were returning home. Having heard Bunkins's tale of what had transpired behind the pawnshop, I was secretly somewhat relieved to know that all had not gone well on their side. In spite of Mr. Perkins's words of encouragement—''Don't worry, lad, for if you got him a good one behind the knee, he'll not go far on a queer leg''—I felt as if I had let the rest down, Sir John most of all. I could not muster much of a comment in response to Bunkins, nothing more than a muttered, ''I know only too well.''

''Ah, you're feelin' queer because Jackie Carver got away, ain't you? Well, you shouldn't. He ran from you, didn't he? You put the fear of that club Mr. Perkins gave you deep into him.''

''Well, I suppose so,'' said I.

We trudged on. The stable was now in sight, well lit in front by two lamps. The horses pressed on eagerly. It was all we could do to keep up with them.

''One thing, though,'' said Bunkins. ''If I was you with Jackie Carver on the loose, I'd watch my back, specially at night. And it'd be wiser to carry that club with you even in the daytime.''

On that happy note we arrived. For certain sure the horses knew the way. They had made the turn into the stable before we were quite ready. Yet we managed well enough and found waiting for us the ostler, a talkative fellow of no grand proportions, who immediately went about unhitching the team from the wagon.

''Well,'' said he, ''that didn't take long. Tell me true, did you catch the villains you was after?''

''We caught a couple,'' said Bunkins, who was far more willing to talk about the matter than I was.

''Right smart hidin' the constables under the canvas like that.''

Bunkins let that pass without comment. But he had a complaint: ''The horses balked, wouldn't go forward, had to lead them down a passage.''

''Was it dark?''

''Indeed it was, but—''

''Well, that explains it, you see. When you led them you carried the lamp with you, I'll warrant.''

''I did, yes, but—''

''It's just that this one''—he cuffed the horse on the left gently on the head—''is afeared of the dark. And this one''—he cuffed the other on the neck—''won't do anything unless t'other tells him to. If you hadn't had that lamp in your hand, you'd still be waitin' for them to move.''

''You never told me that.''

''You never asked.''

''Ain't it proper to tell your customers the peculiarities of your animals?''

''Ah, well, that's another thing entirely. Each one's got so many. Why, they're like people that same way. Why, I could tell you of one that . . .''

Bunkins allowed him to talk on, but I, wearying of their wrangle, went wandering among the stalls of the stable, surveying the sleeping horses, marveling at how they kept their feet as they slept, their handsome heads bowed. All seemed to look in finer fettle than the two old nags we had been given less than an hour before. One of them was indeed a grand animal. It stood taller than the rest—or would have, had all been erect. I stood for a moment admiring it— a beautiful horse, all white it was . . .

I turned and hurried back to the ostler, who bladdered on still, and interrupted him in a manner most excited.

"Here, you, sir," said I, "that horse down the way, the white one, is it a mare?"

"You are buttin' in on a most interestin' story which I am tellin' to your mate here," he scolded.

"Never mind that," said I. "Answer me, and answer me quick."

"Now, ain't you the rude young fella! Well, as any fool should know, since last time I looked she had her hindquarters pointin' out, she's a mare. If she's now turned about, I honor your question as a reasonable one, for she's a mare big as some stallions."

"To whom does she belong?"

"Why, to the owner of this stable, young sir, if it's any of your affair. He bought her about a week or more ago, he did."

"From whom? Whom did he buy her from?"

"I'm sure he never told me. All he said was he expects to hire her out for a handsome price when spring comes and the young blades start ridin' in the park."

"Jimmie B.," said I to him, "I must be back to Bow Street to tell Sir John this bit of information. I'll see you in court tomorrow." Then to the ostler: "Forgive the interruption, sir. Go on with your story."

Then did I quite run from the stable. Though in a great rush to reach my destination, I chose the longer route, wishing to avoid Bedford Street and any remnants of the grogshop crowd. I traveled down Maiden Lane, past the synagogue, then onto Tavistock Street, where Mr. Donnelly's surgery had formerly been located. And all the while

I kept along the middle of the street, taking most seriously Bunkins's warning regarding Jackie Carver. At that time of night, there was little in the way of horse traffic, and that I dodged quite easily.

Thus I came to Number 4 Bow Street. Once inside, I sought Sir John, but he was nowhere to be seen—no doubt in his chambers questioning Mrs. Bradbury or Roundtree. But no, they were in the strong room, whispering together in a corner behind the bars; I was not seen by them. Then I met Mr. Baker, the night man, gaoler, armorer, and the Runners' man in reserve. He was in earnest conversation with young Mr. Cowley, who had just returned to duty following his stabbing of a week or more before. As I approached him he pulled away.

"I'll attend to it just as you say, Mr. Baker," said he. Then, with a passing nod to me, "Jeremy," I watched him go; he limped a bit.

"I'm surprised to see him back so soon," said I.

"Oh, he's a good two weeks from going back to full duty. It was Sir John's thought he might be of use to me here—though I doubted it. I just sent him off to Shakespeare's Head to fetch dinner for the two of us. He's good for that, at least."

Mr. Cowley was not held in high favor by the rest of the Runners.

"I was looking about for Sir John. Is he in his chambers?"

"No, he bade me a good night and went upstairs about a quarter of an hour past. He seemed disappointed when Bailey and Perkins brought in but two prisoners. Seems he was expecting three."

At that my spirits, which had risen with the discovery of the white mare, plummeted like a stone tossed down a well.

"Oh," said I, "then I may as well go up there, too." There was a chance, after all, that he might still be up and about.

"Good night to you then."

A good night indeed. With a heavy heart I said my farewell and began my journey to my narrow pallet before the fireplace. Yet as I passed the strong room, I could not miss Roundtree; he leaned against the bars and beckoned earnestly to me. I went to him. I had no wish to speak with him, still, I could not deny the poor fellow.

"How is she?" he whispered. I had no need to ask to whom he referred.

"Very much better," said I, whispering. "She was up for the first time today. I brewed a cup of tea for her at midday, and she seemed on her way to recovery. That's the last I saw of her, however, for I've been running about ever since."

"Arrangin' my downfall, were ya?"

"Mr. Roundtree, whatever was done by me in this deceit which led to your arrest was done at Sir John's direction. Perhaps you forget that for over a week you've been a fugitive, that you refused a very good offer made for your surrender. No sir, I did not arrange your downfall, nor did Sir John. You yourself, and no other, are responsible for your present situation. Think about it, and I'm sure you'll agree."

Then did I leave him, and as I did I noted that Mrs. Bradbury had risen from her corner of the strong room and was moving over to talk to Roundtree, no doubt to ask the content of our whispered conversation. I wondered if she knew that Roundtree's daughter lay up in my bed. I wagered with myself that she did not.

Up the stairs, then, and into the kitchen. The fire blazed bright. An extra blanket had been laid upon my makeshift bed. I found a bit of bread and cold beef Annie had laid out for me. Having had no dinner, I was as hungry as I was tired. I ate by firelight, then climbed wearily under the blankets, doffing no more than hat, coat, and shoes. I slept warm, and I slept sound.

·   ·   ·

Next morning being Sunday, the household stirred to life a bit later than was the usual, and glad I was for the extra hour or more beneath the blankets which had been granted me. I woke slowly, aware in a vague way of activity about me. The fire had not gone out quite, and so Annie had been able to feed it, rather than wake me to start it anew. She'd got the kettle on the fire, as well, so that it was only when she nudged me with her foot and invited me to a cup of tea that I came fully awake.

To wake to a fresh, hot cup of tea—that indeed is to live the life of a nobleman. I had heard that some such break-fasted each day in the big bed in which they had slept, enjoying the privileges of the sick without themselves being sick. Ah, for such privileges, ah for such a life!

"How is our patient?" I asked Annie.

"Not quite as well as she claims to be, but well enough."

"She got out of bed yesterday and came down to the kitchen," said I. "I brewed a pot of tea so she might have a cup, then had to leave before ever I had a cup of my own."

"Well, she finished the whole pot, then got me to brew another when I came back from my lessons. We finished that one up together. We had a grand time, we did."

"Why, she promised me she would go back up to bed soon as she finished that one cup. That girl's not to be trusted!"

"P'rhaps not, but I don't think it hurt her any. It was warm and snug here through the afternoon, and she told me many stories from her days in the workhouse. Some of them were quite terrible, of course, just what you'd expect—but others were downright funny. Oh, I laughed and laughed, I did. And she just kept working away, and all the while telling stories. But then Lady Fielding came home and shoved her right off to bed."

"*Working?* You said she was working—working at what?"

"Well, at the—"

Then did we hear the unmistakable tread, sure and certain, of Lady Fielding upon the stairs. Annie put her forefinger to her lips instructing me to be silent, and punctuated her command with a wink. When she appeared, our mistress was arrayed in one of her finest frocks, a locket at her throat which hung from a gold chain, a gift from Sir John on the occasion of their last anniversary. Over her arm was her cape. Clearly, she was on her way out, though not, it seemed certain, to the Magdalene Home.

"Oh, m'lady, you look lovely," cried Annie.

"Thank you, dear girl. I'm off to church this morning."

"Church?" We echoed her together rather hollowly. Attendance at holy services was not a routine occurrence in the lives of any of us four who lived above the Bow Street Court.

"Yes," said she with a certain determination, "I've some praying to do on a certain matter, and I think it only right to do it in the proper setting."

"Won't you have a cup of tea at least before you go?"

"No, Annie, I have only minutes to get across Covent Garden to St. Paul's before the service begins."

She threw on her cape and tied it.

"Oh, by the bye, Jeremy, I must congratulate you on getting all the rest of those plaguy begging letters copied out."

"All the rest . . ." I looked at Annie. "Is that what she . . ."

Annie nodded.

I sighed. "Much as I should like to take credit, mum, I made only five copies yesterday before Sir John called upon me for an errand—and one did follow another all day long. I never got back to the task you gave me. It could only be Clarissa finished the rest."

Lady Fielding smiled slyly. "I thought your hand had greatly improved after the first few," said she. "It became more cursive and flowing, less angular—in short, more feminine and less masculine. Altogether an improvement.

You may pass the congratulations I gave you on to her. Has anyone looked in on her yet? Please do." Then, pulling her hat down upon her head: "Well, goodbye all. I must be off."

And indeed off she went. We heard her steps descending the stairs at a perilous rate. She seemed always to hurry down them in just such a way, but had yet to make a mis-step.

I carried a pan of live coals and wood chips up to the top of the stairs to feed the brazier, which had quite gone dead during the night. Clarissa slept as I opened the window wide and emptied the ashes onto the yard below. Whether I had wakened her loading the coals in the brazier, or if she had, as she claimed, been wakened by the smell of bacon cooking, I know not. In any case, she was wide-eyed and smiling by the time I reached the door. I passed on to her Lady Fielding's thanks and praise, which she took as her due. Yet I would not let her off quite so lightly.

"You promised me you would return to bed when you finished that cup of tea I gave you. Do you remember?"

"I remember," said she, then turned away in a sulk.

"Are your promises worth so little?"

"Oh, pooh," said she, as was her wont. "It was in a good cause, was it not?"

"That I cannot contest. But a promise is a promise."

"You're being tiresome. Now, please go, so that I may make use of the chamber pot."

I turned and stalked from the room.

"Shut the door, please—and tell Annie that I shall be along instanter to help her with breakfast."

"You're supposed to stay in bed. Will you not understand that?"

"Mr. Donnelly said that that is a matter of my choice, so long as I keep warm—so there!"

I leaned back and slammed the door shut and then descended the stairs.

Sir John sat, fully dressed, at the table. He was sipping

at a cup of tea as Annie put before him a breakfast plate of hen's eggs and two thick rashers of bacon.

"What have we here?" said Sir John, inhaling deeply. "Bacon *and* eggs? What is it we celebrate with such a morning feast?"

"Well, sir," said Annie, "you and Jeremy were both up late on court matters, and 'twas you who always said if a man don't get his sleep, he must eat well, for he must get his energy from somewhere."

"So I did, so I did."

"Jeremy's will soon be coming."

As Annie turned back to her work, I sat down at the table and pulled my chair close to Sir John's.

"Sir, I have something to tell you," said I in a low voice.

"About last night at Bradbury's? Well, fret not," said he. "These plans of mine sometimes do not go perfectly." He chewed a bit and swallowed, then took another bite, dripping a bit of yolk upon his waistcoat.

"No, Sir John, it's about—"

But he continued: "Mr. Perkins told me how the younger fellow had run through the crowd, and how the crowd had then closed up against him—against Mr. Perkins, that is—and made pursuit impossible. To have leveled a pistol at any of them would have been a mistake. To have fired a pistol would likely have meant a riot. He handled the situation properly."

I paused to think through what Sir John had just told. It took a moment until I understood that Constable Perkins had taken the blame for my loss of Jackie Carver. Should I tell the straight of it? Perhaps later. The important thing at the moment was telling my tale of the white mare.

"No sir," said I, "what I have to tell you has naught to do with what happened last night at the pawnshop. It was what I saw when Bunkins and I returned the wagon and team to the stable."

"Ah . . . so . . . what was it you saw there?"

"A white horse—a mare, big as some stallions, I was

told.'' Then did I tell the tale complete, as Sir John listened, eating, nodding at each detail. In particular he was taken with the matter of time.

''And when did the ostler say the mare had been bought—a week ago?''

''No, sir,'' said I, ''he said a week ago or *more*. I would wager it was something like two weeks past.''

''The owner of the stable would know, of course. He would keep a record of the transaction.''

''And who knows, Mrs. Bradbury could've kept the animal a day or two, wondering what to do with it.''

''This stable—you say it's very near the pawnshop on Bedford?''

''Oh, very near, sir. It's on Half-Moon just before it narrows into the passage to the Strand.''

''Of course, I know the place. I've smelled it a score of times as I passed by.'' He said nothing for a moment, then, with pursed lips, gave a wise nod. ''It could be the very horse George Bradbury rode from Warwick. If we can prove that it was sold to the stablemaster by one of our three conspirators, then we know that he arrived safe in London.''

''And was murdered here,'' I offered.

''That is a bit of a leap, yet one we might take. We shall see.''

''Jeremy!'' Annie called crossly. ''It's not every day you get eggs for breakfast. Don't let them get cold.''

I looked down and found a plate of eggs and rashers before me. How or when it had appeared there I had no idea, so taken was I in communicating my information to Sir John. I nodded to her and fell to the feast.

''When you have finished eating, Jeremy, I should like you to return to that stable on Half-Moon, find the owner, and get from him all the particulars you can. If his description of the seller of the white horse should match one of the two we have in custody, then bring him along to Bow

Street—tell him I insist that he come—and we shall have him identify him or her face-to-face.''

''It will be done, sir, just as you say.''

Then did I hear a clopping on the stairs which I knew well from yesterday. It was Miss Pooh, descending to breakfast in my old shoes.

''But damn,'' said Sir John, ''I fear I must detain you further, lad. I must be shaved again this morning for that Laningham dinner we attend tonight. But then again, it was just yesterday you shaved me, was it not?''

''No sir, the day before that.''

He rubbed his jowls critically. ''Ah well,'' said he, ''I suppose I'm due.''

My return visit to the stable proved only partly successful. When I first looked in at the location, one of the two ostlers present (the night man, who had of course by then gone home, was not one of them) advised me that the owner of the stable was not expected in for an hour or more. I told him that I had come at the behest of Sir John Fielding of the Bow Street Court, and that I would return in an hour to speak with his master then.

I had another matter to attend to. Sir John had also asked me to look in at the pawnshop and give the place a cursory examination—to pay particular attention to the upstairs rooms and look for traces of blood about.

''They could not have separated head from body without spilling blood,'' he had said to me. ''Yet keep your eye open for anything you believe might be of interest. And oh yes, one thing specifically I should like you to bring back to us, should you find it. Our man Roundtree is a carpenter, is he not? If you run across his box of tools, that would be something I should like to have.''

And so, as I walked from the stable to the pawnshop, I reflected upon Sir John's instructions, realizing full well the significance of his request for Roundtree's toolbox.

Bedford Street, at that hour of a cold January morning,

was quite a dismal sight. Though the taverns and grogshops never closed, or so it seemed, they were probably near empty. One or two of them were being cleaned, after a fashion; I saw a door open and a man in the shadows sweeping the filth of the night out onto the walkway. I heard water splashed in another, followed by the rhythmic swishing of a mop passing over the boards of the floor. Far down the street, beyond Henrietta, I caught sight of a single figure, a woman, staggering insensibly on her way to whatever bed or pallet she might claim as her own.

Then to the pawnshop. I took from my pocket the key to the place, given by Mr. Bailey to Mr. Baker and by Mr. Fuller to me. Pleased at how easily it turned in the lock, I stepped inside and locked it again. I found a candle on the counter and lit it, for though it was morning without, it was dusk within. Then did I begin my inspection of the premises. There was far more to the ground floor than I had supposed. Two rooms were filled with oddments of every sort—clothes, musical instruments of every sort and sound, clocks, paintings, even a piece of statuary set in one corner—all of this in no apparent order, simply hung, stacked, and leaned all higgledy-piggledy about, filling the space completely. Looking hopelessly from one room to the next, I realized that I could spend days going through each, and so, for the time being at least, I decided to leave them unexamined, and searched for the stairs to the upper floor.

I found them at the very rear of the edifice and ascended. There were but three rooms above. There was something tight, cramped, and mean about them. They were kept neat enough, which surprised me somewhat considering the disorder below; nevertheless the walls were bare of pictures of any sort (with so many below!), and the furniture, though large and cumbersome, was rather sparse.

Going to the bedroom, I gave considerable attention to the mattress. Sir John seemed to have reasoned that George Bradbury had been murdered in his bed; whether he had been decapitated there was another matter entirely. In any case, when I stripped down the sheet and comforter from it, I gave the mattress a thorough going-over. It was feather-filled and dusty; look as I might, I found no trace of blood on it. Yet I did make an interesting discovery when I took the trouble to search through a high chest of many drawers and the wardrobe beside it—or rather, it was a matter of what I failed to discover. The drawers were filled with shifts, lace undergarments, and nightdresses of the sort worn by ladies of quality, and stockings and garters. The wardrobe was crammed to bursting with frocks and gowns of every sort, color, and weight. There was not a single piece of male attire to be found in the bedroom.

The kitchen was quite ordinary. The only thing worthy of note was that it did not look to me as if it had been used much of late. There was little food in it—a jar of flour and another of sugar, both near full, but no barrel of potatoes, no carrots or turnips, and certainly no meat about. There was a good-sized teapot upon the table; I looked inside it and found it half full of black tea. On a shelf next the unused fireplace, I found a half loaf of bread and a bit of cake covered over with a cloth, still fairly fresh. It seemed that Mrs. Bradbury had done most of her dining in eating places about the town. Perhaps she always had.

As for the parlor, which looked out over the street, it also served as a dining room and had in it a table much too large for such a limited space, and eight chairs. There was a couch, also a bit too large, and two conversation chairs. All together, it made for a rather crowded room. I was about to leave it, when something caught my eye. I turned back to look at the table and saw that it had upon it the only piece of decoration to be seen in any of the three rooms—a small vase, blue and white. I reached over, picked it up, and examined it. It was delicate and thin-walled, of porcelain. I noted the dragon design upon it and determined that it could only be of Chinese origin. Here, though I took no joy in my discovery, was one mystery solved.

I had seen nothing of Roundtree's tools. Perhaps they were not here at Bradbury's. He could as easily have returned them to his room in Half-Moon Passage. Yet I had to look. I descended the stairs to make my search. In that second room of storage, the one farthest to the rear of the house, I found an area hollowed out of the clutter before a fireplace, which must have been located directly below that in the kitchen. Before it was a pallet bed with a wad of clothes at one end which had served as a pillow. This, I felt certain, was where Roundtree had hidden himself from us, close enough to make visits to Clarissa and watch over her after his fashion. This fireplace had had heavy use. There was some evidence he had cooked here, too, though it had no proper accommodation for cooking. Here was a dirty plate, a fork, a spoon. I could picture that poor scarecrow of a man huddling before his blaze, eating what little his protectors (or perhaps, in a sense, his captors) had allowed him to have. This was what it meant to be a fugitive. This was what it meant to mix in murder.

I looked around and located his toolbox with no difficulty. It was tucked in at one side of the fireplace, half hidden from sight—but only half. It was near full, yet there was just room in it, I thought, for the purpose I had in mind. Looking about, I found copies of the *Public Advertiser* which he may have used to start his fire, and tearing up the paper, I wrapped the Chinese vase as carefully as I could. I placed it in an empty spot between the hammer and the saw.

Then was I ready at last to return to the stable.

At my second visit, the owner of the place was indeed present, a man of advanced years but still sturdy and able. He was brought to me by the ostler to whom I had inquired earlier.

"So you're the lad sent over by the magistrate. What is it he wants of me?"

I caught him glancing curiously at the carpenter's box in

my hand, though he said nothing about it. Taking that opportunity, I laid it down upon the floor.

"Your name, first of all, sir."

He seemed to think that rather rude and blunt from one of my years. Still, he answered: "Matthew Gurney." Then, with a frown: "Was it that team you hired last night? Maybe they wasn't the best. I'll refund the cost if that'll make it right. I wish to stay on good terms with the law."

"No, it's nothing to do with that," said I. "But you're right—the horses were not the best. No, I was sent to inquire about the white horse, the mare in the third stall there."

Mr. Gurney gave a little chuckle at that. "Now you *are* talking about the best. Yes indeed, she's the best animal in my stable." A dreadful thought did at that moment assail him: "She wasn't stole, was she? I'd hate to lose her and the sum I paid."

"Nooo, not exactly, but the horse plays a part in a matter that Sir John Fielding now has before him."

"And what matter is that?"

"I'm not now permitted to say."

"Well . . . what do you wish to know?"

"Two things, fundamentally, though I should be happy to hear whatever you may have to add. First, who sold it to you? A man, or perhaps a woman?"

"I've his name on the bill of purchase I made out at the time. It's in my desk in back." He stirred in that direction. "I could fetch it for you."

"Yes, I should like to see it," said I, "but the name he used may well have been a false one. What did he look like?"

"Oh, yes, well, he was a young fellow—not as young as you, I'd say, but young enough."

"Not a tall man of over thirty years?"

"Oh no, not near that age. About ten years shy of it, I'd say. He was about your height but not so broad across the chest, nor stout in the legs as you are."

Jackie Carver, of course. In a sense I was relieved that it was not Roundtree, yet it eliminated the possibility of certain identification of the seller.

With no prodding from me, Mr. Gurney began to expand a bit on the matter of the sale: "As I remembers it, this young fella said he was acting as factor for a third party, a widow out beyond Clerkenwell. Her husband had lately died and left her the farm. She would rent the fields and tend the usual farm animals, but she had no use for the horse, which was her late husband's pride and joy. She had asked this young fellow to sell it for her and had made out a paper giving him permission to act in her behalf—all that legal language. Only thing made me doubt was that if she knew little of horses—as he said—then he knew less."

"Oh? How could you tell?"

"Well, for one thing he didn't ride her in, and anyone knew horses would have counted it a treat to ride so fine a mount. And mind you, he didn't lead her in by her bridle but by a rope tied round her neck."

"He led her all the way from beyond Clerkenwell? Did he say why he had not tried to sell the animal to some stable nearer the farm?"

"No, he did not, and that made me wonder, too. But in all truth, I was so eager to have her—and at such a price!— that I chose to ignore such details. Y'see, that was something else told me he knew nothing of horses. The price he asked for her was not even half her worth. Ah, but I kept my wits about me and haggled him down still further—just so he wouldn't know he was asking too little, of course."

"Of course," said I. He seemed to have told his tale entire. I gave him a moment, but when he added nothing more, I suggested he might now go and fetch his bill of purchase. "That would carry the date of the transaction, would it not? That is the other bit of information I would have from you."

"Oh, that was not so long ago—ten days past or a few more."

"Sir John wants the date exact."

"And you shall have it." Off he went, moving as swift as his old legs would carry him. Though he knew naught of this matter and the implications of the information he had given, he had become eager to cooperate.

I wandered over for another look at the white mare. Awake, she was even more impressive than before. There was keen intelligence in her eyes. She seemed somewhat distrustful, perhaps for good reason. When I extended my hand to touch her long nose, she backed up sharply out of my reach. Perhaps someday I would learn to ride, I thought, and when I did, I would come and ride this very horse. (Alas, reader, neither ambition have I realized.) Returning to my post beside Roundtree's box of tools, I waited, and it was not long before Mr. Gurney made his appearance. He returned waving two pieces of paper quite proudly.

"How times does fly," said he. "I have it on the bill of purchase that it was exactly two weeks ago today that I bought the horse. I had not thought it quite so long ago. But here it is, you see."

He handed it over, and I examined the document with some care. Fourteen days past: on that Sunday, Thomas Roundtree had sat in the strong room there at Number 4 Bow Street, and that evening we had gone off to the Crown and Anchor and watched the late Lord Laningham die a miserable death on the stage before us. Reading on, I saw that Mr. Gurney had acquired the mare, "dubbed Princess," for ten guineas; she had to have been worth much more indeed. At the bottom of the short paragraph which set forth the sale, on the line following "Seller" was a large "X" and the words, "John Cutter, his mark." That would translate easily to Jackie Carver, would it not?

"And this paper here," said Mr. Gurney, "this is the one that made it legal for him to act for her in the sale of the mare. He left it with me, which was the right thing to do, I suppose."

Taking it from him, I merely glanced over it. The document was as he had described it and was written out in a proper "feminine" hand—cursive and flowing, as Lady Fielding had set the distinction. What caught my eye, however, was the name that Mrs. Bradbury had chosen for herself: "Grace Hope." To what would that translate? What else but to one who stands in hope of God's grace. She had then—perhaps the morning after the murder of her husband—some sense of having committed a great sin. I resolved to tell Sir John of this, that he might make the most of it.

"Now, Mr. Gurney," said I, returning the two documents to him, "I return these to you in the expectation that you will keep them safe. They may later be needed as evidence in a trial of law."

"Is that so?" He looked at me most soberly. "But it's got nothing to do with whether the horse was stole?"

"No sir," said I. "That would be the least of it."

"Oh," said he, as he considered what might be the most of it. "I'll put them in my strongbox."

"Do that," said I, "but let me pass on to Sir John that you will say nothing of our conversation to anyone."

"Oh . . . yes . . . certainly . . . nothing at all."

"Then thank you, sir, for your cooperation. I shall now return to Bow Street."

"Well, thank you, young sir, and let me say that if you do carpentry work, there's always plenty of that round a stable. You seem a likely lad for work of any sort."

"Thank you, sir," said I. "Very kind of you to say so."

With that, I picked up the toolbox and politely took my leave of him. Though I made my way at a brisk pace, and in the daylight ventured the shortest route to Bow Street—down Henrietta and across Covent Garden—I dared not run, nor even proceed at a jog trot, for fear of shaking and breaking the Chinese vase that was nestled among the tools. I am not sure that I would have hurried so fast, in any case, for I considered my expedition only partly successful. I had discovered a few things, true, yet I had found no trace of blood upon the mattress, nor anywhere else in Bradbury's upstairs quarters, for that matter; I had also missed the opportunity to summon Mr. Gurney to Bow Street to make a face-to-face identification of the horse seller (John Cutter indeed!).

Nevertheless, I took my findings to Sir John the moment I arrived at Number 4. He was, as I expected, in his chambers, yet alone, which surprised me somewhat. I had half hoped to encounter him in the process of interrogating Roundtree or Mrs. Bradbury. He had seemed so to look forward to it. No doubt he had talked to both of them already, I told myself, made some sort of preliminary examination. After all, I had been gone near two hours.

He bade me sit down and give my report, which I did, telling first of my visit to Bradbury's and then of my interview with Matthew Gurney. His reactions were various. He seemed amused at the way Mrs. Bradbury had removed all trace of her husband from her bedroom, quite interested in the discovery of the Chinese vase, elated that the selling of the horse fitted well in the table of events, yet indifferent to the significance I had placed upon Mrs. Bradbury's false name, Grace Hope. In all, he deemed my expedition a success and congratulated me upon my discoveries.

"I would have you now attend to two matters," said he. "The first is easily done. Take the vase to Mr. Marsden, and tell him to hold it as evidence. There is a chest he keeps for that purpose with lock and key. Tell him to treat it with care, for it is, as you described it, quite fragile, and is very likely the property of William Murray, our Lord Chief Justice." He then paused, as if in some manner he had lost his line of thought. "Lord Murray or someone from his household will have the opportunity to identify the piece eventually. There is no need for that now."

"And the second matter?" I prompted.

"What? Oh yes, the second matter. I should like you to bring the toolbox to Mr. Donnelly. He should be up and about now. He has no patients at his surgery, this being

Sunday, so there should be time enough for him to handle the matter I spoke to him about.''

''There are no instructions to him, then?''

''No, we've discussed the matter. He knows what to do.''

I rose to go, then held back, wondering if Sir John might satisfy my curiosity.

Clearly, he noticed my hesitation: ''What is it, Jeremy?''

''Could you tell me, sir, if you had any results in your questioning of Mrs. Bradbury and Roundtree?''

''What? Oh, no, I haven't talked with either of them yet.''

''You haven't? But you seemed so eager to talk with them.''

''That was when I assumed there would be three to interrogate and not two. You see, there is almost invariably a certain action which takes place when there are three malefactors to be questioned. Two of them will form an alliance against the third. Had all three been there in the cell, I daresay Mrs. Bradbury and that fellow Carver would have united against Roundtree. I should then have informed Roundtree what was said against him and perhaps gotten something approaching the truth from him. In Carver's absence, however, the remaining two have had time to set their stories, and it may take some time to break them down. I intend to convict them on a lesser charge, that I may have that time I need to keep after them on the greater one.''

This was then for me a bit too subtle, I fear. However, I thought his working principle—given three, two will make an alliance against the third—both interesting and sound. But alliances shift, and perhaps in Jackie Carver's absence Mrs. Bradbury and Roundtree would then have made an alliance against him.

With this and other considerations, I entertained myself on my short journey to Mr. Donnelly's surgery and residence.

• • •

The magistrate's courtroom was crowded on that day, for word had gone out that Mrs. Bradbury was to be brought before Sir John. Few in that assemblage had not done business with her or her husband in that pawnshop, and far fewer (even the thieves among them) did not feel ill used or even cheated by them. The pawnbroker is no friend of the poor. He takes from them in their need, and in exchange offers a mere pittance. He acts as a parasite upon their poverty.

Thus it was that when Mr. Marsden called Mrs. Bradbury to stand before the magistrate, a great hum of anticipation chorused through the crowd. Still, it was not loud enough to prompt him to call all to order, nor did it last long. Sir John Fielding began.

"Please state your name," said he.

"Mary Brighton Bradbury."

"You are the true and lawful wife of George Bradbury?"

"I am, sir. We was married a year and a half past at St. Paul's, Covent Garden."

"Are you the same Mary Brighton who was convicted by me two years past of picking a gentleman's pocket to the extent of four shillings and a linen handkerchief?"

Unembarrassed, she admitted it readily: "I am, sir, and I must say you've a good memory for names. But I am a reformed woman now. That two months I spent in the Fleet taught me the error of my ways. Also, my marriage to my dear George altered my situation considerable."

"Perhaps," said Sir John, "but it would seem that your marriage to Mr. Bradbury simply elevated you to a higher place in the chain of thievery, for the charge against you in this magistrate's court is receiving stolen goods—that is, acting, so to speak, as a fence. How do you plead?"

"I plead not guilty, sir," said she confidently.

"Well, then, Mr. Marsden, call the witness."

The court clerk then stood up, pulled himself erect, and called Jimmie Bunkins before Sir John. After the preliminary matters—giving his name and age, establishing himself as a ward of John Bilbo—Bunkins launched into a somewhat truncated version of his first visit to Mrs. Bradbury. What was left out was all that had led to it—our visit to St. Andrew's Churchyard, and his tentative identification of the head at Mr. Donnelly's surgery. (It was given thus upon the request of Sir John, as I later learned.) All the rest was given just as it had happened. He made it plain to her that the goods he would bring her would be property which he would steal from a certain house by means of burglary. Hearing that, she was in no wise discouraged from accepting the goods, and together they made plans on how the loot was to be delivered to the pawnshop—at night, at the back door.

"Then yesterday," said Bunkins, continuing his story, "I went back to her and told her that I would that night return with a wagon filled with what I burgled from this house—though no burglary did happen, for I had told all to Sir John. It was fixed up with him that I'd come back to the pawnshop at midnight with a wagon covered over, but beneath the cover, instead of the swag, was two constables to arrest any and all in sight."

At this, a murmur went up within the courtroom. Though set against Mrs. Bradbury, those in attendance liked not to hear such tales of initiative by the Bow Street Runners, for many of them did themselves engage in thievery from time to time; they seemed to believe such tactics of ambush unfair. Sir John beat with his gavel and brought them back to order.

Bunkins then concluded: "And that was how it happened. After I made sure, for a third time, that she knew the contents of the wagon was stolen goods, and she made it clear she was happy to have them so, I threw back the cover on the wagon, and the constables jumped out and they arrested two—she was one of them—but one of them got away."

At that last phrase—"one of them got away"—a single

cheer arose from the crowd. And hearing it, the courtroom erupted into laughter. Sir John did beat mightily with his gavel until he had hammered all back to order.

"Mr. Marsden," he cried aloud, "did you see who it was gave that cheer?"

"No sir, I did not."

"Should he open his mouth again in such a manner, have Mr. Fuller seize him, and I shall give him thirty days for contempt of my court. And the rest of you out there, I shall have respectful silence from you, or I shall have the courtroom cleared."

Sir John then dismissed Bunkins with his thanks and returned his attention to Mrs. Bradbury.

"Well, then, Mrs. Bradbury, you heard the testimony against you. What say you to it?"

"I do not deny it," said she. "But first off, I would say that I was trapped into it. I did not go out and drag this young fella off the street and say to him, 'Go out and rob some great house, then bring me back the proceeds of your crime and I'll pay you well for the goods you bring me.' No, I said no such thing, for he came to me and proposed that he would do the crime if I should accept the goods he stole. He tempted me, and I, in my weakness—my husband has been absent near a month, with no word from him for two weeks, and business has been bad—he tempted me, and I fell."

"Yet you had time to reconsider your decision," said Sir John. "When he returned to you some time later, he repeated that the goods he planned to deliver to you would be stolen, then repeated it again when he delivered what you believed to be a wagonload of these goods; he told you they were stolen. You had ample opportunity to decline on both of these occasions."

"Business was no better," said she firmly. "I felt I had no choice. But as to that charge you put against me, I deny it completely."

"Accepting stolen goods? You deny that, do you, after

the testimony against you that we have just heard?''

"Of course I do, for you must tell me, what goods was stolen? The wagon brought into our yard contained naught but two constables. What good in resale would they bring?''

Again, the courtroom exploded into laughter. Sir John himself unwillingly joined in, so that he could hardly make good his threat to clear the courtroom. He simply waited until it had subsided and something like quiet had been restored.

Only then did he speak: "Madam, were you a man and had not been caught in this illegal enterprise, I would advise you to read for the bar. You would make a fair barrister, for though you have brought disorder to my courtroom with your remark, you have made a good point. Indeed there were no stolen goods in the wagon. But if and when we open your shop to those who have been robbed in the past year, let us say, then I doubt not that they would discover many items in your store that had once been theirs.''

"If they do, sir," said she, "they will find pawn tickets attached. And how is the poor pawnbroker to know if goods brought into the shop truly belongs to him who brought them in, or has been stolen from another?''

"That is an argument frequently made by those in your trade—and with some effect. So we shall put that aside, at least for the time being, and reconsider, rather, the charge that has been brought against you. I take it from what you yourself have admitted to so far, that while you reject the charge of receiving stolen goods, you would plead guilty to a charge of entering into a conspiracy to receive such goods.''

"Well, I . . .'' She hesitated, searching for a proper response.

"Come, madam, you have said you fell to temptation. In fact, you fell thrice, for on two subsequent occasions when you had the opportunity to withdraw from the agreement you had made, you failed to do so. That agreement constituted a conspiracy to receive stolen goods. You must plead guilty.''

She sighed a most profound sigh. ''I suppose I must.''

''Then I accept your guilty plea,'' said Sir John, ''and I sentence you to sixty days of incarceration, to be served both here in the strong room of the Bow Street Court and in the Fleet Prison, at my discretion.''

There was a bit of whispering at that, for none present had ever heard him divide a sentence in such a way. I, however, understood completely what lay behind it.

''Mr. Fuller, take the prisoner, and, Mr. Marsden, call the next before me.''

''Thomas Roundtree,'' cried the clerk.

He came shuffling forward. Despondent and dejected he may have been, though not yet in despair. There was yet a glint in his eye. He seemed to be a man who yet held out hope. Perhaps he had made an alliance with himself against the other two.

''Thomas Roundtree, you are here as a fugitive from justice,'' said Sir John. ''You fled a guardian appointed by the court and remained as a fugitive for one day shy of two weeks. Is this not true?''

''Yes sir, it is.'' He spoke up strong and steady. No, he did not sound like a man who had given up hope.

''And you were apprehended at Bradbury's pawnshop by the constables who arrested Mrs. Bradbury. How came you to be there?''

''Well, sir, Mrs. Bradbury had given me shelter, which was kind of her. She had a fear that with her husband gone she might be the victim of robbers. So she wanted a man about the house at night to guard against that. Then I took care of the shop when she would go out for a meal.''

''Did you, on those occasions when you tended shop, claim to be George Bradbury?''

He hesitated at that. The question had taken him off guard. ''I might've,'' said he. ''I remembers one such time.''

"Did Mrs. Bradbury know that you were a fugitive from the law?"

"No, she didn't, sir. I kept that from her."

"I see. I shall not ask her to confirm that, for I'm sure she would. When you were captured by the constables, Mr. Roundtree, another man was present who managed to escape. Who was that man?"

"I'm sure I don't know, sir—an acquaintance of Mrs. Bradbury's, I s'pose."

"Well, we shall have occasion to speak of this in the future, Mr. Roundtree, for your penalty for two weeks as a fugitive will be two months in gaol. If that seems severe to you, it should not—for a very handsome offer was made to you to encourage your surrender, and you chose to ignore it."

"I had responsibilities that prevented me, sir."

"Well and good. We shall have ample opportunity to discuss those responsibilities of yours, as well, for I stipulate that you, as well, will divide your sentence between the Bow Street strong room and the Fleet Prison, at my discretion." He brought down his gavel, beating a single stroke upon the table. "Mr. Marsden, does that conclude our business for the day?"

"It does, sir."

"Then my court is adjourned."

As he rose, so also did I and most of those about me. One question remained in my mind as I moved against the crowd toward the door through which Sir John had just passed. That question was this: Why had not Sir John presented the Chinese vase—presumably the property of the Lord Chief Justice—as evidence against either Mrs. Bradbury or Roundtree? Why he had not I could not rightly say, but I was sure that it was not simply an oversight.

Exiting the courtroom through that door into what Sir John did call the "backstage" of his court, I saw Mr. Fuller herding his charges back into the strong room. He turned the key in the great lock and it snapped into place with a loud sound, something between a click and a clang. Round-tree caught sight of me through the bars and greeted me with a sober nod and nothing more.

I made my way back to find Sir John and encountered him in conversation with Mr. Marsden. He broke off at my approach and greeted me by name upon my arrival.

"Ah, Jeremy," said he, "I hope you, too, have not come to tax me on the handling of that Bradbury woman. Mr. Marsden here has said that I gave her far too much rope."

"What I said, Sir John, was that giving her that much rope was an encouragement to every pickpocket and thief who comes before you to give you sauce."

"Well, perhaps," said he. "What do you think, Jeremy?"

"What do I think? Well, you were a bit more lenient with her than I would have expected."

"Should've given her three months 'stead of two," put in Mr. Marsden.

"If I cannot break her down in two months, then I cannot do it in three. She will have bested me. She has a clever mind, that woman. For that reason I mean to take a rest before seeing her. Jeremy, perhaps you could return in an hour or an hour and a half and wake me, if need be. I shall be in my chambers napping at my desk. Until then, Mr. Marsden, allow no one back there, will you?"

"No one at all, Sir John."

He began to move off toward his sanctuary, then turned back and called me to him.

"Yes, sir?"

"Jeremy, it might be good to have a wash and change your clothes. They smell as though you've been sleeping in them."

Stung, embarrassed, I sought to defend myself: "I *have* been doing so, sir. I have had to ever since she occupied my room."

"I know, it could not have been easy for you, sleeping

before the fire. But do freshen up, eh? Must think of others, mustn't we?''

Then did he turn and go, leaving me much abashed.

Well, there was naught to do but attend to it immediately. I rushed upstairs and found the kitchen deserted and the fire dwindling. I heaped on coals, put on a log, and a great pot of water, as well. Where was Annie? There being no concert at the Crown and Anchor this Sunday, she was no doubt off to choir rehearsal—I seemed to recall that. As for Lady Fielding, having made her visit to church, she had probably gone off, as she did daily, to look in at the Magdalene Home. And what about Clarissa?

I dashed up the stairs and found her reading in bed. She looked up, smiled, and returned to her reading—of *Tom Jones,* as I noted. Grabbing my good coat and breeches from the hook where they hung, I started out the room.

"A clean shirt, as well," she called after me. "There's one on the shelf."

"I know where they're kept," said I—yet there seemed no malice in her reminder.

"You'll look quite grand," said she. "I've admired that bottle-green coat these past days. You should wear it more often."

"Well, I—"

"Oh, but I know! You've not worn it because I was here and you did not wish to disturb me."

"That's partly true," said I.

But still she continued: "Jeremy Proctor, I've not thanked you properly for giving me the loan of your room. That was generous of you, more than generous—for Lady Fielding was quick to say that you volunteered it. I am grateful to all in this household—and to that handsome Mr. Donnelly, as well—but to you most especially for giving me, if only for a few days, what I have never before had: a room of my own." Then an afterthought: "Oh, and for *Tom Jones,* too, of course. And whatever betide, I would have you remember that."

All this was delivered in her grandest manner, which was very grand indeed. Lacking her taste for florid statement, I knew not quite what to say. I could but mumble a commonplace response. "You're quite welcome, certainly."

"Remember that always," said she, reaching out to take my hand.

With my arms full of coat, breeches, and shirt, it was no easy matter to give it to her. But then did I remember something that ought be said.

"Clarissa, I shall be taking a bath now. I should appreciate a bit of privacy."

"Oh, pooh!" said she, separating her hand from mine. "D'you think I would spy upon you? I've not the interest in naked lads that you seem to have in nekkid women!" Thus did her nature swiftly shift shape.

"Until later then, Miss Pooh," said I, turning my back on her and departing down the stairs.

A bit farther on, as I soaped and splashed in the narrow confines of the tin tub, I thought upon that speech she had made me and wondered if she had not perchance adapted it from one of her romances. Then, thinking upon it further, something troubling came to me: her speech had the tone of a farewell, and that I thought a bit premature. Mr. Donnelly had not pronounced her well, nor would she likely leave us till a place had been found for her in service at one of the great houses in St. James Street or Bloomsbury Square, or, worse thought, till she was put upon a coach with a guardian and shipped off to Lichfield. Ah, no doubt she had simply been carried away by her own rhetoric. Such excesses were not infrequent with her.

It occurs to me that parts of the interrogation of Mrs. Bradbury which took place that day would be better summarized in part than reported in exact detail. I judged it a disappointment, as did, in the main, Sir John. When an hour and something more had elapsed, I carried down to him a cup of tea with which to rouse him to wakefulness, but found him fully alert, pacing the modest-sized room. The cup of tea, however, was most welcome.

"Is there another in the pot you brewed?" he asked.

"Oh yes," said I, "and it is still warm."

"Then bring it for Mrs. Bradbury, and tell Mr. Fuller upon your return that he is to bring the prisoner to us."

I did as he had directed, and found Sir John in his customary place, seated behind the desk. Mr. Fuller followed quickly with her, and she took the cup from me gratefully enough with thanks. I daresay, however, that there was something in her manner that said such amenities were her due.

The moment that Mr. Fuller had left, Sir John leaned forward across his desk and said in a manner most severe: "Madam, where is your husband?"

"Oh," said she, affecting a style most dramatic and tragic, "would that I knew!" Then did she tell her tale, from time to time taking a sip of the tea to strengthen her and help her hold back the tears. (She did wonderfully well at holding back the tears!) It seemed that George Bradbury had been gone near a month. Except for a letter that she had received from him from Warwick over two weeks ago, in which he told her that his father had died, the will had been read, and his business there would soon be concluded, she had received no word from him. (Sir John interrupted her and demanded to know if she could produce this letter; she assured him that she could.) In that missive he had also reassured her of his trust in her to continue to run the pawnshop in the way that he had instructed her; but as she had said in court, business had been bad, and she had been forced to buy far more than she had sold. It was this, she declared, that had led her to yield to the temptation to buy stolen goods: "For it did seem to me that if I had some truly attractive goods of the kind don't often come our way in our dealings with the poor, then I might resell them quickly. You may not credit it, sir, but there's them who are quite well off who will buy such goods with no questions asked—or so I have heard.'' That, except for a shrill protestation that her husband's absence had caused her much grief and anxiety, ended the story she had to tell.

In a sense, I do Mrs. Bradbury no justice, for putting aside the complete absence of tears, she told her story quite convincingly. There were many asides and digressions (on her husband's fine character, his generosity to her, and the difficulty of conducting trade in such a poor and disreputable area as Covent Garden, et cetera), so that her recital took near half an hour to complete. But then did Sir John begin his attack.

''You talk of your worry at your husband's long absence,'' said he. ''Will you tell me why you have made no inquiries? Have you written no letter to discover what had become of him?''

''I knew no one to write to.''

''You might have tried the magistrate in Warwick. I did and received a long, detailed, and enlightening letter from him.'' Whereupon, Sir John gave her the contents of the letter in question near verbatim. He laid special emphasis on the large sum of money that he had with him from the sale of his father's possessions, the white horse he rode on his journey from Warwick, and the likely possibility of his arrival two weeks past—''or a bit more, say fifteen or sixteen days ago. It was then—that is, upon his arrival in London—that he was cruelly murdered.''

''Why, who could have done such a thing?'' she whined. ''Surely you do not think . . .''

''I believe you were party to it. Indeed I do. Madam, it may interest you to know that the lad who testified against you—''

''There was two of them in the shop that day. And he was the other.'' She pointed at me.

''If you mean he who sits with us now, then you are correct. That, however, is neither here nor there, for the lad who testified against you went on his own initiative to your shop to discover if your husband was alive. He had made a tentative identification of a head found in the Fleet sewer as that of George Bradbury. Yet, as I say, identification was only tentative, since the water and filth of the sewer had altered the features of the poor victim of the decapitation somewhat. There he heard, in substance, the story you have told me. Yet he was suspicious and made it his business to keep your shop under observation. He noted the frequent goings and comings of two men. One of them was Thomas Roundtree who was apprehended with you. The other was he who managed to escape us, one who, I have been told, is quite dangerous with his knife. His name is Jackie Carver, though it may be a fictitious one. Tell me, madam, does the name John Cutter mean anything to you?''

''No, it does not. I know no one of that name.''

''You may have noted, however, how well the two names fit together: John—Jackie, Cutter—Carver. Surely this is no mere coincidence.'' Then did Sir John inform her how one John Cutter had sold a white horse to Matthew Gurney, the proprietor of the stable nearest her pawnshop fourteen days past. He told her that the description of John Cutter fitted well that of Jackie Carver, and further, that the horse, ''a mare as big as a stallion,'' fitted exactly that of the horse upon which George Bradbury had set off for London. Then did he conclude: ''There is but one way that horse could have come to London to be sold, and that is with your husband riding upon him. What say you to that, Mrs. Bradbury?''

''I know nothing of no white horse. I accept it now that my husband died at the hands of robbers on his way home to me. Even the Warwick magistrate said he was taking a great chance going alone, did he not?''

''He did, yet how came the horse to London?''

''I know nothing of no white horse. It must be a different one.''

''We have ways of finding out if it is. It may surprise you to learn that to one who knows it well, a horse can be identified as certainly as can a man or woman.''

She made no reply to that.

"We have time aplenty to send to Warwick for one who knew that horse just that well—a former servant of your father-in-law, or a farmhand who stabled the animal. I have two months before me in which to develop the case against you. And if need be, I can retry you and convict you for accepting stolen goods and have even longer to build my case."

"You can no such thing! I proved to you that there was no sense to that charge. You convicted me on—what was it?—conspiracy. I pled to it."

"Yes, you argued very cleverly, but I failed to introduce a piece of evidence against you for the reason that it has not yet been formally identified. There was found in the upstairs of your shop a Chinese vase, one which had no ticket attached. Just such a vase was stolen from the home of the Lord Chief Justice, William Murray."

"The Lord Chief Justice? Oh, Jesus!" she moaned, for the first time giving evidence of fright.

"I can only suppose that the vase reached the table whereon it was found by the usual criminal process. The thief brought it to you, and you paid him a fraction of its value. And you, liking it well enough, used it as a decoration until a suitable buyer might be found."

"That ain't how it was," said she quickly. "No, that fellow Roundtree gave it to me. I never paid him a penny for it. He said it was in his family for years, that his father was a sailor and brought it from the East. He gave it to me in gratitude for letting him have a place to stay."

"And of course he never mentioned that he was a fugitive."

"He said so himself, didn't he?"

"Ah yes, I seem to recall that he did make such a claim." Sir John paused for but a moment. "Mrs. Bradbury, why did you dispose of your husband's clothes if you expected him back from Warwick?"

Her answer was so patently false, so obviously an improvised lie, that I cannot remember it exact. It was something about him declaring upon his departure that he would buy a whole new wardrobe of clothes for himself if his father's property became his; she then claimed that upon hearing that he had inherited all, she simply carried out his wishes.

Then did Sir John go once again through the list of particulars against her: the tentative identification of the head as Mr. Bradbury's; the appearance of the white mare sold to the owner of the stable just down the street by one John Cutter; the fact that she had thrown out or otherwise disposed of her husband's clothing. He then summed up: ''All of those are circumstantial, I grant, but what I offer you now is the opportunity to confess your part in all this and receive in exchange a recommendation of transportation rather than the gallows to the judge who tries your case. My recommendations have never been refused. Madam, I offer you your life.

''Perhaps,'' he continued, ''your part in it was not so great a one. Perhaps you, in your husband's absence, took this Carver fellow as your lover, and your husband may have returned to find you in his arms. A fight may have ensued in which your husband was mortally struck down. If this or something like it is the case, you have but to tell me, and it will be taken into consideration.''

He seemed almost to be pleading with her. Yet in the space of time that followed, her only response was silence.

Sir John sighed, then posed what proved to be his last question: ''Tell me now, how did you meet this Jackie Carver? What was your relation to him?''

''I know no one by that name,'' said she. ''If that was the name of the one who escaped, then I must accept that. I did not more than hire him off the street to help with the unloading.''

That I myself knew to be a lie, for Bunkins had pointed him out to me entering the pawnshop. And Bunkins had seen him there frequently.

"Jeremy," said Sir John to me, "call Mr. Fuller and have him escort the prisoner back to the strong room. Let him then bring Mr. Roundtree to us—wrist irons, I believe, would be appropriate for him."

I did as I was told and returned with Mr. Fuller, who conducted Mrs. Bradbury from the room. Sir John then stood and stretched.

"Ah, Jeremy," said he, "she will be a hard one, I fear. She has made up her mind, very wisely, to hold with the story she told in the beginning."

"But surely you can break her."

"Not with what I have now at my disposal in the way of facts."

"She did not once weep in her telling of the tale."

"Well, this was a mere rehearsal, a first reading, as it were. I doubt not that she will be able to produce a tear or two when she comes to trial at Old Bailey—if indeed she ever does."

It was indeed a gloomy assessment.

"She did, however, make one mistake," he added.

"Oh? What was that?"

Yet before he could respond, a rattling of chains announced the arrival of Thomas Roundtree. Sir John put his forefinger to his lips, ending discussion for the moment. Then, as the prisoner entered the room, Sir John beckoned me to him.

"Though you may object, Jeremy," he whispered, "I must now send you off on an errand. I should like you to go to Mr. Donnelly's surgery to pick up that which you left with him earlier. He should also have ready for you a written report. In any case, he promised me one."

I did not, of course, object. Though disappointed, I gave my agreement to his wish and left immediately for the surgery in Drury Lane.

Perhaps it was best that I was not about during that first hour or more of Sir John's interrogation of Roundtree, for of course I had some sympathy for the fellow. That alone, however, would have meant little, since after all my only role during these sessions was as an observer. Yet, as Sir John himself later confessed, he had "bullied the fellow unconscionably," and considering the role I would subsequently play, it was good that I be not present for that, even as witness.

Mr. Donnelly kept me far longer than I had expected— yet it was no one's fault but my own. When I arrived, I found him still engaged in the task to which Sir John had set him. He invited me to sit down in his place and peer through his microscope. It was an opportunity never before extended me, so I was not likely to decline. I fixed one eye to it as one might to a telescope and shut the other. I scrutinized what lay below and found a number of rough dark circles, broken circles, and attached circles—and around them bits of pink.

"What is it that I am looking at?" I asked Mr. Donnelly.

"Scrapings from the handsaw in that box of tools you brought me."

"And what is it that I see?"

"You make an excellent distinction, Jeremy," said he. "What you see is blood and bits of bone."

"How can you be certain of that? I mean to say, bone is not pink, nor is blood this dark color—brown, almost black, perhaps some red in it, but only a bit."

"Ah, but that is the color of dried blood. I have seen it often on ship deck. As for bone, it bleaches white, but run a bloodstained saw through it, and the result is what you see before you now."

"Could it not be a mixture of two colors of paint?"

"No. Look closely at the drops of blood, and you will see that there is substance to it. It is not so easy to see in the leavings of bone, but under a stronger microscope this would be evident. You know the adage 'Blood is thicker than water.' Well, it is thicker than paint, too—thus paint is applied in coats."

"Thicker than paint?"

"Yes, paint would flake upon the saw and appear flat. Blood, on the other hand, is the most mysterious stuff in the body. I believe it contains many properties if we could but see into it. We'd need a microscope for that which has not yet been created."

Once again I fixed my eye to the eyepiece and stared down at the dark circles and pink bits and saw that it was as he said.

"It is fair amazing what one can see through such an instrument," said I.

"Yes, isn't it? But now I must to my desk and write the report that Sir John has requested."

So saying, he took up pen and paper and went to his work. As he wrote, I sat apart, considering what he had said. After some minutes, I had a question or two for him.

"Mr. Donnelly, may I interrupt?"

He glanced back at me with some show of annoyance. "Well, you have already done that, so you may as well proceed."

"You said that this is the appearance of blood, but do we not have the same sort of blood in common with all other animals?"

"Well, with warm-blooded animals, at least. That is to say, I suppose that cow's blood would look about the same as human blood, even using the microscope."

"Does it?" I asked.

He sighed and shifted in his chair to face me.

"In all truth, I have never viewed cow's blood, or sheep's blood, or horse's blood under the microscope, but I have often viewed human blood so, and you may take my word on it, what I removed from the handsaw, and what we both viewed, was *human* blood."

"But in all due respect, sir, can you be absolutely certain—that is, not having viewed the blood of other animals? I have seen Mr. Tolliver, the butcher in Covent Garden, cut many a chop from sides of beef with a saw. Wouldn't the blood from his saw look as the blood from the one where you got those dried drops of blood we looked at?''

We then argued the point far longer than was necessary, certainly longer than was profitable. He claimed the physician's expertise; I merely held out the possibility of doubt in the matter. We became quite heated.

"Could not the carpenter have cut up a roast with his saw?'' I insisted.

With that, Mr. Donnelly turned back to his desk and purposefully tore up the sheet of paper upon which he had been writing. I was shocked.

"Why did you do that, sir?'' I asked.

"Because I said in it specifically that I had found traces of *human* blood and bone on the carpenter's saw. I shall now alter that simply to say that I found traces of blood and bone.''

"Oh, well, I suppose in the interest of exactitude . . .''

He wagged his head then and chuckled. "Jeremy,'' said he, "you truly were meant for the law. If ever I questioned it, you banished all doubt during our discussion.''

There was naught he could have said that would have pleased me more.

He did not take long to rewrite his report. And with it in my pocket and the toolbox in my hand, I made ready to go.

"Please forgive me,'' said I to him, "if I was aggressive in my argument.''

"Think nothing of it,'' said he. "It was all among friends and, as you put it, 'in the interest of exactitude.' '' Then: "Oh, by the bye, do tell Sir John that I shall walk over to Bow Street so that we may all ride over to the Laningham residence together. I have just time to change my clothes for this curious event.''

And so, saying my goodbye to him, I took my leave.

It occurred to me as I hurried back in the dark that there was not another of mature years in my range of acquaintance, only Mr. Donnelly, with whom I would have dared to argue as I had. Never once had he said, "You are a mere lad. Who are you to question my opinion?'' He may have argued his superior knowledge as a physician—though he would have done so with any layman who disagreed with him, and that was quite a different matter. He credited my intelligence and had always done so. And for that I would ever be grateful to him.

Entering Number 4 through the door marked ''No admittance,'' I walked down the long hall which led to the court's ''backstage.'' There were constables about. Mr. Baker had replaced Mr. Fuller for the duration of the night. And I saw, passing the strong room, that only Mrs. Bradbury was there inside; she sat in one corner which she had made her own and did not even bother to look up as I passed by. I continued on my way to the magistrate's chambers, sure that I should find him there still deeply involved in the interrogation of Thomas Roundtree.

But no, he was at the door, just leaving the room as I arrived. Above the black band that hid his sightless eyes, his brow was puckered in a frown. The corners of his mouth were turned down in a proper scowl. He seemed altogether quite unhappy. Behind I caught a glimpse of Roundtree, his back to the door, still seated where he had been put well over an hour before.

''Jeremy?'' said Sir John, recognizing me before I had said a word. ''Come over here out of earshot so that we may talk a little. It seems I must go upstairs and change my clothes. What I have on, I'm told by Lady Fielding, is not grand enough for the evening's occasion.''

Thus reminded, I gave him Mr. Donnelly's message regarding their journey to the Laningham residence.

Sir John cackled at that. ''There is an Irishman for you who can pinch a penny hard as any Scotsman.'' But now he whispered: ''Tell me, Jeremy, what does he say in his report? Don't bother to read it. Just give me the content of it.''

''The gist is that he found traces of blood and bone on the handsaw which he took from the toolbox.''

"Damn! I could have made good use of that. He's sure of it, is he?"

"He examined scrapings under his microscope."

"That should make it certain." He bit his lip in indecision. "If I could but stay a bit longer." He sighed. "But I cannot. I have a premonitory notion that something of importance may happen this evening, and I feel obliged to be present if it does." Then did he brighten somewhat: "I have an idea, Jeremy."

"And what is that, sir?"

"You might see what you can do with him."

"Question him?"

"Yes, yes indeed. I played the bear with him. You might play the lamb. Something he said indicates to me that he feels a bit guilty in the way he treated you—cozened you, played the fool until you let down your guard so that he could escape. Use that. Be his friend. Yet try to get from him what truly happened on the night George Bradbury returned from Warwick, and above all, get him to implicate the others. I have promised transportation for him, no matter what his part. That, of course, is all I can promise."

Though I was quite intimidated by the task he had given me, I managed a solemn promise to do my best.

"I know you will," said he. "Fetch me if he breaks, or even if he seems close. I shall let you be the judge of when that might be. But now . . . now I must go."

He grasped for my hand and squeezed it awkwardly between his two. Then he was gone.

I peered inside the room. We had conducted our conversation in whispers at some distance from the door. Yet even so, Thomas Roundtree seemed a shrunken figure as he sat bent in his chair, his bowed head just visible above his narrow shoulders. It seemed barely possible that upright he would stand a good six feet tall. Sir John had advised me to play the lamb with him. Looking at Roundtree, diminished and despondent, I could hardly imagine any other role for myself. My heart went out to him, in spite of myself. I took a deep breath and walked inside.

Turning at my footsteps, he looked at me rather dully and nodded. "Hullo, lad," said he.

"Hello, Mr. Roundtree," said I. "You look as if you might not object to a bit of companionship."

I pulled a chair over, set down the box of tools, and sat down close to him before he could answer in the negative. As I did, I noticed the set of hand irons that he wore were attached to a chain, which in turn had been run through a stout half-link that had been driven into the floor; I must have tripped over that arc-shaped protrusion at least a dozen times without ever once realizing its purpose. It was evident to me, too, why he sat so sagged and bent: his chair had been placed too far back from the link in the floor to which his chains were attached. To keep a purchase on it with his buttocks, it was necessary for him to assume a posture in which he was near bent double. This may have been Mr. Fuller's idea of a joke on Roundtree; he was capable of such petty cruelties to his prisoners. And Sir John, of course, could not have seen.

"Here," said I, rising, "let me fix that chair for you."

I pushed it in close as it would go to the hitch. He was able then to sit erect and relax a bit.

"Is that better?"

"Ain't it though," said he, wiggling his arms. "The gaoler did that. I tried moving the chair with my arse, but that didn't work. Ain't got much arse back there to work with."

It was no doubt true. His clothes did hang upon him. I glimpsed his bony wrists; were it not for his big hands, the irons might have fallen off him.

"I thought you might like to talk a little."

"I wouldn't mind," said he. "I been talked at hard for near all afternoon, it seems. What the magistrate said to me wasn't what I'd call encouragin'. But you know, I been thinkin' on what you said last time I saw you, and it's true, I brought it all on myself. Each time I done something I know was wrong, I sank a little deeper into the shit. Like that time I ran away from you—oh, I laughed and made grand fun of you—but you prob'ly got a great whipping for it, if that's what they do to apprentice constables.''

"No, nothing of the sort," said I.

"But I've done worse."

Rather than ask him direct what worse he had done, which was of course what I wished to know, I gambled that it would be ultimately better to build a firmer foundation of friendship.

"We were greatly puzzled that you had gone fugitive on such a trifling charge as public drunkenness. But then, when I returned to your room and encountered your daughter, we understood."

"That's right. I couldn't go for no month in gaol, for she would've soon been starvin' and out on the street beggin'—or worse."

"And you hadn't the money to pay the fine?"

"Oh, I had the money right enough, but we had other uses for it."

Their passage to the colonies, of course. Though I thought it, I made no mention of it.

"How is she?" he asked. "How is my daughter, Clarissa? You said she was gettin' on well."

"Oh, she's near cured, I'd say, though the doctor still visits."

"She's quite the child, ain't she? Tell me, lad, what do you think of her?"

"I think many things," said I, wondering just what I ought to answer. Then, opting for the truth: "I think, first of all, she's very bright—but I need not tell you that, for you said as much yourself. Yet I also think her willful and headstrong, the sort of girl who will have her way by any means she can. But withal, charming''—a word borrowed from Sir John—''and . . . and interesting.''

"Ahh," said he, laughing despite his situation, "you've come to know her well, I can tell. She is all you said and more—in every direction. Though you may not have guessed it, she likes you quite well. When you gifted her that book, you won her over.''

''Well, she is often quite tart with me.''

''I've no doubt of it. Still, you know, to understand her proper, you had to know her mother. She's most like her in every partic'lar—in her look, in her manner, in her brightness, oh, specially in her brightness.'' He paused then, and I saw tears well in his eyes. He ducked his head, and with his manacled hands, he wiped them away.

Then did he do a most remarkable thing—remarkable, that is, considering his circumstances, and remarkable, too, in that his audience was myself, a youth of fifteen years. He told me the story of his life—or that portion of it he had lived in marriage at Lichfield—of Sarah, his wife, of Clarissa's birth, and the little family they made together. His version differed markedly from the one given us by the Lichfield magistrate, not so much in substance as in tone, for it was not one story but many; these were his store of memories from what he now well knew was the best part of his life. As such, they were, most of them, memories of happy times—Christmases spent with her people, holidays, walks in the country. He recalled their family jokes, told of the bright future he had sketched for Sarah if only he might earn his master carpenter papers, talked of their pride in Clarissa as she grew into the bright girl she is today. Once begun, he seemed unable to stop. He must have gone on so for near an hour. I truly believe he talked to himself, rather than to me.

Yet of a sudden he ended that part of his tale. It was as if he had looked around him and noted who he was, where he was, and why he was here. He sighed a great sigh then and gave forth his *mea culpa*.

''I was not a good provider,'' said he, ''not a bad carpenter, but never a good provider. Y'see, I've had an awful problem all these years with the drink, and I do not think we would've survived, the three of us, if Sarah's father, old

Mr. Gladden, had not helped us along. Then he died right sudden, and the women tried to run the bookshop, Sarah with her mother and sister. She would take Clarissa along, and there, midst all those books, she taught her to read. It weren't hard. It was as if the child had been born to it. But the shop failed, and she had to depend on me, and I was undependable. That's what she called me when she chastised me, and when she did I'd grow angry at her, though I never raised a hand to her, nor to Clarissa. No, I took my revenge by going out to drink some more. Then she took sick with the consumption. Clarissa nursed her, but she lingered on, which was a curse, I truly believe."

By that time tears streamed down his cheeks, and I having listened to him so, they blurred my sight, as well. Yet he pressed on, wailing his guilt to me.

"I have stole, and I have done far worse, but the worst thing I ever done was be a bad husband and . . . father. I drank so when Sarah died, for I was sore ashamed. I drank so, Clarissa went out to the neighbors beggin' for food— my own daughter a beggar! And that's when they took her away from me."

Then, finally overwhelmed, he surrendered to his tears and wept copiously, his shoulders heaving, his chains jangling as he beat down upon his knees with his fists. I knew not what to do to help him. Clumsily I rose, grasped the hand nearest me, and gave it a manly squeeze with my own. I had not felt such sorrow for another since my young friend Mariah went so horribly—nay, more, since my own father died. Slowly, he began to gain control of himself. Yet still he would speak.

"I've been a fool all my life," said he. "Sarah would never have married such a fool as me if I'd not gotten her with child. Her better sense would have prevailed."

With that I dipped into my coat pocket and pulled at my kerchief, loosening the report written by Mr. Donnelly and sending it down to the floor. That was a reminder, certainly, of the onerous task I had been given. I handed him the kerchief, and he made good use of it. I retrieved the report and tucked it away as I sat down and leaned close to him.

"What has Sir John told you?" I asked in a low voice.

"Oh . . ." Roundtree croaked, then cleared his throat and spoke on in a husky voice: "My future ain't bright, I'll tell you. He calculates the worth of that vase I stole at twenty guineas or more. That's enough to hang me. Oh, I stole it, no question, might as well own up since that bitch of a Bradbury woman pointed the finger at me. She'd no need to do that."

"Did the magistrate say no more than that?"

"Oh, he said plenty. He told me he could get me transportation 'stead of the rope if only I would tell what happened to George Bradbury."

"And you hesitate? Why? Exile and forced labor would surely be better than the rope. How can you hesitate when one of the two has already betrayed you?"

"All right, lad, I'll tell you what I would not tell the magistrate. One has betrayed me, true, but I'm afeared of t'other—not for myself but for Clarissa. If I confessed, I would name him, Jackie Carver, and he would have his revenge. He promised me as much. They paid me just so much as would buy our passage to the colonies just to get rid of me and what I knew. Promised to pay more later. But if I was to snitch, and he couldn't get at me in Newgate waiting trial, he would hunt Clarissa out, even down to Lichfield. I'm sure of it as can be."

"But even tonight the Bow Street Runners are searching for him. They will find him. Have no doubt of it. And listen to me, please, Sir John Fielding has it in his power to hold Clarissa from Lichfield, though they want her back in the parish workhouse. He could find employment for her. He could give her the new life you could not."

"He said something of the sort, but if she was here in London, it would be all the easier for that villain to get to her."

"We would keep her safe here with us until Carver was caught."

He took a moment to consider that, then brushed it aside: "He would find a way."

I grabbed the report from Mr. Donnelly from my pocket and waved it at him. "Do you see this? It is a report from a doctor who examined your handsaw and found blood and bone on it. This is the only true evidence of murder we have so far—and it points to you. It says that *you* murdered George Bradbury."

"I murdered no one. 'Twas him, Carver, who done it. He told me so himself. Boasted of it, he did."

"Then how was it the blood and bone got on your saw?"

"The problem was, Carver puts it to me, 'How do you fit a five-and-a-half-foot man in a three-foot box?' No, George Bradbury was dead when they showed him to me. I cut off his head with the saw and sent Carver off to be rid of it. He come back, and says he dropped it in the Fleet sewer. I told him that was no place to be done with it, for there was too many places for it to bump up against and stop. And ain't that just what happened?"

"Yes, it was, but where, then, did you dispose of the box of Bradbury's remains?"

"We threw it off the Westminster Bridge late at night when they was nobody about. I went out and got good and proper drunk—had to after that. I did a terrible thing, and I knew it, but I did it for the passage to America. But I managed to get so drunk that I was arrested, and you know all the rest."

I kept silent for the moment, giving him time to recover himself. "Mr. Roundtree," I said at last, "I want you to tell Sir John Fielding what you told me. I promise you, as he will promise, that we will keep Clarissa with us until Carver be caught, no matter how long it may take."

"You mean upstairs of here?"

"Yes, where Sir John himself dwells. There she has a room to herself and she eats well, probably better than she has ever in her life. She passes her time reading.''

"Oh, she would, she would do that." He said nothing for quite the longest time. Turned away he was, considering what I had said. I waited. "Well"—he spoke at last—"I suppose not even Carver would dare to go there."

"Mr. Roundtree, I know Jackie Carver, and he is not near so bold as you think him."

"P'rhaps you're right. He murdered Bradbury while he slept." Then with a sigh: "All right, bring the magistrate, and I will tell him what I told you—and more. But I will tell him nothing at all if he does not promise to keep Clarissa safe."

I rose from my chair and grasped his hand once again.

"This is what it is right to do, Mr. Roundtree. It is what Clarissa herself would have you do, believe me. I shall return soon with Sir John—as soon as ever I can."

ELEVEN

*In Which I Encounter
a Villain Named
Jackie Carver*

Though Sir John had left no instructions with me as to
the disposition of Roundtree should I feel it propi-
tious to fetch the magistrate from the Laninghams', it
seemed to me wrong to return him to the strong room. Who
could say what might transpire between him and Mrs. Bradbury were they to be thrust together again? She might remind him of Jackie Carver's threats and thus discourage
him from proceeding with his confession; he, on the other
hand, might throttle her for her casual betrayal of him. No,
some other place must be found for him. I went to Mr.
Baker with the problem.

He listened, nodded, and asked, "Is he secure there?
Chained to that link in the floor?"

"Oh yes, but Mr. Fuller had the prisoner so far back he
was stretched out and could barely move. I put him forward
so he could at least sit upright." I was quite indignant on
Roundtree's behalf.

"One of Fuller's little tricks," said he, with a wrinkle
of his nose. "But as to the question of where the prisoner
should be put, I'd say where he is now is as good as any

place. He'll need a guard—and I've got just the man for you.'' Then did he raise up and shout, ''Mr. Cowley!''

So it was that Roundtree was left in the care of Constable Cowley, he who had returned to limited duty while the knife wound in his leg did heal. I last saw Cowley armed and limping visibly as he walked toward Sir John's chambers. And so I was off to the Laningham residence in St. James Square.

Had a hackney been somewhere in sight as I left Number 4 Bow Street, I might have jumped inside, yet so charged was I by what I had accomplished that, seeing none, I set off at a run, assuring myself I could flag one down on the way. But having gone half the distance without success, I settled down to a fast jog trot and covered the remainder on foot, as well. As a result, I arrived at the door of the great house overheated and perspiring there in the cold night air. I took a moment to catch my breath, yet not so long, for I did not wish to catch a chill. I rapped hard with the knocker, waited, then rapped again. The door opened, and I caught the sound of music within—an instrument I had not heard before, somewhat like a harpsichord yet without the jangling sound of it. I recognized the man at the door as the butler of the house. I recalled his name.

''Mr. Poole,'' said I to him, ''I am come on an urgent court matter for Sir John Fielding. Can he be called away?''

''Not perhaps at this moment, but come in, lad, and I'll get you to him quick as ever I can.''

I thanked him and followed him past the grand winding staircase and down the long, wide hallway. As we approached our destination, the music swelled louder, an intricate weaving of a single theme at a slow, quite majestic tempo. It was, as Lord Laningham had promised, quite funereal in tone. The book-lined room, when reached, was quite deep—and wide as it was deep. Great double doors opened onto it. Before we entered through them, Mr. Poole held me back and bent close to whisper in my ear.

''I shall seat you just left of the door,'' said he, ''away

from the rest. As soon as the musician is done, you may simply go up to Sir John and deliver your message. He sits, I believe, in the first row of chairs.''

Nodding my agreement, I thanked him and was led in through the double doors. He pointed out to me three empty chairs placed against the wall and gave me my choice of them. As I seated myself in the nearest of them, I glanced back at the butler and saw that he had taken a place beyond the door on the other side. There he stood—though not for long. I saw him waved over by none other than Lord Laningham himself. The lord—perhaps exercising the host's prerogative—sat in a corner apart from his guests and a bit out of their sight. That struck me as a bit odd, though never having attended such an affair as this one, I had no particular reason to suppose it so. He gave to Mr. Poole an instruction of some sort and sent his servant out the double doors.

The music continued somewhat monotonously. It seemed to have had a soporific effect upon the dozen or so who were seated in the chairs directly before . . . what was it? The fortepiano? Yes, that was the name of the instrument; I recalled it from the invitation. A few young men in the second row of chairs seemed to be nodding, though Mr. Donnelly seemed quite alert. Of those in the first row, Thomas Trezavant, the coroner—whose abundant form quite overwhelmed his chair—rested his chin upon his chest, evidently deep in slumber; Sir John may have appeared to those who did not know him well to be dozing, yet I knew him well enough to recognize his attitude as one of cogitation; the women—Lady Fielding and the black-clad females of Lord Laningham's immediate family—were all of them admirably attentive.

I confess that the seemingly endless repetitions and minute variations of the music also began to have a dulling effect upon my own brain. No doubt I was tired from my great rush to arrive at this place. In fact, I myself had begun to nod, so that I missed the butler's reentry into the room.

Yet shaking myself to a wakeful state, I made a swift survey of the room and saw Mr. Poole bending to offer Lord Laningham a wine bottle and an empty glass upon a serving tray. So the lord had sent his butler off for a tipple—how ignoble of him! He would drink while his guests thirsted. Perhaps that was why he had chosen that secluded corner to listen to the concert. Yet he made no further effort to hide his purpose. He allowed the glass to be filled, then indicated by his sign that he wished the bottle to be left on a small table nearby. Immediately the butler had left him, he gulped down the contents of the glass and poured another—even shaking the bottle a bit as he did so. (To what purpose? I wondered.) I should not have thought him so keen for claret—yet of course I hardly knew the man. But then did I remember a detail told by the late Lady Laningham: that when the late Lord Laningham had called for the bottle of wine from his table, Arthur Paltrow had insisted on drinking from it before he would allow it to be taken away. Perhaps he who had hosted this dignified occasion was a secret sot, as much a slave to good claret as Roundtree was to common gin. I resolved to mention this to Sir John.

He drank as a sot would drink, gulping down the second glass as quickly as the first. But then, his greedy desire temporarily satisfied, he sat back as if he intended to relax—yet could not. Something in him denied him repose. Was it an immediate thirst for another glass of wine? Or had perhaps guilt possessed him that he had given in so completely to his need. In any case, though tense, he remained back in his chair and made no further move toward the wine bottle.

Had only I seen this? I looked at Mr. Poole. He was back at his post, erect, head turned neither to the right nor to the left, the serving tray now tucked under his arm. Apparently he had witnessed nothing. Not wishing to stare (I had attempted to see all I had seen by means of repeated glances), I willed my attention elsewhere, focusing for the first time really upon the musician who, after his fashion, entertained us. Mr. John Christian Bach was a short, thickset man who wore a wig, no doubt to cover a balding head and perhaps for warmth, as well. Though much of him was hidden behind the great large instrument that he played, I judged him to be thickset by the size and movement of his wide shoulders, and I knew him as short by the fact that his feet bare touched the pedals of the fortepiano. Mr. Bach must indeed have been famous, for even then I, who had no real knowledge of the London music world, had heard his name. (In fact, he was Music Master to the King, and his appearance that night must have cost Lord Laningham dear.) Nevertheless, I liked his music little—monotonous it seemed, with none of the joy of Handel. Still, I listened closely, attempting to judge him fairly. And listening closely, I soon began again to nod.

Then, of a sudden, I was brought up sharp by a sound, a most remarkable sound, which issued from that corner of the room which the host had taken as his own. It was a long, sustained "Ohhh," which was moaned out in the most frightening way that could be. I looked immediately to my right and saw that Lord Laningham was on his feet, swaying uncertainly. Others looked, too, turning in their chairs, mouths all agape. Mr. Poole hurried to his master. Yet too late he was, for just as he arrived, Lord Laningham collapsed upon the floor and began most hideously to vomit.

I rushed to him, as did the rest. It took but a moment for all to be crowding about him in much the same manner as the musicians and members of the chorus had pressed upon the dying man on the stage of the Crown and Anchor. And Lord Laningham—that is, Arthur Paltrow—did regurgitate the contents of his stomach just as violently as had his uncle before him. One paramount difference there was, however, between the two occasions, and that lay in the fact that through all this turmoil, indeed for many minutes after it had begun, Mr. John Christian Bach continued to play in the same manner as before; this lent a bizarre element to all that transpired—the shouting of the men, the screaming of the women, and with it the repeated revolutions of the fortepiano.

Because I was perhaps a bit closer, or quicker on my feet, I reached the prone figure just after Mr. Poole. Seeing the vomit gush forth from his mouth and spread upon the carpet, I called out one bit of advice—"Turn him on his side that he may not drown!"—and saw it promptly followed by the butler. Then there was much more advice shouted.

"Give him room!"

"Give him air!"

"Call a doctor!"

But of course, a doctor was present. Mr. Donnelly was down on his knee beside the sick man, attempting to push back the rest of the people. Then did I hear my name called in a voice most familiar.

"Jeremy! Jeremy Proctor! Are you here? Did I hear your voice?"

It was Sir John. I glimpsed him on the periphery of the encroaching circle where he had been led by Lady Fielding. I fought my way out of the crush, and in a moment I was by his side.

"How long have you been here? Did you see what happened before his collapse?"

"I did, sir. I came because Roundtree—"

"No, listen," he interrupted. "Lead me away from all this mad shouting, and tell me what you saw."

And suppressing my desire to tell of my triumph as an interrogator, I did exactly as he had instructed me. Again, as I had done at the Crown and Anchor, I gave him all the events that I had witnessed—the call for the bottle of claret, the rapid guzzling of two full glasses, and, oh yes, the shaking of the bottle ere he poured the second glass. The last detail interested Sir John greatly.

"You say he shook the bottle? As if to mix its contents?"

"Well, yes, more or less, I suppose."

"Then, Jeremy, I must have that bottle from which he drank."

"But Mr. Donnelly said there is no proper test for . . ." Somehow I dared not say the word.

"Get it, lad, for I have a test of my own."

Taking that as a direct order, I hastened back to those clustered round the fallen Lord Laningham and saw immediately that the bottle remained still on the small table, and remained also—*mirabile dictu!*—upright; not a drop of its contents had spilled. I leaned over and grabbed it, and with it firmly in hand I stepped back. And as I did, my eyes came in direct contact with those of Lady Laningham. She looked sharply at me, though her expression registered neither shock nor disapproval. Then she shifted her gaze to where it properly belonged: to her distressed husband. He was at that moment being raised by Mr. Poole and the largest of the young gentlemen, under the direction of Mr. Donnelly.

"Put him in his bed," said the medico to them. "I shall fetch my bag and do all I can for him."

Then did I return to Sir John and tell him that I had the bottle, and it was half full.

"Good. Now I believe I heard Mr. Donnelly say that he was going off to tend Lord Laningham. Has he left? Can you bring him to me?"

I could, and I did, detaining him at the door as he was about to make his exit. He came willingly enough, though he obviously felt his duty lay with him who was at that moment borne into the hallway.

"Yes, Sir John, what would you with me?"

"I'll not detain you long," said the magistrate in a voice low as a whisper. "What I have heard from Jeremy leads me to believe that Lord Laningham himself may have purposely brought on his condition."

"Poisoned *himself?* That seems a bit far-fetched, Sir John."

"Perhaps, but could he not produce the same symptoms with a simple emetic? The vomiting, of course, is real enough, but could not the extreme condition be performed as a bit of theater?"

"Well, it is possible, I suppose. I'll look for signs of it. Still, it does seem quite like a repetition of the same fatal disorder I saw in the late lord."

"If he lives, I shall be suspicious," said Sir John.

"If he lives," said Mr. Donnelly, "you may attribute it to my powers as a physician."

And then, ducking his head sharply in a hasty bow, he turned on his heel and left us. I fear he was somewhat miffed at Sir John.

"Now, Jeremy, you may tell me what you wished to regarding Roundtree."

That I did very quickly, emphasizing that we had but to promise that we would keep Clarissa safe with us until Jackie Carver be caught, and Roundtree would tell all he had told me and more to Sir John.

"So that was why he held back from me so resolutely!" said the magistrate. "He feared for his daughter. I had not thought him an altogether bad sort. Sad, is it not, what poverty will force a man to do?"

"He awaits you, Sir John."

"Ah, but I cannot go just yet. I must put questions to the butler—Poole, I believe, is the fellow's name. I must find out from him if the bottle from which Lord Laningham drank was taken from the general supply, or if it had been laid aside specially for his master's own consumption."

"Would you like me to remain for that, sir?"

"No, I think it best that you go back to Bow Street. Lady Fielding can help me about this place. You, I think, should continue to talk to Roundtree—no need to question him further, simply keep his spirits up. Tell him I accept his condition and promise to keep his daughter safe. Tell him also that I shall be with him in less than an hour.''

"I will do so, Sir John.''

With that, I turned to go, but was detained by his hand upon my arm.

"But one thing more. Take that bottle of claret with you. Find a cork and stopper it. It might be safest to take a hackney for your return. I'll not have you dropping it along the way. Have you enough for the fare?''

"I have, sir.''

"Then on your way.''

I found Lady Fielding at the door, Mr. Trezavant beside her. Both were engaged in murmuring comforting words to Lady Laningham and their daughters, Charity and Felicity. I waited patiently by her side until the moment when her inspiration flagged and a pause came. I then touched her on the shoulder, and having her attention, pointed into the room at Sir John, who waited alone where I had left him. She nodded to me, excused herself, and went to him.

And I, reader, I went off in search of a cork.

Upon my return I went direct to Constable Baker and handed over to him the bottle of wine. He took it and held it up to the light.

"Half full, I see,'' said he with a wink. "Good stuff, is it?''

"You might not think so if you'd seen what happened to him who drank from it.''

"Oh? What did happen, then?''

"Poisoned him.''

"Is he dead?''

"Not yet. But last I looked, he seemed on his way.''

"Ah, well, then no need to sample it. I'll put it away under lock and key in Mr. Marsden's evidence box.''

"You might label it poison, as well, lest Mr. Marsden be similarly tempted in the morning.''

"I might indeed, or leave him a note.''

"Any word from Mr. Cowley on our prisoner?'' I asked.

"Not a word. No news is good news, I reckon. I did hear the chains rattling a bit some time ago. Most likely your prisoner's asleep."

"If not, I shall talk with him a bit more until Sir John arrives."

"Do send Cowley back to me, would you?" said Mr. Baker. "Though it's a bit early, I feel a great hunger coming upon me. I believe I'll send him out for dinner."

And so, with a wave, I left him. Having remarked upon his hunger, he had reminded me of my own. Far more than keep company further with Roundtree, I should have preferred to go upstairs to the meal that I was certain Annie had saved for me. Still, I saw the good sense of Sir John's instruction. I had led Roundtree to the water of salvation. It would not do to allow him now to back away.

Upon reaching the door, which was but half open, I did hear heavy breathing—a light snore—that indicated he I had come to visit was indeed asleep. I hesitated a moment, considering whether it might not be better to allow him to sleep a bit longer that I might go up and eat my cold dinner; but indeed no, I had received my orders, and I would carry them out—even if it meant wasting an hour sitting by a sleeping prisoner. I pushed the door gently open so as not to waken him. What, then, did I find?

Not Roundtree, but Constable Cowley it was who slept— quite comfortably in a chair set in a far corner of the room.

The prisoner was nowhere to be seen.

I leapt to the place he had been—to the empty chair— and found chains and hand irons still attached to the link driven into the floor. Then, looking about, I saw the box of tools was also gone. Had I left it within his reach? No, I was certain I had not. Yet I examined the hand irons and the chain, and I was relieved to find no marks of a file upon them. What I did find, however, was bits of shaved skin and blood smeared over them, and I immediately understood that somehow he had made those long hands of his narrow enough so that he had managed to squeeze out of the irons. The gore and scrapings left on the manacles was the price he had paid for his freedom. It must indeed have been a painful escape. Yes, of course, I saw the open window, and the chair standing to it. He had gone out there, taking the toolbox with him—all that while Cowley slept. Well, he would sleep no longer.

I went to him and shook him roughly.

"Mr. Cowley," said I, near shouting in his ear, "*awake!* You have let the prisoner escape."

Even so, I had to shout his name a second time before his eyes came open.

"What . . ." said he, the thickness of sleep still upon him, "what did you say?"

I repeated the plain fact of the matter and pointed to the prisoner's empty chair.

Then did his sleepy eyes widen. Then did he jump from his chair.

"Oh, God," he wailed, "oh, dear God!"

At that moment came the sound of running footsteps, and Mr. Baker leaned through the door. "Did I hear it aright? The prisoner's gone?"

This time I pointed to the open window.

"Oh, Cowley," said the constable, with a shake of his head, "you've crapped it for certain this time. We've never before lost a prisoner out of Number Four Bow Street. Could you not stay awake for once?"

"What can I do? What shall we do?" he moaned. I feared he might commence to weep.

"The first thing you can do," said I, "is go out and search every part of the yard in back and make sure the prisoner is not hiding somewhere there. That's where these windows lead."

"I'll do it!" he yelled—and ran from the room.

"And don't forget to look in the privy!" Mr. Baker called after him.

But then we heard the door slam and could not be sure Mr. Cowley had heard or no.

"What can be done?" I asked Mr. Baker, appealing to him as the wisest and most experienced of us three.

"Well, where would this fellow, this . . ."

"Roundtree."

"Where would Roundtree go? Think on it."

That I did, concentrating most hard upon the question. At last I said: "I can think of only two places."

"Then go to them. Take Cowley with you. He's armed, got a brace of good pistols by his side. You'll need a constable with you to take your prisoner back again."

No doubt he was right. "But what of his leg—the wound? Can he travel?"

"Bugger his leg and his bloody wound. If he don't bring back the prisoner, he'll have no job to return to. If he'd showed a bit of sense, he'd not have gotten that knife in his leg in the first place."

I nodded my understanding, yet perhaps withheld my agreement. I was not at all sure Sir John would let him go over such an offense, for he had treated it lightly when Roundtree escaped from me. On the other hand, the fellow was then not known to be witness to murder. And as for the other, I knew not the exact circumstances of his wounding.

"And yet a thing more," added Mr. Baker. "When you get out there with him, chasing your man, you take command. Tell Cowley what to do. That poor cod can follow orders right enough, but without someone to tell him, he's plain lost. You hear me, Jeremy?"

"Yes, Mr. Baker, and I'll do as you say."

A minute or two more and Constable Cowley had returned, shaking his head. "He ain't nowhere about out there—and yes, I looked in the privy. He had but a low wall to climb to get from here. No telling where he'd be now."

"Jeremy's got a couple of ideas about that. You go with him, and do as he says."

Constable Cowley looked at me and then at Mr. Baker. "Yes sir, I'll do it just so."

And so we started for the door to Bow Street. Mr. Cowley grabbed his greatcoat and was pulling it on when Annie, of all people, came racing down the stairs.

"Jeremy," said she, "have you seen Clarissa about?"

I looked at her rather stupidly. "Down here? Why, no. Is she not upstairs?"

"No, and I've looked everywhere."

"She's not up top in my room?"

"I've looked everywhere, I tell you—even in the sitting room, the dining room, and the bedroom of Sir John and Lady F. I've looked in cupboards and wardrobes—everywhere. She's nowhere up there."

My thoughts raced. Did Clarissa perchance know that her father was in detention down here? Could she have known her father would escape? Could she have aided him in some way? Had not her last conversation with me had the tone of farewell? Yes, I had remarked that a little afterward. Then, from somewhere deep in my memory, came Roundtree's voice in my head, and the words that echoed there were these: "Some way or other, I'll get her in five days." That was what he had said when he waylaid me outside the chemist's shop. I inferred that it was in five days that their ship sailed for the colonies, nor had he gainsaid me. Then, counting back, I realized that tomorrow might be counted as the fifth day—or might so by Roundtree. This meant that their ship would depart tomorrow—no doubt on the morning tide. They thought to board her tonight and sail away undetected on the morrow.

All this came to me in less than a minute. Annie stared at me impatiently, reasonably expecting some response from me. When she was about to turn away, I at last managed a reply.

"She will be with her father," said I to her.

"Well and good," said Annie, having no notion of the circumstances. "You must find her father then, for she is not yet well enough to go about on such a night as this.''

Then did she start back up the stairs.

''Come along, Mr. Cowley,'' said I. ''We now have a third possible place to search for the prisoner.''

And with neither a question nor an argument he followed along behind me out the door to Bow Street. As we tramped along together, I considered the situation of father and daughter in greater detail. It was just possible that Clarissa had known her father was down below in the strong room. If she had been in the kitchen, and the door to the stairs was open, she might have heard his voice—but that seemed unlikely. Could she have crept downstairs merely out of curiosity and unexpectedly found her father staring out at her from behind the bars? Could they then have made their plans together? Also unlikely, for neither Mr. Fuller in the daytime nor Mr. Baker at night (both of them quite vigilant) would have allowed her to go walking about, exploring their domain; even less would they have allowed her to talk to a prisoner. And had any such event occurred, I should have heard about it from either one of them, or from Sir John. No, I thought it far more likely that father and daughter had acted independently; each knew the date and time of the ship's departure; their passage had been paid in advance; each had confidence in the other to meet—but where?

We had made it past Russell Street and now walked along Tavistock Street. Not far along, I realized that in my haste I had set too swift a pace for Constable Cowley. Though he was taller than me by a good many inches and had a longer stride, he now moved with such a pronounced limp that he was having great difficulty keeping up. He had not complained, yet his face—his tight mouth and the determined set of his jaw—made plain the strain upon his wounded leg.

''Here, Mr. Cowley,'' said I, slowing to a pace not much better than a crawl, ''let us not go so quick. I've a need to think, and I find it difficult to do so at such speed as is natural to you.''

''Oh . . . sorry, Jeremy, I'd no idea.''

''Your legs are longer than mine.''

''Aye, so they are, but one of them's got a hole punched in it with a knife by that villain Slade. Quite throbbin' it is now. I'm happy to move along slower.''

What I had said to him was, in one sense, true enough. I did need to think a bit on where we might go first to look. Had it been Roundtree alone we sought, I should have thought it likely he would go to Bradbury's pawnshop—or go there first, at least. Though it was locked, he might gain admittance by breaking a back window or forcing the door. He would know where the cash was put, since he had kept shop for Mrs. Bradbury. Indeed he might even have some idea where the trove of treasure taken from the late George Bradbury was hid. He would reason that he and Clarissa needed money, as much of it as could be found, if they were off to start a new life in Boston or Baltimore, or wherever their ship might put in.

I stood upon the corner of Maiden Lane with Mr. Cowley, still considering this urgent matter. To the right lay Bedford Street and the pawnshop; to the left was Half-Moon Passage and that sordid warren of a court wherein father and daughter had lived for months in a single room.

What did Clarissa know of the pawnshop? Simply that it was the place where her father went to hide from the law—if indeed she knew that. It seemed to me most likely that they would expect to meet in the room. They would collect their belongings, and then perhaps he would take her to the pawnshop to rob it.

''Tell me, Mr. Cowley,'' said I, ''is it still January?''

''So it is,'' said he. ''Tomorrow's the last day of the month. Rent's due.''

Then the room would still be theirs. They would know that. They would meet there.

''This way,'' said I, starting off toward Half-Moon Passage. "We shall go here first, then try another place on Bedford if our first visit yields naught."

And if our visit to the pawnshop should also prove fruitless? That was another question altogether, one that I put to myself as we two trudged on, past the stable and into that fearful stretch where the street narrowed into a tight passage which came out into the Strand. I'd not visited this stretch at night, and I was grateful to have an armed constable with me on this occasion. Two or three men lurked in a passageway—to no good purpose, I was sure—and ahead I saw the great hulking figure of one even larger than Mr. Cowley. Could Clarissa have come this way? I doubted it.

If Roundtree was not to be found here, nor in the pawnshop, then I must find which ship sailed for America on the morning tide. Who could tell me that? And then a sudden inspiration: Mr. Humber would know. He, a broker at Lloyd's Coffee House, had all such information in his head; none knew sea commerce better than he. I would wake him, if need be, and learn the name and wharf of their ship.

Yet it would have to be in the company of a different constable, I feared, for Mr. Cowley fared quite poorly. Even at a slow pace, a snail's pace it was, he limped along badly. I doubted at that moment that he could even make it down Bedford Street to visit the pawnshop. Yet we had at last arrived at the old court building which was our destination.

"This is the place, Mr. Cowley." I pointed us in at the entrance.

"And glad I am for it. This leg of mine . . ."

Indeed that leg of his. He hobbled on with me into the stinking courtyard, yet when we came to the stairway he hesitated, then came to a full stop.

"Jeremy," said he, "stairs give me particular pain. You go ahead, why don't you, and I'll follow quick as I can."

Why not, after all? It was not at all certain that the two of them were up there—nor even that I might discover

Roundtree alone. And should I find him, I vowed to use persuasion, rather than try to overpower him.

"Very good, then," said I. "Follow if and when you can. If the prisoner is present, and he flees, I shall chase him, and he will have to come this way. Have your pistol out, threaten to shoot, and if shoot you must, shoot to wound. We need him for a witness."

"I'll do it just so," promised Constable Cowley.

With that, I left him leaning on the balustrade, his wounded left leg elevated upon the first stair step. Indeed, I thought, I would chase Roundtree, if necessary—if he did not first jump out the window. No, I would not allow that. Somehow I would station myself between him and that exit. He would not elude me again in such a way.

Proceeding up the long hallway, I went softly as I was able. It would not do to have them hear approaching footsteps. Them? I hoped to heaven that if I found Roundtree, his daughter would not also be present; Clarissa would likely do all she could to impede her father's apprehension.

I stood before the door, which was slightly ajar. Light flickered in the few inches of space where it stood open. I held my breath, listening—and what did I hear but the sound of weeping, a girl's light sobs, followed by footsteps. I wondered, was Clarissa perhaps pleading with her father to return to Bow Street and give up this mad plan of escape? I should have liked to think that of her.

How to enter the room? Quietly, or should I rush in and get myself between Roundtree and the window? Then, of a sudden, did such considerations seem meaningless. I simply threw open the door and walked swiftly into the room— yet not deep into it, for what I encountered therein surprised and shocked me so that I was no more than a few paces inside before I came to an abrupt halt.

What I perceived first by candlelight was Thomas Roundtree on the floor, dead or dying, a great stain of blood upon his plaid waistcoat. Clarissa knelt over his body, mourning him in tears; I was uncertain whether she had

even noted my entrance. There was another in the room—
there had to be, those footsteps—and I had a sense of who
it must be. Yet it was not until I had caught movement out
the corner of my left eye that I had any idea where he might
be. I whirled then to face him and found a figure about five
and a half feet away.

Little more than that did I see in the dim light—except
the blurred glint of something in the right hand—for I was
leapt at, charged, before my feet were set proper on the
floor. Yet I pushed away with my left foot and staggered
awkwardly out of range as my assailant lurched past me.
Though he tried to stop himself, he could not. Tripping over
Roundtree's body, he fell in a tumble with Clarissa beneath
him. She fought to free herself and screamed a great, loud,
full-throated scream.

At the same time, I reached behind my coat to the small
of my back, where I kept my club—and grasped at nothing.
I realized instantly that when I bathed and changed clothes
I had left it behind. How could I, remembering Bunkins's
warning, have done something so stupid? Now I would
have to fight him with no more than fists and feet.

Yet I was not even to have that chance, for as I was
about to leap upon him, he righted himself and grabbed at
Clarissa and pulled her to him in a passionate though love-
less embrace. His knife was at her throat. They were then
on their knees. He pulled her to her feet as he himself rose
with some difficulty. There, where the candles burned on
the fireplace mantelpiece, I saw his face plain.

Jackie Carver it was, though from the moment I had
spied Roundtree on the floor I knew it could be no other.

"Make a move on me, chum," said he, "and I'll cut her
throat."

I said nothing, merely backed away, giving him room,
trying to think how I might detain him. Clarissa's large eyes
grew larger with fear—and fury.

"Ever see anyone get his throat cut?" he taunted. "You
get a gush of blood at the wound, but it comes out their

mouth, too, like they're drowning in it. You never seen such a lot of blood.''

"I believe you'd do it, right enough," said I to him. "You need not convince me. Only one as stupid as you would do such a thing."

"I ain't stupid," he snarled. "I kilt the only witness against me."

"And now you have two more witnesses to your killing of the first."

He frowned at that, as if he had not previously considered it. The fellow was truly not very bright.

"I ain't worried about that just now. You I'll get some night when you're out on the Beak's business. Her I might not have to crap at all—give her a bit of the ol' lovey-dovey, turn her out proper, and make her one of my bawds—just like I done with that little blowen Mariah. There's them like a bawd young as this one here."

There were voices in the hall and footsteps. Clarissa's scream had aroused her neighbors.

"Now, what I want you to do is move away slow while me and her go to the door."

I did as he bade me, leaving a path open to him. He took it, dragging the girl along with him. I noted that he moved with a pronounced limp.

"You'll not get far on that leg," said I, echoing Mr. Perkins's prediction.

The two stood in the doorway now. His back was to the hallway.

"I owe you for that," said he. "Oh, and I'll pay up. Count upon it, chum. I ain't been able to straighten that leg proper since you whacked me on it. Oh, but I'll get you. I'll get you some night for fair."

"Why not get me now?" said I, taking two swift steps toward him.

"Easy, easy," said he, grasping Clarissa tighter, putting the point of his knife to her just under her ear so that he drew blood. "Oooh, I seem to have made a tiny hole in 'er. Just think how she'd bleed if I cut her proper.''

I made every effort to disguise my surprise and relief when I saw Constable Cowley appear in the doorway behind him, his pistol raised so I might see it—and yet I failed.

''What're you smilin' at?''

''I was just thinking how you'll dance when the crap merchant hauls you up high.''

To what purpose I know not, but at that point Clarissa shouted: ''Will you two stop jawing and *do* something?''

At that, Carver, quite nonplussed by her remark, turned his head and looked down at her in surprise.

That must have given Mr. Cowley the more satisfactory angle he sought, for he then put his pistol to the back of Carver's head and pulled the trigger.

Simultaneous with the loud, dull report of the pistol, I saw Jackie Carver's face—the top half of it, specifically— quite disintegrate before my eyes. Flesh, bits of skull and brain, were scattered across the room. The sudden eruption of blood stained Clarissa's cape and frock, yet she did not scream as her former captor fell lifeless to the floor. She did no more than give a yelp of surprise and take but a moment to gape at the body at her feet; then did she begin quite mercilessly to belabor it with kicks, laughing a bit hysterically as she did.

Once I had calmed her, I removed Clarissa to the hall and left her in the care of Bessie, the neighbor who had nursed her. Then did I make certain there was no life left in Roundtree—there was none—and pulled Carver's body deeper into the room; I shut the door upon them both. Then did I attend to Mr. Cowley. He leaned against the wall of the hallway, his weight off his wounded leg. I saw that a dark stain had spread there on his breeches just above his knee. Something had to be done for him.

''How do you fare?'' I asked him.

''Not good. I opened the wound coming up quick as I could when I heard the girl scream.''

"Can you make it to the Strand? We can get a hackney there. We must get you to Bow Street."

"I can try."

"You did well to shoot him. He would have killed the girl soon as he got clear."

"I did well to shoot him because he's the bastard punched this hole in my leg."

"What do you mean?"

"That's Jonah Slade lying on the floor in there. I reco'nized him by his voice. I still remembers how he laughed and jeered at me as I tried to pursue him with his knife in my leg."

Why not? Jonah Slade? John Cutter? Jackie Carver? They were likely all false names. He had probably had his partners in crime give it out he had gone off to Ireland while he hid out at the pawnshop with Mrs. Bradbury.

"Well and good," said I. "He's best dead whatever his name."

And so I assembled us for the journey back to Bow Street. Bessie fetched from the room the roll of clothing that Clarissa had put together for her voyage to the colonies, and she added one of her own frocks to the bundle. And as she did that, I explained sternly to Clarissa what must be done. She nodded and—rare for her—said not a word. We set out, supporting Mr. Cowley between us, I on his right side, giving greater help to the wounded leg which he could put little weight upon. For the most part, he hopped along down the hallway. The stairs were a problem, yet somehow we managed. In Half-Moon Passage that great, threatening figure materialized of a sudden from the darkness—a dark man who was near the size of Constable Bailey but built heavier.

To Clarissa I said: "Keep going. Pay him no mind."

And, grabbing the loaded pistol from Mr. Cowley's holster, I pointed at him who blocked our path.

"Put it from your mind, friend," said I.

"Pass, brother—and a good evenin' to you."

Then into the Strand, where a line of hackneys waited before that notorious brothel where the seamen from the H.M.S. *Adventure* had rioted a year or two before.

I pointed to the nearest. Mr. Cowley hopped and hobbled to it between us. I demanded that the driver take us to Number 4 Bow Street.

"I can't," said he. "It ain't my turn in line. Go up to the head. Besides, how do I know you can pay, a lad like you?"

"A lad I may be, but I am a lad with a pistol, and if you do not come down now and help us get this wounded constable inside, and then take us, I shall shoot one of your horses dead."

I then brandished the pistol, that he might take me in earnest, and reluctantly he climbed down and gave assistance.

Thus went we to Bow Street, Clarissa and I sitting on facing seats and Mr. Cowley lying on the floor between us.

At one point on our short journey, she leaned forward and, peering closely at me, asked: "Would you truly have shot the horse?"

"I don't know," said I in all honesty.

Upon our arrival, I sent her inside to summon Constable Baker for his help in bringing Mr. Cowley inside. Together we eased him out, and with Clarissa opening doors before us, we managed to get him inside and into the chair nearest the entrance; as it happened, it rested opposite the strong room; Mrs. Bradbury was up from her corner and at the bars in a trice, determined to hear all. Well, thought I, let her.

Sir John was summoned by Mr. Baker, and came hurrying back to us.

"You are safe, both of you?" he asked. "But I understand Cowley is unwell?"

"His wound has opened."

"At this late date? Someone feel his forehead."

Sir John himself groped toward his face, but Mr. Baker slapped a sure hand upon Cowley's brow.

"He's burnin' with fever, he is."

"How long have you been feverish, Mr. Cowley?"

"A few days, sir."

"Then why did you—" Sir John halted. "Wait! Who is here with us? I sense another present."

"It is I, Clarissa Roundtree," said she, in a voice most subdued.

"Well," said he, "I understood from Annie that you had fled from us."

I had prepared my lie in advance. "No, Sir John, that was Annie's mistake, as it was mine. Clarissa waited for us to join her. She informed us of where we might find her father. It was her intention to persuade him to return to bear witness and confess. She led us to him."

"Is this true, Mr. Cowley?"

"It was her scream led me up there." He said it weakly; quite near a faint he was.

"And why did you scream, young lady?"

"Because, sir, I found my poor father dead," said she.

Sir John seemed about to offer her a word or two of condolence when, of a sudden, a wild peal of laughter burst forth from behind us. It issued from Mrs. Bradbury, who had hung upon the bars of the strong room, listening close to every word spoken. Clarissa rushed to her and attempted to pummel that harpy through the bars. Yet the evil woman stepped back, smirking, and retired to her corner of the cell. Mr. Baker informed Sir John of what had just happened, and Sir John ordered Clarissa upstairs. She complied without a word of protest. The rest of our discussion was conducted in whispers.

I told of how Jackie Carver, to call him by but one of his names, had threatened Clarissa's life with a knife at her throat; and that Mr. Cowley had come up behind him quite undetected and put a bullet through his brain. Sir John could bare disguise his consternation at the news.

''My last witness,'' he whispered.

Then did the door to Bow Street fly open, admitting a jubilant Mr. Donnelly.

''I saved him, by God!'' he crowed. ''I believe I have brought him through.''

He fair did a jig to us, so happy and proud was he.

''You refer, of course, to Lord Laningham,'' said Sir John.

''I do, yes, and it was on the advice of an old professor on the medical faculty in Vienna. He wrote in answer to a letter I wrote some time back. *'Geben Sie dem Nächsten Milch, soviel er trinken kann.'* ''

''Come, come, Mr. Donnelly, you know I have no German,'' said Sir John.

''Milk! Milk! No more than that. I kept pouring it down Laningham, and he has begun to rally. I believe he will pull through.''

''Then, as I told you, sir, I will be suspicious. But that is neither here nor there for the moment, for we have another patient for you.''

Mr. Donnelly looked down at Cowley, truly surprised. ''What is the trouble here?''

''That knife wound opened up, sir,'' said he, pointing down at the stain on his breeches.

''At this late date? Cut away his breeches. Let me look at it.''

Mr. Baker produced a knife and began ripping away at the knee of Cowley's breeches. When it was pulled back, a dirty bandage was exposed.

A look of anger appeared upon the surgeon's face. ''Mr. Cowley,'' said he, ''this looks like the bandage I put upon the wound these many days past. I recognize the knot with which I tied it. Did you not change it every other day as I instructed? Did you not apply alcohol to it from the bottle I gave you?''

''Well . . .'' said Mr. Cowley, ''my wife was afeared to

touch it, and I thought 'twould heal of itself. It was not so great a wound, after all.''

"I trusted you to have the good sense to follow my instructions.'' Mr. Donnelly clapped a professional hand upon his forehead. "You've a high fever from it. Cut away the bandage.''

Again Mr. Baker did as he was told, and then, at the surgeon's direction, ripped off the bandage. Mr. Cowley let out a howl of pain—and I could well understand why. The wound, though not large, had festered and swollen in a nasty way. Pink pus oozed from it, encrusting an area at least three inches round it. It smelled most foully.

"Take him out to the hackney in front, and send word to his wife in the morning that he will not be coming home to her until he is well.''

"Is there a hackney in front?'' I asked.

"Yes, the driver is yelling to be paid. Said he would not press his demand for fear his horse might be shot. Can you imagine such a thing?''

When at last, having eaten my dinner, I prepared myself to sleep, I was fortunate enough to be given back my own bed. When Lady Fielding heard what Clarissa had experienced in that bare, shabby room in Half-Moon Passage, she pronounced the girl no longer infectious and sufficiently well to share Annie's bed with her. The three of us—Clarissa, Annie, and myself—had by then put our heads together and revised the circumstances of our guest's unexplained absence. When asked again, as I was sure we would be, we would at least all tell the same story.

You may well ask, reader, why I had in the first place lied to Sir John. It was no impromptu fib: I had given consideration to it on the journey to Bow Street in the hackney coach. It seemed to me then, as it seems to me today as I write this, that had Sir John known that she had fled intending to sail with her father to the colonies (as she later admitted to me), then he would have sent her posthaste

back to Lichfield and the parish poorhouse. To put it simply, I thought she deserved better than that. And so, though
a liar, I felt justified in my lie, and I slept well in spite of
it.

Next morning early, I was sent off on the queerest errand
I had ever been sent on by the magistrate. It included a visit
to the Bilbo residence to learn the exact location of the
destination I sought. It continued with a visit to the worst,
the smelliest, the most squalid hovel in all London, I'm
sure, where I made a purchase of—well, let us say, some
animals. It concluded with the delivery of said animals to
Sir John in his chambers. He then bade me go to Mr. Donnelly's surgery and invite him to come to Bow Street at his
earliest convenience. Mr. Donnelly agreed, saying that
Cowley had just fallen asleep after a bad night and that he,
the physician, would soon be leaving for the Laningham
residence and would stop off on his way.

He arrived at Bow Street only a few minutes after my
return. Sir John had only just had time to outline his plan
to me; I thought it bizarre in the extreme, yet sensible and
worthy. Mr. Donnelly knew nothing of it at all as he seated
himself. I remained standing, for I, as I knew, was to take
an active part in what Sir John was pleased to call his "experiment."

"Now," said the magistrate, "you have said that there
is no proper test for the presence of arsenic."

"That is what I have learned—no chemical test known,
and I trust him who told me."

"Well and good," said Sir John. "I propose now to
make an experiment which, though not a proper chemical
test, should nevertheless be convincing. As you know, sir,
when Lord Laningham fell stricken after drinking from a
bottle of wine, I suspected and suggested to you that he
might have taken an ordinary emetic to cause the vomiting
and have shammed all the rest. I told you that if he recovered I would be suspicious."

"And I told you," put in Mr. Donnelly, "that if he recovered it would be due to my skill as a physician, for I had by then received the advice of my old professor and meant to put it to practice."

"I quite understand. But because I had some notion of this little experiment, I asked Jeremy here to seize the bottle of claret from which Lord Laningham drank and take it here as evidence. Now, Jeremy, has the bottle been tampered with, or added to, in any way?"

"No sir," said I, "it has been under lock and key in Mr. Marsden's evidence box."

"And what have you done with it to prepare for the experiment?"

"I poured a good bit of its contents into this bowl, which contains chunks of bread from our kitchen. The bread is well soaked in wine now."

"Just one more question: Did you first shake the bottle of claret?"

"Yes sir, just as I had seen Lord Laningham do before he poured and drank his second glass."

"There, you see, Mr. Donnelly, it's all been prepared just so. Do you accept that?"

"Yes, certainly, of course I do."

"Then, Jeremy, take the cover from the cage."

I did as he directed, revealing the three good-sized rats I had purchased from the ratcatcher who had so efficiently ratted Mr. Bilbo's kitchen. So long as they were in the dark, they had lain dormant. Now, with the light upon them, they were stirred to activity. It took but a moment until they seemed in an absolute frenzy. Mr. Donnelly, at first startled by their sudden appearance, leaned forward and studied them, quite fascinated.

"Now, Jeremy, drop the bits of bread into the cage— but I caution you, be careful. I would not have you bit by one of those filthy creatures."

I was careful as could be. I dropped the claret-soaked bread through the top of the cage. Each morsel fell with a wet plop to the bottom, so heavy was it with wine. The liquid spread. The rats lapped at it and tore at the bread. I continued to drop food to them until the bowl was empty, then I poured the residue of the liquid into the cage, where it splattered and ran.

"They have it all now, Sir John," said I.

"Then," said he, leaning back in his chair, "we have naught to do but sit back and wait for the result."

It did not take long for the ugly long-tailed, furry things to finish the bread and lick the floor of their cage dry. That I also reported.

"It should not take long," said Sir John. "You see the sense of this, do you not, Mr. Donnelly? If the rats are made sick merely, then the bottle of claret contains an emetic. If, however, they become sick and die, arsenic being the commonest rat poison, then I shall concede that arsenic is what the bottle contains, and I shall laud your healing powers to the very heavens."

By that time, the three creatures roamed their cage restlessly, hoping in vain to find some morsel or drop that had earlier escaped their notice. Then, one after another, they began to stagger, fell down upon their bellies, and began to regurgitate the contents of their stomachs. All a purplish red it was, exactly the color of the wine and wine-soaked bread on which they had feasted only minutes before. Indeed they vomited so copiously that the bottom of the cage was soon awash in their foul puke. I informed Sir John of this development.

He nodded, a patient smile upon his face. "They should be sick for a time, in great discomfort no doubt from the emetic, but as I predicted, they will recover."

Mr. Donnelly said nothing. He simply leaned forward and stared in fascination, waiting.

Then one of the rats, the smallest of the three, rolled over, his tiny legs in the air, went rigid, and died.

"Sir," said I, "one of the rats has died."

"*What?* Are you sure? He might revive."

"Oh, I think not, Sir John," said Mr. Donnelly, "for there goes another."

It was so. And then the third. All three adopted the same unnatural posture in death—upside down and quite stiff.

"I'm afraid, sir," said Mr. Donnelly, "that you must begin now to praise my skill as a physician."

"Why, that I have always done, as you must know. But truly, sir, I am amazed, for that knave Paltrow, who has assumed the Laningham title, seemed to have arranged it all. He specified the bottle from which he drank. It was waiting for him to drink during the musical entertainment. I know this from the butler. Paltrow shook the bottle in a most suspicious way, according to Jeremy, who saw all. And God knows the fellow had motive enough for murder."

"Well, then, perhaps the butler did it—heaped in the arsenic before serving the bottle."

"Perhaps, yet I trust him far better than I do Paltrow."

"Or, since the bottle was waiting to be drunk, no doubt it had been uncorked, and any one of the household staff might have had access to it."

Sir John said nothing. He simply sat, shaking his head slowly.

"Well, if you will now excuse me," said Mr. Donnelly, rising from his chair, "I must attend him whose life I saved last night."

"Yes, yes, of course," said Sir John. "Forgive me for wasting your time, sir."

"By no means was it time wasted. I concede that the effect of arsenic could have been counterfeited with an emetic. Now we know that it was not. Goodbye then, Sir John, Jeremy."

He picked up his bag and started for the door. Yet then did the magistrate detain him with a last query.

"Mr. Donnelly, I cannot let you leave without inquiring after Mr. Cowley's condition."

"Between us three," said the physician, "it is not good.

I've got all the pus from it I could and washed it down with alcohol. Now I have on it a poultice of fungus and leaves which I was given by an Indian medico, one of the few whom I respected.'' He sighed. "The infection has entered Cowley's body. I hope I can at least save his leg.''

"Pray God you can.''

With that, he departed, leaving us two to share a glum silence.

"Well, Jeremy,'' said Sir John, "it would seem that we must now take seriously the tale we were told about him who had sworn vengeance upon the entire Laningham line.''

"Yes sir,'' said I. Then, after a bit: "Shall I take the rats and perhaps bury them in the yard?''

"Not immediately. I'm hoping yet that they will revive.''

TWELVE

*In Which Lord
Laningham Receives an
Unexpected Visitor*

A day passed. As news came that Lord Laningham was swiftly recovering, Mr. Cowley's condition steadily worsened. Whereas Mr. Donnelly had previously said he hoped he might save the constable's leg, he now said he hoped merely to save his life. The leg had gone gangrenous; it would have to be amputated. Mr. Bailey and Mr. Brede, both of whom had assisted in such horrendous procedures on the battlefield, volunteered to assist the surgeon. It was to take place at night, that the constable's screams, if and when they came, would not be heard by many. Two bottles of gin were purchased in hopes that they might not come at all. Mr. Cowley began drinking in the late afternoon. I heard later that by the time the operation was begun he was quite insensate.

And indeed I heard little more than that. When Mr. Bailey and Mr. Brede returned at about eleven, exhausted and blood-spattered, they informed Sir John that all had gone well in that there were no unexpected complications. Mr. Brede, who was by nature quite taciturn, was moved to speak in praise of Mr. Donnelly.

"He learned his craft well in the Navy, sir," said he. "I never seen nor heard of it done better."

"Should I ever be needful in the same way, which God forbid," said Benjamin Bailey, "I pray God it's Mr. Donnelly does the job."

"Yet an ugly business at best," said Sir John.

"Aye, sir. But he gives young Cowley a good chance for recovery."

"Thank God for it. Go now, both of you. Your return to duty on this night will be a matter of your own choice."

With that they took their leave of us.

"And so," said Sir John, rising from his seat at the kitchen table where he had taken their report, "the awful thing is done."

"Yes sir." Then did I come forth impulsively with a thought which had greatly troubled me: "I feel somewhat at fault in this, Sir John."

"Oh? How can that be?"

"Had I not taken Mr. Cowley with me in the search for Roundtree, his wound might not have opened. And he—"

"If it had not," he interrupted me, "the poison from it might have taken an even firmer hold in his body and killed him outright. We heard the message passed on to us by Constable Bailey: Mr. Donnelly gives Cowley a good chance for recovery."

"Yes, but recovery with only one leg to stand on? What can he do? What will become of him—and his young wife?"

"That, Jeremy, is a question to which I have given much thought and which I intend to address in a letter I shall dictate to you tomorrow morning early. But now, let us to our beds—for we both of us have gone short on sleep of late."

The letter to which Sir John referred was directed in his chambers to William Murray, the Lord Chief Justice. It pled in well-reasoned terms that a pension be bestowed upon

Constable Cowley of no less than three-quarters of his pay as an active member of the Bow Street Runners until such time as he could find employment or earn by his own enterprise an amount comparable to his monthly salary. He made the point that even though the amputation was necessitated some time after the wound was inflicted, it had been inflicted in the line of duty. The infection had come about, said he, from Constable Cowley's premature return to his duties. And even on the night on which he had become incapacitated, he had performed admirably, shooting dead a villain who, seeking his escape, had put a knife to the throat of a young girl of good character.

(Glad I was to take down in dictation this description of Clarissa; I thought it boded well for her future.)

He concluded: "I shall be happy to discuss this matter at your earliest convenience, and remain your humble and obedient servant, et cetera."

I presented it to him for his signature, which he did put where I placed the pen. Then did I fold it with my usual care, drip sealing wax upon it, and seal it with his signet.

"Take this to him to whom it is addressed," said Sir John to me. "You needn't, of course, wait for a reply, for the Lord Chief Justice will likely think about it for some time and summon me to argue it in person. I would, however, like you to bring with you the Chinese vase which Roundtree filched from his residence. Do not simply deliver it. Before you hand it over, insist on sure and certain identification of it as the one that had been stolen."

So intrigued and delighted was I by this final instruction that in taking my hurried leave, I nearly bumped into Mr. Donnelly at the door. I paused but to make an urgent inquiry into Mr. Cowley's state.

"The surgery went well," said he. "His wife is with him now, quite overcome she is. *He* is comforting *her*. A good sign, that. I think he will pull through."

Thanking him, I went off to find Mr. Marsden that he might hand over the vase to me. Yet I was still near enough to hear Mr. Donnelly say: "Sir John, I have received another letter from my old professor at the medical faculty, an addendum to the first, which I believe will interest you greatly."

That, of course, interested me greatly, as well. Yet the importance of the letter I carried and the pleasure of returning the vase urged me go forth at all speed, rather than find some excuse to dawdle and thus hear what Mr. Donnelly had to report.

It was one of those days in early February which offer a hint of the coming of spring. Oh, it was still winter, and have no doubt of it. I was happy to have my muffler tucked tight about my neck. My hands were thrust deep into my pockets, one of which contained the letter and the other the small porcelain vase. Yet the sky was blue, the air was clear and dry, and the sun shone down upon us all who walked the streets. My steps were buoyed by this slight change in the weather, so that the journey to Bloomsbury Square seemed not to last near so long.

I arrived and beat confidently upon the door. The butler, with whom I had fought so many engagements in the past, was as quick to arrive as he usually was. He opened the door no more than a foot or two, and stared out at me with the same air of imperturbable sobriety that he always showed me.

"What is it you wish, lad?"

"I have a letter for the Lord Chief Justice."

"I see that you wear your bottle-green coat," said he. "You may wait inside for your reply, if you will."

"There is no need for that, or so I was told by Sir John."

"Then give it me."

He held out his hand, and I delivered the letter into it. Yet just as he was about to shut the great door, I piped up once again.

"There is another matter."

"Oh? And what is that?"

"I have here a Chinese vase," said I, producing it from

the other pocket. "Would this be the same one was taken from the house when the carpenters were working here?"

He looked at it, though not closely, and offered his hand again.

"I suppose it is," said he. "I'll take it."

I pulled it back out of his reach.

"I'm afraid, sir, that your supposition will not do. Sir John instructed me that I was to have sure and certain identification of it before I surrendered it to you or anyone else in the house."

"But . . . but," he sputtered, "the proper place for it is in Lady Murray's bedroom. I've had no cause to enter there but once or twice."

"Perhaps, then, Lady Murray's maid might identify it."

He stood frowning at me a bit longer than I thought necessary. Then at last he said, "Wait here," and shut the door upon me.

I returned the vase to my pocket and waited quite happily. I turned and surveyed the street, whistling a ballad, a tune from Annie's inexhaustible supply. As it happened then, my back was turned when the door came open again—exactly as I'd planned it.

"Lad, here, lad, I have brought Lady Murray's maid."

I turned with a smile and one was returned me by the woman who crowded the doorway with the butler. Quite plump and motherly she looked, but her eyes were eager as a child's.

"Do y'truly have the vase?" she asked.

"I may," said I, taking it from my pocket. "Would this be it?"

She took it from me carefully and examined it, turning it round to examine it this way and that.

"Oh, it is, it is! I'd know it anywheres. Wherever did you find it?"

"Sir John Fielding recovered it in the execution of his duties."

"Well, you must thank him for all of us. M'lady will be

so pleased. Egbert,'' said she to the butler, giving him a nudge with her elbow, ''have you no sense of justice? Give the lad a reward.''

Yet much as I should have liked to remain to witness his discomfiture in this situation, I stepped back and bowed deep to her. ''The smile on your face is reward enough,'' said I to her, ''for I was, after all, but the bearer. Goodbye to you, then.''

And so saying, I left them both with a wave. The sour look on the butler's face was one which I can picture to this day. He knew he had been bested. And I, oh yes, I knew it, too. I fairly danced back to Bow Street.

Upon my arrival, I was informed by Mr. Fuller that Sir John wished to see me. I hastened off to his chambers, found the door standing open, and entered. Immediately he rose from his desk.

''Jeremy? Come along. We're off to visit Mr. Donnelly's patient.''

''You mean Mr. Cowley, sir?''

''Ah no, that will have to wait, I fear—though not so long, to be sure. I meant his more illustrious patient, Lord Laningham. There are a few things I wish to find out from him, and thanks to the admirable speed with which you performed the task I gave you, I have just enough time to make my inquiries before I hold my court. Perhaps it's best if you precede me and bring a hackney to our door.''

''I shall have one waiting, Sir John.''

Perhaps I was a bit optimistic in my promise, for I found it necessary to go all the way to Russell Street before I encountered a hackney for hire; when I rode back in it, I spied Sir John before Number 4, leaning upon his stick. He had his head up high, and wore a broad smile upon his face. As I helped him up into the coach, he remarked upon the day.

''There is the breath of spring in the air,'' said he. ''I truly wish we might walk the way to St. James Square, yet time is against it.''

He settled back in his seat, I shut the door, and we were off. We had not gone far when I timidly approached him on a question to which I was eager to have an answer.

"Sir John?"

"Yes, Jeremy, what is it?"

"Would this visit to Lord Laningham, these few things you wish to find out—would all this have something to do with the letter from Vienna which Mr. Donnelly brought to you today?"

"Ah, you heard that, did you?"

"Only that he thought its contents would interest you."

"And you, too, are interested, eh?"

"Oh, yes sir, very keenly interested."

"Well, I fear I must disappoint you for now as to what was said in the letter. Perhaps it will not be long, however, until all will be revealed to you."

With that, he fell into that deep silence so like sleep. As we bumped along over the cobblestones his head bobbed loosely, though his chin never rested full upon his chest. I knew him to be deep in thought. No doubt, I surmised, he was planning his strategy for the battle that lay ahead.

Battle? Nay, when it came, I considered it more in the nature of a skirmish. In truth, I was rather disappointed at the magistrate's gentle handling of a fellow whom he held in low regard. In spite of the outcome of the experiment with the rats (which now lay two feet beneath the weeds and furze of the yard behind Number 4 Bow Street), I felt that Sir John still held Lord Laningham suspect.

We were met at the door by Mr. Poole, the butler, who conducted us to the bedchamber of the master, a grand room by any measure. And it was one decorated in the grand manner: there were paintings and statuary, with furniture of the size and sort one might more likely expect to find in a drawing room; a fire blazed in a fireplace wide as it was tall. In the midst of all this inherited splendor, Lord Laningham sat up in as large a bed as I had ever seen. He leaned against a whole mountain of pillows and smiled wanly as Sir John was ushered in.

"Ah, Sir John," said he, "so good of you to come. In fact, I so hoped you might that I left instructions with Poole that should you make an appearance, you were to be shown up to me without formalities or delay."

"Mr. Donnelly cautioned me that until today you were in no condition to accept visitors," said Sir John.

"Ah, Donnelly, I owe my life to the man! Do you know the medicine he prescribed? The elixir that brought me from death's door?"

"Milk, as I understand."

"Uh, yes, so it was," said he, somewhat deflated. "It somehow acted against the poison. Ah, the miracles of modern medicine, eh?"

Though the curtains had been drawn against the blue sky and morning sun and the room was quite gloomy, I saw Lord Laningham plain by candlelight and the blaze of the fire. He looked indeed as if he had passed through a great ordeal. The dark discoloration I had earlier perceived round his eyes seemed darker still. His face seemed thinner, drawn. Nevertheless, though his voice was low and seemed somewhat strained, his words were more confident, perhaps, than ever before.

"Lord Laningham," said Sir John, "I wonder, did you take any of the steps I urged upon you when you reported the shot fired at you through the window?"

"Unfortunately for me, I did not. No, I took what you told me quite seriously, and I was grateful for your advice, yet there were a number of matters which intervened—my aunt's funeral, for one, preparations for that near-fatal musical evening, for another. I do recall, however, that you recommended that I engage a bodyguard."

"A bodyguard would have done you little good those few nights past. It seems you must, like some Oriental potentate, now also employ a food and wine taster."

"Oh, surely not. Perhaps now that this enemy of the

Laningham line has attempted to poison me and failed, he will leave me be for a time.''

''Do you truly believe that, m'lord?''

''Having done his worst? Why not?''

''Not his worst,'' said Sir John. ''His worst would have been to have succeeded. Or perhaps to murder your wife and daughters as well as yourself.''

''Oh dear!'' Lord Laningham appeared appropriately shocked at the suggestion.

''May I put forth a plan?''

''Please, oh please do.''

''Your butler, whom I tend to trust, has informed me that the bottle of wine from which you drank had been chosen specially by you some time before, uncorked, and left to air at a place in the pantry to which the entire household staff had access. So was it with your aunt's tonic, and so might it also have been with those bottles of wine taken to the Crown and Anchor by your uncle. Having endured what you have, you must now believe that both of them were poisoned?''

''Well, I must, I suppose, though there is that curious discrepancy: I drank from my uncle's bottle that night of his death and suffered no ill effects from it.''

''Yes, of course, that is a curiosity, is it not? Yet the manner of his death, the sudden attack of vomiting, was quite like what you experienced two nights past.''

''Indeed, it's true.''

''My point is this,'' said Sir John. ''This enemy of the Laningham line, as you call him, is either on your household staff or has a close confederate working here. Have you prepared that list of your servants?''

''What? Oh, that. No, as I said, so much has intervened. Poole could provide one, I'm sure.''

''Have him do that. And I suggest you take yourself and your family elsewhere and give me the opportunity to interrogate each one. My methods are such that I firmly believe I shall be able to find our man—or woman. If I cannot prove the case, then my suspicions will be such that you may discharge the person.''

"But why should it be necessary for us to go elsewhere?''

"Why, m'lord, to remove you from further danger. I take it that your estate in Laningham is independently staffed. You would need take none of your servants from your residence here in London with you, thereby leaving your London staff, among which is undoubtedly our poisoner, to me and my powers of interrogation.''

"Yet what about that shot fired at my uncle up in Laningham? You remember? When he was out riding?''

"Ah yes, of course, that was the first attack, was it not? Well, perhaps you would not be entirely safe there. Let me think.'' He paused a moment to stroke his chin. "I have it,'' Sir John exclaimed. "Why not take your family for a tour of the Continent? You need not do it with a great retinue of servants. Two would suffice. I would suggest the butler and your aunt's maid, both of whom I've already talked to and seemed to me trustworthy. Your daughters would find it quite elevating, and Lady Laningham, as well. Perhaps you yourself have not had that opportunity?''

"Ah, but I have,'' said Lord Laningham, as a smile of recollection appeared upon his face. "My uncle may have had his faults, but he was no skinflint. When I reached the age of majority he sent me off on the Grand Tour. An entire year I spent touring the capital cities—Paris, London, Vienna, Venice, Rome, Naples—viewing the art, tasting the wine, trying the ladies, mere flirting, you understand.''

"Oh, quite. Ah, how I envy you, for you must have seen the great sights—the Mediterranean, the great castles. Lake Como, I have heard, is quite beyond compare. But do you know, had I my sight, I would like most to gaze upon the great mountains of Switzerland and the Austrian Tyrol. Have you . . . Did you see them?''

"Ah yes, both—such magnificence! Quite beyond description! Switzerland itself has little to offer but a confusion of languages—except for its mountains. Austria, on the other hand, has Vienna and the equally magnificent mountains of the Tyrol. They are very friendly to the English there.''

''And why not? We fought a war on their behalf,'' said Sir John. ''But there, you see. You have such pleasant memories of that year abroad. Why not give them to your wife and daughters, too? You yourself could serve as their guide.''

''Ah, would that I could. And in a few years perhaps we shall make a trip just as you describe. But for the time being, alas, it is out of the question. I have not yet been presented at court, nor have I properly assumed my seat in the House of Lords. And make no mistake, sir, I mean to be a most active member—acquaint myself with the issues, speak out on them.''

''And will you align yourself with the Whigs or the Tories?''

''That I have not decided quite yet. But when the time comes, I shall choose the party that is in the right.''

''Ah yes, of course you will,'' said Sir John. ''Since it is your determination to pursue an active political life in London, I can only advise you to engage the services of a bodyguard.''

''I'll do as you say. And please feel free, Sir John, to enter here at any time and talk to any members of the household staff. I'll have Poole prepare that list for you.''

''We shall leave it at that, shall we, Lord Laningham? I wish you a goodbye and a swift recovery.''

''Goodbye to you, Sir John Fielding, and I thank you again for your visit to this poor bedridden patient.''

A bow from Sir John, a weak nod from Lord Laningham, and we two made our way through the door, where Mr. Poole materialized of a sudden to lead us down the stairs. At the great door to the street, the magistrate paused and addressed the butler.

''Mr. Poole, you will no doubt be asked by Lord Laningham to prepare a list for me of the members of the household staff. He may present it to you as an urgent matter, but between us there is no great urgency to it. I may come by to talk to the servants one at a time, but they are not to dread these conversations. Please assure them of that. I have even now a fair idea of who is responsible for these attacks upon the late Lord and Lady Laningham and the present lord.''

''That is good to hear, Sir John. And may I pass word of that on to the staff?''

''You may if you care to.''

We said our goodbyes and stepped out into St. James Square. The day was no worse; if anything, it had grown a bit warmer. We set off for Pall Mall, where we might easily find a free hackney.

''Well, Jeremy, what did you make of that?''

''Very little, I fear, sir,'' said I. Then did I mention the darkness about Lord Laningham's eyes, his drawn visage, and his general appearance of weakness. ''He seemed truly to have undergone a great physical strain.''

''Oh, I've no doubt of that. His voice was weaker toward the end of our interview, quite husky, as if it were a strain upon his throat to talk.''

''Yes, but he seemed more confident somehow.''

''Mmmm,'' said Sir John, and no more than that.

We walked on in silence until we were quite near Pall Mall, where two hackney coaches stood free for hire. Then did I burst forth in exasperation.

''Sir, was that interview of any use at all? Was what you told Mr. Poole true?''

''Mmmm,'' he repeated, yet this time he continued: ''Well, those are two separate but related questions. To answer the second, yes, I shall no doubt be dropping by the Laningham residence to collect details, evidence if possible, and yes, I do have a good idea of who bears guilt in all this. It is up to me to build a case now. And as for your first question, indeed the interview was useful, for Arthur

Paltrow told me just what I needed to know.''

And thus ill informed, I guided him to the waiting hackney and aided him inside.

Next morning I was with Sir John, once again taking in dictation a letter of no little importance. It was directed to William Bladgett, Esquire, Magistrate of Lichfield, and it gave to him the circumstances of the death of Thomas Roundtree. And it did so in some detail, explaining that though he was party to the disposal of the body of George Bradbury, he had in no wise participated in his murder. (In this, Sir John took what Roundtree had told me as true.) Further, he attributed to the late Roundtree a not altogether reprehensible motive for his actions—that of earning sufficient to take him and his daughter away to the American colonies (again accepting as true that which he had heard from me). Sir John was frank to say, however, that when given the opportunity to escape, Roundtree took it.

''And now,'' dictated Sir John to me, his amanuensis, ''we come to the matter of Clarissa Roundtree. As chance would have it, she was at the time of her father's escape in our household recovering from a fit of pneumonia. In spite of her condition, she aided those who went out to search for him. It was her intention to persuade him to surrender. When she arrived in the room they shared, which was where he was first sought, she found her father dying, only a minute or two earlier struck down by him who had done the murder of George Bradbury. Her scream at this shocking sight brought the constable and another who had aided in the search. The constable shot the murderer dead.

''Because of Clarissa Roundtree's aid in this matter, and because Lady Fielding has taken an interest in the girl, I have decided on her behalf to decline your kind offer to welcome her back to the Lichfield poorhouse. Though she is young, she is exceptionally bright, and may even at her present age of twelve be put out for service on the staff of one of the great houses hereabouts. My wife and I have access to a few of them and should be able to find a place suitable for her. Thus it should not be necessary for the Parish of Lichfield to bear the cost of her upbringing. That, I am sure, is a resolution that should satisfy you and the parish board. In my firm certainty of this, I remain, Yr. humble and obedient servant, John Fielding, Magistrate, City of London and City of Westminster.''

I had just written so far and was blowing upon the paper to dry the last lines, when a great commotion was heard in the hallway outside—a familiar voice shouting loud, ''Where is he, damn it?'' followed by thunderous footsteps. Then did William Murray, the Lord Chief Justice, come bustling into the room. His entrances seemed ever to be made in this fashion.

''Ah, there you are!'' said he, as if he had discovered Sir John in hiding.

''Indeed, here I am, and ready to discuss with you the matter of the letter I wrote you yesterday. That, I assume, is why you have come.''

''That and another matter, as well.''

''Very kind of you to come to me, my lord. I should have gladly made the trip to Bloomsbury Square.''

I stood awkwardly to one side, the unsigned letter in my hand. Sir John did not invite me to leave. The Lord Chief Justice paid me no mind. And so I slipped off to one corner to listen and heard all.

Lord Murray threw off his greatcoat, tossed it aside, and dropped into the chair I had lately vacated. He leaned forward so pugnaciously that he seemed near ready to engage in fisticuffs with his blind opponent.

''Let us put all such pleasant preliminaries aside and get down to it, shall we?'' said he. ''Now, as you well know, when one in the Army or the Navy is wounded past service, he is paid a lump sum and put out on his own.''

''Put out indeed with a bowl to beg, my lord. It is a national disgrace.''

''Be that as it may, the precedent has been set. What

makes you think that your constables deserve better?''

"I have reasons, right enough, and they are two. First of all, they are constables, whose work it is to keep peace in the Cities of Westminster and London. They are not many, but they do a good work of it. Could any gainsay that? I believe not. Just think of the criminal disorder in the streets before my brother, God bless his memory, put together this force—robberies in broad daylight, shootings, knifings. Why, one had to go about with sword and pistol to protect what was in his purse. The only force against the lawless was the independent thief-takers who were themselves criminals. The community knows this, and they are grateful to the Runners. Why was I knighted but for their work? The community makes the distinction between my Bow Street Runners and soldiers and sailors even if you do not. They hold them in higher esteem because they protect them directly. The poor wretches who take the King's shilling or are pressed into service, the public regards as mere cannon fodder sent off to fight in foreign wars whose outcome affects them only indirectly—if at all.''

To give him credit, the Lord Chief Justice listened attentively through all this. He even nodded once or twice, whether in agreement or to signal his understanding, I know not. Yet when Sir John had concluded, he gave but a cold response.

"You said that you have a second reason.''

"I do indeed.''

"I await it.''

"It is this: Mr. Cowley should be given a pension as an example to all the other constables. If he is not given one, if he does, as limbless soldiers and sailors do, appear as a beggar on a street corner—then think of the effect this would have upon my Beak Runners. They would look at him and say to themselves, 'There is my future.' They constitute a small force, my lord, yet they quell riots, they hold mobs at bay, they pursue murderers into dark corners. Would they do this so willingly, so fearlessly, if they knew that a serious wound, the loss of a limb, would put them on a street corner opposite Mr. Cowley, begging, hoping to collect enough each day that they might survive the next? No, my lord, I think not. Would you? *I* would not. If, on the other hand, they hear that Mr. Cowley has been granted a pension—if they meet him on the street and hear from him that he is learning a trade and will soon be able to support himself and his young wife with it—then they will know that whatever happens, they will be provided for. And they will pursue their duties as boldly as ever.''

"From what you say,'' said the other, ''I suppose that should a married constable be killed in the line of duty, you would argue that his wife should receive a pension.''

"Though I had not considered it,'' said Sir John, ''I think that an excellent suggestion, for all the reasons I have just given, and I thank you for it.''

The Lord Chief Justice, having tasted Sir John's tart irony, offered him a rather sour look. "I believe that some years ago one of your constables lost an arm. What became of him?''

"That would be Mr. Perkins, an altogether exceptional man. You're right, my lord, he did lose his arm just about at the elbow in that notorious melee in the bookshop. Yet he trained that remaining arm of his so that it had the strength of two in it—perhaps three. He proved to me that a one-armed constable can be as aggressive, as capable as any with two. But really, there is no comparison between a man with one arm and one with one leg. You must see that.''

"Couldn't you find work for this fellow Cowley here at the court? Something to justify paying him something?''

"I could try. I will try. But a man with one leg cannot handle prisoners, and Mr. Cowley has not education enough to be of much help to my clerk—though perhaps that might be possible. We shall see. Let me say that Mr. Cowley was exceptional among the Runners only in that he was the youngest of them, and that he had no military experience.

He performed bravely when called upon, as he did on his last night of duty, but he lacked initiative. He made errors. I shall even reveal what might turn you against him somewhat. The amputation of his leg was necessitated because he did not care for his wound, as any man with military experience would have done. I shall not take another onto my force of men who has not previously soldiered. But I argue for Mr. Cowley's pension not because he is the most deserving, but rather for the respect the Runners are due and the need to maintain their moral integrity and high standard of performance.''

At last the Lord Chief Justice leaned back in his chair, still frowning, yet now in deep consideration.

''You know, sir, you should have been a barrister,'' said he.

At that Sir John laughed most heartily. ''Forgive me, Lord Murray, but I recently said the same thing to a quick-witted woman who has quite confounded me. And I fear that neither I then, nor you now, meant it as flattery.''

''No indeed, sir, I meant it as plain fact. You plead your case most persuasively—and all on principle. I tremble to think what this may cost us, but I am inclined to yield to your arguments. But good God, three-quarters of his established wage! That is simply too much. Why not half?''

''Why not? Because Mr. Cowley, being the youngest and least experienced constable on the force, received the lowest wage. He married recently, however—not so much impetuously as it was out of moral obligation. His wife, as I have heard it bruited about among the constables, was with child at the time of their wedding. The two of them—nay, three—simply could not survive if he were put on half-pay. He would soon be forced to go begging to make up for what he lost.''

Silence, scowling silence from the Lord Chief Justice. Until at last: ''What would you say to two-thirds?''

Leaning back in his chair, Sir John elevated his chin in an attitude of concentration. One would think that the magistrate was doing sums in his head. "Well . . . yes," said he. "I believe that they can make do on that."

"Two-thirds it is, then. But let it be understood that you will make some effort to find work for him at your court, or get him with someone who will teach him a trade. In other words, sir, it should be understood that I do not see this as a pension for the term of his natural life."

"Understood and agreed." Had Sir John had his gavel at hand, I believe he would have pounded the table with it; in lieu of that, he gave it a resounding slap with the palm of his hand. "Now, what more have we to discuss? You said, as I recall, my lord, that you brought two matters with you."

"Indeed. Word has reached me that you are holding back from me a murderess, Sir John. Do you do this out of some special consideration for the weaker sex? For if she be truly a murderess, then she is strong enough to hang for it."

"No, I hold her back so as to save us both from embarrassment. I simply do not believe that there is evidence enough against her to convict her."

"Do you believe her guilty?"

"I do, yes. Though she likely did not plunge the dagger, I believe she conspired in her husband's death."

The Lord Chief Justice gave an indifferent shrug. "The same thing," said he.

"Perhaps, but the two witnesses who could make her party to the crime are both dead. We have no body, only an uncertain identification of the victim's head. We cannot even prove on direct testimony that murder was committed, though we have it on hearsay from one of the dead witnesses that murder was done."

"This is all rather confusing. I tell you, what I should like is a memorandum from you laying out the crime and whatever evidence, uncertain or hearsay, that you may have against her. I'll look it over, and if I feel there is a fair chance to convict, I'll ask for an indictment and put her on trial. I'll try the case myself. I like a good murder."

"I have her incarcerated in the Fleet Prison on a lesser charge. Would it not be better to wait a bit? I *might* be able to break her story with repeated interrogations."

"You seem somewhat doubtful."

"Well, I have talked twice to her, and she has not altered her account, not one jot or tittle. Twice is not many, and she might tire and weaken sometime in the future, though she shows no sign of it now. She is wily, clever, and stubborn. She is, in fact, the one whom I told that she should have been a barrister."

"Then on that alone I should consider her worthy for trial. Please do as I suggest and prepare the memorandum, Sir John. I think matters such as this are best handled when they are hot."

"My lord, your wish is my command, your whim my desire."

Then did the Lord Chief Justice let out a great chortle as he rose from his chair. *"Ha!"* said he. "Would that it were so. I seem to lose as many to you as I win. This time again I believe I've made even with you."

Then, with no more goodbye than an indifferent wave, he turned and left for the coach-and-four that awaited him in Bow Street—swiftly as he had come.

Sir John listened to the departing footsteps, then turned in my direction, knowing exactly in which corner of the room I had taken shelter.

"There is a lesson for you, Jeremy," said he. "In negotiating, you must always ask for more than you expect to get. I did not suppose for a moment that Lord Murray would agree to three-quarters pay. Mr. Cowley can scrape by on two-thirds, even with a child. I'll tell him so myself. And if he cannot, I'll raise my fines a bit. We'll not let him down."

"And the other matter, sir?"

"There I believe the chief judge is making an error of judgment." And to that he would add no more.

•   •   •

Upon my return from posting the letter to Lichfield, I hied
upstairs to the kitchen in search of Clarissa. She had lan-
guished somewhat since her ordeal. Her recovery from her
pneumonia was complete, said Mr. Donnelly, yet still she
wore a bandage about her neck to protect that prick beneath
her ear given her by Jackie Carver. That, too, mended well
under our care. Yet her mental state seemed low: she was
unnaturally silent, especially at meals, which she now took
with us; only with Annie, with whom she now slept, did
she enjoy any degree of companionship. They had told one
another their life stories, and Annie's was every bit as sad
as hers; thus they had become sisters in tragedy. To me she
had had bare ten words to say since that terrible night. That
troubled me.

I found her in the kitchen next the fireplace, book in
hand; she had progressed to the sixth and last volume of
Tom Jones (her reading, at least, had continued apace). At
my entrance, she looked up and mumbled my Christian
name in greeting, and then returned to her book.

"I have good news for you, Miss Pooh," said I, with a
teasing smile. "Would you like to hear it?"

"I'm sure I must, since you seem determined to tell it."

Undeterred by her waspish reply, I gave forth: "Only
this moment I've returned from the letter office, where I
posted a letter from Sir John to the Magistrate of Lichfield."

She sighed a deep sigh. "Then is my fate sealed."

"Not so," I protested. "Did I not say that I brought
good news? Since I myself took the letter in dictation from
Sir John, I know its contents. In it, he said that because
of the help you volunteered in returning your father to
custody—"

"Which we both know to be a pack of lies," she interrupted.

"—and because Lady Fielding had taken an interest in
you," said I, pressing on, "he had decided *not* to return
you to Lichfield, but rather to find a place for you on the

household staff of one of the great houses of London. There! Now what do you think of that?''

Quite expecting her to jump from her chair in joy at my news, I was more than a little disappointed at her listless reply: ''Well, I suppose that is better than returning to the poorhouse. But then, anything would be.''

''Surely you cannot mean that,'' said I. ''Why, there are hundreds of girls in London—thousands—who would be eager for such a chance as you are offered now.''

''Then they are wrong,'' said she, ''for they know not what awaits them—as kitchen slaveys, scrubbing away at pots and pans, or perhaps as maids of all work to be chased by the master or the butler until they yield, then leave in disgrace with their apron high.''

''You're quoting from the romances now,'' said I, though I knew there was some truth in what she said.

''Annie's experience was not so much different, and in some ways worse.''

''Her master did monstrous deeds, and he was punished for them.''

''Those were not the deeds for which he was punished.''

She was difficult in argument, no doubt of that. Yet I persisted: ''There are many houses with decent masters—and reasonable butlers, though as a class of men I do not think highly of them myself. I'm sure Sir John and Lady Fielding would install you in a good situation—perhaps . . . oh, perhaps in the staff of the Lord Chief Justice in Blooms-bury Square. Now there is a man who would tolerate no untoward behavior among any in his employ. Oh, and there are others—many others, I'm sure.''

She said nothing, simply looked up at me quite dubi-ously.

''And as for Annie,'' I added rather irrelevantly, ''things turned out well for her, did they not? She is happy, is she not?''

''So would I be—*here*.''

Ah, so that was it. Once in our little domestic circle, she

had no wish to leave it. Well, I could not blame her for that. I remembered my own feelings when I, not much older than Clarissa was at that moment, looked forward to an apprenticeship in the printing trade (one that I knew well, for my father was a printer). Though I had come to London hoping for just such an appointment, once I had moved into Sir John's orbit I felt a gravitational pull as with some great heavenly body, a pull which I was loath to break. I, too, wanted to stay at Bow Street—and I was quite overjoyed when it was permitted me. Was it so with her? Or did she but fear the unknown?

I did at last manage a response, albeit one that avoided altogether the issue raised by her: "Well, I brought you the news of the letter because it concerned you and because I thought you would be eager to know it."

"And I thank you for that," said she with a curt nod, which I took to be one of dismissal.

That annoyed me so that I spoke to her rather harshly. "What right have you to treat me so rudely?" I demanded, "sending me on my way like some servant. Why, were it not for me and the lie I told, you would be on your way to Lichfield in the company of a constable or a beadle, or whatever. Yet ever since your return from that terrible night, you have been quiet. I can understand that, considering what you witnessed and how you were threatened. But you have been rudely quiet to me. Miss Pooh, you have snubbed me, and I wish to know why."

Then did she rise from her chair and meet me face-to-face. "Why? I will tell you why. You knew that my father was captive down on the floor below us that entire day, and yet you did not so much as whisper it to me. I hold that against you, and I always shall."

"If I had told you, what then? What would you have done?"

"Why, I should have gone to see him. I could at least have comforted him, told him I was safe and well now, and that I would wait for him until he'd served his sentence."

"You truly have no idea in what evil he was involved, do you?"

"Evil? Why, naught but drunkenness and flight. You pursued me, and I—to my everlasting shame—led you to him."

"Nothing of the kind. I knew you two would meet to leave together for the colonies."

"How did you know? Did he tell you that?"

"No, he merely confirmed what I had guessed."

She was silent for a moment, her wide eyes shifting this way and that. Then did she say: "Murder—he was witness to murder. That horrible fellow who slew him said as much, did he not?"

"He did, yes, but Clarissa, you would not want now to hear the full story, nor should you hear it from me. Yet there will come a time when you will want to know. Then you must go to Sir John and ask him. He is the one to tell you—not me."

I did then turn from her and leave her where she stood. Through the door I walked and down the stairs, having no particular destination, wishing only to be away from this troublesome girl.

Near a week went by. It passed between Clarissa and me as a state of armed truce. Whereas previously she had snubbed me, we now snubbed one another, yet we were now more careful not to let our feelings show. At table with the rest, we feigned friendliness, presented false smiles, and occasionally offered innocuous comments and remarks to disguise what I perceived to be mutual hostility. It could not go on forever so, but until she was sent out in service it seemed a satisfactory *modus vivendi*.

As for matters of greater import, all went well. The very evening of his interview with William Murray, the Lord Chief Justice, Sir John went to see Mr. Cowley. He made the visit in the company of Constable Bailey, and so I know not precisely what was said, but the purpose of the call was to inform Mr. Cowley of the pension he would receive. The young constable (or perhaps better put, former constable) was most gratified. Mr. Donnelly, with years of experience behind him in the Royal Navy, was quite surprised to hear of such generosity, as he stood by his patient's bedside. He later told me that whenever he had been forced to amputate a leg in the past, it had seemed to him that rather than saving a life, he was simply condemning the victim to a slower death by starvation. The news of the pension so cheered Mr. Cowley that it hastened his recovery. A week after his surgery, he went home with a crutch made for him by Mr. Brede, who had a talent for making things of wood, and stern instructions from Mr. Donnelly on the care of his stump.

Sir John and I worked closely together on the preparation of the memorandum for the Lord Chief Justice regarding the case against Mrs. Bradbury. A good deal of it he left up to me, since I was better acquainted with such matters as Bunkins's identification of the head of George Bradbury, the purchase of the white horse, and Thomas Roundtree's confession. I wrote drafts of these parts for his approval. It was for me a most instructive exercise. Though I enjoyed the work and took it most seriously, I certainly saw the inadequacies in the case which Sir John had argued. I was also a bit disappointed when, while I was thus engaged, he made a visit to the Laningham residence to interview some of the staff—particularly so in that he had invited Clarissa to accompany him in order to acquaint her with the life belowstairs in the great houses. I saw the sense of that, of course, yet I could not but feel that my position had some-how been usurped by her.

Taking my drafts, adding to them where necessary, he composed a lengthy but nevertheless precise and cogent document which I took in dictation. This, signed by him, I delivered to the Lord Chief Justice. Next day a letter was delivered to Sir John instructing him to bind Mary Brighton Bradbury for trial on a charge of homicide; she would be tried as soon as a place came open on the high court docket. That was done swiftly, to the astonishment of Mrs. Bradbury, and she was sent off to Newgate, where all prisoners awaiting trial on capital crimes must needs go.

As for Arthur Paltrow, Lord Laningham, his recovery continued. A few days after our visit to him, Mr. Donnelly pronounced him fit to be up and about, though he was to continue upon the mild diet he had prescribed. When Sir John returned from his visit to the Laningham residence in the company of Clarissa, I asked him if he had turned up anything of interest. "One or two things perhaps," said he—and no more, nor could I pursue the question further, for he changed the subject swiftly to the memorandum, and that, of course, concerned me more directly. He did later indicate, however, that he would be returning to St. James Square, perhaps sometime next week, and that I might go along with him then.

In sum, he seemed not to be moving along with much speed on the matter, yet he seemed curiously untroubled by this. It was as if he were waiting for some new development or some essential bit of information, confident that it would come.

Therefore we were all surprised—Sir John perhaps most of all—when Mr. Perkins interrupted our evening meal toward the end of the week to inform us that a footman had arrived from the Laningham residence bringing news that someone had been shot.

"Jeremy," said Sir John, rising from the table, "get your coat and bring my cape, if you will. I must go down and talk to the fellow." Then to Mr. Perkins: "Is Mr. Bailey about?"

"He just left the downstairs, sir. He can't be far. I'll fetch him."

"Do that and bring a coach around. I want you both with me—armed with pistols."

When next I saw Sir John, he was downstairs attempting

to extract from the footman the most basic sort of information—without much success.

"...understand all that, my good fellow," said he. "There was a great struggle for a pistol and someone was shot. But I put it to you again: *Who was shot?*"

The footman's face was flushed, whether from the ride in the chill evening or from plain embarrassment, I could not say. "Well, sir," he attempted to explain, "that I can't rightly say. When Mr. Poole sent me off to you, the ladies was all crowding round the door and making such a racket so I could not get a proper look inside."

"All right, then, well and good. Ride back and tell them I'm on my way. Jeremy?"

He spoke my name with the assurance I was nearby. In answer, as the footman hurried for the door to Bow Street, I threw the cape round Sir John's shoulders and secured it with a knot in front.

"There you are, good lad. I want you to run for Mr. Donnelly. Find him, if he be not at some grand dinner party, and bring him—by hackney, mind—to Laningham's. Do you have sufficient in coin to pay the fare?"

"I'm sure I do, Sir John."

"Good, he's become rather pinchpenny of late. On your way then."

So it was that we two, Mr. Donnelly and I, again arrived at the Laningham residence after the rest. Yet on this occasion, due to their difficulty in finding a coach free for hire, we arrived directly after they had. In fact did I see their hackney pull away as we dismounted ours. Nevertheless, Sir John and Constable Bailey were already inside the house. Constable Perkins had been posted as a guard at the door.

"I can't tell what's going on inside," said he to us, "just a lot of shouting and screaming. Don't bother to knock. Nobody'd hear if you did."

We burst in upon the Paltrow women—Felicity and

Charity and Lady Laningham. It was they who supplied the screams. The shouts were Sir John's.

"Get these women out of here, my lord, I beg you!"

In truth, what seemed to have possessed the three was a fit of tearful wailing. Who had been shot, indeed? They seemed, in their hysteria, to be keening for the victim, who was clearly not Lord Laningham.

He was now herding them away toward the great winding staircase, addressing them in soothing tones, urging them to get a hold on themselves and wait for him above. The shooting must have taken place in the room just to the left of the vestibule, for there the door stood open. Sir John and Constable Bailey stood half in, half out of it, blocking the interior from my sight. This, I recall, was the study, so called, the room in which Lord Laningham had been when, as he had told it, the shot came from the street, narrowly missing him whilst he sat at his desk. Sir John turned toward us.

"I heard the door open and shut when those women were caterwauling their worst. Was that you, Mr. Donnelly? Jeremy?"

"It was," said Mr. Donnelly. "We seem ever to meet disaster in this house, Sir John."

"We do indeed. Come through here and take a look at this poor fellow. Mr. Bailey assures me he is dead, but you may be able to supply a few interesting details. That is, I hope you can."

Sir John and the constable stepped aside, making a path for Mr. Donnelly and giving me a glimpse of the victim. He lay face up on the carpet and bore the vacant, expressionless look carried by most dead men. Though he was burly of bulk, there was naught of the laborer about him. He was well dressed in a warm cape, beneath which he wore a coat of bottle green quite like my own; and beneath that a waistcoat of a lighter green which bore a stain of crimson in the area of the heart. That was all that I saw, for once Mr. Donnelly had been admitted into the room,

Sir John and Mr. Bailey closed up the gap and blocked my view. Yet I heard all.

"Describe the victim to me, if you will, Mr. Donnelly," said Sir John.

"He is a man of about forty, perhaps a year or two less, well dressed, still wearing a cape, his hat fallen aside on the floor."

"He is dressed for the street, then."

"Yes sir, quite evidently," said the medico, and then continued: "He is a good-sized man about two inches less than six feet and thirteen or fourteen stone in weight. He looks to have been fit, but . . . here, let me see—" There was a pause of short duration. "His hands bear no signs of calluses or roughening, but the fingers are slightly stained with yellow and red. Hmmm—Oh, and by his right hand lies a pistol of no great caliber. The barrel of it points toward his hand. And one other detail: He wears a wedding ring on his left hand."

"The pistol," said Sir John, "is indeed an important detail, sir. I'm glad you did not omit it altogether."

"I nearly did, didn't I?" said Mr. Donnelly with a chuckle. "I was so taken with the stains on the fingers. I wonder what they are. It seems to me I have seen them before and that I should be familiar with them."

By this time Lord Laningham stood behind Sir John, waiting with obvious impatience to speak.

"And the wound?" prompted the magistrate.

"Ah yes, the wound. It is in the region of the heart. The bloodstain about it is relatively large, indicating that death was not quite instantaneous—though it must have come soon enough placed thus."

"Thank you, Mr. Donnelly. You may leave, if you like. I hope my summons did not ruin your plans for the evening."

"Nothing of the kind, Sir John. I do have plans, but this lamentable occasion has brought me quite near my evening's destination. I shall walk the distance from here." All this was said as he passed between Sir John and Mr. Bailey and made his way to the door. There did the surgeon pronounce his goodbye to each of us, myself included, and then did he depart.

As the door banged shut, Sir John turned to Lord Laningham and addressed him direct. "My lord," said he, "I have sensed your eagerness to talk. You may do so now, but I must ask you to restrain yourself to replies to my questions. Is that agreeable to you?"

"I suppose so, yes—if I must."

"Then let us proceed. Who is this man who lies on the floor?"

"I know not his name. Indeed I searched his pockets, yet found nothing to provide that information."

"Did you ask him? Mr. Donnelly said that he did not die immediately."

"He lived perhaps a pair of minutes at most and died with a curse for me upon his lips."

"Because you had shot him, I suppose?"

"Why, it was not near so simple as that. We struggled for the weapon. I suppose I had managed to gain control of the weapon, but—"

"That is to say, butt and trigger were in your hand?"

"I suppose so, yes, but he jerked the weapon in such a way as to wrench it from me, yet in doing so, he caused it to discharge direct into his heart."

"Whose weapon was it? Yours? His?"

"His! His! Good God, Sir John, this is not working well at all. He cursed me in his dying breath, because this is the man I told you about, he who swore vengeance upon the Laningham line, he who poisoned my uncle and aunt, and attempted to poison me, he who shot at me through the window in this very room, no doubt with this very pistol!"

"And how do you know this?" (This, as all Sir John's questions, was put to Lord Laningham in a cool and disengaged manner, thus inspiring Lord Laningham to greater excitement.)

"I know it because he told me. Please allow me to present this to you as it happened without interrupting me at every sentence with a question."

"Do it so, if you insist, though I cannot promise you that you will have no questions put to you in the course of your narrative."

"I suppose I must accept that." He paused to organize himself. "Well," he began his tale, "I was sitting at that desk, going over the household accounts—when of a sudden I heard a knock upon the door." His left hand shot up and cupped his ear in the universal gesture of listening. Then did he continue: "I heard Poole answer the door, and—"

"Oh, by the bye," interrupted Sir John, "where *is* the butler? I should like to talk with him once I have concluded with you."

"I really have no idea, sir, somewhere about. Servants are notoriously absent when you want them, and underfoot when you don't."

"So they say—but by all means proceed, and do forgive my intrusion."

"Yes, well, Poole answered the door, as I said, and I heard a positive row ensue—one can hear all from this room here. 'I would see Lord Laningham'—this in a deep, gruff voice, the voice of a villain—'nor will I be turned away!' Poor Poole tried to reason with him, get him to state his business and so on, yet it was all to naught. Then I fear I acted foolishly, for I went to the door, opened it, and—"

At this Sir John raised his hand and halted him. "You say you acted foolishly, and I agree. What could have prompted you to act as you did?"

"I have given thought to that, Sir John," said he, raising a hand to his brow, "and I believe my excuse lies in the fact that I was only moments before involved in the household accounts."

"I beg pardon, my lord?" Sir John did seem truly puzzled by the response.

"It was just so, sir, that I had noted that my uncle had been quite dilatory in paying a number of accounts—tradesmen and suppliers of one kind or another. Now that I think back, it seems to me that having just noted this, I somehow assumed that it was one of these come to demand payment. Yes, having given the matter some consideration, I believe that is why I opened the door and invited him into my study."

"Oh, invited him in, did you?"

"Oh yes, and dismissed Poole, as well."

"That was also foolish of you, wasn't it? But do continue."

"He entered, and I shut the door, inviting him to sit down. Yet he refused and said that he would not be staying long. I thought it odd of him not to remove his cape, and quite rude to keep his hat atop his head. But then he got to the point, launching into a venomous attack upon the Laninghams, giving instance after instance in which my family had cheated and plundered his family through generations."

"But did he never name his family?"

"No, no, he never did. He would simply say that his grandfather had this tract of land seized, his uncle had lost his farm, his father had lost all his holdings, et cetera—all to my family. Most of these supposed wrongs had been done his forebears in the territory surrounding Laningham. I, who had resumed my place at the desk, rose then from my chair and declared that though I sympathized deeply with him for the wrongs done his family, I knew nothing of them and could hardly be held accountable. By this time, of course, I knew who he was and what his probable purpose was, as well."

"And you did nothing to dissuade him?"

"How could I? I saw him a man obsessed. I made placating gestures, and yes, I did attempt to dissuade him, for

I suggested that I might look into these matters when I went to Laningham Manor, as I planned to do quite soon. All this, however, was mere subterfuge, for my true purpose was to free myself from the hindrance of the desk that I might position myself for a bold attack upon him. He soon made it plain that this was my only recourse.'' Then, once again adopting the gruff villain's voice: '' 'Lord Laningham,' said he to me, 'your family has tormented mine for over a century. Now I have taken my revenge upon them. Your uncle I poisoned, and his widow, as well. You survived my attacks by pistol and poison, but my lord, you shall in no wise escape me now.' ''

"He confessed all this to you?"

"He did, yes, he did," declared Lord Laningham. "And then having said it, he drew a pistol from beneath his coat, and I knew that the time for action had come. I leapt at him, threw myself across the room with all my strength, and toppled him down. We struggled for possession of the pistol in the manner I have described to you, and he was shot, mortally wounded. I should point out to you, sir, that it was not my intention to shoot him. It was his action, and not my own, which caused the trigger to be pulled. I wished only to save myself. If I had had any intention beyond that, it would have been to hold him prisoner with his own pistol and send for you."

"Well, I came in any case," said Sir John dryly. "What you are saying, then, is that you did not purposely kill the man on the floor."

"Oh, certainly not!"

"Nevertheless, he is just as dead as he would have been if you had planned and executed the whole affair quite by design. In other words, my lord, since your finger was on the trigger, there should be—at least by custom—an inquest by the coroner into this matter. I daresay you have nothing to fear from Mr. Trezavant if you tell the story as you told it me now."

"Well, of course I shall, for it is the truth."

"No doubt, no doubt, yet I fear this means that you will have me underfoot tomorrow, and I must interview any and all who were witness to this unfortunate event—that is, to what preceded and followed it. This would include your daughters and Lady Laningham. They are obviously in no condition now to answer my questions."

"I fear not."

"It will mean, also, that we must leave the corpus where it lies. Have the room locked, if you will, and see that nothing is disturbed. It will be taken in the morning."

"It will be done as you say, Sir John."

"And finally, we must take the pistol with us to Bow Street. Mr. Bailey, will you take charge of it?"

"Oh? Must you? I had thought . . ."

Mr. Bailey had already stepped into the room to fetch the weapon.

"What had you thought, my lord? Surely you did not wish to keep it as a remembrance of this dreadful occasion?"

"Oh no, nothing of the kind. I had thought merely . . . oh, that since you would want nothing disturbed, you would want that also where it lies—perhaps for Mr. Trezavant's viewing."

"No, I fear that Mr. Trezavant is totally dependent upon us for his information. So far we seem to have given him more than he wishes." Then, with a rap of his stick upon the floor, Sir John concluded the interview. "And so, Lord Laningham, we shall depart," said he. "I wish you a good evening, certainly a more tranquil one than you have so far had."

"Let me show you to the door. I do wonder where Poole has got to."

He went the few steps to the door and opened it, permitting us to trail out.

"Goodbye to you, then, Sir John. I look forward to your visit in the morning."

Then did the great door slam behind us.

Immediately did Mr. Perkins take Sir John aside and mutter low: "Sir, there's a poor cod been freezing out here in the cold for the chance to talk to you."

"Take me to him at once, Mr. Perkins."

It was Poole, the butler. He popped out from behind a bush that had quite obscured him. He was dressed for the house; he wore neither greatcoat nor cape, but stood chafing his hands and shivering.

"Sir John," said he, "I must be swift ere I be missed."

"Then quickly, Mr. Poole."

"The gentleman who lies dead—well, he was a trades-man, but he conducted himself as a gentleman—you could tell he was expected. He even said as much. He gave his name and offered his card. But before I could announce him proper, Mr. Paltrow, who calls himself Lord Lan-ingham, came out of the study. He greeted the fellow by name rather somber and took him into the study. It was a short time afterward, not much more than five minutes, that I heard the shot, but the ladies of the family were already there when he emerged—smiling. Yet the women imme-diately set up an awful racket of wailing and crying, like it was all planned among them. He then orders me off to send Sam for you. Now, I know not what was told you, sir, but that's the truth of it, though you likely heard different from him."

"I did indeed. Tell me now, since you did not have the opportunity to announce the caller, do you perhaps still have his card?"

"Why, as a matter of fact, sir, I do." Wherewith, Mr. Poole dipped into a pocket of his waistcoat and produced the card in question, which he placed in Sir John's hand. "As I recall, the caller's name was Mr. Pugh. But now, I must back into the house."

"Just one thing more, Mr. Poole. Did the late Lord Lan-ingham keep a loaded pistol in the study—perhaps in his desk?"

"He did, sir, in fact two—a boxed set. I know them well,

for he called my attention to them and said that if it was ever necessary to drive an unwelcome caller from our door, then here was the means.''

''Then I have a request. You have the keys to the study. Sometime during the night, when you will not be noticed, I want you to take the boxed set—one will no doubt be missing—and steal it. Sequester it and give it me in the morning.''

''I will do that, sir. But now I must go.''

''Go indeed, and may God bless you as a truth teller.''

Then did Mr. Poole take his leave, departing swiftly down a narrow pathway to the side of the great house to some rear entrance of it.

Sir John then handed the card to me and asked me to read it him. The light was not good, yet I made out the name, Peter Pugh, chemist, and an address on King Street, Twickenham, all of which I read aloud to Sir John.

''Gentlemen, are you ready for a long coach ride?'' he asked. ''We've a distance to go this evening, but we must reach Twickenham before murder is again committed.''

THIRTEEN

In Which an End of
Sorts Is Put to
Both Matters

We three—Constable Bailey, Constable Perkins, and myself—knew as little of the reason for our expedition to Twickenham at our arrival as we had at its beginning. Sir John had kept his silence as we huddled against the cold, bumping and bouncing along the road that followed close along the great river Thames. It seemed to me there were a score of questions that needed answer. Yet who was I to ask them if two of the Bow Street Runners—to my mind, the two finest of their number—were content in their ignorance of Sir John's plan? What I least understood was the urgency of this journey. Why could it not have been undertaken in the morning when it was a bit warmer?

Reader, if you are not acquainted with London and its environs, then you should know that Twickenham lies well into the County of Middlesex, beyond Richmond. Because of its location on the river and its handsome natural surroundings, there are a few great houses there, but the town itself is not much more than a village; and as we entered it, though the hour was not truly late, it gave every appearance of being a village asleep. Lucky for us that our destination lay on King Street, for it proved to be the chief street of the town, and the driver of the hackney had no difficulty finding the chemist's shop of Peter Pugh.

As we climbed down from the coach, Sir John paused to speak with the driver.

"We shall need you for the return trip to London," said he.

"And I shall need a return fare, for I'll not find one here."

"Well and good," said Sir John. "Here is an extra two shillings added to what we agreed upon." He passed the coins to Mr. Bailey, who reached them up to the driver. "Find a tavern or an inn hereabouts and wait there. One should be open at this hour."

"Aye, the Coach House Inn, or the Eel Pie House perhaps."

"Wherever you choose, but come back sober . . . oh, in an hour. But I must make it clear that I do not wish you waiting for us here within sight. Is that understood?"

"Understood and agreed."

Then did the driver urge his horses forward, leaving the four of us standing together before the chemist's shop. What was it, I asked myself, that demanded immediate attention but could be accomplished in an hour? Well, I would soon know.

"Tell me, gentlemen," said Sir John, "does a light burn in the floor above the shop?"

"It does, Sir John," said Mr. Bailey. "Someone's up and about."

"Are there pebbles about? Perhaps in the roadway?"

I was nearest the curb. I bent down and, looking closely, found a few near at hand.

"I have some, sir."

"Nothing large enough to break a pane of glass, I hope."

"Oh no, mere chips off the cobblestones they are."

"Then if you will, Jeremy, throw them one or two at a

time up at that lit window. Perhaps we can get attention from up there without raising a rumpus and rousing the neighbors.''

I threw up two together: one fell short, and the other clicked against a pane. I had the range; the next hit the mark, as did the next after that. I had returned to the road to search for more ammunition when sounds came from above. As I looked up, the window came open and the head of a woman emerged; she peered down in the darkness at us.

''Who is there? What do you want?''

''Madam Pugh?'' asked Sir John, his voice barely louder than it had been when he had spoken to me a few moments before.

''That's who I am, right enough, but who are you?''

''I am Sir John Fielding, Magistrate of the Bow Street Court, serving the Cities of Westminster and London. These men are constables. I wish to speak to you regarding your husband. Come down and open the shop door.''

''Oh dear, oh dear,'' said she, most fretful. ''But . . . but how do I know you are who you say you are?''

''I can tell you what you know to be true—that Peter Pugh this day went to London to meet with Lord Laningham.''

''Oh dear,'' she repeated. ''What—Well . . . all right, I'll be down in a moment.''

We gathered at the door. And in truth, it seemed little more than a moment until light showed vaguely below as through a frosted glass. Then did she throw a curtain back and proceed into the front of the shop. She bore a lit candle in one hand and a great ring of keys in the other. She had no difficulty finding the proper key to the door. Throwing it open, she bade us enter, and we trooped inside.

''Close the door,'' said she, ''for it's terrible cold out there.''

I, who was last to enter, pulled it tight shut behind me, noting as I did that she was probably warmest-dressed of any of us. She wore a thick winter robe over a wool night-gown, and a wool scarf tied round her head.

Mrs. Pugh faced Sir John square on. "What is it, then? Tell me the worst."

"Since you put it so," said Sir John, "I shall be direct. Your husband was shot to death by Arthur Paltrow, Lord Laningham, no more than two hours ago."

She seemed at first to take the news stoically, for she said nothing during what seemed a great while. Holding her face still, she kept her jaw so rigid that it seemed to bulge. Then, of a sudden, she lost control, and her face crumpled in an excess of tears.

"Oh, God," she wailed, "what is to become of me?"

"That, madam, is one of the reasons we have come. I have good reason to believe that Lord Laningham is on his way here at this moment with the intention of murdering you."

"But . . . but . . ." She strove to gain control over the great hiccuping sobs that now racked her. Then at last she mastered them to ask: "Why . . . should he do . . . that?"

"You knew, did you not, of the considerable quantities of arsenic your husband had sold to Arthur Paltrow?"

Recovering herself, she admitted that she did: "Peter began to suspicion him when he kept coming back for more. 'No house has that many rats,' says Peter to me."

"Yet your husband continued to supply him, did he not?"

"Out of curiosity he did and because there was no reason not to. One time he followed him from the shop, that he might know where was this house with all the rats. What he found was that the fellow marched off to the Coach House and took the post coach to London. That struck Peter as passing strange. If the fellow wanted arsenic, why did he not buy it in London, where he could get it in any chemist's shop?"

"When did these visits begin? How frequent were they?"

"He first came six months ago and would visit each month to buy a good half-pound, or more, but he wanted more each visit. On his last, he bought more than a pound."

"And when was that?"

"About a month ago," said she. "Now, sir, it was always my husband's dream to escape Twickenham and open a shop in London. He would read the *Public Advertiser,* so he knew all the news and tittle-tattle just as any who lived there might. One day he read to me the story of the death of old Lord Laningham in the Crown and Anchor, and he says to me, 'May,' he says, 'that sounds to me like arsenic, it does, and I'm going into London next Sunday to the concert to see if this Arthur Paltrow fellow is the one comes each month to buy it of me.' Well, he went, and he had his look, and it was the same fellow. Then did my husband read of the death of old Lady Laningham, and that made him still more certain to proceed with his plan."

"His plan of extortion, you mean?"

"Is that what you call it? Well, Peter didn't ask for much—just a hundred pounds each for the lord and lady. He wrote in the letter he would only require thus much, and would not ask later for more. But he said if this amount was not paid, he would bring what he knew to the attention of some magistrate or other. It may even be you he mentioned, sir."

"When was it this letter was sent?"

"Less than a week ago. He got a prompt reply which invited him to call tonight at seven. Oh, I begged him not to go, said it could be a trap. I counseled him against it, I did, but he was determined. He said it would give him enough to move us to London and open a shop in a good district."

"Nevertheless, madam, you knew your husband's unlawful intentions, and you failed to report them. That made you a silent conspirator in the criminal act. Yet I promise you that all will be forgiven you if you take part in my plan to apprehend your husband's murderer."

She thought a moment upon his proposition. "I'll do it," said she. "I'll do whatever you ask."

"Very good. You have made a wise decision. We expect this man Arthur Paltrow, who has taken the title of Lord Laningham, to come here soon. I want you to go upstairs and allow him to halloo you down. Be reluctant, but allow yourself finally to be persuaded. Open the door to him, but retire to a place near the entrance to the back of the shop. We will wait there. Get him to talk truthfully of what has happened, and at the first sign of danger to your person, cry out, and we shall be there to rescue you. Is that clear?"

"It's clear," she said, yet she wavered: "But . . . what is this of danger to my person?"

"Don't you understand, madam? He's coming here to murder you, too, for what you know of this. But never mind that now. Go upstairs, for this villain may come along at any time."

Then, somewhat wide-eyed, she turned away and left us. I heard her footsteps on the stairway a moment later.

"Come along, gentlemen. Take me to the rear of the shop so that we may find a less visible place to wait. Is there a curtain? Ah, good—even better."

We had not long to wait. Sir John amended his plan in one particular. At Mr. Perkins's suggestion, he placed the constable in one corner behind the counter. There he would be invisible unless Arthur Paltrow himself stepped behind the counter, which was not likely. Then, satisfied, we took our place behind and to one side of the curtain, leaving Mrs. Pugh an easy path past us.

"Now you, Jeremy, I make responsible for Mrs. Pugh's safety. Should she cry out that she is in danger—or at my command—I wish you to reach round the curtain, or even through it, and grab the woman and pull her back. Pull her down if you must, but get her out of harm's way. Understood?"

"Understood, sir," said I.

"And you, Mr. Bailey, have your pistol out and cock it

soon as she goes by, so that you are ready to step into the gap and shoot, if necessary. Understood?"

"Aye, Sir John, as you say."

We waited, though as I have written, not long. The first sign that our expected visitor had made his appearance came from Sir John: a smile spread across his face. Then came a nod from Constable Bailey, and at about that time my own dull ears picked up the sound of hoofbeats on the cobblestones.

"From the sound of it," I whispered, "there is but a single man on horseback."

"That's as I would have expected," said Sir John. "Had he come in his coach-and-four, he would have had his driver and footman as witnesses to murder. The horse he rides, however, cannot bear witness against him."

The hoofbeats stopped before the shop. The conversation that ensued after a minute or two between the rider—the sound of his voice identified him certainly as Lord Laningham—and Mrs. Pugh was rather difficult to follow in that we were unable to hear clearly what was spoken by her. She had shut the door at the top of the stairs, and I at least was only able to make out what was said by him. He lured her with a promise of payment, saying that her husband had fallen ill and had put up with them for the time being, but had insisted that he, Lord Laningham, ride out to Twickenham and inform his wife of this and make payment to her direct so that she might not worry about his absence.

"I am only conforming with Mr. Pugh's wishes in this, madam, so please open the door that I might pay you and be gone. I have had a long, cold ride, and I would be done with this, and done with it as quick as possible."

Though I heard not what she responded, she must have allowed that to persuade her, for it was but an instant later that I heard the door open and her footsteps on the stairs. She looked quite apprehensive as she approached us.

"I hope I ain't sorry for this," she muttered.

"Just stand with your back into the curtain," whispered Sir John.

Then she stepped past us, and into the front of the shop. I heard the key rattle in the lock and the door swing open on its dry hinges. She had no need to urge this visitor to shut the door: he closed it sharply behind him.

"Ah, madam," said he, "you've no idea how good it is to be in out of that chill night air. There's even a bit of wind up. I had a frightful ride here."

"And all to deliver a certain sum of cash. Well, tell me, where is it?"

A frown appeared on Sir John's face. Was she not rushing things a bit? I asked myself. And why had she not backed up against the curtain, as she'd been told?

She, too, must have realized that her pace in the matter was somewhat precipitous, for she amended her question: "But tell me first what ails my husband."

"You seem quite agitated, madam, if I may say so. And why do you back away so?"

"I ain't sure I did right to let you in."

"Let me assure you that you have little to fear from me. You will have your cash. I wish only to ascertain a thing or two first. But let me now tell you that Mr. Pugh suffered some pains in the region of his heart. A physician has examined him and prescribed rest merely. At this moment he sleeps peacefully in one of our best rooms."

At last the curtain stirred and bulged ever so slightly inward. She was at last where she ought to be.

"When will he return?"

"Oh, you'll be seeing him soon, I'm sure."

"He's not been poisoned, has he?" She put it to him right boldly.

"Ah, now that was one of the things I was curious to know. I wondered, did your husband tell you anything of the little arrangement he proposed to me? Your question indicates to me that indeed he did tell you. The question, madam, is how much do you know?"

"I know enough," said she, in a manner most sullen.

"That suggests to me that you know all." He sighed somewhat dramatically. I speculated he might have practiced a few of these remarks on his ride to Twickenham. "Such a pity," said he. "I might have spared you had you said you knew nothing at all of the proposition your husband had put to me—though probably not, for a man in my position must expect the worst. I cannot, alas, afford to gamble."

"What do you mean?"

"What I mean, madam, is that I fear I misled you a few moments ago. I led you to believe your husband was, let us say, healthier than he in fact is. I said that he sleeps peacefully in one of our best rooms. That is true, as far as it goes, yet he sleeps the sleep of death, lying on the carpet of my study. And when I said he had pains in the region of the heart, well, that much is true, for I caused them by shooting him there. And that, dear madam, is where I now intend to shoot you."

"Oh, dear God, what is that?" she shouted. "A *pistol?*"

With that, I grabbed at her body through the curtain. With a slippery hold on her, I pulled her back and down so that she tumbled upon me—and the curtain, ripped from where it hung, came down atop both of us. Nevertheless, there was a shot: it rang forth loud as a clap of thunder and sailed above us both, smashing through glass behind us before it came to rest in the far wall. And near simultaneous with it were two more shots, equally loud, from the two constables in separate corners. When the smoke had lifted, and I had fought clear of the weighty female form that rested on my chest, as well as the yards of cloth that covered us, I heard Sir John shout out, demanding a report as I myself took a look about.

"Mrs. Pugh is well, as I am, too," I called out. "Is that not so, Mrs. Pugh? Speak up, please."

"I've felt better than I do now after that fall on my backside, but I ain't shot."

"Well and good," said Sir John, "and what about you, Mr. Bailey? And you, Mr. Perkins?"

"I'll do well enough," said Mr. Perkins.

"Good as can be," responded Mr. Bailey.

"Which leaves our friend Arthur Paltrow. What is his condition, Mr. Bailey?"

"Well, Sir John, from the look of him, cringing and twisting there on the floor, I'd say he took Mr. Perkins's ball in the upper arm and mine in the other shoulder."

"I demand you take me to a surgeon before I bleed to death."

"Oh, I doubt you will. Mr. Donnelly has treated his share of gunshot wounds. He'll save you for the hangman." Sir John then cocked an ear and listened. "And if I do not mistake, then that is our hackney returning to take us back to Bow Street. Gather up the prisoner, gentlemen. Put him on his feet and march him out to the coach. Mrs. Pugh, you played your part in our little drama quite well. Soon you will receive a subpoena to testify against this knave who took your husband's life and sought to take your own. Extortion of the sort your husband attempted is a serious crime, but murder is far, far worse."

It was in the course of our return journey to London that Sir John clarified all. From time to time, in the course of his explanation, he would prod Paltrow with his foot, demanding confirmation on this point or that—demanding but never receiving, for the pretender to the earldom, who lay on the floor in the space between the facing seats, kept an angry silence the entire distance as he bled onto the floor of the hackney. Sir John did not begin his disquisition immediately. He remarked upon the crowd we had attracted upon our departure. He inquired, that he might be reassured, whether Paltrow's horse was tied securely to the rear of the coach. Then did he lapse into silence for a time. It was not until we were passing through Richmond that he commenced to tell just how he had reached his various conclusions. He directed his remarks to me, though all the rest, I'm sure (including Mr. Paltrow), were fascinated by what he had to say.

"Try as I might to keep an open mind in the matter, Jeremy," said he, "I continued to suspect poisoning in the deaths of Lord and Lady Laningham. And since Mr. Paltrow here had most to gain, it seemed likely to me that he was the poisoner. Was that not so, sir?" he inquired of his prisoner. Paltrow merely grunted. "But to continue," said Sir John, "because this was my state of mind, I was quite skeptical of the tale told me by this one here of him who had sworn vengeance upon the Laningham line. Though by my attitude I may have let show my skepticism, I nevertheless gave him practical advice on how he might protect himself—advice which, significantly, he never chose to follow.

"Yet," Sir John went on, "I received a surprise—perhaps better put, a setback—to my line of reasoning. It was occasioned by Mr. Paltrow's collapse at the musical evening soon after his aunt's funeral. I say it was occasioned because the collapse—the vomiting and so on, so much in the same manner as those earlier deaths—did not surprise me. I had had a premonition, or perhaps just a feeling, that we had been invited there for a purpose—that is, to witness some great event. And so, when it came, the event itself did not surprise me, for I reasoned that the symptoms of poisoning could be produced with an ordinary emetic, one strong enough to produce vomiting of a quite violent nature. No, what surprised me and set me back a bit was the result of our little experiment with the wine drunk by Mr. Paltrow and the rats in the cage. I was forced to admit that it appeared that indeed Mr. Paltrow had himself suffered poisoning by arsenic. I was confused by that, quite at sixes and sevens, ready to take seriously the tale told us of that shadowy figure who had sworn death to the Laninghams."

Then did Sir John prod Paltrow once again with his foot. "Thought you had me there, did you not, sir?" Yet again there was no response.

"But," Sir John resumed, "Mr. Donnelly, or rather his former medical school professor, came to my rescue with that second letter of his. Do you recall it, Jeremy? You were most curious about it. Well you may have been, for that letter provided an explanation for Paltrow's recovery from arsenic poisoning. No, it was not milk that rescued him, not entirely, though he assures me that it helped. Remember the letter came from Vienna—from Austria. The professor simply added to his first letter a matter he thought of general interest on the subject of arsenic. To wit: the people of Austria's Tyrol region, mountain people they are, have the custom of eating arsenic upon their food. They believe it gives them strength. He went on to say that he knew not whether it made them stronger, though indeed they are a hardy lot, but it had been proven that the eating of it over a period of time made them resistant to doses of the poison that would prove deadly to any other man or woman. You will recall, Jeremy, that we went off directly to call upon Paltrow, ostensibly to inquire into his recovery. Yet I managed to turn our conversation to travel in foreign lands, and he admitted having visited the Tyrol region—quite enchanted he was by it. Well, the fact that he had visited there was in no wise proof that he had learned there of that curious local practice, but I revisited the Laningham residence in the company of Clarissa Roundtree—you recall the occasion?—and learned from the servers that Lord Laningham, as they called him, had been in the habit of sprinkling a white powder over his food, a powder which he called his medicine. He did this, of course, to build up his resistance to the poison, having foreseen that in order to escape detection as a poisoner, he would one day have to poison himself, or make some show of it, as he did when he took a bit of his uncle's wine. In the past days, however—that is, since his fit of vomiting—he no longer made use of the powder. Those dark circles round his eyes, by the bye, which you mentioned to me, were said by Mr. Donnelly to be a likely result of arsenic eating.

"Well, what to do? If he no longer took arsenic—and he had no need to do so, for he thought he had already made his point—then he had no need to have it about and had probably disposed of it. Yet rather than gnash my teeth in frustration, I simply sat back and waited for him to make a mistake. That he did soon enough, but he must have congratulated himself beforehand on the marvelous opportunity he'd been given. He must have felt indeed that Mr. Pugh's threatening letter and his eventual appearance provided a way out of all this nonsense he himself had created."

"You mean, sir," I asked, "the creation of that shadowy figure who had sworn to kill all the Laninghams?"

"Exactly, for the man who presented himself to Paltrow, if shot dead, could be offered to us as the avenger. Paltrow wished to be rid of this fiction he had formed from his imagination. The avenger had served his purpose. Now let him be destroyed, in the person of this troublesome fellow who sought to extort money from him. He had received a letter, and so had thought things out quite well by the time Mr. Pugh arrived. Yet when the visitor did arrive, he proved to be a good-sized, strapping fellow. And Paltrow—Mr. Perkins, what would you judge Paltrow's weight to be?"

"Oh, not much more than ten stone, Sir John."

"About what I had reckoned from his height and the sound of his voice. I doubted, of course, that such a one could so easily wrestle a pistol from another so much larger. And then, too, there was the information given me by Mr. Bailey when he checked to see if there was still some life in Mr. Pugh. What was it you whispered, Mr. Bailey?"

"I told you that judging from the spread of powder it looked like he'd been shot from a distance of about five feet or so."

"And that would put it just out of arm's reach—contrary to Paltrow's testimony. Yet it was not until the butler presented me with the card of the man who lay dead in the Laningham study that all became clear. First of all, Mr.

Pugh was a chemist. One who contemplates poisoning with arsenic needs a supply of it, and one who sprinkles it atop his food to develop a resistance to it needs a goodly supply. Now, where was he to come by it? Not in London, though it could be got there in any chemist's shop, for those he intended to poison were well known in the city, as he would eventually also be. A London chemist might eventually remember Paltrow's purchases, and should he become suspicious, report them. Then no, not London—he would go someplace far outside the great city and choose a chemist at random. His mistake was that in traveling to Twickenham, he did not go far enough, and in choosing a chemist, he happened upon one who kept up on all the news from the capital. I knew that once we knew whence Peter Pugh had come, we must make haste there, for Mr. Pugh wore a wedding ring, and that could not have escaped the notice of Paltrow. Mrs. Pugh may even have presented herself in the course of one or more of his visits. She would know what her husband had planned, and so she, too, must die. The rest you know, of course, for all of you played your parts well.''

Having thus concluded, Sir John sought confirmation from his prisoner one last time. ''What about it, Mr. Paltrow? Would you care to add or subtract anything from my account of the matter? What have you to say?''

''I will neither add nor subtract from your account,'' said Paltrow, giving an answer at last. ''I would but point out to you that the deaths of both my uncle and my aunt have been put down as resulting from natural causes. It will be difficult to prove them otherwise.''

''Difficult, but perhaps not impossible,'' replied Sir John. ''But not difficult at all to prove willful homicide against Peter Pugh. That I'll gladly leave in the hands of the judge and jury.''

Arthur Paltrow had no more to say, nor, as it happened, did Sir John Fielding. The magistrate fell silent for the rest of our journey. Mr. Bailey dozed, and Mr. Perkins kept a

sharp eye on the prisoner. For my part, I went through each
step of Sir John's summary, and saw the logic of it. I ap-
preciated, too, that though he may have had the suspicion,
even the conviction, early on that murder by poison had
twice been committed, it was quite another matter to bring
convincing proof against Paltrow in these deaths. Having
thus considered the question thoroughly, I concluded it
most likely that Arthur Paltrow would be indicted and tried
only in the death of Peter Pugh. And in that I was proven
correct.

   We came at last to Number 4 Bow Street. There I exited
the coach in the company of Sir John, who left the prisoner
in the charge of Constable Bailey and Constable Perkins.
"Take him to Mr. Donnelly," said he to them. "I trust the
surgeon will have returned from his revels. Then back here
with your charge, and into the strong room with him. I'll
see him in my court tomorrow."

In the matter of the Crown versus Mary Brighton Bradbury,
the Lord Chief Justice tried the case himself, as he had
promised he would. That he weighted it at every opportunity against the defendant could hardly be denied; that he
did so unfairly should also have been plain to any who
heard it from beginning to end. That number, as it happened, included myself. I had been called as a witness for
the Crown, as had Jimmie Bunkins. He gave his testimony
early in the trial. I was not summoned until its second day
but had to be there the opening day, for the trial was not
expected to last more than a day. Few in those days that
were tried before the Lord Chief Justice went so long.

   That it had gone to such a duration was due largely to
the diligence and eloquence of her barrister, William Ogden. She was allowed counsel, as the charge against her
was technically one of treason, as the murder of a husband
by his wife was and is judged to be. Mr. Ogden was then
at the beginning of his great career, and I was quite inspired
by watching him at work. There was a rumor about that

Mrs. Bradbury had promised him twice his fee if he got her off the charge of murder, and nothing if she went to the gallows. Knowing that she had a small fortune from Mr. Bradbury's sale of his father's house, lands, and goods hidden away, and that she no doubt could not uncover it until she was released, I thought there was probably a good deal of fact to the rumor. Mr. Ogden must have taken a good look at the case against her and accepted the challenge—double or nothing. He went at it like a gambler, giving all to the great game of it; he tried the case not on Mary Bradbury's guilt or innocence but rather on the merits of the case, which I knew to be weak.

He was especially aggressive on cross-examination. He played hard upon the fact that Bunkins's identification of the head had not been positive (Bunkins, of course, had never claimed that it was), but he managed also to use this to impugn his identification of Jackie Carver as one who made long and frequent visits to the Bradbury pawnshop. He forced the stablekeeper Matthew Gurney to admit that so much of Carver's face had been destroyed by Mr. Cowley's shot that he could not give certain identification beyond allowing that "it looked like it might have been him who sold the white horse to me." I, too, felt the sting of Mr. Ogden's wit and intelligence when I was called as a witness for the Crown. Because I had seen enough of him by then to know what he might do to my testimony in cross-examination, I was very careful and precise not to claim to have heard or seen more than I actually did. I had to admit in cross-examination, however, that neither Thomas Roundtree nor Jackie Carver had mentioned the part, if any, Mrs. Bradbury had played in the murder of her husband. And he did attack the single weak spot in my identification of Jackie Carver as one who had been present at the scene when the Runners made their midnight raid upon the pawnshop.

"How could you be sure it was this fellow Jackie Carver?" he asked.

"Because he was known to me by sight and by his evil reputation."

"You had met him? Seen him often?"

"I had met him once or twice, seen him often in the region of Covent Garden, and heard his reputation as one who used a knife to threaten and to do physical harm."

"Were you friends with him?"

"Certainly not."

"Enemies perhaps, then?"

"Certainly not friends," I repeated. "I would say, however, that my contacts with him were brief. He gave me a wide berth, not because he feared me personally but because of my known association with the Bow Street Court and Sir John Fielding."

Then, happily, Mr. Ogden went on to other matters, leaving at that my past relations with Jackie Carver.

In presenting his case for the defendant, he first read in full to the jury a document they had heard only in part from the prosecution. It was the letter from the Warwick magistrate. Mr. Ogden gave great emphasis to the fact that the magistrate had warned George Bradbury against making the trip to London on horseback, and repeated this line, "Though it is no great distance from here to your great city, the roads between are known to be infested by highwaymen," and another, "He may have been caught in some ambuscade and now lies in some shallow grave in a wood between here and there."

Then did Mr. Ogden call Mary Brighton Bradbury to the stand in her own defense. He led her through the same story that she had told Sir John: that her husband had never returned from Warwick and that in her desperation she had agreed to take a load of stolen goods, which she otherwise would not have consented to do. And as for Jackie Carver, she claimed again that he had simply been hired off the street to help unload the wagon which supposedly contained the booty taken in burglary. It was a simple tale, one which every member of the jury could grasp. She stuck to it tenaciously during cross-examination by the Crown prosecutor. He railed at her, bullied her shamelessly, but she did not break, nor did she alter her story. Yet she was in no wise cold, for she presented herself as a bereaved widow and wept for her lost husband. As the prosecutor's attack intensified to a climax at the end, she cried out, "No, no, I would give all if George would return to me—and I pray that one day he may. Perhaps he was hit on the head and his brains was addled, or he may be recovering from a gunshot. He may come back!"

With that thought firmly set in the minds of the jury members, the Crown prosecutor had to strive mightily to assemble the bits and pieces of the case against Mrs. Bradbury in such a way as to convince them of her guilt. Yet strive he did, rumbling darkly of her infidelity, shouting of her final betrayal of her husband in her collaboration in his murder, demanding finally that "this Jezebel hang for her sins."

Mr. Ogden, by contrast, was calm, the very voice of reason, as one by one he pointed out the flaws and gaps in the Crown's case: that the identification of the head was uncertain; that no one had seen George Bradbury arrive on his white horse; that a white horse had been sold to a stable near the pawnshop, but he who had sold the horse could not be certainly identified as the one who was present when the Bow Street Runners made their raid on the pawnshop; and as to the hearsay confessions of Thomas Roundtree and Jackie Carver, that neither gave mention of Mrs. Bradbury in the alleged murder of George Bradbury. "We know not truly if such murder took place," said Mr. Ogden, raising his voice just slightly, "because *there is no body*. It was good of Mrs. Bradbury in her reply to the prosecutor to remind us of an important point. Though even the Magistrate of Warwick seemed to think it unlikely that George Bradbury would return unscathed or indeed at all, he may indeed someday return. Will it be that he comes back the day after his wife has been hanged for his murder? Think of that possibility, gentlemen of the jury. The decision in this matter is yours, and yours alone.''

As the Lord Chief Justice gave his summing-up and instructions to the jury, it had the tone of a second statement from the prosecution. Nevertheless, he seemed in a sense almost apologetic for the flimsy case brought by the Crown, noting that, yes, it was unusual to try a case of homicide when the victim's body was nowhere to be found, yet a head had been discovered and given approximate identification—and if it was not George Bradbury's head, then whose was it? None, to his knowledge, had reported one missing. (This brought uneasy laughter from some in the courtroom, though not from the jury.) And if the testimony regarding the murder was in part hearsay, he had admitted it because it was of a convincing nature and from a good source. (I puffed a bit at that.) It may be that it did not directly implicate Mary Brighton Bradbury, yet it proved to his satisfaction, at least, that murder had been committed—and what did they suppose she was doing as her husband was being killed and sawed in parts? Tending the shop below? And so on. The Lord Chief Justice had insisted on bringing the case to trial, and he had no wish to feel on the morrow that he had wasted two days of his life.

And so the jury went out to determine the fate of Mrs. Bradbury. I, one among many, was prepared to wait to hear the verdict no matter how long it might take; nearly all in the courtroom, save those leading actors directly involved in the drama we had witnessed, reseated themselves, relaxing somewhat, beginning to talk in hushed, respectful tones.

The fellow next me, perhaps a few years older than I, turned to me of a sudden and surprised me by telling me that he had been quite favorably impressed by my testimony.

''How often have you given testimony before?'' he asked.

''This is my first time ever,'' said I, in a manner quite naive, ''that is, my first criminal trial. I'd never even visited this court before, though I've sat more often than I can count through Sir John Fielding's sessions at the Bow Street Court.''

''Why, then I'm doubly impressed—giving testimony at your first trial in Old Bailey—imagine! But after all, a magistrate's court must be much different.''

''Not so much, no.''

He was a good-looking chap, sandy-haired and well dressed, with an eager manner. ''I was a little unclear as to your relationship to Sir John. It was not made specific.''

Unable quite to help myself, I laughed at that, then said rather hastily: ''Forgive me for laughing, but it is something I have wondered at myself. In truth, I am but one of his household, yet I help him sometimes in court matters.''

''Did he truly allow you to question that man Roundtree?''

''Yes, he trusts me sometimes to carry out such duties. He advised me on the approach I might take, and I followed it.''

''With good results.''

''Satisfactory,'' said I, alas, a bit smugly. Then did I make bold to add: ''I am preparing to read law with him.''

''Ah! Preparing? In what way?''

''He has assigned me the task of reading twice through Sir Edward Coke's *Institutes of the Law of England*—the first time to acquaint myself with the matter and the second time to take notes and prepare questions for next year, when we begin reading through it together. Then, he says, we shall be on to other things. But I have time. I am yet young.''

''Fascinating,'' said he, ''but let me introduce myself. I am Archibald Talley, and I, too, am preparing for the law. I'm reading with my uncle Benjamin, who is a common-law judge. I clerk in his office, as well.''

I quickly presented myself, and I said how pleased I was to meet one who, like myself, was aiming for the law.

''But between us,'' said he, ''you know, surely, that your

Sir John should never have sent such a weak case up to be tried in felony court.''

"He argued against it to the Lord Chief Justice, and when he set me to writing drafts of the parts of it I knew best, I saw that he was right. It was indeed weak.''

"You helped him prepare the case?''

"A memorandum outlining it—and only the parts I knew well. It was the first time he had asked me to do so.''

"Even so, that is most impressive. I envy you your participation, Mr. Proctor.''

"But didn't Mr. Ogden tear into it remarkably well?''

"He was quite marvelous!'' said Mr. Talley. "I'd heard he was worth coming to watch—and I certainly wasn't disappointed.''

We then spent well over an hour discussing the trial—or more specifically, Mr. Ogden's handling of it. As we did so, I gradually became aware how beneficial it was to me to discuss such matters with one who was formally engaged in the reading of law. He brought an insight and a variety of reference to his comments that I could only envy. Yet he was neither pedant nor peacock. He did not parade his knowledge; it was simply there, and he used it to good advantage. I swore to myself that I would go at Coke more diligently in the coming months.

Then, with the entrance of the bailiff and the clerk, came the first hint that the verdict of the jury would soon be forthcoming. Mrs. Bradbury, in the company of a second bailiff, the Crown prosecutor, and Mr. William Ogden followed them, and the room went silent as the jury filed in. All stood as the entrance of the Lord Chief Justice was announced; not until he, too, was seated did we resume our places. Then was the formal request made for the jury's verdict. The foreman stood, a shopkeeper by the look of him, and after clearing his throat, said as follows: "M'lord, in the absence of a body, we find the defendant not guilty.''

There was no demonstration of approval or disapproval in that august hall. The only emotional response came from the judge himself, whose expression turned from grave to sour as he dismissed the jury and called Mary Brighton Bradbury before him.

"You, madam, are a very fortunate woman," said he. "I, for one, was convinced of your guilt and am still. That, however, matters little, for the jury has spoken otherwise. You are free on this charge, but I return you to the Fleet Prison to serve the remainder of your sentence for conspiracy to receive stolen goods."

Then he brought down his gavel. Mrs. Bradbury was ushered out; then we all stood once again as William Murray, the Lord Chief Justice, made his departure.

As we were taking our leave, Archibald Talley declared his pleasure in meeting me; and I impulsively invited him to come sometime for a visit so that I might introduce him to Sir John. (My true purpose, I confess, was to extend our acquaintance.) He brightened at the suggestion and promised to do so sometime soon. Then, pleading work awaiting him at his uncle's, he hurried away with the crowd. I left Old Bailey that day with a sense of elation. Though a guilty woman had gone free, I had watched a brilliant barrister reveal the paltry nature of the case against her: the law had been served. And I had made the acquaintance of one who might prove a friend. I felt more certain of my future and the profession I had chosen than ever before.

But to end the tale of Mary Brighton Bradbury, let me move swiftly a month ahead to her release from the Fleet Prison. It was said—and I've no reason to doubt it—that William Ogden was waiting for her at the prison gate when she passed through. They proceeded together to the pawnshop, which she opened with the keys that had been provided her by the Bow Street Court. Asking him to wait, she disappeared into the rear of the shop. After an absence of many minutes, she reappeared with his fee, doubled as promised, in gold guineas. He left with thanks. The next day she appeared at the offices of the *Public Advertiser* and purchased an advert putting the shop up for sale. She had a buyer within the month, and it was sold for a goodly price, lock and stock, and the building, as well. And then she disappeared—quite vanished, she did. None seemed to know where she had got to; none seemed to care. When I asked Sir John if he had any idea of her whereabouts, he simply shrugged and said, "More than likely to the colonies. They seem to accept most of our trash. If there be any true justice, perhaps she has been washed overboard on the voyage, or having arrived, been scalped to death by some red Indian."

Arthur Paltrow did not fare near so well. Though, as Sir John predicted, Mr. Donnelly had no difficulty removing the pistol bullets from his arm and shoulder, Mr. Perkins's ball had broken the bone when it entered. It was necessary to set the left arm, causing Paltrow greater pain, and fashion a sling for it. The right shoulder wound was not near so serious, for the ball was embedded in the fleshy part and had nearly passed through altogether. It made quite a gouge, but Mr. Donnelly cleaned it thoroughly and bound it up.

Next day he was indicted by Sir John for the murder of Peter Pugh and directed to Newgate to await trial at Old Bailey. Mr. Paltrow protested grandly, claiming the right to be tried in the House of Lords. Sir John, wishing all to be done properly, detained the prisoner an extra day in the strong room so that he might hear from Parliament on the matter. He was informed that while the House of Lords had received his "letter of patent" to the Laningham title, it had not yet issued to him the Writ of Summons to Parliament. Mr. Paltrow, in other words, had made his application, but as yet had not been given his invitation—nor would he be. It was proper, then, to try him in felony court and improper to address him by the title Lord Laningham. So off he went to Newgate to await trial. It seemed strange to me that he should have wished to be tried in the House of Lords, for if found guilty, as he most certainly would have been, he would have surrendered his head to the executioner's axe; hanging, the mode prescribed by the felony court, seemed infinitely preferable to me.

Eventually, his case came up for trial. Lord Murray, who wanted no part of a matter involving anyone who had even a claim upon a title, handed the case to one of his lesser judges, Francis Seward. Having no such compunction, Justice Seward dealt swiftly with Mr. Paltrow. The defendant undertook his own defense. Among the witnesses called against him were Mr. Poole, Constable Bailey, and Mrs. Pugh. The first two established that the shooting had taken place, and that Peter Pugh was the victim, though Paltrow had sought to hide the identity of the man he had killed. Mrs. Pugh gave the motive for murder, repeated the confession she had heard from Paltrow's lips, and told of the shot he had aimed at her. It became obvious in his cross-examination of Mrs. Pugh, or so I understood from Mr. Talley's later report, that Mr. Paltrow's line of defense was that he was justified in shooting Peter Pugh, for in demanding money from him Mr. Pugh was committing a crime. This was made quite explicit in a statement Paltrow had prepared in his own defense which the judge permitted him to read. "In effect," his statement concluded, "this man Pugh was attempting to rob me of two hundred pounds, a considerable amount—a small fortune—just as surely as if he had held a knife to my throat. Had this happened on some dark street, would I not have been justified in protecting myself and my money? Of course I would! You, gentlemen of the jury, would have done the same, would you not? Of course you would!"

He seemed most confident at that point, but later Justice Seward put to him a few questions which caused him some embarrassment.

"Mr. Paltrow," said the judge, "Mr. Pugh did not hold a knife to your throat, did he?"

"No, I used that merely as an analogy."

"He used the force of revelation, did he not? That was the analogical knife to your throat?"

"Well, yes, but I—"

"Then this revelation must have had the strength of deadly force. Now, we know from Mrs. Pugh's testimony that the information with which her husband threatened you was your purchase of great amounts of arsenic, which is a poison. Why, sir, was it of such urgent importance to you to keep that information away from investigating authorities? Why did it have the strength of deadly force?"

"With all due respect, my lord, I'd rather not go into that."

"You decline to answer? I must caution you that there is only one basis on which you may do that and that would be if, in answering, you ran the risk of incriminating yourself. Is it on that basis that you decline to answer?"

A silence ensued. Arthur Paltrow seemed quite tortured by the decision put to him. At last said he: "Then, if I must, I decline on that basis."

Wherewith, Justice Seward charged the jury and sent them out to make their deliberations. They returned a verdict of guilty in about a quarter of an hour's time. Mr. Paltrow was sentenced to be hanged the day next but one. All his property was made forfeit to the Crown.

Allowed then to have a final word, the condemned man said something which struck me as strange and rather pathetic. "All I did," said he, "was done for my daughters, that they might make good marriages."

Then was he carted off to Newgate, whence, the day next but one, he was hanged on Tyburn Hill in the company of thieves and burglars. His left arm was still in a sling when the noose was put about his neck.

What became of his wife (the putative Lady Laningham), and the daughters for whom he did all, I never heard. Managing to salvage sufficient funds from the uncle's fortune, perhaps they, too, may have shipped off for the American colonies.

• • •

I recall the evening well. We had just supped well on mutton and spring potatoes. There were, as there had been for near two months, five of us round the table, for Clarissa Roundtree was still with us. Inquiries had been put out on her behalf to a number of houses; none seemed suitable—at least not to Lady Fielding. And so, the matter of her future had hung fire for a number of weeks. For her part, Clarissa was outwardly much different; physically, she was not just recovered from her illness but in the full bloom of good health, as well. She had put weight onto her spare frame, her cheeks had taken on some color, and her face had filled out a bit so that she no longer appeared quite so like a waif. Inwardly, however, it was difficult to tell, for she was one, it seemed to me, who hid her true feelings well. She would be laughing at table at some story of Annie's of choir practice or her lessons with Mr. Burnham, and I would catch a watchful look in Clarissa's eye as she glanced about the table, as if she might be asking herself if it was proper to laugh, or laugh quite so boldly. She seemed always anxious of the impression she might make upon the others. For that matter, she had made an excellent impression upon Lady Fielding. She pitched in to relieve Annie and me of some of our more burdensome household tasks, helping with the cooking and proving herself capable as a floor scrubber; indeed, after dinner each night she and Annie retired to their room, where she drilled her on her reading lessons; and she had made herself quite useful to Lady Fielding, both in our household and at the Magdalene Home, writing letters, running errands, doing in short whatever she was asked. With me, to whom she had come nearest to presenting her true self, she was for the most part unchanged. She was civil, even easy with me in the presence of others. Yet she had thrown up an invisible wall—nay, something more in the nature of a scrim—between us; I could not penetrate it, and she apparently had no wish to.

And so we sat, all of us at table, on that particular evening. We had reached a kind of comfortable hiatus between the completion of our meal and the clearing of the table. It was in this space of time that Lady Fielding leaned forward toward Clarissa and said in a manner not in the least unfriendly, "My dear, I wonder, would you mind leaving the table and going upstairs to your bedroom?"

Clarissa rose without hesitation, or even surprise, and said simply, "Yes, mum." She moved swiftly across the kitchen and disappeared up the stairs. A moment later we heard the bedroom door close.

"Was that necessary?" asked Sir John of his wife. "What is it we have to discuss that she ought not to hear?"

"Yes, Jack," said she, "I think it was necessary, for it is her future I wish to discuss, and I wish us all to feel free to speak without the restraint we should naturally feel if she were present and listening."

"Ah, well, I see. Since you have initiated this, you must have something quite particular to say. By all means, Kate, let us hear it."

With that, she took a deep breath and expended it all in a short sentence. "Jack, I need a secretary."

"A what?"

"A secretary, one to help me at the Magdalene Home with correspondence and to keep things in order there, ordering my schedule, reminding me of what must be done on a particular day or during a certain week. And . . ." Here she hesitated but a moment, then went bravely on: "And young though she may be, I believe that Clarissa could perform such work for me. Why, she's already demonstrated it! My office was in chaos, my desk piled with unanswered mail and unpaid bills, and in those days she has spent there with me, she has put everything right, showed me where I might look to find everything. The girl has a knack for it. It's something that can't be taught—or not easily, in any case. In short, I would like her to stay with us here. She could spend, oh, a certain number of days each week with me there, and the rest of the time she could help out with housework here.''

''You wish, then, to give up the notion of placing her in service?''

''Girls in service have an uncertain future at best,'' said Lady Fielding. ''You know that as well as I. Besides, even if we found the best possible place for her in all London, one free of the usual influences, putting her in service would still be a waste of her talents—her reading, her writing, her mind. The girl has a fine mind, and it should not be wasted.''

''Hmmm,'' said Sir John, and only that for a long moment. At last he spoke up: ''I understand your point now in sending her away. This is a matter that concerns us all. The bit of extra food she eats is of no concern to me. We can well afford it. She shares a bed with Annie. But to add permanently to our number a new person, a new personality, that is something that affects us all. I should like to hear from Annie and Jeremy on this matter. Annie? What say you?''

''I'm for her,'' said Annie, quite immediately. ''She's been a good chum to me, helped me with my reading and with my cooking, as well. Oh, but not just for that. We get along well, well as any two who ain't the same age can. And for a girl who's had a life hard as she has, she knows how to make a bit of fun. She can set me laughing anytime she wishes.'' She paused then, frowning. ''And, well, she's a good bedmate, too—doesn't pull off the covers of a cold night. That's all I can think of to say.''

Sir John took all that without comment, simply nodded a number of times, thrusting out his lower lip in deep consideration. At last he said: ''And you, Jeremy?''

I had dreaded the moment when I, too, would be asked to speak, and I had resolved to say as little as possible.

''I have no objection,'' said I.

''No objection?'' repeated Sir John. ''Does that mean

you are for it? Do you wish her to remain with us permanently?''

"Well . . . yes.''

"Forgive me, Jeremy, if I mistake, but have I not de-
tected something strained and distant between you and
Clarissa in the past weeks?''

"Well . . . perhaps.'' And I thought we had kept it so
well hid. The man amazed me.

"Why, Jeremy,'' spoke up Lady Fielding, clearly disturbed, "I had no idea! Whatever could you—''

"Please, Kate, those are matters with which you are not
acquainted.'' And then to me: "Does she blame you for
what happened to her father?''

"Partly, I think, yes.''

"Did you tell her his part in the crime?''

"No, I told her that only you should do that.''

"Well, you were right in saying so. Nevertheless, you
should not have carried that burden all these weeks. But do
you stand by what you said? That you have no objection
to Clarissa joining our household? That you wish her to
remain with us permanently?''

"Yes, I wish her with us. I know she has a great desire
to do so. I know that she is bright and has great talents.
And I know, or suspect, that what Lady Fielding said is
true, that girls who go into service have an uncertain future
at best. And I believe that whatever difficulties Clarissa and
I may have between us will be resolved with time.''

"But Jeremy,'' said Sir John, most insistently, "do you
want her here?''

"Yes sir, I do.''

"Well and good,'' said he, "it is settled then. Clarissa
Roundtree may remain with us if she chooses. The division
of her time between the Magdalene Home and here can be
worked out satisfactorily, I'm sure. If you like, you may
go up and tell her that, Kate.''

"Why don't you tell her, Jack?''

He sighed. "Yes, perhaps I should.'' He rose and started

across the kitchen. At the stairs he paused. "We may be a while," said he.

We heard him knock upon her door, a few murmured words, and then there were footsteps in the upstairs hall, just a few. I knew that he had taken her to the small room between the two bedrooms which he called his study. He would invite her to light a candle if she liked or sit in the dark, for it was all the same to him. And then he would tell her that she was welcome to remain with us if that was her wish. After she had said that indeed it was her wish, he would tell her that since that was the case, it was only fitting that she know the truth about her father. I was as sure as could be that this, or something quite like it, was what would pass between them.

As I cleared the table, Annie busied herself stowing the leftover mutton for tomorrow's stew, then heated the water for my washing up. Lady Fielding left us, giving a curious look to me as she bade us good night. She went straight to her bedroom and shut the door. Once the water was warm, Annie took it off the stove and set it out for me there to do what more had to be done. Then, in taking leave of me, she grasped me by the hand.

"You did right, saying what you did, Jeremy," said Annie. "Sometime you must explain to me that matter between you and Sir John about her father."

"Sometime perhaps I shall."

And so Annie, too, left the kitchen and went up the stairs.

The task of washing up seldom took much more than half an hour under ordinary circumstances. On this night I lingered over it a bit, giving extra effort to the greasy pan in which the mutton had been cooked; grease, fat drippings, blackened bits of meat covered the bottom of it. With soap and brush I won the battle, however, and I was just drying it down with one of the rags I kept for that purpose, when quite without prior notice Clarissa appeared next me, giving me a bit of a start.

"It's only I," said she. "I did not mean to startle."

I laughed in embarrassment. "Only that I was surprised," said I. "I heard no closing of the door, no step on the stair."

"You were busy banging that pan about. Making a terrible racket, you were. You couldn't hear me coming for all the noise you made."

"Well, you might have whistled a tune, or at least cleared your throat—something to let me know you were near."

Then and only then did I notice the tears that dampened the corners of her eyes, and I remembered where she had come from and what she had no doubt heard.

"You must forgive me. I fear I'm a bit tetchy this evening," said I.

"No," said she, "it is you, I hope, will forgive me, for I misjudged you and took for ill what you meant in kindness. I do apologize to you most sincerely."

"Were you urged to make this gesture? Told to say what you've just said?"

"Of course not. Then it would not be a sincere apology."

"True," said I. "So I accept and offer you my hand on it."

Briefly we clasped hands and made peace, each with the other.

"This will do much better," said she, "for I've been driven near to distraction being always so cheerful, so falsely cordial, with you. What I've missed most is our quarrels."

"I'm sure," said I, "that we shall have time in the future to make up for all those lost opportunities."

Later, years later in fact, when we were fast friends, I had the chance to ask Clarissa what it was that attached her so to her father. "Probably," said she, "it was that with my mother gone, he was all I had." I told her that he had said the same thing of her. "But there was something more," she added, "something quite especial that my mother often commented upon. No matter what our state, no matter how low our condition, he could always make us laugh."

Let that, then, be his epitaph: He could always incite laughter.

A Sir John Fielding Mystery

DEATH
of a
COLONIAL

BRUCE
ALEXANDER

PUTNAM

MURDER IN GRUB STREET
A New York Times
Notable Book of the Year

"A fine tale . . . Historical fiction done this entertainingly is as close to time travel as we're likely to get."
—*Newsday*

"First-rate, original, and persuasive." —*Boston Globe*

"Alexander has a fine feel for this earthy period, with its interplay of serene reason and irrational cruelty and violence. A bewildering time, to be sure, but Sir John's judicious insight and Jeremy's naïve fascination supply a novel perspective on it."
—*New York Times Book Review*

"Noteworthy . . . A stunning double climax."
—*Publishers Weekly*

BLIND JUSTICE

"*Blind Justice* is as much fun to read as it must have been to write. Bruce Alexander has done a fine job of depicting mid-eighteenth-century London."
—*Washington Post Book World*

"A shocking solution . . . Lively characters, vivid incidents, clever plotting, and a colorful setting . . . A robust series kickoff." —*Publishers Weekly*

"Alexander works in a vigorous style that captures with gusto the lusty spirit of the era. Sir John and young Jeremy are an irresistible team in what promises to be a lively series." —*New York Times Book Review*